TOKYO EXPRESS
USS BULL SHARK NAVAL THRILLER SERIES, BOOK 4

SCOTT W. COOK

Copyright © 2022 by Scott W. Cook

All rights reserved.

Book cover and formatting provided by Trisha Fuentes

No part of this book may be reproduced in any form or by any electronic or mechanical means, including information storage and retrieval systems, without written permission from the author, except for the use of brief quotations in a book review.

CONTENTS

Preface   v
Prologue   ix

PART ONE
TOJO TIME

1. Brisbane, Australia   3
   August 15, 1942 – 0530 local time
2. Henderson Field, Guadalcanal   17
   August 18, 1942
3. The Slot – 120 miles W, NW of Sealark Channel   29
   August 18, 1942 – 2155 Guadalcanal time
4. S-52 – 300 miles S, SW of Guadalcanal   43
   August 18, 1942 – 2135 Guadalcanal time
5. Guadalcanal – August 18, 1942, 2000 local time   57
6. Nouméa, New Caledonia – 1,100 miles S, SE of Guadalcanal   71
   August 19, 1942, 0530 local time
7. Cocumbona, Guadalcanal   83
   …hours earlier
8. USS Bull Shark – The slot   95
   August 19, 1942 – 1230 ship's time
9. USS Bull Shark – The Slot   109
10. S-52 – 200 miles S, SW of Guadalcanal   123
11. Goettge's Revenge – First Battle of the Matanikau, part 1   139
    August 19, 1942 – 0515 local time
12. Goettge's Revenge – First Battle of the Matanikau, part 2   153
    August 19, 1942 – 0815 local time
13. Goettge's Revenge – First Battle of the Matanikau, part 3   165
    August 19, 1942 – 1315 local time
14. USS Bull Shark – The Solomon Sea   181
    August 19, 1942 – 2130 local time

15. Taivu Point, Guadalcanal 195
August 20, 1942 – 0330 local time

16. New Georgia Sound – Northeast of San Christabel Island 209
August 20, 1942 – 1130 local time

17. Norambao Village, Guadalcanal – Between Taivu and Coli Points 223
August 20, 1942 – 1715 local time

18. The Slot – 90 miles NW of Savo Island 237
August 21, 1942 – 0022 Guadalcanal time

19. S-52 – Sealark Channel 253
August 21, 1942 – 0330 Guadalcanal time

20. S-52 – Sealark Channel 265

21. Guadalcanal – west of Taivu Point 281
August 21, 1942 – 0930 local time

22. Guadalcanal – Battle of Alligator Creek 295
August 22, 1942 – 0217 local time

PART TWO
BATTLE OF THE EASTERN SOLOMONS

23. The Slot – 25 miles North, Northwest of Savo 315
August 22, 1942 – 1130 Guadalcanal time

Chapter 24 329

25. Truk Harbor – Truk Atoll 339
August 22, 1942 – 1630 local time

26. Pacific Ocean – 100 miles east of Guadalcanal 353
August 22, 1942 – 2230

27. S-52 - 100 miles northeast of Tulagi 365
August 23, 1942 – 0810 local time

28. S-52 – 100 miles north of Tulagi 375
August 24, 1942 – 0620 local time

29. The Savage Islands 387
August 24, 1942 – 0930 local time

Chapter 30 399

31. Kido Butai – 250 miles NE of Guadalcanal 409
August 24, 1942 – 1220 ship's time

32. Kido Butai - 150 miles N, NE of Guadalcanal 421
August 24, 1942 – 1525 ship's time

33. The Savage Islands 435
August 24, 1942 – 1920 local time

Chapter 34	447
Chapter 35	463
Epilogue	477
A Word From the Author	485

PREFACE

Once Allied forces had landed on Guadalcanal and seized control of the Lunga Point airfield, it became clear to the Japanese that they had a tiger by the tail. With 20,000 Marines, Army and Navy personnel spread out on the islands of Guadalcanal, Tulagi, Gavutu and Tanambogo and Florida… the Allies held the upper hand when it came to the Sealark Channel. The waters of New Georgia Sound, colloquially known as "The Slot," stretched between the Japanese holdings at Rabaul and Bougainville and the Sealark Channel.

Although Admiral Richmond K. Turner's surface fleet and Admiral Frank "Jack" Fletcher's carrier task force departed shortly after the invasion of Guadalcanal, the carriers would return and with the completion of the airfield, named Henderson Field; the Allies held all the cards when it came to controlling the theatre during the day. Their air superiority would prove difficult to combat and deadly to any Japanese shipping that attempted to supply ground forces on the big island.

In order to overcome this disadvantage, Admiral Isuroku Yamamoto devised a plan to use fast destroyers to run down the slot in the darkness, using their speed, maneuverability and anti-submarine

PREFACE

capabilities to thwart U.S. planes and ships from sinking them. In this way, at over thirty knots, men and supplies could be funneled to Guadalcanal to fight the well-established American presence there.

As the defeat at Savo Island had shown, the Allies might have held the advantage during the day, but by night, the sea belonged to the Japanese. The destroyer supply runs came to be called *Nesumi Yuso* or rat transportation. To the Allies, this stream of ships became known as the Tokyo Express.

Ultimately, the tactic would prove ineffective. Destroyers were not built for supply missions. Their capacity was far smaller than cargo ships. Their great speed was effective but used a large amount of oil which was already so precious to the Empire. Only so many Japanese soldiers and Marines could be loaded onto the ships in addition to the cargo. This cargo, carried in sealed metal cylinders, was often simply dropped overboard as the destroyers sailed by. Although meant to be washed ashore or picked up by boats at night, a large percentage of precious supplies never made it to their intended recipients. Like the Allies, the Japanese on Guadalcanal were plagued by a shortage of food and other necessities.

By day, Japanese fighters and bombers from Rabaul, Bougainville and what carriers could be spared punished the new Allied holdings. The American airmen at Henderson Field became known as the Cactus Airforce, daily defending their islands while ground crews repaired the damage by night. It was a long and bloody war of attrition that the Japanese were doomed to lose… but not without making the Allies pay for every inch of territory.

The Japanese had one more problem as well. By day, they couldn't run ships due to the presence of Allied airpower. By night, although air attack was unlikely, there was danger from another quarter. When the sun sunk below the rim of the world, a ravenous predator whose lust for Japanese blood could not be satiated rose to the attack. Steel sharks with Torpex teeth prowled The Slot for new victims.

It's an all-out war. Brutal fighting in the jungles of Guadalcanal… vicious duels in the skies over The Slot… deadly games of cat and mouse beneath the waters of the Solomon Islands… courage,

PREFACE

dedication, sacrifice and dogged determination are inadequate to accurately describe the struggles of these brave men.

This tale is dedicated to them. And although it's a work of fiction, the made-up portions… as fanciful as they might often get… struggle to keep pace with the true facts of history.

PROLOGUE
OUTSIDE THE SLOT – 450 MILES FROM NEW BRITAIN

AUGUST 9, 1942 – 0330 GUADALCANAL TIME

"Ah, Sato," Captain Kenji Igawa said cheerfully when his short but burly executive officer entered his at-sea cabin, "you're just in time! Have you heard the news?"

Takashi Sato knew all too well what his captain was so elated about. The moment he'd exited his seaplane and been hoisted aboard along with his guests, he'd been told by no less than half a dozen exuberant officers. Told the tale of the Battle of Savo Island. Told the tale of how another fleet under another Japanese officer had dealt a devastating blow to American ships earlier that morning.

He'd *also* learned about the strike carrier *Sakai's* own duel just after sunset the previous day. How a single Yankee submarine had found them and sent one of their two remaining destroyer escorts to the bottom and all but crippled his own ship.

Fortunately, although fire room number one had been flooded, the seawater had prevented a boiler from exploding. The carrier was even then on her way to Rabaul at two-thirds speed to have a patch welded into place, and the boiler room recovered.

Arthur Turner's submarine, *Bull Shark,* had dealt Sato and his task force several shrewd blows and had gone virtually unpunished. Because of that one ship, his swift *Sakai,* a ship he'd served even since she was still on the drawing board, had been forced out of the Guadalcanal action as well as the Savo Island fight.

In his mind, the ship's executive officer found no cause for celebration. Further, the fact that his captain had managed to blunder and foul things up repeatedly… and yet could stand there in the midst of his comfortable cabin and smile was galling. The fool should be on his knees, prostrating himself before Yamamoto and begging for forgiveness. Rather, the man acted as if it had been *he* who had won a great victory, rather than possibly losing the Sealark Channel Islands single-handedly.

"I have indeed, sir," Sato said with masterfully feigned comradery. "A great victory! Admiral Mikawa has sent no less than four American ships to the bottom and perhaps damaged others!"

Igawa laughed, "Yes indeed! What have you there, Yakuin?"

Sato held a manilla folder in his hand, allowing it to hang absently at his side, "Oh, just a report. I thought you might like to look it over. It refers to my time ashore."

"Very good, I shall do that… but first, a celebratory wet is in order, eh?" Igawa replied genially.

Igawa poured the remainder of a tokkuri of warm sake into two large low-ball glasses. Not the usual chokos for the rice wine. He smiled at Sato and handed him one of the tumblers.

"And we have beaten off an attack from an American submarine," Igawa said, "Our carrier sustained a direct torpedo hit, and we're still running under our own power, Takashi! A few days at Rabaul, and we'll be ready to hunt once more! Isn't it grand?"

"Grand, sir," Sato said and drank his wine. He set the tumbler down and held out his other hand, which contained a bottle as well. "I brought something of my own with which we might have a toast."

Igawa grinned, "What have you there?"

"It was found in a village on the west side of the Matanikau River, perhaps left by one of the English. Eight-year-old scotch. I thought it might be appropriate to salute the defeat of the round eyes with something of their own making, eh?"

Igawa laughed and reached to open the bottle. By the redness in his eyes and the vermillion flush on his face, it was clear to Sato that his captain had been imbibing for some time, "Excellent! Oh… were you able to retrieve Osaka and Hideki?"

"Indeed I was, sir," Sato said. "Commander Hideki was injured when their airplane was shot down. He is currently in sick bay. As it is late, Commander Osaka elected to accompany him and then proceed to his stateroom. It shall be just us enjoying this small spoil of war."

Igawa appeared concerned, "I sincerely hope the commander will recover. We need all the good men we can get."

Sato lifted his tumbler up before him. The soft illumination in the cabin danced briefly in the pale liquid, "Here is to victory and the glory of good men."

"*Kenpai!*" Igawa chuckled and tapped his glass to Sato's. He then swallowed a generous portion and exhaled so hard he nearly coughed, "My word… powerful drink these British enjoy… perhaps we might use it as torpedo fuel, eh?"

Sato touched the rim of his glass to his lips and then lowered it again, smiling, "Perhaps, Captain. It is a powerful brew, indeed. Some might say life-altering in large enough quantities."

Igawa laughed. He drew in another sip and smacked his lips, "Quite a difference from our sake… but I approve. The Brits know how to do more than just organize a fleet, eh, Yakuin?"

"Indeed, sir," Sato said, once more pretending to sip. "Are you all right, Captain? Perhaps you should sit down."

Igawa's flush was deepening, and his eyes roamed, seemingly at random. He chuckled drunkenly and managed, after a fashion, to sit on his small sofa, "I believe I may've… over-indulged… Yak… Yak… Sato."

Sato set his drink down on the table and stood before the captain. By now, Igawa's face was losing its red hue in favor of a pallor that did not… *was* not, in fact… at all healthy. Igawa blinked up at Sato stupidly, not quite able to focus his sight or his thoughts.

"The British are also known for their ideas... I believe it was William Shakespeare through the mouth of Julius Caesar who said, 'Be not afraid of greatness; some are born great, some achieve greatness, and others have greatness thrust upon them,'" Sato told his captain. "For such men, obstacles must be removed, Captain. As I must now remove you. You had your opportunity to defeat the Americans... to defeat *Turner*, and you failed. As Osaka failed. Now *I* shall have my chance. And *I* will *not* fail."

"Sato..." Igawa croaked, the true import of what was happening beginning to push through the damp fog in his mind. "What... what have you done...?"

"What was necessary," Sato said, not without at least a modicum of regret in his tone. "Forgive me, Captain... but what I do I do for the greater good of our Empire."

Igawa was beyond the point where he could either understand or object. His eyes had gone glassy, and his breath ceased. It did seem to Sato, however, as he regarded the dead man slumped against the arm of the sofa before him that a lingering vestige of reproof remained in those dead eyes.

With quiet efficiency, Sato went about his work. The cabin had large bay windows that could be slid aside to allow fresh air in. He slid open the one that looked out over the starboard side of the ship and began to rid the room of any evidence.

First, he pitched the two drinking glasses and the poisoned bottle of scotch out into the blackness. Next went the body of Igawa himself. This was no easy task, as the captain was at least as robust as his first officer. However, with an effort, Sato muscled the limp body up and over the low sill, and it plummeted into the darkness where it would plunge into the sea along the carrier's side. At night and moving at fifteen knots, it would neither be seen nor heard.

Next, Sato moved to the captain's typewriter. From the folder he'd brought, he removed a typed sheet of paper and fed it into the machine. He carefully positioned the message so that it was sure to be found by the steward at first light. The note said that Igawa felt great shame. That he had failed, and in order to save face for his family and his ancestors, he had thrown himself into the sea. With a final touch of dramatic license for which he felt particular pride, Sato had written that the emperor had been forced to endure too much failure of late… but unlike Nagumo, Igawa would not multiply his shame by avoiding seppuku.

With a grin of satisfaction on his lips, Sato inspected the cabin one last time and then went out, locking the door behind him. No one noticed as he descended the companionway down one deck and then into his own cabin. Even should anyone have seen him, it was known that he had gone to visit the captain. He was the first officer, after all. This was simply routine. For a brief moment, Sato entertained the notion of going to sickbay and visiting Hideki.

He dismissed this notion out of hand, however. With no body and no way to perform an autopsy to detect the poison, no one could prove that Igawa's plunge into the nighttime depths was anything but what it appeared to be… a shame-fueled ritual suicide. A regrettable situation that left the ship without her captain… but Sato would stoically step in and fill that role with pride.

The smile was still on his face when sleep overtook him only five minutes later.

TRUK ATOLL: – 1,000 MILES AWAY

Isoroku Yamamoto found it impossible to return to sleep. He stood alone on *Yamato's* port bridge wing, a strong cup of tea in his hand, and contemplated the warm darkness around him. It was a scene of serenity, this well-protected anchorage blanketed in the pre-dawn night.

Truk was, for all intents and purposes, a virtually impenetrable fortress. The great harbor was home to dozens of ships and ringed by an impressive array of naval guns and anti-aircraft batteries. Truck Lagoon was rightfully becoming known as the Gibraltar of the Pacific.

Yet the Admiral's spirit was not at peace. For although the word of Admiral Mikawa's victory at Savo Island was what had roused Yamamoto from sleep… it wasn't the elation of victory that kept him awake… it was the implications of the larger future that occupied his restless mind.

The Americans were now on the warpath themselves. No longer satisfied with beating back Japanese attacks, they had chosen to implement a bold and decisive plan. And they had come in great force, as Yamamoto had foreseen. Over eighty ships, it was believed, had fallen upon Sealark Channel. Three aircraft carriers at least. It must be at least three because there had been too many aircraft over the theater of operations. And reports from pilots and ground forces alike estimated between sixty and eighty surface vessels constituted the Allied invasion fleet.

It meant that perhaps fifteen or even twenty thousand Marines had landed on the Florida Islands and Guadalcanal. Yamamoto shivered slightly as he remembered the words of that young radioman from Tulagi…

"Enemy troop strength is overwhelming," the man had reported. "We pray for enduring fortunes of war and pledge to fight to the last man…"

The great heritage of the Shogun era. The Japanese fatalism and belief in their divine right. That the winds of fortune should always blow in their favor.

Yamamoto harrumphed at that. Hadn't this myth been repudiated? Hadn't Hirohito and Tojo learned the hard way that this simply wasn't so? We send a devastating force to obliterate the American fleet at Pearl Harbor… and they come after us with a terrible resolve for vengeance. We once again plan an overwhelming strike at Midway, where our fleet is to crush the remaining American carriers and seize the island… and thanks to incompetence and a good deal of luck on both sides… we lost half our carrier fleet!

And now, finally, the United States has come to the Solomons with a lust for Japanese blood. And do they send a few troops to grapple with his own naval infantry? No! They send a massive force to simply overrun the Japanese and seize and, more importantly, *keep* those islands. Even now, as the fleet celebrates Mikawa's victory, it is but a candle in the wind. As soon as the sun rises, Fletcher's carriers will send hundreds of aircraft to find Mikawa and punish him. They will rule the skies by day; of that, there would be no doubt. And once the airfield they captured the previous day was completed, the Americans would have what Yamamoto sought to have.

An unsinkable aircraft carrier that would provide a stable base of operations for the Eastern Solomons. Where Japan sought to control the shipping lanes between the U.S. and Australia, now the U.S. will have control over the Solomons. And they won't be satisfied with this, of course. They'll come for Bougainville and Rabaul next. Who knows? They might be so bold as to attack Truk as well.

And through all of this, Yamamoto's people would fight. They would bravely and foolishly make the Allies pay for every inch of ground they took… for every sea mile to which they could lay claim. It would mean *years* of brutal fighting. It would mean young Japanese men committing atrocities that would bring shame to their people for generations. In the end, though, it would be all for *nothing!* Yamamoto knew this as surely as he knew the sun would rise in little more than an hour. Sunrise… The Rising Sun… it showed brilliantly for a time, but the sun must always set, must it not?

And where would it end? The trouble with fanatics is that they never seem to know when to quit. They refuse to acknowledge the reality of their situations, believing that they *must* win. And like all fanatics, the Japanese Emperor and Prime Minister will do what all such men have always done… they'll build a wall around themselves and hide behind it while others die for their cause. A wall constructed not of stone or iron or barbed wire… but a wall built from the bones of the tens of thousands of young men who gave their lives for someone else's cause.

Yamamoto found himself chuckling sardonically. Here he was, only hours after hearing that one of his fleet commanders had sunk three Allied heavy cruisers and damaged another so severely it would no doubt be required to be scuttled. Mikawa had damaged several other ships as well… and his thoughts were as black as the water below him. Yet how could it be otherwise?

"Good morning, sir," Admiral Matome Ugaki said quietly as he exited the navigation bridge. "Have you just arisen, or have you been awake since the announcement?"

Yamamoto turned to consider his chief of staff and friend. He grinned, "You already know the answer, Matome."

Ugaki bowed ever so slightly, Two steaming mugs in his hands. He extended one to his superior, who accepted the fresh tea gratefully.

"You're troubled," Ugaki said.

"You know me too well," Yamamoto spoke wistfully. "Perhaps nearly as well as my beloved Chiyoko. Would that she was here now to comfort me...."

Ugaki smiled at this. Yamamoto was well-known for his particular diversions. Gambling and geishas. Those who knew him well knew that Chiyoko was far dearer to the venerable admiral than his own wife.

"Would that we all had such companionship," Ugaki said and then smiled. "Perhaps we might organize a game of bridge later this evening? It might take our minds off things a while."

Yamamoto chuckled, "Perhaps I'll send for my Chiyoko, and we'll leave this war, Matome... go to Monaco and open that casino finally. The once-mighty Admiral who ruled the waves will now dominate the craps table, eh?"

Ugaki laughed and then grew somber again, taking his cue from his friend, "Sir... what is it that troubles you so? What is it that keeps your spirit from finding solace?"

Yamamoto sighed. The man really did know him too well.

"Matome... Mikawa achieved something tonight... but he could have achieved more," Yamamoto explained. "This seems to be a theme, does it not? A thread of... timidity perhaps... that runs through our fleet commanders. Hara did not press his advantage when we took Tulagi in May. Had he not become fearful that his fleet would be lost, he might have also seized Port Moresby. Had Nagumo not been such an old woman at Midway, he might have finished the job he started, and the Kido Butai might not be at half strength now. Hell, had he sent up another sortie at Pearl Harbor, none of this might now be necessary! *Nagumo*... how is it that this man is *still* in command of my combined fleet? And now, Matome, Mikawa ceased his attack right when a little boldness could have seen an *end* to this! He had the invasion fleet in his sights! He could've destroyed them or at least crippled them and left the Americans on the island without any support!"

Ugaki remained silent. He knew enough not to interrupt when Yamamoto's anger came to the surface.

"Again, and again and *again*, Matome, victory or at the very least, stability is ripped from our grasp!" the Admiral continued. "And not because our enemy is superior… but because *we* grow too cowardly to press our advantage! How can we expect to defeat a nation whose industrial might is so enormous with such foolishness? How can we hope to overcome a people who are so doggedly set upon crushing us beneath their boot heel? And this great American resolve, Matome, was created by *us!* All we did at Pearl Harbor was enrage a sleeping giant who now wants nothing more than to grind every *jap* between his teeth. Rather than *frighten* the Americans, we angered them into action. And rather than use our superior technology and forces to frighten them further, we continue to back down before them… even when we *win!*"

Ugaki could not argue. As much as he didn't like to admit it, the truth of the matter was plain. Yet he couldn't allow himself to become as fatalistic as his superior. The tide of war ebbed and flowed, and with faith, Ugaki believed his people could prevail.

"It, therefore, falls to us, Matome," Yamamoto said, resignation creeping into his voice. The steel that had made him whom he was slipping into place and relieving Ugaki of a great deal of his worry. "We must act now. Here is the situation as I see it… the Allies have the islands; that's not going to change soon. However, we can dominate what the Americans call The Slot by night, as Mikawa has demonstrated. We can also punish them by day. By sending bombing sorties from Rabaul each and every day, Matome, we can hound the Americans and further strangle their operations. We must get more men and supplies to Guadalcanal by night. That's the most important objective."

"But we can't send in slow transports, sir," Ugaki advised. "Either the Allied warships or planes will take them out easily. Not to mention the presence of that notorious American submarine, *Bull Shark*. Igawa nearly lost *Sakai* to them."

Yamamoto nodded, "Precisely. We must therefore make use of faster and better-protected ships. I want to send destroyers to Guadalcanal, Admiral. Every night, they'll come down from Rabaul loaded to the gills with men and supplies. Arrange this so that the line of ships reaches the island well after dark and exits the area well before light. At thirty knots, this is most certainly feasible. By night, we funnel men and materiel to Guadalcanal, and by day, we smash the Lunga Point airfield and keep the Marines there bottled up. This should give us time for yet another operation I wish you to plan."

"Sir?"

"We must order the Kido Butai here," Yamamoto said, beginning to pace even as he made his plans. "We will assemble a carrier strike force, escorting surface battle force and troop and supply convoy to Guadalcanal. This is in addition to our destroyer convoys, Matome. No doubt it will take upwards of two weeks to put this together, so we must act immediately. Our objectives are to get substantial troops to the island and to locate and smash Fletcher's carriers. We *must* maintain air superiority over the Americans, Matome. With these combined efforts, we have a chance to turn this disaster to our advantage."

Ugaki smiled with hope. Seeing the fire in Yamamoto's eyes bolstered his own flagging faith, "Yes, sir! And… what of the American submarine?"

Yamamoto smiled thinly, "My great adversary, Captain Turner? In our report from *Sakai,* we learned that Osaka and Hideki were found and recovered. Hideki was injured, sadly… but with him aboard the strike carrier, we may have an advantage. Once *Sakai* is repaired at Rabaul, she will go forth once more. She can escort our destroyer train and seek out *Bull Shark.* No doubt this will make Igawa happy in all events. That is now *Sakai's* primary mission. To locate and destroy this submarine. It has been a thorn in our sides and will continue to do so unless dealt with, I fear."

"Yes sir," Ugaki said. "Do you think this Turner fellow will be kept in the area?"

Yamamoto smiled, "Oh, I think so, Matome. Perhaps it's fate or destiny or God… I don't know. Yet I sense that Arthur Turner and his *Bull Shark* have been placed in our path."

"Let us hope that we're dealt the better hand, sir," Ugaki observed, a crooked smile playing at his lips.

"Indeed, my friend…" said Yamamoto thoughtfully as he looked toward the faint light glowing in the east. "Indeed…"

PART ONE
TOJO TIME

"To Defeat the Japanese, we shall have to throw away the rulebook of war… and go back to the tactics used in the French and Indian Wars."

— MAJOR GENERAL ALEXANDER A. VANDEGRIFT

1

BRISBANE, AUSTRALIA
AUGUST 15, 1942 – 0530 LOCAL TIME

"Good morning, gentlemen," Admiral Charles A. Lockwood said genially as Art Turner, Elmer Williams and Pat Jarvis were shown into the small conference room.

The chamber was located in the superstructure of the submarine tender USS *Zachary Taylor*. Three large portholes looked out to starboard over Morton Bay and were just beginning to lighten with the soft glow of false dawn.

Already a faint gray raft of cigarette smoke clung to the overhead, and the smell of strong coffee and burnt tobacco filled the room. In it, aside from Admiral Lockwood, were three men. One was obviously the Admiral's aide, a slightly grizzled and square-jawed CPO serving as his yeoman. The other two were dressed in working khakis and had gold dolphins pinned to their breasts. Submariners both, Turner noted with approval but not surprise.

"Come on in and have a seat, gents," Lockwood said, gesturing at the table around which the others were seated. Faintly visible steam rose from a large silver coffee pot and service at the table's center. The three *Bull Shark* officers sat, and Turner began to pour coffee for them all.

"Allow me to introduce Lieutenant Commander Bernard 'Salty'

Waters and Lieutenant Chris Savage, torpedo officer. Both from the S-52," Lockwood said. "Barnie, Chris, this is Anvil Art Turner, Elmer Williams and Pat Jarvis. Skipper, Exec and torpedo officer of USS *Bull Shark*."

The men stood and shook one another's hands. Waters was of medium height and heavily built with a tendency toward plumpness. He was a year or two below forty and had the faint beginnings of crow's feet and gray at his temples. His hair was medium brown, as were his eyes. His face was square and pleasant, and when he smiled, Turner thought he noticed that the smile didn't quite reach the eyes. Or perhaps that the deep melancholy in the eyes resisted the smile's power.

Savage, on the other hand, was in his late twenties, a little taller than his captain and lean. His blonde hair framed a boyishly handsome face with wide-set green eyes.

"So, you're Captain Waters," Turner remarked as everyone sat once more. "I just read the report on your last patrol, Captain. Sunk two oil tankers and a destroyer right outside the harbor at Balikpapan. Well done, sir."

"Long as the Japanese hold Borneo and the great oil reserves there," Lockwood stated, "we'll have boats prowling those waters."

Waters nodded slightly. When he spoke, his voice resonated deeply with Texas cattleman, "It came at a high cost, though, Captain Turner. I lost my executive officer, chief of the boat and ten more men… a quarter of my crew. We used our last four fish on those oilers and tried to shake that DD… but the bastard hounded us all the way down the Makassar Strait. We took enough depth charge damage that I decided we had no choice but to go up and fight him with our deck gun."

Jarvis grinned, "Our skipper likes to do that too. Charge into battle with guns blazing."

Williams and the Admiral smiled, but Turner noted that neither of the S-52 officers did. Waters only lit a cigarette and inhaled deeply before continuing.

"Yeah, but you've got a fancy new fleet boat," Waters replied to Jarvis, sounding a little miffed. "We're in an old pig boat with a single four-inch. I sent my Exec and COB up top with gun crews and machine gunners to harass the destroyer. He cut us up pretty bad before a lucky shot from our deck gun hit his fantail and detonated the ashcans there… sunk the bastard, but his own gunners took down just about everybody on deck. We went in to look for survivors… found a few, too…."

"One of the fuckin' Nips had an Arisaka," Savage said heatedly. "We get close, and he opens up on us! Took out Mr. Daniels, our XO, Tucker Kafflen the COB and two more men… sons of bitches… pardon me, Admiral…."

"It's okay, son," Lockwood said kindly. "War can be a dirty business."

"Yeah, and those damned Japs love to fight dirty," Waters added indignantly. "No sense of honor, whatever they say about it."

The men of *Bull Shark* fell silent. They could understand the other men's frustration and pain. They too had seen their fair share of the grittiness of war. Turner himself, along with several of his men, had recently spent a week slogging through the jungles of Guadalcanal and seen that side of things up close and personal.

"We've been working around the clock to get Barnie's boat back up to snuff," Lockwood explained. "As we've been doing for yours, Art. Although your Exec here treated *Bull Shark* pretty badly in The Slot…."

Williams flushed, and Jarvis grinned. Lockwood chuckled and gave Turner a wink.

"Tore up the upper after deck… had a nasty squeal in the stern planes, too," Lockwood went on. "Don't know how many light bulbs and gauge glasses we replaced… that shit ain't cheap, son."

"Sorry, sir," Williams said and grinned crookedly. "I'll try and do better."

Lockwood laughed, "Two freighters and two destroyers with only ten fish. Shameful, Elmer."

Williams hung his head in a reasonable facsimile of disgrace. Then he smiled and tapped the new Silver Star beside the Bronze one pinned below his dolphins, "I've got this to remind me of my shame, sir."

Everyone laughed then. Once more, Turner noted that while Waters and Savage joined in, there was a definite note of reserve in them. Both men had received medals for their last patrol. Savage sported a Bronze Star of his own, and Waters had a Navy Cross pinned to his chest beside a Bronze Star. They shouldn't be jealous… but clearly the two officers were not as exuberant as they might be.

"All right, gents," Lockwood went on, lighting a smoke and allowing the yeoman to refill his coffee. "As you're no doubt aware, the Guadalcanal campaign has just gotten started. The Marines have gotten the airfield operational. They've named it Henderson Field, after a Marine pilot, Lofton R. Henderson, who went down at Midway. A good thing too… the field being open, I mean… because the damned Japs have been flying harassment sorties every damned day since Admiral Turner pulled his fleet out. Admiral Nimitz has kept Fletcher's carrier groups in the area to provide air cover and has been slowly ferrying in fighters and bombers to build up what the men on Guadalcanal are calling The Cactus Airforce. By day, we still hold the upper hand… but we've got some problems."

Turner harrumphed, "Yes sir. I was there. Supplies are short because Admiral Turner didn't unload but half of what was supposed to go ashore."

Lockwood sighed, "Right. And that attack near Savo the night the Marines took the airfield was a hard blow. I can't blame Turner for leaving. Because if anything, that attack proved that at night, the Japs hold the high cards. All that garbage about them not seeing well and not being good night fighters is a bunch of bunk, as you gents well know. They're *excellent* night fighters, and after the sun goes down, The Slot is not safe for any Allied shipping."

"So we're to go out and teach them a lesson, sir?" Savage asked.

Lockwood nodded gravely, "In a way, Lieutenant. Station Hypo and the Ultra boys have come up with something and brought it to my attention. As you know, the Japs have updated their JN-25 code, so Joe Rochefort and his team are once again busy trying to decipher it. As I understand it, Art, your wife is a WAVE now and working on that team. From what I've heard, she's got a real head for it."

"Yes sir."

"Anyway…" Lockwood continued, "what Ultra has discovered is that Yamamoto has ordered that supply missions to Guadalcanal be run at night. Right down the slot but not with freighters. He's using destroyers and taking advantage of their speed. They run down from Rabaul, Bougainville or the Shortland Islands loaded with men and supplies and drop them off in the dark. Somewhere to the east of the Teneru River. Taivu Point, maybe."

"Christ…" Turner muttered, thinking of the situation he'd seen on the island for himself.

"I think it was somebody on Guadalcanal, maybe one of the Marines, who labeled it the Tokyo Express," Lockwood said. "Logistically, it's a problem for us. It does commit a lot of Japanese resources for small gains… but it's *effective,* and that's the point. So I want your two boats to high tail it out to The Slot and derail this train."

"A wolfpack, sir?" Williams asked.

"Not exactly," Lockwood replied. "Your two boats will be working together, but not in tandem. My thinking is to station one of you in the Sealark Channel and one further up new Georgia Sound. Maybe halfway between Rabaul and Guadalcanal. One boat tries for the destroyers before dark, and any that slip past, the second boat gets them in the channel. I'm working on getting more assets in the area as time goes on, but we're spread thin, and there's a helluva lot of Jap shipping to take down in the Pacific. As noted earlier, Borneo is a key holding for them because of the oil reserves. In the meantime, if you two captains can at least *slow down* the Tokyo Express, it'll be of great service to our Marines."

"Glad to, sir," Turner replied.

Waters nodded solemnly.

"My thinking, Art, is to put *Bull Shark* further up The Slot," Lockwood stated. "Your boat is half-again as fast and has a greater range than an S-boat. If you go northwest, you'll be in position about the same time as Salty here gets into Sealark Channel."

"Yes sir," Turner stated. "Makes sense."

"Once you two get in position, I'll leave local command up to you, Art," Lockwood stated.

Waters frowned, "With all due respect, sir… I'm senior… perhaps I should be in operational command?"

Lockwood drew in a breath, "Your promotion to O4 came before Art's, it's true, Barnie. But Art has seen more action thus far in the war. He's got four war patrols under his belt, one on *Tautog* and three on *Bull Shark*. Eleven confirmed kills."

Waters flushed with anger at that. Savage was clearly distressed as well but managed to clench his jaw and say nothing. Lockwood noticed and smiled disarmingly at Waters.

"I'm not in any way denigrating you, Barnie," Lockwood said gently. "But you've only run two patrols and sunk three ships. I've got to go with experience on this one."

"Sir… my patrols were full length," Waters protested. "*Bull Shark's* were all short."

"I know, Barnie," Lockwood said, his patience beginning to thin. "And for the most part, you're running independent. As I say, this isn't a wolf pack… although, in my opinion, the Germans have had a lot of success with that tactic, and I feel we should adopt it. The higher-ups aren't so convinced yet, though… at any rate, Art is in overall command. That's the final word."

"Yes sir," Waters said smartly, almost snapping to attention in his seat.

"For what it's worth, Captain," Turner tried to soothe. "I respect your experience. On the rare occasions we will communicate, your input will be invaluable. For my part, I think of this as a team effort."

Waters nodded. He wasn't mollified but had enough self-control to contain himself and even appreciate the peace offering Turner was extending. Their superior had made Turner the CO for the mission, and he wasn't obligated to make peace. Waters was expected to follow orders whether he liked it or not. It said much about Turner's character that he was making such a concession.

"I appreciate that, Captain," Waters said.

Lockwood drew in a breath and a pull on his Newport, "There's one more thing that may ruffle some feathers… but I believe it's vital. The reason I asked for Mr. Jarvis' presence here is that S-52 is short one executive officer and one Chief of the Boat. With Mr. Jarvis' experience and seniority, I'm assigning him TAD to S-52 as her XO.

I'd also like you to send along one of your chiefs as temporary COB as well, Art."

"Sir… Lieutenant Savage has been acting exec for me since the attack," Waters stated. "In my opinion, he's done a fine job."

"Good," Lockwood said. "But for this mission, Barnie, I need experienced men in these vital billets. If you feel that Mr. Savage is ready, then after this patrol, I'll consider sending him off to PXO School. I know all this is a lot to absorb, but like Operation Watchtower, this little op here, which we'll call Operation Switch Track, is equally slapdash. You two skippers are my finger in the dike for now. I'll arrange for more assets to cover this situation in time, but for now, I want both your boats on station by Thursday. A lot is happening out at Guadalcanal, and keeping those islands is absolutely *critical* to our war effort. Which means… as usual… the submarine service is the lynchpin. You put yourselves right in the cannon's bore and smile big as you charge into it. And hardly anybody knows what brave deeds you do. That's the silent service for you."

"Yeah, we can't all get a write-up in LIFE magazine," Savage quipped, casting a cutty-eyed glance at Turner and his XO.

"Sure you can, Chris," Lockwood attempted to smooth over. "You'll get your shot. War's young yet. All right, gents, I want your boats the hell outta my harbor by sundown. Repairs are complete, and crews are loading supplies and fish as we speak. Any ideas on who you'd like to take with you, Mr. Jarvis?"

"I think Chief Brannigan, sir," Jarvis said. "Our chief electrician's mate. I'd love to take Chief Rogers, but…."

"No way, no how, Pat," Turner said. "Besides, Harry could use a change of scene, and I think he's ready for a COB's duties."

"Excellent," Lockwood said, clearly indicating that the meeting was over. "Oh, Art, would you stay a moment, please?"

The four other men filed out, and Turner was left alone with Lockwood. The Chief yeoman was still there, of course, but the man knew how to make himself inconspicuous.

Lockwood drew in a breath, "Art… I'm sorry to have to put you in this position… but I don't have a lot of options right now."

"What position is that, sir?"

"Having to deal with potential personality conflicts with Captain Waters," Lockwood said. "He's seven years older than you. He was promoted to Lieutenant Commander a full year before you… but that was fairly late, even in peacetime. He's a good submariner. Knows his business. But he is, for want of a better term, one of the old-guard sub drivers. Likes the book. Believes in the doctrine. No night surface attacks, put yourself in front of a convoy… play it safe, in other words. You and I both know that the war has changed things. Aggression wins the day, not caution. Waters is going to resent you, I imagine. Younger skipper, better boat… and I don't envy Pat Jarvis. It's going to take a strong man to stand between Waters and Savage."

Turner smiled thinly, "Pat's not a man to trifle with, sir."

Lockwood nodded, "That's my impression, too. Frankly, I think he's ready for PXO school himself. We'll see how things go this mission."

"Aye, sir."

Lockwood drew in a breath, "There's something else you should know, Art. Reports from air recon and decoded transmissions, what little we've got, indicate that *Sakai* is at Rabaul now and being repaired. In all likelihood, she'll be back in The Slot before you get there."

Turner scowled slightly, "Yes sir that makes sense… and her executive officer, a man named Takashi Sato, is gunning for me."

Lockwood nodded, "I read your report. There's something else, too… believe it or not; I think your wife might actually have decoded this of all people… the captain of the strike carrier committed ritual suicide the morning after *Bull Shark* attacked. Sato is in command now. Watch out for him, Art. What little intelligence we have on him says he's a smart and ambitious man."

"And he wants my hide," Turner added. "He wants to play a game of wits with me… which means he's out for blood."

Lockwood nodded, "Be careful. Get him if you can. It wouldn't hurt my feelings, and CincPac agrees, to have one less Jap carrier afloat, even a small one. Because, as if all this isn't enough… I've got other units out near Truk. They keep an eye on things, and over the past few days, there's been quite a lot of shipping entering the lagoon, including Nagumo's carriers. Yamamoto is up to something, Art. And I'll bet my right arm it's directly related to Guadalcanal."

"An invasion and assault campaign," Turner said. "Jesus…"

Lockwood nodded, "I'd say so. As to what, where and when… that remains to be seen. I know for a fact that Admiral Nimitz is somewhat unhappy with Fletcher. His leaving the area to refuel and taking his sweet time about it isn't sitting well with Admiral King, either… but I'd also bet my right arm that those carriers will be back in the Guadalcanal area within a week or so."

"Sounds like we've got our work cut out for us, sir," Turner observed wryly.

Lockwood snorted, "Yeah… don't we all. Well, I'll let you get back to your ship, Captain. Good luck and Godspeed."

Pat Jarvis watched with a heavy heart as *Bull Shark* eased herself away from S-52's side, her gray and black paint job gleaming in the late afternoon sun. She'd been moored outboard of the older submarine, which herself was moored alongside the big submarine tender. The gangplanks had been removed, and all lines cast off. The big fleet boat cleared the ships, threw her starboard engine back and port engine forward and spun toward the channel that led out of the harbor. On her main and cigarette decks, the officers and special sea detail waved their hats at S-52 and the tender.

"Exec, take the deck and con her out," Captain Waters said from beside Jarvis, a Pall Mall clenched in his lips. "You think you can handle that, Mr. Jarvis?"

Jarvis, not easily goaded nor discommoded, smiled at his new skipper, "I'm willing to give it a try, Skipper."

There was a snort of derision from behind them. Jarvis knew Chris Savage was there, watching and probably smirking.

"Chief, cast off four, standby on two," Jarvis called down to Harry Brannigan, S-52's new and likely temporary Chief of the boat. He thumbed the bridge transmitter himself rather than using a quartermaster to relay orders. "Helm, bridge, port back one-third, starboard forward one-third."

The order was acknowledged, and the ship vibrated as her two Busch-Sulzer diesels revved up to increase electrical power to her twin Ridgeway electric motors. The stern began to slowly slide to the right, increasing the distance between the boat and the ship beside her.

"Cast off two!" Jarvis called. "Helm, bridge… all back one-third. Five degree left rudder."

S-52 eased backward now, pulling away from the tender and out into the open waters of the harbor. With the wind southerly, the odor of burnt diesel exhaust wafted over the submarine's decks. It mixed with the salty iodine scent of the sea and made Jarvis smile.

"All stop," he ordered. "Right full rudder… all ahead one-third. Helm, steer one-one-five for channel entry. What's our speed?"

"*Bridge, helm… Bendix log indicates four knots.*"

"Very well," Jarvis said.

"*Bridge, navigation,*" came the voice of the quartermaster of the watch, a middle-aged first-class petty officer named Jack Cleghorn. "*Final channel leg turn is comin' up… one-half mile. Standby to mark the turn. Turn bearing will be zero-seven-five.*"

"Standing by," Jarvis replied. "COB, dismiss the special sea detail. Set the normal watch."

"Aye-aye, sir," Brannigan said and hustled his men below decks. With the ship about to enter the open sea and no lifelines rigged, it was best to get all unnecessary personnel below before the sea state was known.

"You act like you might've done this before, Pat," Savage said.

"I read a lot, Chris," Jarvis quipped. He knew that both the captain and the torpedo officer resented his presence there. How the rest of the crew felt, he couldn't be sure. Even as he sat in the meeting with Admiral Lockwood that morning, Jarvis decided he wouldn't give them any reason to doubt his abilities. Further, as was his nature, he couldn't help but return the volley a little. Making flippant remarks that were carefully crafted to make Savage nervous. He doubted a seasoned sub driver like Waters could be tweaked.

"*Bridge, navigation…. Mark the turn.*"

Thankfully, the harbor passage was well marked with large brightly painted red and green buoys. Jarvis had been watching the next red approaching the submarine's portside. He didn't know exactly how the S-class boat would handle… although he'd served aboard similar craft earlier in his career. Theoretically, this submarine should have a slightly better turn rate than *Bull Shark,* as she was seventy feet shorter and six hundred tons lighter on the surface. However, it was better to be safe than sorry.

"Helm, bridge, full left rudder," Jarvis ordered.

The boat's bullnose bow began to swing to the left. Jarvis picked out the twin red and green markers that were the first of those marking the final leg of the channel out to the inlet. By eyeing these, as well as the red buoy passing to the boat's port side, he could judge the turn rate. He could see that the sharp forty-degree turn was going to carry S-52's stern a bit too far to starboard. Waters could see it too but kept his face carefully neutral, waiting to see if Jarvis would correct.

For his own part, Savage seemed to take no notice. He just stood there, smiling scornfully and didn't seem to realize the boat was in danger of over-swinging. Jarvis made a mental note of that.

"Maneuvering, bridge," Jarvis thumbed the speaker. "Stop port engine."

The bow began to turn faster now. Out of the corner of his eye, Jarvis saw the captain nod ever so slightly. The boat's bullnose was now pointed nearly dead center for the two quad-pole channel markers.

"Maneuvering, bridge," Jarvis said. "All ahead standard. Helm, meet her."

S-52 eased into the channel, nearly dead center. The diesels revved, and the ship accelerated to eight knots. Ahead of them, just passing between the breakwaters and out into the Pacific, Jarvis saw *Bull Shark* begin to accelerate. There was only an hour or so of daylight left, and Art Turner was using every bit of speed he had to get out to sea and head for the Solomon Islands.

"Thank you, Exec," Waters said neutrally.

"Yes sir," Jarvis replied with equal professional detachment.

"You didn't run us aground, Pat… that's something anyway," Savage jibed.

Jarvis turned and locked eyes with the younger man, "You didn't run us aground, *sir.* If you're gonna be a snotty little shit, Lieutenant, then you and I are not on a first-name basis, and you do not have permission to ride me."

Savage flinched at this rebuke, and his face colored with anger, "Yes *sir*."

"Now, Pat," Waters said evenly. "Chris here didn't mean no harm. Just some friendly ribbing. You're the new guy, after all."

Jarvis nodded but kept his eyes on Savage, "I'm all for camaraderie and busting balls, skipper. Nothing wrong with guys tossin' a few nifties at each other in fun… God knows I'm known for it… but there's a line between friendly teasing and kidding around and blatant disrespect. I won't tolerate it."

"Hey, I was just joshin' ya'," Savage tried to play it off.

Jarvis was having none of it, "You're dismissed, torpedo officer."

Savage once again colored and looked to his captain. To his credit, Waters didn't defend him. He simply stood by passively, watching.

Savage chuffed and went down the bridge ladder. Jarvis sighed and returned his focus to the channel and the inlet ahead.

"You might want to cut the kid a little slack, Pat," Waters said calmly. "We had it rough on that last patrol. Chris was my acting exec for the past few weeks. All things considered, he's taking this whole thing kinda hard."

"Captain…" Jarvis withdrew a Camel from a pack in his duty blouse and cupped his hands around his zippo as he lit up. "Please don't take what I'm about to say as me diminishing what you fellas went through. It sounds like you had it hard. Believe it or not, I know what that's like. It ain't exactly been a cakewalk on *Bull Shark* either. And I know that Harry and I are the new kids here and that just being here steps on some toes. But I'm here to do my duty, sir. I'm the executive officer. I like a boat where we can kid around, even with the troops. But you and I both know there's a line. If a junior officer disrespects a senior, it erodes good order and discipline. And as XO, I need to be able to command. Wouldn't you agree?"

Waters nodded, "Fair enough. Just so long as you keep all that in mind, it's nothing personal, Pat. I've read your jacket, and you're brave, tough, smart and capable. An asset to any boat, I'm sure. But as *you* know full well, a submarine is a family. Maybe more so on an S-boat with two-thirds the number of men as on yours. You gotta give these guys a chance to get used to you. Don't come off all Captain Bly, or it'll totally fuck up what I've built here. This is still my boat, and I'll have it run my way."

"Understood, sir. You let me know your policies, and I'll see they're carried out," Jarvis said and smiled in spite of himself. "In point of fact… I know what having a Breadfruit Bly is like all too well. We had a temporary XO during the Midway operation. Him and his buddy were a couple of hot-headed tyrants who turned our family into a shithouse. I won't go out of my way to push my agenda. But neither will I bend over backwards and let some punk mouth off. I'm a good-natured guy, sir… but I'm also a hard-ass. If that kid below can't swallow his pride and do his job, then I'll damned well take him out on the after deck and teach him a lesson. You all right with that, sir?"

Waters actually grinned, "I think we'll get along, Pat. Don't worry about Chris. He's young and hopeful. In spite of his disappointment, he's a good gunner. He'll come around; you'll see."

"Good," Jarvis said with a smile of his own. "Then what do you say we go out and sink some Japs, sir?"

Waters smiled, but as Turner had noticed before, the smile didn't quite wipe away something in the man's eyes. Yet another mental note for the new XO.

2

HENDERSON FIELD, GUADALCANAL

AUGUST 18, 1942

"How you feelin' sailor?"

Lieutenant Porter Hazard yawned and sat up in his hospital cot. His body was sore and stiff, but he felt stronger that morning than he had in a week. He smiled at the man who was strolling down the ward toward him.

"Like I've been crucified, Dick," Hazard joked. "How about you?"

Richard Tregaskis chuckled. A unique man in a number of ways, Tregaskis wasn't a combat soldier but a war correspondent for the International News Service. He was twenty-six years old, and reports were that he was always with the Marines, either working alongside them or even standing with some of them along the defensive perimeter set up around the airfield. Tregaskis was a good-natured man with a ready smile and quite easy to pick out in a crowd, as he was six feet seven inches in height.

"Doc says you're okay to go ambulatory now," the correspondent stated. "Feel like schlepping over to the mess hall and grabbing a bite with me?"

Hazard groaned as he stood. After capturing him a week before, the Japanese had worked him over pretty thoroughly. As if that weren't bad enough, after speaking with Captain Turner, the maniacal

Japanese Navy officer had instructed his men to nail his palms to a couple of trees, tie his feet and then work him over some more. They'd then stabbed him with bayonets in both thighs, his left foot, right shoulder and right bicep. The wounds weren't fatal, as they were intended not to be, but Hazard had lost a good amount of blood. Thanks to some stitching and some of that new penicillin, he'd recovered nicely. Though his wounds were still sore, especially when he walked. The bruising from the multiple beatings had subsided into pale yellowish blotches and whose traces would soon be gone.

Except on his soul, of course. Aside from the Navy doctors and a handful of army nurses, the airbase also sported an army psychiatrist. The shrink warned Hazard that he may suffer longer-term effects from his ordeal than just his physical wounds.

"I don't suppose there's biscuits and gravy, pork sausages and fresh fruit, is there, Dick?" Hazard asked after the throbbing subsided enough for him to take a hand off the wall.

"How about powdered eggs, canned peaches and corned beef hash?" Tregaskis smiled. The smile faltered momentarily as he saw the grimace on the sailor's face when he stood. He thought about offering Hazard an arm but refrained for the moment.

"Sounds ducky," Hazard said, steeling himself and standing erect. "All right, Dick, lay on. All ahead two-thirds. Not quite up to full power yet."

They moved down the ward, Tregaskis slowing his long gate so as to keep pace with the submariner's limping progress. Hazard saw the troubled look flitter across the younger man's face, and he grinned crookedly.

"Don't fret, Dick… I'm all right," Hazard reassured his new friend. "Just hurts more when I first start hobblin'. Few minutes and it levels down. Better today than yesterday. Probably ought to go for a run, if anything. Get these muscles workin' again."

"You're a better man than I, Porter Hazard."

"What've I been tellin' you all week?"

It was more than an hour after dawn and the morning sun bathed Henderson Field in its blazing golden light. All around the two men, the business of the day ebbed and flowed in a tide of seemingly chaotic activity. Aircraft were being readied for takeoff as what the men of the base called the Cactus Navy prepared to meet the daily Japanese air assault. This was known as "Tojo Time" by the Marines. The narrow-gauge railroad… they called this the Turnerville Trolley… was in use, its small locomotive hauling supplies from one end of the airstrip to the other. Construction vehicles growled, farted and smoked as they worked. Jeeps, cars, trucks and bicycles by the dozen went to and fro on a dizzying variety of errands. Marines were marching, calling cadence and organizing as the round-the-clock perimeter guard was changed and men went about their training.

Fifteen thousand men, most of whom were Marines, gave life to the new base, and the overall impression was comforting. Joining the Marines were Navy pilots and crews, Army pilots and crews as well as a handful of non-combatants like the dozen Navy nurses and four doctors and Tregaskis himself, of course.

"Sir! Sir!" a faint voice called out from the two men's left.

They stopped and looked around to see who it was that had called them. Of course, the shouter could've been referring to any number of sirs in the area, but Hazard somehow knew it was meant for him. He spotted Davie Taggart and Ted Entwater trotting toward them from the enlisted bivouac area down the field.

"Mornin' fellas," Hazard said.

"How ya' feelin', sir?" Taggart asked as he and the younger Marine stopped and saluted. "Mornin', Mr. Tregaskis."

"Morning fellas," Tregaskis replied amiably.

"I'm still vertical," Hazard said. "What're you boys up to today?"

"We just come from the radio station," Taggart explained. "Got word that the skipper and Chuck should be here inside of a week. Either on the Navy's next supply run or by air."

"That's great news… for us," Hazard jibed. "How're they doin'? Better'n me, I hope."

"Chuck is okay," Entwater explained. "Took a stick in the leg, but he's up and about like you, sir. Wasn't as badly hurt, so he says he's fit and ready to jitterbug again."

"The skipper is doin' good, too," Taggart added. "They got him walking around a bit. Probably not ready for any strenuous duty… but he's requested he be allowed to rejoin us here. Even if all he does is sit on his kiester and shout orders. Better than sitting in a Navy hospital in New Caledonia and bawlin' for more Jello."

"Good news," Tregaskis said. "You Raiders did a helluva thing the morning of the invasion. Could've been messy otherwise."

"Well, things were messy enough across the channel," Taggart said. "Colonel Edson is still rooting out Japs."

"Did you boys get your breakfast already?" Tregaskis asked.

Both men grinned. Taggart cleared his throat, "Yeah… but considerin' the duty we're tasked with this morning…."

Hazard crinkled his eyes, and then they went wide in understanding, "Don't tell me you're on latrine duty?"

Entwater flushed, "Yes sir… we volunteered, actually. On account of me and Davie haven't had even a touch of dysentery. We Raiders are made of sterner stuff. So, we agreed to help dig new trenches this morning."

"Then we get to take the afternoon off before heading out on special assignment," Taggart said.

Hazard raised his eyebrows, and Tregaskis appeared befuddled as well.

Taggart drew in a breath, "We're headed out with Jake Vousa and headed for the Matanikau, sir. You heard about Colonel Goettge?"

"Yeah, I spoke with Arnt and Spalding," Tregaskis said glumly. "Their reports were not good… and it's been a couple of days now."

"The General wants to send a couple of companies across the Matanikau to at least learn the colonel and his party's fate," Taggart said. "And give the Nips what-for… wish we knew what *really* happened out there…."

"Still no word?" Tregaskis asked.

The two Marines shook their heads in the negative. A few days before, Lieutenant Colonel Frank Goettge had led a team of twenty-five marines to Point Cruz, just to the west of the mouth of the Matanikau River. Intelligence reports… and the testimony of a prisoner… indicated that a platoon of Japanese soldiers was starving there and radioed to indicate that they would surrender in exchange for food. Goettge had been dispatched to recon the situation and bring the Japanese Marines back.

However, contact had been lost, and there were unreliable reports from locals that the entire thing had been a setup to draw Marines into an ambush. Word was that Colonel Goettge's entire patrol had been wiped out.

The only word had come from a couple of Marines that Goettge had dispatched to go back to base and report. The news had not been uplifting, to say the least.

"I ain't surprised," Hazard said gruffly, his face reddening. "Them fuckin' Japs ain't to be trusted. Ever. They're vicious, treacherous goddamned animals. I hate to say it, but I doubt you'll find Colonel Goettge or any of his men... alive. Christ... I wish I were goin' with you guys."

"Us too, sir," Taggart said, no small amount of empathy rising up within him for Hazard. The man had not only proven to be brave, strong and good in combat... he was a former Marine as well as a submarine officer... he'd suffered badly at the hands of their enemy. "Give it a few days, and you'll be ready to suit up again."

"Ooh-rah to that," Entwater said and smiled.

"Which means we need to get some chow into this boy," Tregaskis said, patting Hazard on his shoulder. "I still want that interview with you guys, by the way. Your story about coming ashore before the invasion is one I think the American public would love to read about... *needs* to read about, in fact."

"Fine by us, sir," Taggart said. "Although I'd rather it all be done at once. Maybe when the skipper and Chuck Lider get here, we can have ourselves a pow-wow."

"Wish Captain Turner and the others were in on it, too," Hazard said. "Wonder where they are now?"

Tregaskis shrugged, "Last I heard, *Bull Shark* was in Brisbane. Another correspondent I know there let me know. Said that they pulled out a couple of days ago. Where they're headed, though... well... it's the silent service, after all."

Hazard frowned, "That's true... and maybe before you write up an article about our doin's here we might check in with Webster Clayton. You know him, Dick?"

Tregaskis nodded grimly, "I do… and you may be right. He'd no doubt read my article before it was published in any case."

"Well, we gotta get movin', sir," Taggart said. "You fellas enjoy your chow. Try to keep it on the inside, huh? There's only so many trenches can be dug on this rock."

The four men split back into two groups; one another's laughter trailing behind. Hazard and the correspondent continued on to the makeshift mess hall set up not far from the Pagoda, the administration building constructed in the Japanese style of architecture.

By now, the hall was nearly empty. Shifts had been changed, and mealtime was nearly over. In fact, there was only one occupied table where four white men and half a dozen Melanesians clustered together over their garbage catchers.

"Porter!" Martin Clemens sang out, springing to his feet and beaming. "Happy I am to see you on your own two, mate! Grab a bite and join us, eh?"

Ever since Clemens and his people had come down from Vungana several days earlier, they'd been working closely with the Marines to arrange scouting parties, liaison missions to local villages and other island-centric logistical tasks. Clemens himself, who'd lost over forty pounds since the Japanese invaded the Solomons, was doing his best to pack it back on. This in spite of the two meals per day rationing instituted by Vandegrift to stretch out the Marines' meager supplies.

Clemens had cut his hair and shaved, and gone was the wild Grisly Adams mountain man and in his place a clean-cut, clean-shaven Scotsman who spoke with an English accent and now looked younger than his twenty-six years.

Hazard and Tregaskis grabbed trays of food-like substances that included a heaping pile of powdered eggs and cheese, a couple of canned peach halves, coffee and a healthy scoop of coconut rice. The latter being the result of leftover Japanese supplies supplemented by the ubiquitous nut found all over the northern coast and the former coconut plantations. They moved to the table and set their trays down as the ten men stood.

"You already know these lads, port," Clemens indicated the six dark-skinned island men with their four-inch-high hair tinged with yellow or red on top. These included Jake Vousa, who gave the two a thumbs up. "These three blokes here are some of my fellow coastwatchers. Aussie Commander D.S. McFarlane and fellow Britishers L. Schroder and F. Ashton Rhodes. Say hello to one of the gents that saved our backsides before the Yanks arrived, gents."

Hands were shaken, and introductions made. The twelve men sat and attended to their meal. After catching up a bit, Hazard cleared his throat.

"I understand Jake here is headed out on a scouting patrol tonight."

"That I am," Vousa said. "Dave and Ted and me. Headed east to scout out past the Teneru and maybe all the way to Taivu Point. Rumors are that the Japs are using it as a major drop-off point after dark."

"Something about using destroyers to ship in men and supplies," McFarlane commented in his heavy Australian drawl. "Bloody Nips are coming right down The Slot after sunset and dropping off men and barrels right off the beach there."

"The Tokyo Express," Tregaskis said. "Yeah, the rumors are they've been doing it since almost day one of our landing."

"Where'd you hear these rumors, Marty?" Hazard asked.

"Well, it's partly from our contacts here among the populous," Clemens replied. "And partly from decoded intelligence reports, as I understand it."

"From who?" Hazard asked although he suspected he knew.

"From me, Lieutenant," a new man's voice said from a few paces behind the sailor.

Both Tregaskis and Hazard turned to see a young Marine in olive drab utilities escorting a thirty-something man in an unadorned khaki uniform. The second man grinned at Hazard.

"Mr. Clayton?" Hazard gawked. "What the hell...?"

"Figured it was time I got back in the game," Clayton said and then turned to his guide. "Thanks, Treadway, I'll sit with these gents for a bit."

PFC Joe Treadway came to attention, "Aye-aye sir. Sure you don't need me for anything else, sir?"

"Not for now, Treadway," Clayton said and smiled at the friendly and somewhat over-enthusiastic young man. "And for the love of all that's decent… stop calling me sir."

"Yes sir!" Treadway said. "I'll see to our gear and locate Sergeant Oaks and the rest of the team, sir."

"Our gear, Treadway?" Clayton asked, a little bewildered.

"Yes sir," Treadway replied excitedly. "I've been accepted into the Raiders, sir. With Major Decker and Corporal Lider out of action, for the time being, Captain Simard thought that since I was accompanying you out here anyway, my weapons training would come in handy on Major Decker's team, sir."

"I thought you were admin, Joe?"

"Oh, that was just TAD for the Midway op, sir," Treadway replied. "My designator is infantry with a specialization in small arms, sir."

"Well, I'll be damned…." Clayton muttered. "Okay then, Joe. You'd better go and explain all this to Sergeant Oaks."

"Yes sir!" Treadway said and stood there silently at attention.

Clayton sighed and shook his head indulgently, "You're dismissed, Joe… and stop calling me sir."

"Aye-aye sir!" Treadway said and fast-walked for the door.

Clayton chuckled along with the other men, "Well then… I guess that's that."

"You're going on the scouting mission, Mr. Clayton?" Hazard asked dubiously.

The Office of Strategic Services man nodded, "Sometimes you've got to do what's necessary, Mr. Hazard. Not the first time I've put myself on the front lines, either. Seems only right."

Hazard introduced Clayton to the others. After another round of how-dos, he sighed, "I wish I were going with you fellas… I hate hanging back here where it's safe."

That got a laugh from the group. Although staying within the perimeter around Henderson Field certainly lowered one's chances of being shot… it did dramatically raise one's chances of being bombed.

As if to underscore Hazard's irony, a metallic clanging began from somewhere outside. The clanging reminded Hazard somewhat of the general quarters alarm aboard *Bull Shark*.

"What the hell's that?" Clayton asked. "Breakfast is over, right?"

Tregaskis snorted, "That, Mr. Clayton, is the camp-wide announcement that it's Tojo Time."

Hazard gulped down the last of his meal and stood, "It means we're about to get bombed."

"Yeah, and he doesn't mean it in any positive sense, Cobber," MacFarlane quipped. "Like a tall cold beer in one hand and a little hot Sheila in the other."

"Time we headed for the hills, as you lot say," Clemens told Clayton.

"Just about this time every morning, a group of Zekes, Vals and Betties heaves into view and tries to annoy us," Tregaskis told Clayton. "No worries, though… plenty of trenches to dive into. Just hold yourself up on your elbows, and it reduces the chance of concussion."

"Maybe this wasn't my best notion…." Clayton grumbled as he moved out of the hall in the wake of Clemens and his men. He and Tregaskis walked at Hazard's speed, ready to give him a hand in order to speed things along.

Already the Cactus Airforce was staged to meet their enemy. First to go were the nineteen Wildcats. Ready behind them were the dozen SBD Dauntless dive bombers stationed wherever they could be staged. The airfield didn't yet have much in the way of tarmac or taxiways. Yet the planes were ready to go, and the Marine pilots were eager to get into the air for the first time and face the Japanese on their own two feet, as it were.

Although the Dauntlesses weren't designed as fighters, they were rugged and without a bomb payload, more than nimble enough to face off with the Japanese Val dive bomber and Betty level bomber. The Wildcats, on the other hand, would engage the Zekes and attempt to down as many bombers as they could before they reached Henderson Field.

The gonging of the makeshift air raid alarm, an old dinner bell somebody had found and hoisted near the Pagoda, was drowned by the roar of radial engines as the Wildcats raced down the runway and into the air. Hazard, Clayton and Tregaskis angled toward the nearest foxhole, placed between the barracks and the runway. There were several Marines already in the trench, and they helped the wounded Hazard down and handed out extra combat helmets. All ten men turned their gaze skyward as the thirty-one aircraft of the Cactus Airforce soared north out over Sealark Channel and met the oncoming dark specs of enemy airplanes.

From the beaches ahead of them and from positions to the west of the landing strip, machine guns and anti-aircraft cannons began to chatter and pop. Red tracers lanced into the sky, and the world once more filled with the fury of the mechanical thunder of war. Engines roared, guns clattered, and men shouted. Then, inevitably, came the gut-wrenching whistle that every man there knew all too well.

Through the voices of battle, the swishing and whistling of deployed bombs blanketed the landscape all around. Even as some Japanese planes exploded overhead or cartwheeled into the sea, their deadly payloads plummeted hungrily toward the Earth. They tasted the soil and found it good… exploding in catastrophic flashes of incandescent death and great volcanic plumes of dirt, gravel and concrete. Mostly the bombs fell on open ground, gouging jagged craters in the earth. However, some did find the runway and, in a second, undid many hours of work by scooping out great hunks of landing strip and flinging it skyward in a cloud of destruction. One or two impacted with a building, but for the most part, the major structures were built to withstand such an assault. Here and there, though, a temporary or hastily set up structure would fly apart in a spinning cloud of wood splinters or aluminum sheets.

The attack drew out time into a seemingly endless and merciless cacophony of thunderous explosions, flying debris and the angry hornet roar of nearly a hundred aircraft. Then, as it so often happened, the noises vanished or diminished so significantly that what remained was a comfort as compared to what had gone before.

As the Cactus Airforce drove the Japanese away, the ack-ack fire ceased, and in the relative quiet, the sounds of men calling out for sucker and the rumble of construction equipment took over. Even as the Japanese planes turned back for Rabaul, medics were dispatched to see to the men, and the construction crews were dispatched to repair what damage had been done to the airstrip.

"Sweet Jesus…" Clayton coughed out as he stood from his hiding place and began to dust himself off. "That was… indescribable. Everybody okay?"

Tregaskis helped Hazard to his feet and spluttered, his breath cutting visible eddies in the hovering dust around them, "Yeah, it's quite a shit show… ahem… keeps the boredom away, though."

Clayton smiled at the bravado of the men around him, "John Ford's movie, as good as it was, didn't prepare me for that."

"Hell, we got off easy," a lantern-jawed Marine Sergeant stated wryly. "That was a light dustin' compared to yesterday's Tojo Time."

"Now we got our own birds," Hazard stated. "Feels good to see our boys kicking the jap up his slanted ass, don't it?"

Tregaskis laughed and glanced down at Clayton, "You *sure* you want in on this madness, Mr. Clayton?"

Clayton's belly was still twitching, and he seriously considered replying with a resounding hell no. But seeing the resolve and high spirits of the men around him, he could never bring himself to admit fear. Instead, he grinned crookedly and said: "It's a livin'."

3
THE SLOT – 120 MILES W, NW OF SEALARK CHANNEL
AUGUST 18, 1942 – 2155 GUADALCANAL TIME

A handful of long and narrow nimbus clouds sailed placidly high over a tropical sea. Their misty keels turned leaden gray in the dying twilight, yet each had just a hint of glowing gold at their bows as the last faint rays of sunlight caress them gently from over the horizon. Below these great and ethereal skyships, the waters of New Georgia Sound rolled gently, impelled by a moderate trade wind.

From between two of the gentle two-foot swells, something cold, hard and unnatural rose, its single unblinking eye peeping about, turning a complete circle before once again vanishing. This small stalk, no thicker than a man's arm and whose length, at least what could be seen of it above the surface, was no longer than a tall woman's leg. It might appear innocuous, hardly hinting at the true size of the monster to which it was attached, nor to the deadly potential of the thing which commanded it.

The stalk vanished, and then the sea foamed and churned and writhed as its deadliest predator, a leviathan more than three hundred feet long and weighing two and a half thousand tons when submerged rose from the depths. Its sleek shape and purpose all too clear, its voracious appetite for steel hulls impossible to slake.

The bridge hatch opened, and six men popped up. Three continued to climb, swarming up the steel webbing of the periscope sheers and clipping into the perch there. The three other men crowded together on the small bridge, and tiny flames glowed momentarily near their heads. Behind them, four rapid coughs and growls broke the peace of the evening as the submarine's four mighty General Motors' diesel engines came to life, pouring their power into the great batteries and electric motors as well.

"Ship rigged for surface, Captain," Elmer Williams said as he drew on his Winston.

"Very well, Elmer," Art Turner said formally and then grinned as he puffed his Lucky Strike. "Gorgeous evening. Warm, pleasant sea breeze… and we got Hotrod to look at…."

"It is my great pleasure to allow my beauty to be an object of admiration, *señor*," Quartermaster's mate first-class Ralph "Hotrod" Hernandez drawled in an over-the-top Mexican accent. "I have been much sought after by the young women in my humble village."

Williams snickered, "Your humble village of Long Beach, California?"

"Lotta rich dames scoping you at the beach, were there, Hotrod?" Turner asked with a chuckle.

"*Si…*" Hotrod intoned. "*Muy bonita con chichis grande, Tambien!*"

That broke everyone up, even the men in the lookout perch. Although most didn't speak Spanish, except for Turner, they got the gist. The captain shook his head tolerantly.

"Okay, XO, where are we?" Turner asked as if he didn't already know.

"In The Slot, about a dozen miles southeast of New Georgia Island and Munda Point, to be exact," Williams said. "I figure we can do a west to east and back again route by night. Bound to catch something driving down for Guadalcanal."

"Roger that," Turner said. "I think we can plan this so that by day, we take a peek at New Georgia. From what I've heard, there are several useful points on that island. Munda Point, as you say… could be a sight for another damned Jap airfield. Then there's a harbor on the northwest side…."

"Bairoko Harbor," Hotrod added. "Deep water."

"Yeah, great place to land troops and supplies from Rabaul," Williams opined. "Probably gonna be another stop on the Solomons hit parade someday. God... can you imagine... hopping up these islands one after another and fighting tooth and nail for each damned inch?"

Turner drew in a breath and let it out slowly, closing his eyes for a moment, "All too well, Elmer. Well, it's time I took the reins. Go down and grab yourself some supper, XO. Henrie has whipped us up something special for our arrival back at the shit show. Cajun snapper filets, last of the fresh broccoli and dirty rice."

"Yum," Williams said. "You boys behave up here. And if you see any japs, wait till I'm done eating before sounding the alarm, huh?"

"Shoulda eaten when we did," Turner jibed.

"*I* was on watch, Art... not lounging around like the Prince of Timbuktu," Williams jibed.

"Hey... it's not *my* fault I'm the captain!" Turner pretended to whine.

"Oh yeah, mister?" Williams asked in his best annoyed mom. "Then who's fault *is* it, mister?"

'Uhm... Hotrod's..."

"That makes sense," Williams said and then laughed. "Try to be a good influence, huh, Hotrod?"

"*Si.*"

Williams dropped down the hatch, and Turner leaned against the starboard bridge rail, "Ahh... lovely evening. Well, Hotrod, best we get up off it and get on with it. Put us on a track to cross The Slot. Let's keep one and two on charge and three and four on an 80/90."

Aye-aye," Hotrod said. He quickly consulted his maneuvering board and thumbed the bridge speaker. "Helm, all ahead standard. Come right and steady up on course... zero-seven-five."

"*Bridge, helm, maneuverin' answiz' all ahead two-thirds, steadyin' up on course zero-seven-fivuh,*" Richard "Mug" Vigliano, the helmsman of the watch, reported.

Bull Shark turned slightly to her right and drove on toward the deepening indigo of eastern darkness. At a modest eight knots, she'd cross the main shipping lane of The Slot shortly and could then accelerate once her batteries were fully charged. Before dawn, the submarine would cross the shipping lanes and then back again. She'd also follow the path for a while as well, hoping to be overrun by the Tokyo Express destroyers either headed for Guadalcanal or returning.

As the men stood their watch, the sea breezes occasionally carried with them the scent of the land. The Solomon Islands archipelago was one of the largest in the world, with over a thousand islands ranging from low-lying coral atolls to higher volcanic islands like Guadalcanal. Being tropical, … even now the boat was only a few hundred miles from the equator… the biomass was immense. Tropical rainforests and jungles, palms and hardwoods along with ubiquitous seaside scrub exhaled their perfume into the atmosphere so profusely that even from over the horizon, the heady aroma of chlorophyll, flowers and moist earth found its way to the nose of the mariner.

Down in the wardroom, Elmer Williams sat at the head of the table with the rest of the off-duty officers. With both Pat Jarvis and Porter Hazard away from the ship, *Bull Shark* was short-handed at the top level, and a few minor changes had been made. For one, Paul "Buck" Rogers, the ship's Chief of the Boat, or COB, was also acting electrical officer. As an acting officer, he was also slated to stand watch and was currently acting JOOD for Turner. Andy Post had once again resumed his former position as assistant engineer and Joe Dutch as acting torpedo officer. Frank Nichols was still engineer, and not much had changed for him.

Dutch, Nichols and Post were dining with the XO, therefore. Each man also had a small pocket notebook ready to hand. It was a working meal, to be sure.

"You know you boys need to relax once in a while," Eddie Carlson, the officer's steward, chided as he set out the food. "You gonna give yourselves an ulcer."

"You our mom now, Eddie?" Nichols asked genially.

Carlson smiled, "Well, sir… it's my job to sort of look after y'all. Any you valuable officers breaks down on account of me slackin' off, and Uncle Charlie will hang my black butt from the nearest flagpole."

"There's an interesting mental image…." Post chuckled.

"Yeah, great… now all I'm gonna see when I close my eyes tonight is an image of Eddie mooning all of us!" Dutch chortled.

Carlson made a rude noise, "No appreciation for beauty."

"Damn," Williams enthused as he took a bite of his snapper. "Flakey and with a nice flavor. Henrie sure does know his way around the galley."

"He'll be happy to hear that, sir," Carlson said, moving into his pantry for a fresh pot of coffee.

"Okay…" Williams began. "The Skipper and I have a list of concerns and items to go over. The most pressing, as I'm sure nobody will be surprised to hear… is our pickles. How we doing on that, Joe?"

Dutch consulted his notebook, "Well, we all know that the reloads we got in Brisbane are the *unmodified* Mark 14s. We also know that BeauOrd would have our nads nailed to a barn door if they ever get wind of what we're up to…."

"Yes, but thankfully Admiral Edwards gave us carte blanche on that," Nichols pointed out.

Williams harrumphed, "That was six months ago, Frank. We're not in his command anymore… not even in his *ocean,* for that matter. I'm not so sure that ComSubLant's influence will keep us safe. I think we should all understand that. Maybe not let that leak down to Sparky or Murph… what they don't know can't hurt them… but technically we *are* in violation of regs."

Dutch shrugged, "And we got eleven kills, something like sixty thousand tons of downed shipping to back us up. Anyway, the damage is done. All loaded fish have been modified. COB has been working with Sparky and Murph, and me to get those magnetic exploders deactivated. There are still two to be done in the after room and half a dozen in the forward. It's kind of a slow process. It's not overly complicated, but the work has to be done slowly and carefully, as you might imagine. I'm hoping that by noon sights tomorrow we'll have the after fish completed and two more in the forward room. That gives us ten good fish loaded and a complete modified reload. So far."

"Let's hope we get a chance to burn through 'em quick," Post said around a bite of rice. "I, for one, wouldn't mind putting into Pearl for two weeks. Would be nice we got a full R and R stint for once."

The other men laughed, even Carlson. They all knew that Andy Post was engaged to a tall, buxom blonde named April and that the two were anxious to get hitched. There was little doubt among anyone who knew the pair that their wedding night wouldn't be their first foray into coital bliss… but then again, sampling the goods beforehand probably made the waiting all the harder.

"Roger that," Frank Nichols said, who also missed his pretty young wife.

"Here, here," Dutch added, hoisting his coffee mug. "Even us married guys like to see our wives every few years."

Williams chuckled along with the others, yet he felt a mild twinge of loneliness as well. Unlike the other men in the wardroom, Williams had no sweetheart to return to. He'd been engaged to a pretty young woman named Margaret when he'd been assigned to oversee *Bull Shark's* final construction and fitting out. Yet the time constraints of PXO school, which he hadn't even finished until later on, fitting out the boat and other duties left little time for him and Madge.

She'd quickly grown resentful and bitter and had left him only to fall into the arms of a man named Tom Begley. Williams had served with Begley, and the two men had not formed a friendship. Partly due to Begley's poor attitude and partly because he blamed Williams for losing a wargame in which they both served on the same S-boat in Panama.

Somehow, in spite of being at PXO school himself, Begley had found time for William's ex. However, things came to a head at a local New London bar one night. Elmer and Pat Jarvis had mixed it up with Begley and his buddy Burt Pendergast. It had shown Madge, who was there, what type of man Begley really was… but that had done nothing to heal the rift between her and Elmer.

"Your chest full of medals isn't enough?" Williams jibed. "You want *sex* too?"

They all looked at him and grinned broadly. That got another laugh, and the meal proceeded on in the usual good nature of the boat's wardroom.

Williams climbed into the lower rack in the stateroom he shared with Pat Jarvis a little after twenty-hundred. It was odd to have the entire stateroom… hardly enough room for the two bunks and chest of drawers… to himself. Once more, Williams felt a bit lonely. At least when Pat was around, he had a fellow bachelor to talk to.

It seemed like only seconds after he'd closed them that William's eyes snapped open. The melodious cathedral-bell gong of the ship's general alarm banishing any tendrils of sleep and impelling the XO to shoot to his feet and begin pulling on his shorts and uniform blouse. A quick glance at his watch showed him he'd only been asleep for a little over an hour.

"Leve it up to Art to find a Jap ship before his first watch on station was even over…" Williams muttered bemusedly as he slid his feet into his sandals.

The control room was bathed in blood-red light, a standard procedure when the ship was surfaced at night. The red light allowed men to work without affecting their night vision. Williams caught the COB's smile as he entered and gazed around to assess the situation.

"Skipper's last sugar jig sweep made contact with possible multiples to the northwest, sir," Rogers reported before the XO could even ask. "He's got me on a new plot."

"That my little Elmer down there?" came a faint voice that filtered down from the bridge hatch, through the conning tower hatch and still reached their ears.

Williams chuckled, "How the hell could he possibly… yeah, I'm here, Art!"

The control room phone talker grinned, "Captain asks you report to the bridge, sir."

Rogers laughed as he bent to his plot on the big master gyro compass table. Even as he started up the ladder, Williams noted that Nichols and Dutch were ducking into the control room from the forward battery compartment, as was Chief yeoman Clancy Weiss. Weiss took up station at the plot, and Dutch followed Williams up the ladder where he slid into Pat's usual seat at the torpedo data computer.

"Welcome back, Elmer," Turner said as William's head popped up from the glowing crimson circle of the bridge hatch. "I think we've got ourselves a convoy."

The XO stood behind and between the captain and the quartermaster, "Definite multiples, sir?"

"Not yet," Turner said. "But I'll bet it's a group of tin cans running in line ahead formation. Wouldn't make much sense to send just one, I'd think."

"Concur," Williams said. "Well, I'll go below and assist with the plot, shall I?"

"That's a negative, XO," Turner replied amiably. "We're gonna do it the Mush Morton way. I'll con the approach; you manage the attack."

Williams grinned, "Works for me. What's our strategy?"

Turner drew in a breath, "We'll see how the land lies, so to speak. But if I'm right, and they are running in a line, then I'd like to either swing around or duck under and send a couple of fish up the rear vessel's skirt. You know what we've been talking about, Elmer. It's one thing to shoot freighters and tankers… but going after warships, especially DDs that are designed to sink *us,* will have to be a different ball game. We might not be able to get them all in one go. More likely than not, we've got to be happy with one kill and then get the hell outta Dodge. Hopefully, S-52 will be waiting near the end zone and take out another. Not tonight, of course… they won't be on station for a day or two… anyway, let's see what happens. I've got us cutting away from their course at a fifteen-degree angle for a little while."

"Putting enough angle off the track so that the radar can pick out the ships astern of the first one?" Williams asked by way of confirmation.

Turner grinned, "Exactly. Teddy says they're running about one-two-zero at thirty knots. Range right now is twenty-thousand yards. Which means they'll be on top of us in twenty minutes."

Williams nodded, "Understood."

"*Bridge, radar!*" Ted Balkley reported over the transmitter. "*Two targets, repeat* two *targets headed one-two-zero at three-zero knots.*"

"Only two…" Turner mused. "Running balls to the wall, though.

Be tough to hit them even from their flanks. Too easy to evade at that speed. I think it's plan-B, Elmer."

"Aye-aye," Williams said and dropped down the hatch. As he did, he heard the order come down from Hotrod to alter the boat's course to put her directly in the line of the destroyer's track. Once done, the diving alarm was sounded, and the lookouts dropped down the hatch, followed by Hotrod and the skipper.

"Phone talker, alert maneuvering to standby to answer bells on batteries," Turner ordered. "Mug, all stop. Close main induction, rig out bow planes… All ahead two-thirds helm…."

"Green Christmas tree!" Nichols reported from the diving station in the control room. "Pressure in the boat!"

"Make your depth one-five-zero feet, diving officer," Turner ordered. "Open main vents, flood safety, flood negative…."

With admirable efficiency, the crew of *Bull Shark* rigged their ship for dive. Within thirty seconds of giving the order, the boat was angling down below the dark surface, still using the remnants of her surface speed to drive down more quickly. When done smartly, a submarine's momentum from a high-speed run would still be pushing her faster than her electric-only operations could. In this way, she could dive at greater than her maximum nine knots of battery-powered speed and get below the surface in a hurry. With a well-drilled and well-seasoned crew like *Bull Shark's*, this complex maneuver became a matter of smooth routine.

"Forty-five feet," Nichols reported.

"Close all vents, blow negative to the mark," Turner ordered. "Mug, right full rudder, bring us around to one-two-zero. Keep your ears peeled, Chet."

Chet Rivers, the boat's leading sonarman, focused on his controls and the sounds filtering in through his headphones. Mounted to the upper bow and slung below her forward torpedo room, the JP and JK soundheads respectively were turning and collecting sound waves from the ocean around them. As this wave energy was converted to electrical signals, it was filtered through a series of amplifiers and transformers to be slowed down and reproduced at the sonar station in the conning tower as audible sound.

"Fast light screws, sir," Chet said calmly, speaking a little quieter in spite of no silent running order having been given. "Now bearing one-eight-five... turn rate steady and matches thirty knots from radar... range now one-four-triple zero yards."

"Joe, alert the forward room to open their doors," Williams said from his position beside Turner at the periscopes. "Speed high, depth six feet."

"Helm left standard rudder," Turner ordered. After a few seconds, he said: "Come back to one-two-zero... Chet?"

"Contact bears one-eight-zero exactly, sir," Rivers said with admiration. "Dead nuts."

"Yeah, let's hope we ain't all a bunch of dead nuts...." Vigliano jibed.

"What're you scared, Mug?" Turner asked wryly.

'Not so much for me, sir," the helmsman tossed off, "but there's this cute little broad I met in Brisbane... oh, Madone... I'd hate to deprive her, y'know?"

"I love a man who's humble," Williams chuckled to himself.

"Mug, back us down to ahead one-third," Turner said after a moment. "Chet, any echo ranging from the tin cans?"

"Not at this time, sir," Rivers reported, sounding a bit bemused.

"Yeah, that is weird..." Williams opined, "you'd think they'd at least do a regular scan."

Turner shrugged, "Moving as fast as they are, they probably figure there's not much danger from a submarine. A set of good lookouts should be able to spot the torpedo wakes with enough time to evade, even at night. Speed is life, I guess."

"Then won't they spot ours coming up on their tails?" Dutch asked.

"Maybe... so that's why we need to be crafty," Turner said. "Our fish run at forty-six knots. Our targets are running at thirty. Our fish have to run a minimum of four-hundred and fifty yards to arm...."

"One train leaves San Diego traveling at sixty miles per hour...." Balkley muttered and snickered.

"Exactly, radar," Turner acknowledged. "So, Joe and plot down there… and Hotrod… with a sixteen knot overtake, when is the earliest we can fire and have our fish reach the sternmost DDs screws at just over four-five-zero yards?"

"It's a trick question," Hotrod replied with a smile of triumph. "Since it's a straight line shot from astern, we fire at four-hundred and fifty yards. That gives enough time for the fish to accelerate to top speed, so they should reach the target a little past the arming point."

Turner laughed, "Good work, Hotrod."

"Still lookin' at two minutes run time, Art," Dutch said.

"Chance we have to take, Joe," Turner said. "Hopefully the prop wash from the tin can will mask the torpedo wake. Guess we'll find out. Order of tubes is one, two. Give me a zero-gyro, zero-degree separation. Rig ship for silent running."

The order went out, and all unnecessary equipment was turned off. That included the hydraulic gear that controlled the steering surfaces and sound heads, as well. Which meant the planesmen and helmsman would have to steer using muscle power alone. It also meant that three men in the forward torpedo room would be spinning the overhead JP control wheel and the JK and WCA control wheels below the platform deck.

Turner could just imagine Sparky grumbling and swearing in his heavy Alabama drawl. It put a smile on his face.

Rivers' report of the approach of the first destroyer was entirely redundant. Even from several hundred yards away, the swift swishing of the screws began to fill the quiet submarine's long tubular hull.

Shoo, shoo, shoo, shoo, shoo, shoo…

"Here's number one…." Rivers whispered.

"Hang tight, Mug, you might get some wash turbulence," Turner advised.

Mug was a brawny Bronx Italian, and Turner could already see that his biceps were bulging beneath the cotton of his skivvy shirt. Strangely, a portion of a fouled anchor tattoo on Vigliano's left arm stretched as his muscles bunched with the strain of holding a twenty-six-hundred-ton ship steady through the eddies of another vessel's propellors little more than a hundred feet over his head.

The entire boat shivered as the Coriolis effect created by the passage of two-thousand tons through seawater at high speed and the thrust of twin screws buffeted the submarine. Turner alternately watched the rudder angle indicator and the gyrocompass repeater and Mug's tattoo. Admirably, the helmsman held the boat perfectly on course. After a moment, the screw noise began to fade and the tattoo to deflate.

"Number two is nine-hundred yards astern and closing," Rivers said.

"Firing solution set," Dutch stated.

"It's your finger on the button, Elmer," Turner said, leaning against the bridge ladder and lighting a cigarette.

Turner smiled to himself as a memory of himself as XO of *Tautog* conning his first *real* attack appeared before his mind's eye. He recalled Captain Willingham, leaning against the ladder and lighting a butt just as he was doing now. Ah, the circle of life…

"Hang tight, Mug!" Rivers hissed.

Again, an unnecessary announcement. Once more, the churning of rapidly spinning propellors grew louder and louder until it became as thunderous as a high waterfall. It was joined by the shuddering of the boat and the nearly inaudible squeak of small gear in shock-absorbing mounts. Finally, the sound began to diminish.

"Call out fifty-yard marks for me, Chet," Williams said. "Standby Joe…"

"Fifty yards… one-hundred yards… one-fifty," Chet intoned. At first calm and metronomic, but as the range opened and the firing point drew near, he couldn't keep the excitement from his voice. "Three hundred… three-fifty… four hundred… four-five-zero yards!"

"Fire one," Williams ordered.

Instantly, Dutch pushed the firing plunger for tube one, and the boat shuddered as three-thousand pounds of torpedo was blasted from her nose. Williams counted to six.

"Fire two!"

Again, everyone felt the surge of force through their feet and legs as another twenty-foot-long Mark 14 was expelled. To a man, jaws opened and closed and worked to equalize the pressure as six-thousand pounds of compressed air was sucked back into the boat and expelled into the pressure hull from the Poppet valves.

"Periscope depth," Turner ordered. "Chet, get that Kodak ready. Frank, be ready for a hard dive when I give the word! Secure from silent running. Mug, all ahead two-thirds."

The boat rose slowly toward the surface, planing up through the dark waters until her cycloptic eye could pierce the waves and observe what havoc she would hopefully wreak.

"Up search scope," Williams ordered. "You want first look, Skipper?"

"Nope, that goes to the man who gave the word, Elmer."

"Twenty-seconds," Dutch said.

An explosion thundered in the distance. In his scope, Williams saw a plume of dark water erupt, foaming ghostly silver in the moonlight.

"Damn!" Rivers cranked. "Premature detonation on number one, sir!"

"Fuckin' BeauOrd pickles…." Buck Rogers was heard to grump from below.

"Let's hope the next one—" Williams was interrupted by a brilliant flash in his eyepiece and then an even more devastating explosion. "Got him! Take a look, Skipper!"

Turner pressed his eye to the piece and laughed in triumph, "Christ! He must've been carrying some ash cans… blew his ass right off! Quick, Chet, snap a pic before he goes under!"

Rivers pressed his camera to the eyepiece and snapped off three quick shots.

"Frank, full down angle!" Turner ordered. "Mug, hard right rudder. Chet, let me know what his buddy is doing."

The problem with sinking destroyers or other warships, as every submariner knew, was that it was like stirring up a hornet's nest. All other ships would know that an enemy submarine was near and would go on active alert, doing all they could to punish the offender.

"No change," Rivers said. "Still heading one-two-zero… no, turn rate increase. Must've gone to flank. I think he's high tailing it, sir."

"Probably more important to get to the island than to hunt us down," Williams mused. "Well… that was easy." Turner grinned,

"Good work everyone. Well done. I think, though, that this one's gonna be the easiest. We've shown our cards now, and God knows Tojo doesn't take much lying down. It's only gonna get harder the longer we go."

"Funny, Skipper," Mug tossed off, "that's the same thing I told Henrietta just four nights ago."

4

S-52 – 300 MILES S, SW OF GUADALCANAL

AUGUST 18, 1942 – 2135 GUADALCANAL TIME

Although there was no reason to think so, pat Jarvis was firmly convinced that S-52 was louder than his own boat. No reason to think so because, for one thing, the pig boat had only two diesels instead of four… yet to Jarvis' ear, the twenty-year-old submarine was a rattletrap.

It was nearly the end of the second dog watch, and he was slated to take over the deck from the Skipper in less than half an hour. It had always been Jarvis' habit to take a turn through the boat before he went on watch. To check over the equipment and to get a handle on the mood of the men. That way, at least, if there were any maintenance issues, mechanical casualties or personnel problems, he'd know the score before taking over the ship. Especially if his watch was to be stood on the bridge, as it would be since the sun was even then going down.

While the Navy did classify the S-class submarines as fleet boats… they really weren't up to the job these days. They were smaller, slower and less heavily armed than their modern fleet boat descendants. And if anybody thought a *Gato* or *Balao*-class boat was cramped, Jarvis mused, they ought to squeeze into this stinking pipe for a few days.

S-52 was the very last S-boat to ever have been built. This meant that she was the youngest of her class, commissioned in 1922. However, it also meant she was twenty years old and, in spite of upgrades, showed her age in just about every conceivable way. Her soundproofing was a joke; the clatter and rattle of her diesels and electric motors at near full power easily reached the torpedo room forward. Her ventilation system, although good, could do nothing to alleviate the stinks that accompanied submarine life. Body odor, diesel and lubricant fumes, frying fat from the galley, stale cigarette funk and even the occasional waft from the two heads that served over forty men could nearly gag a person when they first came aboard. Thankfully, one's nose grew accustomed to this unique bouquet… desensitized was more like it, really.

S-52, at least, wasn't one of the earlier designs with the fuel and ballast tanks *inside* the pressure hull. Jarvis had done a tour on S-15 when he was a fresh-faced ensign, and the boat reminded him of a complex lead pipe full of machines that somebody, at the last minute, had stuffed a couple of bunks into just to be an asshole.

S-52 was smaller than *Bull Shark,* of course, and had only six compartments in the pressure hull rather than the normal eight. There was the torpedo room forward, of course. Then the forward battery compartment, which held the first of S-52's sixty-cell lead-acid batteries beneath the deck. Above the deck, crammed in as tightly as Electric Boat could make them, were the crew's berths. Twenty of these, which meant that the men had to share them, or "hot bunk" as it was known. There was the crew's head and shower, the tiny officer's wardroom and the captain's stateroom. A dog box hardly large enough for his bunk, fold-out desk and enough room to very carefully slide into a pair of pants.

There was the control room aft of this compartment, of course. Above it was the conning tower. These two compartments were not dissimilar to the newer boats except that the gear was older. One interesting feature of the S-boats, or some of them, was that there were two small portholes in the conning tower to either side of the bridge hatch. These were remarkably thick and watertight… unlike the periscope barrels, both of which seemed to leak terribly. So much so that if a man didn't don a rain slicker and sou'wester rain hat while dancing with either one-eyed lady, he'd be soaked through in seconds.

Aft of the control room was the after-battery compartment. This was where the galley and mess were located, to port. To starboard were a number of switchboards, the officer's head and shower and two staterooms for two officers each. These snugs were the lap of luxury and privacy, save the captain's lone cabin, and allowed two officers to lounge in their racks and take turns dressing so as not to stamp one another's toes.

Next came the engine room with the boat's two eight-cylinder diesels and associated Allis Chalmers machine electrical generators. This extremely loud and hot compartment, when on the surface, also held the auxiliary engine, water evaporators and a variety of tanks. Finally came the maneuvering room. The boat's two big electric motors drove the propellor shafts, and all engine, motor and battery systems were controlled from a cubicle not unlike *Bull Shark's*, although somewhat smaller and more ancient.

Sitting on the padded bench before the pipe-organ-like control console was Chief electrician's mate Paul Cantone. Cantone was a swarthy man of about forty whom it was rumored had been with S-52 since she slid off the ways. He was a hard-faced man from South Boston and had little tolerance for screw-ups, newbies or officers with two notable exceptions. He admired the skipper and had accepted their now dead executive officer. So, it followed then that he was not a fan of Jarvis.

"Evenin' chief," Jarvis said casually, intent on breaking through the man's wall of hard-ass with kindness rather than a right cross. Although he had yet to rule that path out entirely.

"Sir," Cantone replied stiffly in his thick Boston. "Come back to learn somethin', sir? Or just make sure we ain't screwin' off back here?"

Leaning against the barrel of number five torpedo tube, Chief Machinist's Mate Archie Lockner lit a cigarette and chuckled irreverently. Where Cantone was somewhat short and squat in build, Lockner was a bit of a bean pole. Standing at about Jarvis' own six-two, Lockner couldn't weigh more than a buck seventy. But although stringy in appearance, he was tough and knew how to run his engine room. He was a generally good-natured man of thirty with reddish-brown hair and a no-nonsense midwestern outlook.

"Don't mind him, Mr. Jarvis, sir," Lockner said. "He ain't ever in a good mood. Hates everybody and everything that don't flow with lectristy or come with a pair of hooters."

"Long as he keeps this boat running smoothly," Jarvis said, "I don't give a rat's ass what he thinks about any goddamned thing."

Cantone harrumphed and studied the arrays of switches, gauges and levers before him. The boat was about to surface, and he'd be called upon to switch from batteries to diesels and would have to divert power from the generators to recharge the batteries as well as answer all engine bells from the conning tower. He didn't have time to verbally fence with no smart-ass from Rhody.

"How about you, Chief?" Jarvis said. "You hate officers too? Think I'm a shithead because I'm here and your former XO isn't?"

Lockner puffed and shrugged his bony shoulders, "Frankly, sir… I'm just an engine snipe, y'know? I don't get into politics and all that. Mr. Daniels was a decent officer. I didn't have too many troubles with'm. But we wasn't friends and didn't always see eye to eye. Don't mean to speak ill of the dead, understand. Man gave his life for the ship, and that ain't no small thing. So… like you say, sir. You do your job, and I'll do mine."

"Good enough," Jarvis said. "Everything here and forward looks ship-shape as usual. Well, you boys enjoy your off watch. Gotta go and take the reins."

Jarvis ducked through the forward hatch into the engine room and was gone. His backside had hardly cleared the hatchway when Cantone snorted in derision.

"Thinks he's the cat's ass, don't he?"

Lockner made a non-committal sound, "Dunno, Pauly. So far, he been doin' his job. Heard some stuff about him from our new COB, though. Member, he does my job aboard *Bull Shark*. Anyway, he says Mr. Jarvis there is a good dude. He don't micro-manage and knows how to let a workin' man work."

"Uh-huh," Cantone did not sound convinced.

"I *also* hear that he don't suffer fools gladly," Lockner said, waggling a finger at his friend. "You ride him, and he will kick your ass for ya'. Way Harry tells it, Pat Jarvis is a great man to have in your corner and a heller to have on your case. Somethin' to think about, buddy."

Cantone made a rude noise, "I ain't worried."

"Well," Lockner said with a chuckle as he moved away from the oddly placed single aft torpedo tube. "Then I'm afeared you might be headed for what we in Saint Looey call a con-ffron-tation. See you at chow."

"I wouldn't want to get on that guy's bad side, Chief," Jimmy Kintner mused from beside Cantone.

"Did I ask your opinion on the matter, numb nuts?" the Chief grumped. "You just sit there and do ya' fuckin' jawb."

In the cramped wardroom, Jarvis found Savage and two other officers enjoying their chili mac. It had been no surprise to Jarvis to find that he and Savage had not yet been able to find any common ground. Jarvis was learning that this boat was not just a close-knit community but almost phobic of change.

A few of the men had actually been pleased to have *Bull Shark's* torpedo officer. Strangely so, as many others were sore about it. This strange dichotomy extended to the officers as well. While Savage was certainly no fan… Jarvis suspected it had far more to do with the fact that he hadn't gotten the executive officer's billet than it did any love for the now-dead man. Savage talked a good game, but his grievance was all too clear, and he wore it like a charm bracelet for everyone to see.

S-52 was a smaller boat and had only forty-five officers and men. That meant fewer officers, as a matter of course. It meant that Harry Brannigan, now acting COB, also stood JOOD with the captain. The remaining two officers, Lieutenant Crawford Lutz, engineer and Tony Skaggs, communications and commissary, were all there were.

Lutz was a thirtyish man of average height and build. Pretty much average in every way. Medium brown hair that matched his eyes, plain looks and a mostly neutral disposition. Although he'd only been aboard a few days, however, Jarvis did sense a certain lack of zeal for his work. It was nothing overt, such as neglecting his duties… it was more a sense that Lutz would neither slack off nor would he go the extra mile. He did his job as engineer and diving officer without either enthusiasm or creativity.

Tony Skaggs, on the other hand, was a different animal all together. Twenty-four and a real eager-beaver. He'd just been promoted at the end of the S-52's last tour and was all gung-ho to go out and kill him some Japs. He'd been one of the men who was fired up about Jarvis coming aboard. Tales of *Bull Shark's* exploits were tearing through the fleet, and to an ambitious youngster like Skaggs who was perhaps over-eager to attain some glory, they were like gasoline on a campfire. Skaggs was paired with Jarvis on his watches, and the new XO thought that he might be a good source of insider dope on the boat and her men. He also thought that with the obvious hero-worship Skaggs held for him, Jarvis might be able to caution the man into a bit more circumspection for his own good.

"How's the grub, gents?" Jarvis asked as the steward, a Philipino man named Apolinario Avellino, handed him a cup of coffee.

Avellino was one of the refugees who'd escaped with MacArthur and had joined up with the Navy as soon as he could. He was a cheerful young man whom the men and officers either referred to as double-A or Apollo.

"Fills the belly," Lutz replied.

"You tell us, you already had yours," Savage said. "Figured you'd be on watch already. New XO and all."

"Just came to pick up Tony here," Jarvis said, making an attempt not to rise to Savage's standoffishness. "Ready for the excitement, Tony?"

Skaggs grinned around a forkful of chili and spaghetti, "Aye-aye sir. Though we're kinda far for any action yet, ain't we?"

Jarvis grinned, "You never know."

"That's right, Tony," Savage said with a sneer playing at his lips.

"Might need to dive under a couple of frigate birds, huh, Craw? They can be *deadly*."

That story, too, had been making the rounds. How on Jarvis' watch a day out of Panama on her way to Pearl back in May, *Bull Shark* did an emergency dive to avoid what the lookouts thought were Japanese aircraft. It had turned out to be a couple of sea birds, and the then XO Tom Begley had wanted to bring up Fred Swooping Hawk… the man who'd sighted the birds… before a captain's mast. Fortunately, cooler heads had prevailed.

Lutz chuckled but made no comment. Skaggs frowned and shot a withering look at Savage. He said nothing but quickly polished off his dinner.

Jarvis grinned at Savage, "Better safe than sorry, Chris. I'd much rather have a sharp-eyed man misidentify a bird than slack off and miss a real threat."

Savage scoffed, "Maybe those men were better trained, and they'd have known that there wouldn't be any Japs five thousand miles east of Pearl, huh, Pat?"

"We live and learn, Chris," Jarvis replied calmly. "And by the way… since you refuse to yank that pole outta your ass and accept the situation… me bein' the XO and not you… then I think that *you're* well-trained enough to know that you refer to me as *sir*. Long as you keep actin' like a spoiled brat… or a hard-on… we ain't on a first-name basis. So, I strongly suggest you remember that or drop the tude. Clear?"

Savage's face erupted into a vermillion flush of fury. He barely managed to stiffen and, through clenched teeth, replied: "Yes *sir!*"

Jarvis sighed and looked to Skaggs, "You ready to go, Tony?"

"Yes sir," the younger man said eagerly.

"We've got a few minutes yet if you want to eat a little more," Jarvis said kindly.

"I'm all topped-off, sir," Skaggs said, almost jumping to his feet.

Jarvis nodded to the other men and led the way out through the mildewed green baize curtain and into the passageway. As they were about to duck into the control room, Jarvis placed a friendly hand on Skaggs' shoulder.

"*You* can call me Pat, Tony," Jarvis said kindly. "Except for formal situations. It's good for officers to have a friendly working relationship, I've found."

"Thanks sir… Pat."

"Welcome to the party, gentlemen," Captain Waters said from around a cigar as Jarvis and Skaggs climbed up into the conning tower. "You fellas ready to face the night?"

"Yes sir," Skaggs enthused.

Waters rolled a considering eye toward Jarvis, "How about you, Exec? Young Tony here would love it if we came topside in the middle of a Jap battle fleet. Maybe bag a flattop or two… maybe even *Yamato*. How about you?"

"Well sir," Jarvis said, still uncertain of how to best approach Waters. "We've got fifteen fish aboard… figure that's enough for at least a task force."

Waters uttered a short chuckle around his Panatela, "Uh-huh… God save us from men lookin' to make their mark on somebody else's tree… thought I had my hands full with young Anthony here."

"I didn't come to the Pacific to play cribbage, Captain," Jarvis said with a smile. "I came out here to kick some Jap ass. But neither am I some Hollywood war movie hero who can't wait to run out into battle yellin' yahoo while the enemy mows me down."

"Good to know," Waters replied thoughtfully. "Well, we're at periscope depth, and I just did a sweep. Looks all clear up there, so you fellas should have a nice quiet watch while we put the spurs to'er. She's all yours, Exec."

"I relieve you, sir," Jarvis said.

It's all in my night book and on the watch board," Waters said. "Hope you boys took a peek before you came up?"

Jarvis nodded, "Yes sir."

"Very well," Waters said. "Me and the COB are gonna get some supper. Good night, Mr. Jarvis."

"Exec has the con," Jarvis announced. "Tony, stand by to rig ship for surface."

The watchstanders went down the ladder as the new men came on duty. Skaggs took up his place at the diving station and reported ready.

Jarvis had him sound the surfacing alarm… three blasts on the diving alarm… and then ordered main ballast tanks blown and an up angle.

The old boat broke the surface and, on Jarvis' word, maneuvering switched over to diesels. After one more high look on the search scope… far less drippy now that the boat was on the surface… Jarvis ordered a sweep on the sugar dog. Unfortunately, the S-52 did not possess the newer SJ surface-search radar but only, the older and less specific SD.

However, with no returns, he and the quartermaster of the watch, Jack Cleghorn, went up to the bridge followed by the lookouts. The sun had disappeared below the horizon by then, but some twilight remained. Enough to show a sea that bulged with long and gentle six-foot swells.

"What do you feel is the best method, Jack," Jarvis asked as he lit a Camel. "Charge the batteries as fast as possible or split the difference? What's this boat like best?"

Cleghorn lit his own cigarette and pondered for a moment. Like many men on board, he still wasn't quite sure of what to make of Jarvis and the new COB. Cleghorn had been friends with the now-dead chief of the boat, but he tried not to let his grief and anger cloud his judgment. More likely than not, unless Harry Brannigan was permanently assigned, Cleghorn would be promoted to the position himself after this patrol. He was wise enough to understand that you can't hate a man who's brought in to do a job. *Ordered* to do it. Long as he did a good one and didn't come aboard with a big case on.

"Best would be just to run the rock crushers at full power and top off the banks," Cleghorn opined. "Just shove as much juice in as you can, and then get on with your life. Still, we gotta make progress. The advantage of bein' topside is makin' as much progress as we can in the dark… so finding a balance between chargin' and runnin' looks good on paper."

"Yeah, ten knots and charge all night," Jarvis said. He almost wistfully pointed out that he missed having four engines to play with but stopped himself. It wouldn't do to draw comparisons with such a prideful and touchy crew. "Still, if we can run at two-thirds, we can top 'em up faster. Say two-thirds for six hours, and then we can run at full power for the next five."

"Works out about the same distance made good, sir."

Jarvis nodded, "Yeah, but it means we have full charges sooner, just in case. Other option is to go dark for the middle watch, save as much power as we can and shunt some of the auxiliary juice into the cells."

"Yeah, but the skipper don't like that, sir," Cleghorn stated. "The guys gotta eat and relax and what not."

Jarvis nodded, "Yep."

"Skipper's night book says we go half and half until the batteries are charged anyway," Cleghorn replied. "And he don't like it when anybody goes against his ways. Not even the XO."

Jarvis smiled grimly, "I get that sense. That ever happen before?"

Cleghorn seemed to grow pensive for a moment. Jarvis thought that maybe he'd crossed another of the many invisible lines that seem to be laid out all over this boat like tripwires. Finally, the older man sighed, "Not more'n once, sir."

"I read ya'," Jarvis said. "Continue on course. Alert maneuvering to proceed all ahead full with a fifty-fifty charge and propulsion split on engines one and two."

"Aye-aye," Cleghorn said, sounding mildly relieved.

Jarvis began to wonder what would happen if somebody didn't do things exactly the way that Salty Waters wanted. He began to wonder how the man might behave in combat, as well. Would he be open to suggestion from the first officer? Not for the first time since coming aboard, Pat Jarvis was troubled by vague doubts.

Then again, it could just be his own discomfort at being the new kid in school. Time would tell.

It was around 2330 when Skaggs came up to the bridge to make his final report to Jarvis before the end of the watch. He relieved Cleghorn to go to the head and handed the XO a cup of coffee.

"Thanks, Tony," Jarvis said as he sipped. "All's well below?"

Skaggs nodded, and in the dim, red glow from the open hatch, Jarvis thought he saw something on the younger man's face. An uncertainty or hesitation barely under control.

"What's on your mind, Tony?"

"Sir…" Skaggs shifted from one foot to another. "Well sir, it's about the boat and…."

"If there's somethin' on your mind, just come out with it, Tony," Jarvis prodded gently. "I can keep it between us if that's what you want."

Skaggs closed his eyes and then seemed to come to a decision. He leaned in close and whispered, "Be careful, sir. Things ain't what they seem on this boat."

"Meaning what, exactly?" Jarvis asked with narrowed eyes.

Skaggs glanced around as if there would be somebody to listen in, other than the lookouts above and behind them, "You noticed how about a third of the guys on this boat think it's a keen idea you and the Chief came over from *Bull Shark,* right?"

Jarvis nodded, "Yeah, and how the other two-thirds think we're pissin' in their bug juice. What's your point?"

"Lotta the guys in your camp are new, sir," Skaggs went on in hurried silence. "Just came aboard *after* the last patrol. Replacements for the guys we lost. Most of the guys who aren't onboard are older ones."

"Okay… been with the boat longer and more loyal to the skipper… not unusual," Jarvis admitted.

"Yeah, but the thing of it is, sir—"

Skaggs stopped abruptly when Cleghorn began climbing the ladder from the conning tower. The conversation had to be cut short by necessity. Jarvis was intrigued and wanted to know more, but a submarine, especially an S-boat, was no place for private confabs.

"Everything come out okay, Jack?" Jarvis quipped.

"Like a well-found trim pump, sir," Cleghorn said. "Be glad to get below, though. Pretty bushed."

"Sir!" one of the lookouts called down excitedly. "I think I just saw a light… yeah, bearing zero-three-zero horizon! Possible steaming light, sir."

"Way out here?" Cleghorn asked. "Nothing in the Coral Sea I know about…."

Jarvis thumbed the bridge speaker, "Radar, bridge… give me a scan with the sugar dog."

A moment went by and then: "*Bridge, radar... nothing sir. Dead scope.*"

Jarvis pulled the pair of 7x50 binocs from their holder below the speaker and trained them off the boat's starboard bow and toward the horizon. He swept them back and forth several times, then lowered them and used his unaided eyes. Nothing there. If the lookout had spotted the light intermittently, then it was probably only popping up when the boat or the source ship rose on a swell.

"I got it, sir," the lookout called down. "Steady now... must be gettin' a little closer. About thirty degrees to starboard of the bow, sir."

Jarvis frowned, "Jack... order the helmsman to reduce speed to all ahead one-third. Have sonar train the sound heads and sweep between zero-one-five and zero-four-five."

The XO was remotely aware of the petty officer speaking to the men below. He finally saw it, a brief glimpse of a white point of light that popped up and then was gone. He wondered if it might not be a planet.

The boat's diesels reduced their power and throttled back to a more sedate rumble. With the engines powered down, the sonarman would be able to hear distant screw noises more effectively, or so Jarvis hoped.

"*Bridge, sonar! Contact! Surface contact bearing zero-three-three, range twenty-thousand yards!*" Crackled the tinny bridge speaker excitedly.

Jarvis reached out and thumbed the transmit button, "Gaines, keep your ears on him. Let me know if he's comin' or goin'."

There was a long pause after the acknowledgment. It stretched on to two and then nearly to five minutes. Jarvis frowned and thumbed the speaker again in mild annoyance.

"Sonar, bridge... what's the story down there?"

"*Exec, this is the captain,*" Waters' voice filtered through the speaker, sounding terse. "*Clear the topsides. Dive the ship.*"

"Sir?" Jarvis asked in confusion. "We've only just—"

"*You got hearing problems, Mister? I said dive the goddamned ship! That's a Jap destroyer out there... Asashio-class! I recognize the screw noise. She's moving closer, and we can't afford to get picked off! Now move it already!*"

Jarvis looked questioningly at Cleghorn. For an instant, the quartermaster appeared as bewildered as Jarvis, but in the next, a mask of stoic neutrality set in. The first officer swore inwardly and pulled the diving alarm lever twice.

"Clear the bridge!" he said and pressed the transmit button again. "Control, bridge… rig ship for dive! Emergency deep."

5
GUADALCANAL – AUGUST 18, 1942, 2000 LOCAL TIME

"How's the leg, Phil?" Porter Hazard asked as he and Web Clayton entered the small arms magazine.

Sergeant Philip Oaks stood at a worktable near the entrance with Entwater, Taggart and Treadway. Each man was in the process of field stripping and re-assembling Springfield 1903 rifles. Jacob Vousa, who had also volunteered for the mission, was gathering ammunition and filling magazines at the other end of the table.

"Hardly gives me a twinge now," Oaks said. "How about you, sir?"

Porter grumbled, "Feel like a damned old man… and I ain't happy about you boys headin' out into the bush without me."

"Yeah, but we got our very own spook, sir," Treadway said with a grin. "Mr. Clayton will keep an eye on us."

That drew a laugh from all the men. Clayton wasn't sure if he was being ribbed good-naturedly or if there was some veiled disapproval in the joke.

"Just so you know, boys," Clayton said. "I'm not just some civvy yahoo Washington weenie. I joined the Army back in twenty-eight. Right out of high school."

"So you probably won't shoot yourself in the foot then, sir?" Taggart jibed.

"Not *my* foot, Taggart," Clayton joked back and winked.

That drew another laugh. Hazard clapped Clayton on the shoulder, "Web here ain't no softie, fellas. He was aboard *Bull Shark* when she went up against that Jap submarine carrier. Was on board when the boat went down to eight-oh-five. He's got some nuts bouncin' around in his skivvies."

"Good to know," Oaks said.

"However," Hazard went on, looking at Treadway. "As the new kid on the team, Joe, I'm makin' it your job to sort of… watch out for Mr. Clayton here. You stick with him and keep him outta trouble, hear?"

Treadway smiled, "Yes sir. Been doing that since I met him back in July… isn't that right, sir?"

This last was directed at Clayton, and the OSS man smiled, "Pretty much. One thing, though, Joe… you really need to stop calling me sir."

"Yes sir," Treadway replied snappily as he reseated the trigger mechanism in his rifle.

The other Marines snickered. Vousa laid out a row of magazines and other gear. He then brought five Colt 1911 semi-automatics over and laid them on the table.

"Whose logistics man for the team?" Hazard asked.

"That'd be me, sir," Entwater said. "Although Joe has proven good at the paperwork."

"What's your loadout?" Hazard asked.

"Everybody gets a 1903 with four extra mags," Entwater explained. "A .45 with two extras. Packs will have extra ammo, too, boxes of shells for the rifles. Their magazines only hold five. The exception is Mr. Clayton, who'll get the Thompson. He'll have two extra mags."

"Why me with the SMG?" Clayton asked.

"Well, sir," Entwater said. "All of us are figured as crack shots. Marksmen, sir. We don't have many automatic weapons. Couple of Thompsons from *Bull Shark* that we brought, and the First and Fifth have a few BARs… Browning automatic rifles… so we can really only take one. Figured you'd be more comfortable with the extra firepower, sir."

"Okay," Clayton said, not sure he followed the logic, but he *did* like the idea of carrying the Chicago typewriter.

"Then we got some standards," Treadway put in. "Ruck with D-rats, some C-rats, bottled water, halozine tabs, couple pairs of socks, skeeter gear and like that. E-tools, ground cloths, tent, the usual bit. Enough stuff for four days out there."

"How long you boys plannin' on stayin' in the jungle?" Hazard asked Oaks.

"Taivu Point is about thirty-five klicks from here," Oaks said. "And you know how slow going it is on this rock. There are some roads and trails… but we're avoiding them for obvious reasons, sir. So, it could be a couple of days just to get there and another couple back."

"Tricky part is the field radio," Treadway stated. "Can't imagine that the Japs won't hear us. That and the chances of our broadcasts making it back here…."

"Not unless we can get out to the beach," Entwater said, pushing his horn-rimmed cheaters up on his nose, "or up in the mountains to high ground and transmit. The radio is bulky but has the range… but as we know, in the jungle, it's dramatically reduced."

"Wouldn't be any fun if it were easy," Oaks said wryly. "Well, that looks like it… let's mount up, boys."

Hazard sighed, "Sure wish I were going with you fellas…."

"Us too, sir," Taggart said. "Just not the same blowin' up japs without you."

As the men gathered their equipment, a pair of booted footsteps approached from outside the open magazine doors. All five men turned to see none other than Major General Alexander Vandegrift step into the storage facility. With him was a young and robust-looking Captain.

"Gentlemen," Vandegrift said after everyone, including Clayton, came to attention. "At ease. Allow me to introduce Captain Lyman Spurlock. Lyman here is headed out with a couple of companies of my finest tomorrow to find out what really happened to Colonel Goettge. And I have a request, Mr. Clayton."

"General?" Clayton asked, raising his eyebrows.

Vandegrift looked to Spurlock. The mid-twenties captain cleared his throat, "I understand that all of you men, except Mr. Clayton here, of course, are pretty familiar with Guadalcanal."

"We've been here since the first of the month, sir," Oaks replied for his men. "Came in with a landing force aboard a submarine in order to make contact with Captain Clemens."

Vandegrift grinned, "Did a helluva thing. Lieutenant Hazard's skipper came in too, Lyman."

Spurlock smiled thinly, "I read those reports. Anvil Art Turner, they call him. Sounds like he made a pretty good Marine."

"That he did, sir," Hazard said. "With any luck, he's out in the channel right now, or soon will be, giving them Japs a lesson in humility."

"Well, I'm taking men into an unknown situation tomorrow," Spurlock explained. "And the fact that we lost over twenty Marines there a few days ago… it's not sitting well. Colonel Goettge and most of his men were intelligence. So, I thought that maybe you, Mr. Clayton, would consider changing your plans and taking men out toward the Matanikau for a little scouting run. Nothing too dangerous, just a quick peek to try and give us an idea what we're in for."

"Normally, I wouldn't consider sending in a civilian," Vandegrift said. "But since you did come here to see things up close and personal, Web, and since you've got Army training… well, I thought that all of this would dovetail nicely."

"Sir…" Clayton began cautiously. "You make a good point. Yet heading out to scope Taivu Point is also critical to my overall mission here. There are… things in the works in The Slot. Japanese ship movements, and we've got a couple of boats headed out there to put the kibosh on it."

"The Tokyo Express?" Vandegrift asked.

"Yes sir," Clayton said. "And as Porter here says… Art Turner is tasked with derailing that operation. At least spearheading that effort. But the Tokyo Express doesn't end at land's edge, sir… Knowing what type of ground forces are gathering to the east and seeing what's coming ashore might give us more clarity on the big picture, sir. And as it is, this mission out there and back looks to be one of at least four days."

"What if we split up, sir?" Treadway blurted and then flushed, appearing chagrinned that he'd spoken without being spoken to in the presence of so much brass.

Spurlock smiled at him, "Might work, son. There are six of you, Mr. Clayton. Suppose we sent half of you to Taivu and half to the Matanikau? We can get you out there in a couple of hours by boat. Scope the sitch and then hot-foot it back here inside the perimeter. Could be done by breakfast. Give me enough intel to better organize my troops."

"It is better for scouting ops to have fewer personnel, Mr. Clayton," Oaks observed.

"I'll go to Taivu," Vousa volunteered. "It's not far from my home village, and I know the area between here and there. Give me one man. That's all I need."

"Dave, Teddy and I have some boots on the ground experience with this area, too, sirs," Oaks said. "Maybe I take the two of them, and then Mr. Clayton and Treadway can go with Jacob? Joe knows the gear, and while I'd put Teddy's technical knowledge up against anybody's… we don't need that on a scouting patrol."

Spurlock nodded in approval. Vandegrift looked to Clayton, "It's your op, Web. Your choice… but we're spread so thin right now and already have patrols out in every direction… short-range… you guys are just too handy not to use. It also sounds like the best use of resources. You still get to scope Taivu, Web. With Mr. Vousa's expertise, that gives you a good chance of success. On the other hand, with the sarge, the corporal and PFC Entwater's familiarity with the island, that gives *that* team the best shot."

Clayton nodded slowly, "It's your arena, General. I'm just a guest punter."

Spurlock grinned, "Outstanding! I'll see to getting you boys a ride over to the Matanikau. We'll also escort you to the eastern edge of the perimeter, Mr. Clayton. We can at least see you across Alligator

Creek… and there's a bridge across the Teneru on the Coast Road. That'll be the easy part, I'm afraid."

WEST OF POINT CRUZ – 2217

"We was s'posed to land here in the first place," Sergeant Charles Arndt told Oaks as they sat together on a bench in the Higgins boat. "But it was dark that night… poor vis… and the coxswain misjudged where we was in the dark. Ran us aground and took a good fifteen minutes to get us off the bar again."

Oaks cast an eye toward the boat's pilot and engineer. He then looked back to Arndt. The Sergeant had been added to the mission at the last minute. Neither Spurlock nor Vandegrift wanted to send him, but the sergeant volunteered. He felt he owed it to Colonel Goettge and the other men… since he made it out, and they didn't.

"Not them," Arndt said quietly. "Not the guy's fault anyway. As I said, it was darkern'n Tojo's asshole out here. Problem, though, was that the Colonel was warned not to go ashore between the Matanikau and Point Cruz on account of the Japs were holed up there. Even our Jap prisoner, the guy who told us some Japs were hidin' out and wanted to surrender, warned us off… but…."

"Don't it seem dumb for the four of us to go strollin' right through the same Indian country, Sarge?" Taggart asked dubiously.

Arndt drew in a breath, "It's four guys, well set up and at night. My opinion, all that noise we made tryin' to get the boat off the bar alerted the Japs ashore. This time, we'll put ashore where we were *supposed* to on the twelfth. Cocumbona isn't occupied now, far as we know. And tomorrow, when Baker, Item and Love companies put ashore, they'll come there."

Oaks nodded, "That's what Captain Spurlock said. They'll hit Cocumbona, the sandbar at the mouth of the Matanikau and a bit upstream. A three-pronged attack to catch the Nips in the crossfire. Wipe 'em out so they can't run west and escape. Our job is to start from Cocumbona and head east and back to our lines. It being night, we should be able to do it by dawn. Or at least get across the river and send a runner. Give the attack some good info."

"Sarge, we're headed in," The boat's coxswain said, a waft of pipe tobacco floating to the waiting Marines as the boat turned and the wind shifted.

"Sure wish we had the kind with the bow ramp," Entwater muttered as the four men moved to the bow.

"Afraid of gettin' your feet wet, Poindexter?" Arndt teased.

Taggart frowned at the sergeant and leaned in close, "You lay off that kid, Sarge. He's a Raider, and he's earned it. Kid can shoot a wart off your ass at three hundred yards, too. Don't let them birth controls fool ya'."

Arndt raised an eyebrow and smiled. He clapped Entwater on the shoulder, "Sorry, Ted. Just funnin' ya' a little bit. No hard feelin's, huh?"

Entwater nodded, pretending to focus on the dark patch of beach slowly approaching. The bow gently bumped and scraped along the sand, and the four Marines leapt over the side, holding onto the plywood gunwales of the boat to try and slow themselves and reduce the splashes. The coxswain gave a thumbs up and reversed his engine, backing the boat away from the shallows and out into the channel.

In less than a minute, the low rumble of the Higgins boat's engine was swallowed by the sound of the surf and the eerie quiet of the tropical night.

"Okay," Oaks said, huddling up with the other men. Although he and Arndt were the same pay grade, Oaks was in operational command. "There's an open area ahead before we hit any jungle. Not far in, there's a series of ridges and shallow canyons and shit. I say we go in about a hundred yards or so and sweep west, staying within fifty to a hundred feet of one another. Every half hour or so, we'll close in, and two of us will penetrate inland for half a klick or so and then come back. We continue west and keep repeating this, each taking turns on the penetration sweep. Any questions? Suggestions?"

"Yeah," Arndt whispered. "If the squids put us down where we're supposed to be… then Cocumbona is only about three klicks east. I say when we get there, we do a complete perimeter sweep around the village. It's supposed to be free of Nips, but…."

"Yeah," Taggart put in. "Our experience on this godforsaken rock is that not much is as it seems. We had trouble with locals pretty much since the day we landed."

"Not to be trusted," Oaks said. "Not really their fault… the japs make their lives a living hell if they resist. Okay, let's move out."

Guadalcanal's landscape was odd in many places. Although covered in tropical rainforest and jungle, the island was the result of eons of volcanic activity. As such, its topography wasn't a smooth and orderly rise from the sea to the mountains. Even on the north side, where most of the flatland lay, the land could dramatically change without any rhyme or reason.

One might come ashore on a placid golden sand beach bordered by tropical plants and trees and swaying palms only to walk a hundred yards inland and find a hundred-foot-high cliff rising straight out of the jungle. Or walk up a gently rising slope only to come out into a clearing where a jagged gash appeared to slice right through the land as a sharp-edged fifty-foot-deep canyon blocked your path. It made moving in a straight line quite difficult, even in daylight. At night, it was treacherous, to say the least.

Oaks' Raiders did their best to sweep across the moonlit plains and through jungle paths. They moved slowly, attempting to make as little noise as possible. For behind every densely packed clump of jungle or from the top of any craggy volcanic ridge, Japanese soldiers could be waiting. Arndt's story of how Colonel Goettge's patrol had been jumped from a two-hundred-foot ridge only a little way in from shore was unnerving.

However, by midnight, the team had covered several kilometers of rough terrain and had made it to the village of Cocumbona. The village was like most small settlements on the Island. A haphazard collection of thatched-roof cottages raised a bit above the ground to keep them dry during heavy rains. There was an open field on the western side of the village where some food was grown and a small stream on the south side that connected to the Matanikau river not far off to the east. The village was bounded on all sides by rainforest and palms, with a steeply rising ridge to the west and a sort of road on the south that ran parallel to the stream. The road crossed over the stream near the village and continued along the edge of the crops and up and over the hill to be swallowed by more jungle.

Being late, the village was dark and quiet. A light odor of burnt firewood hung over the open land from that evening's cooking, no doubt. The scene, bathed as it was in silvery light from the moon that hung almost directly overhead, was tranquil. Crickets chittered, and nocturnal creatures called out from the dark jungle. An oppressive pall of moist heat hung over the land as if wrapping it in a woolen blanket. All was still, especially the four Americans who crouched together at the edge of a jungle trail, watching carefully.

"Looks peaceful enough," Taggart whispered.

"Yeah, for now," Arndt said disdainfully, "but who knows what's in them huts."

"I say we go and find out," Entwater offered.

Oaks chuckled softly, "Got somethin' to prove, Ted?"

Entwater jerked his head in the direction of Arndt and shrugged.

"Okay, here's my thinking," Oaks said. "Me and John Wayne here'll cut across the field to the stream. Charlie, you and Davie cut around the far side of the huts. We'll meet on the other side and compare notes. Then we can cross the stream there and follow it to the river, using that road. If there are any Japs between here and the Matanikau—"

"You can bet on that," Arndt said.

Oaks nodded, "Yeah… then they'll be near the road."

From a nearby hut, not more than ten yards away, a door opened, and a figure in light beige stepped out and down the three steps. With the door open, a soft glow of yellow light spilled out along with muffled laughter and voices. Voices that sounded a lot like Japanese. What sounded like a yelp or scream drifted through the open bamboo door before it closed as well.

The man in the light khakis stumbled around to the rear of the hut, standing between it and the jungle and began to urinate. The Marines elbowed each other as they watched the Japanese soldier only thirty feet away. As he pissed, the man mumbled to himself and began to sing in a soft drunken discord that blended perfectly with his swaying.

"We could take him out, Phil," Taggart hissed into Oaks' ear. He held up his KA-Bar for emphasis.

"Don't know how many there are," Arndt whispered.

"Let's find out," Entwater hissed, holding up his own KA-Bar.

"We didn't come here to kill Japs, only locate them," Oaks said in an attempt to be the voice of reason.

"Fewer Japs tomorrow, the better, right?" Entwater asked.

Oaks grinned and sighed, "Okay, Ted… why not. Blades only, though, no guns. Probably just a patrol bunking down here for the night. Probably getting' shitfaced on sake and taking turns with a local woman or two. Who wants to take down Tinklin' Tom over there?"

Arndt grimaced, "I'll go first. I owe these yellow fuckers anyway…."

Oaks nodded and pulled out a second blade that he and the other Raiders carried. It was a slim dagger-like Stiletto with cutting edges on either side. He held it out to Arndt.

"Before we got these new KA-Bars," Oaks explained. "We Raiders used these… good for the job if you see what I mean."

EAST OF THE TENERU – 0215

The advantages of moving through Guadalcanal's dense foliage by night could not be overstated. Jacob Vousa had done so more times than he could count and preferred trekking by moonlight rather than sunlight whenever possible.

For one thing, although the swelter of the damp jungles and rainforests still clung to the land by night, it was somewhat cooler. Often, after a heavy rain, the heat would steam the wet forests and coat the land in a dense mist that cut visibility down to as little as a dozen feet at times. For one who was familiar with the landscape and knew the ways of moving through it stealthily, this delivered a tremendous tactical advantage.

Vousa had been born and bred in the Solomons. First on his home island of Malaita, and later on Guadalcanal. He knew how to move and move silently. He also knew that, for the most part, the Japanese soldier was a city dweller. Not raised in the ways of nature but in the ways of the artificial environment of carefully organized cities. This wasn't always the case, and God knew the Japs were fast learners.

Still, even on clear nights like this one, free of clouds and mist and rain, the bright moonlight was enough to navigate by. There were also plenty of shadows so that men could make use of the rough roads and trails to move more quickly by night.

From Alligator Creek to Taivu Point was about nineteen miles. Even at a modest pace, walking along the best roads and paths available by day, this was a minimum of a six-hour sojourn. And on Guadalcanal, by night or by day, the heat and humidity would sap a man's strength like nothing most people had ever known. A six-hour walk in a temperate climate could easily become a two or even three-day journey on what the Americans were now beginning to nickname "the Canal."

So being able to cover more ground by night would get Vousa and his teammates to their goal all the faster. The former protectorate officer had no doubt that both of his comrades were tough men. Treadway was young and fit, and Clayton, although ten years older, was still more than a dozen years younger than Vousa's forty-seven. But they weren't acclimatized yet. The night was simply easier on new men.

That and there were fewer Japanese roaming about as a matter of course. Fewer islanders to report to their Japanese overlords, for that matter.

Nothing was entirely certain, of course. Things could change rapidly. At least in the darkness, the odds of three camouflaged men to duck away and hide should they encounter something went up substantially.

This could become an issue shortly, as Vousa knew that the road they were currently plodding along ran through Aola. The large village, once the headquarters of the British Solomon Islands Protectorate on Guadalcanal, had been abandoned almost as soon as the Japanese came ashore on the island back in the early part of the year. Vousa hadn't been back to the village since he assisted Martin Clemens in his evacuation, but he'd heard enough to know the place was literally crawling with Naponapo.

Vousa saw a break in the forest ahead and thought that this might be where the road opened up onto what had been a coconut plantation and the farmland around Aola. He stopped and held up a fist for his men to halt as well.

Treadway and Clayton came near and stood to either side of Vousa, their shoulders almost touching. For a long moment, all three men simply stood on the side of the rutted track under the shade of some tropical trees and listened.

"What's up?" Clayton hissed.

"I think we're nearly to Aola," Vousa explained softly. "Reports are that Japanese are occupying the town… We may need to move inland to skirt the place or…."

"Did you hear that?" Treadway broke in with an urgent and alarmed hiss.

"What?" Clayton inquired.

Vousa stiffened. The young man obviously had exceptional ears. He hadn't heard it at first, but he did now. There was something moving in the jungle just ahead of them and on the other side of the road.

Something large.

"I vote we duck into the salad," Clayton hissed.

"I'm with you, sir," Treadway said almost inaudibly.

Vousa nodded, "Champion… who's got a rope?"

"I do, sir," Treadway said, reaching behind him and pulling something from a pocket in his ruck. "Just a length of twine, sir… got more in my pack, but…."

"Good, PFC," Vousa said quietly, edging toward the trees. "Tie three loops in it, about six feet apart. Then we each take a loop. I'll go first, then Mr. Clayton and then you. Savvy?"

"Yes sir," Treadway whispered as he began to work the line of thin cord.

"And don't call me sir, Joe," Vousa said.

"Yes sir…"

Clayton had to stifle a snicker. Treadway handed the first loop to Vousa and then another to Clayton.

"Just follow me," Vousa said. "It's black as pitch in there, so this way we don't get separated. We move slowly and quietly as you can."

Treadway had just stepped between a huge Bird of Paradise and a teak tree when the rustling seemed to grow in intensity. This was joined by Japanese voices—a *lot* of them.

"Butterheads sir..." Treadway hissed, nearly bowling Clayton over as he tried to get further into the cover of the jungle.

"Yeah, no shit, Dick Tracy... and for the love of the sweet baby Christ... stop calling me sir!" Clayton implored.

"Yes sir..."

"Down!" Vousa urged, pulling on the twine and pressing a hand to Clayton's shoulder.

The three men dropped to the damp floor of the jungle and went still. From no more than fifteen yards away, quiet but urgent Japanese voices were chattering.

"It sounds like a squad, sir," Treadway whispered.

"Agreed," Vousa said. "Keep quiet, lads...."

Webster Clayton, Office of Strategic Services, lay on his belly on a carpet of leaves, twigs and who knew what else. The jungle floor was damp with dew, moldering vegetable decay and moist loam. The entire front of his BDU trousers and blouse were already beginning to soak through. Something hard and sharp was poking uncomfortably into his crotch. On top of that, the chorus of uncounted millions of tiny tropical denizens called out to him, singing a song not of welcome but of hunger.

As tiny crawling things began to touch him, Clayton had to wonder just what in the *hell* he'd been thinking. He didn't need to be here... what was that... didn't need to be lying face-down in a jungle with... was that a spider walking on his back... with all manner of things trying to bite him. He didn't need to be here trying to control his terror as a dozen armed Japanese soldiers stood nearby, itching to stick a long sharp bayonet into his guts.

Intelligence man... phooey... What was so intelligent about being eaten alive by mosquitos... God, they itch... while his enemy closed in on him in the dark...

The Japanese were so close now that the three men could smell their body odor and hear their soft, cloven-hoofed boots squelching in the mud at the road's edge. One man was nearly on top of them. He took several steps into the jungle and stopped.

Treadway's heart was jackhammering in his chest. The Jap was not more than five feet from his head. He hadn't been on this damned island a single day yet, and he was about to die.

"Banzai…" the soldier growled softly and then unleashed his attack.

6

NOUMÉA, NEW CALEDONIA – 1,100 MILES S, SE OF GUADALCANAL
AUGUST 19, 1942, 0530 LOCAL TIME

"Sir? Sir, you awake?"

Albert Decker swam up through a warm sea of darkness toward a faint and cold light. This irritated him for some reason… ah, yes… the warmth of the darkness had not been one of solitude.

A moment before, a rather pretty, dark-skinned Melanesian woman had been lying beside him on a warm tropical beach, the silver glow of the moon caressing her naked flesh. She'd been saying something to him, but he couldn't understand it at first. He struggled to comprehend, sensing that it was important, yet his mind just didn't want to cooperate. He was also mildly confused because he had no idea who she was, and yet he also sensed that he did…

"Major?"

Decker opened his eyes and blinked away the gossamer threads of sleep. Standing in a dimly lit doorway was the frame of a man he thought he should know, "Wha… who's there?"

"It's me, Corporal Lider, sir," the man spoke in a thick Alabama drawl that snapped Decker's mental faculties back into place.

"Chuck? Hey… come on in," Decker said, blinking and yawning. "How's the leg? What time is it?"

"Just a little sore, but otherwise, I'm 4-O sir," Lider said, ambling in and coming to stand by Decker's bedside. "It's zero-five-thirty, sir."

Decker groaned, "Then what the Christ are you doing waking me up from a nice dream at this hour, Corporal? Don't you know I was lying on a beach with a naked native woman?"

Lider grinned, "Sorry sir… but I have some news that might interest you, and it's kinda timely."

Decker sat up and groaned. His entire upper body felt like he'd gone a dozen rounds with Jake LaMotta. Eleven days earlier, he'd taken a bullet through his back on Guadalcanal. The round had passed through his left shoulder blade, pierced his lung and exited between his BDU blouse pocket and his collarbone. A bad hit that had cost him a great deal of blood but thankfully hadn't struck any vital vessels. He'd been rushed into emergency surgery aboard the *McCawley,* Admiral Richmond Turner's flagship, within an hour of being hit. Then he'd accompanied the fleet, along with Lider, who'd been bayonetted in the leg, back to New Caledonia.

"How you doing, sir?" Lider asked.

"I'm ambulatory," Decker said. "I move like a damned old fart, but at least I can walk on my own. What's the story, Chuck?"

"There's another supply run scheduled to head to The Canal today, sir," Lider said, his hands absently wringing on the bed rail. "Transports and some DD escorts. I hear Admiral Fletcher's already out there with his carriers supporting Henderson Field while they get squared away."

"Yeah, I heard they opened it up," Decker said.

"Yes sir," Lider continued. "I guess there's a Jeep carrier going with us with some more fighters and whatnot. A flight of Fortresses flying out in a day or two as well."

"Why you telling me this, Chuck?"

"Cuz our guys are still at the field," Lider said, lowering his voice conspiratorially. "Lieutenant Hazard is with them. Too wounded to be taken off the island and travel back to Brisbane with *Bull Shark.*"

Decker looked confused, "Porter…? What do you mean wounded?"

"I just heard the poop on what happened after we were sent off," Lider said. He then explained about Turner having to go and retrieve Hazard and the crazy Jap Naval officer.

"Jesus…" Decker groaned. "I hope Art nails the prick."

"Point is, sir… the *Cavalier*, one of them new *Fletcher*-class jobs, is part of the advance convoy," Lider explained excitedly. "She's scheduled to shove off in a couple of hours and get to the Sealark Channel in like three or four days, sir… and there's room aboard for a couple of riders."

Decker's eyes lit up. The chance to get aboard a fast ship and get back to the fighting and to his men was a mouth-watering proposition. He'd heard plenty of general scuttlebutt about the fighting on Guadalcanal and was going bananas not being a part of it.

Almost all of Edson and Carlson's Marine Raiders were out there, digging the Japs out of the Florida Islands and fighting with the First and Fifth Mar Bats on The Canal. He knew that Oaks, who was himself wounded, Taggart and Entwater were at Henderson Field. His men needed him, and he needed them.

"Problem is I'm not cleared to be released out of this Lysol factory," Decker grumbled.

Lider looked around as if somebody would be listening in and leaned in close, "Why I came at oh-dark-thirty, sir. Not many staff on right now. Land hospital and all. I gave the petty officer at the intake desk twenty bucks to stick his nose in a comic when we go past… but we gotta move out now, sir… I mean, if you think you're up for it."

Decker scoffed, "Shit, Chuck… I can lie on my ass or relax aboard a ship easy as in here. Docs cleared me to walk around some, say I'm over the worst of it and no infections. Just gotta change my dressings and take my pills. Let's mount up!"

Decker didn't exactly shoot to his feet. Rather, he struggled out of bed and had to hold onto the rail for a few seconds while the wobbling in his legs stopped. However, he managed to slip into a clean pair of khakis and shoes from the room's small closet. Decker also had a small seabag with what few personal items he could lay claim to. What little he had brought with him aboard *Bull Shark* was either still aboard the boat or had come to Guadalcanal with him. When he'd been evacced, the only thing he or Lider had was the dirty combat utilities on their backs.

The Navy, thankfully, had provided them both with a new kit containing essential toiletries, a couple of changes of clothing, some pay and other odds and ends. With this slung over his shoulder, Lider led the way out into the hall and down to the lobby. The recovery unit was located on the first floor.

Lider was right. All was quiet at a little before six in the morning. The lone nurse at the station outside Decker's door smiled at them and said good morning, and asked what the two men were up to.

"Gonna take the air for a bit," Decker replied. "Nice to be able to get up on my own shin ponies again."

The attractive blonde Navy nurse smiled, "I'm sure. You just take it easy, though, Al. Don't overdo it."

"Wouldn't dream of it, doll," Decker said and winked at her. "Not without your guidance, that is."

This bit of flirty bullshitting complete, the two grifters moved down the hall and into the small lobby. As expected, the beefy Navy petty officer shot them a grin and buried his schnoz in a Captain Marvel. Paying no heed as the two sauntered out the door without signing the register.

"See there, sir? Cool as cucumbers," Lider said and chuckled.

Decker grinned, "Okay, great job, Chuck… but what about orders?"

"Orders, sir?"

Decker rolled his eyes, "Yeah, man… orders! It's one thing to grease a security guard and to use my overwhelming animal magnetism on a dish of a navy nurse… I mean, who could resist… but it's another to shlep on over to the docks and stroll up the brow of a destroyer with nothing more than a smile. Master at Arms ain't so easy to bamboozle."

"Oh… oh geez, sir… I wish you'd said something sooner…." Lider appeared flustered and confused. When Decker stopped and glared at him, the Corporal grinned wickedly and pulled a pair of envelopes from his own seabag and handed one to his CO. "Just gas-lightin' ya' sir! I got these cut yesterday. Nice French broad works over in admin… schmoozed her but good."

Decker snorted and guffawed, "Jesus Christ, Chuck! Not funny. Somebody's been busy while I've been laid up, I see."

"Leg wound goes a long way in some circles," Lider said and winked. "We're due to report aboard by zero-seven-hundred, sir. Just enough time to get ourselves a last good French breakfast before ship fare and whatever rats they got left on The Canal."

"You might need a pay raise for this, Chuck."

"Might? No doubt *about* it, sir."

SHORTLAND HARBOR, SHORTLAND ISLAND – 320 MILES NW OF GUADALCANAL

Commander Takashi Sato leaned negligently on the observation bridge railing aboard the strike carrier *Sakai* and puffed languidly on a Cuban cigar. The cigar had been a part of Captain Kenji Igawa's personal effects. However, like his ship, the cigars now belonged to her new captain. Captain pro-tem, it was true, but at least for the moment, Sato was in command.

He'd officially been in command since sunrise on the fateful morning when the carrier's former captain had committed ritual suicide by flinging himself into the sea. Or at least… that was what was believed to have happened.

Sato had been awakened from a rather deep sleep by pounding on his stateroom door. The noise had awakened him instantly, and there was no doubt as to the reason for the disturbance. Of course, he had played his part well.

The ship's *Yakuin* had flung the door open and barked at the Master at arms and Lieutenant Goro Arawi, the officer of the watch. His ire was wiped away by shock when the younger man explained what had occurred. They'd gone to speak with the captain and found the door to his stateroom locked. When no answer came to their knocking, the Master at arms had been called with his master key.

"A terrible thing has happened, sir," Arawi explained, looking haggard and out of sorts. "The captain… he has committed seppuku."

"What!?" Sato had blurted in disbelief. "For what reason?"

Arawi bowed his head, "He left a note stating that he felt that he failed… that he couldn't live knowing he had allowed the carrier to be damaged and the American submarine to escape."

"No… it was not his fault…." Sato had bemoaned, lowering his face into his hands and even managing to squeeze out a tear or two. Quite a brilliant performance, even if he did say so himself. "I spoke to him just last evening… he was somewhat down in spirits… but not to that degree… at least I didn't think so… Oh God… if only I'd—"

"Sir, you cannot blame yourself," Arawi had tried to soothe.

"Are you *sure*, Lieutenant?" Sato asked. "Sure this is true?"

Arawi nodded grimly and led the executive officer to the captain's sea cabin. There was the typed note still in the typewriter where Sato had left it. There was the open port that let moist tropical air into the cabin. The cabin, whose emptiness seemed heavy.

"There's no chance anyone saw…?" Sato asked hopelessly.

Arawi shook his head, "In the dark… no. Even if this had happened five minutes ago, the odds of finding him would be small… but the room is damp with humidity… it must have happened sometime during the night. He's… he's gone, sir."

There had been mourning. A ceremony for all hands on the flight deck. Yet life went on, and necessity insisted that Sato take over. Arawi offered to have his things moved into the captain's cabin. Sato had adamantly refused, even growing angry at the mere thought of this. *He would not be so arrogant as to assume himself fit to take his captain and friend's quarters.* No doubt Yamamoto would send a new captain soon anyway.

Yet, as Sato hoped, this had not happened. He'd stayed in his stateroom until arriving at Rabaul. Even as the carrier was sent into drydock and work began on welding new hull plating over the torpedo hole and refurbishing the boiler room that had been hit, Sato was contacted by Admiral Ugaki himself. Yamamoto's chief of staff informed him that as the first officer and the man most familiar with

Sakai, that Yamamoto expected him to step up and fill Igawa's role. It would be Sato's job to aid the supply runs to Guadalcanal. It would also be his job to, if possible, sink the damned *Bull Shark.*

Of course, there had been no promotion. That would be impolitic, evidently. However, Ugaki assured Sato that should his next patrol be successful, his promotion to full *Kaigun Daisa,* Captain, would be a certainty. Sato had humbly accepted this role and said that even should no promotion come, it was his duty and his honor to continue Igawa's great mission.

So, when Sato *did* assume residence in the former captain's cabin, no one batted an eye. It was proper. Even when he smoked one of Igawa's cigars, it bothered no one. After all, that's what cigars were for, and when asked, Sato would explain that it made him feel closer to his departed friend. As if with every puff, he was sharing the rich flavor with Igawa in the afterlife.

Not only did the officers and crew buy this bit of melodramatic bullshit… they actually seemed to respect Sato more in consequence. As if their usually hard-edged former executive officer had mellowed somewhat and was showing a human side. It was a perfect situation.

Almost.

There was one annoying fly in his ointment, unfortunately. That fly came in the form of Lieutenant Commander Ryu Osaka. His friend, Omata Hideki, was perhaps a concern, but not nearly to the extent that was Osaka.

In a move that Sato believed was both clever and inspired, he'd contrived to, if not drive a wedge between the two men, at least separate them by duty. *Sakai's* air group commander had been wounded during the submarine attack. Badly enough that he'd been required to go ashore and recuperate at the hospital in Rabaul. Hideki's flying experience, rank and carrier experience offered Sato an opportunity. He could make Hideki *Sakai's* CAG. Since the man was there anyway, he might as well be given something to do. This would keep him busy and isolate Osaka somewhat.

Osaka, though, was still something of a thorn. In recognition for his service and his being shot down, Yamamoto had promoted him to a full Commander. This then put both Osaka and Sato on the same footing, as now they were both of the same substantive rank.

Of course, Sato had been made a ship's captain. And ship's captains, in every navy, were special creatures. Aboard their ships, they had almost unlimited authority. Authority that extended even over higher-ranking officers not in their direct chain of command at times. So this still put Sato in a position of command over Osaka, in spite of their ranks.

Still… while Sato's position as de facto captain brought him new power, he was not such a fool as to ignore Osaka's own influence. The man was a favorite of Yamamoto's. A *personal* favorite and this was no small thing. Sato could and *would* flex his professional muscles, yet he must also know when to ease up and not push too far. A well-placed word from Osaka might deprive Sato of his ship and perhaps more.

This was galling, to say the least… yet it was nothing new. A career in the Imperial Japanese navy was as much about whom you knew as what you knew. When it came to Ryu Osaka… both came into play.

Osaka had chilled toward Sato since that fateful morning the captain had been discovered missing. He didn't come out and say anything, but Sato sensed that Osaka had his suspicions. At worst, the man believed that Sato was complicit in Igawa's death… not that he could prove it. At best, Osaka believed Sato to be an overly ambitious rung climber who didn't mind standing on the back of a dead man to move up in the world. Not that the man had said anything, but the implication was there all the same.

Sato moved to the portside railing as the sound of Mitsubishi radial engines roared to life. Twenty feet below him, on *Sakai's* five-hundred-foot flight deck, a flight of six Zeroes was being spotted for takeoff. Moored outboard of these were another half-dozen fighters. Fully half of the ship's airwing. Each of the ready fighters was, he knew, armed with two one-hundred-and-fifty-kilogram depth charges each. These charges, whose depth settings could be adjusted by the pilot, were earmarked for a certain American submarine and her commander. A man that Takashi Sato had chosen to battle in a personal contest of wit and skill.

Ever since he'd read Arthur Turner's intelligence file, Sato had been intrigued. In Sato's mind, Turner was like him. A man who had risen quickly as a result of the war and who demonstrated aggressive skill, cunning and courage. A perfect adversary for a ship that could both act as a carrier and anti-submarine platform. A new American boat and new American captain against whom *Sakai's* formidable capabilities could be tested. A captain proven to be successful and, in Sato's estimation, a worthy opponent for his own genius.

Turner had struck first in their contest. Just the night before, his submarine had obliterated one of two destroyers racing down the new Georgia Sound to Guadalcanal. There was no proof that it was Turner, of course. The leading destroyer hadn't even slowed down to look for survivors, so vital was her mission. But Sato knew. He felt it in his *bones*. Turner and his steel predator were out there. They were out there right now, lurking below the surface and waiting for their next meal.

Of course, now that it was known that a submarine was prowling The Slot, precautions must be taken. Destroyer convoys would be larger, and they would be on high alert, especially after dark. It was a fortunate stroke as well that *Sakai* had been repaired and rushed out of the dock. For although the engineers were still having some issues with the new boilers… why she was anchored in Shortland harbor instead of on patrol… her airwing was invaluable during daylight hours.

Submarines liked to attack during the day as well, but they were at a distinct disadvantage. In the clear tropical waters of the Solomons, a boat at periscope depth could be easily seen by scout aircraft. Of course, the "rat cargo" missions, as the IJN sailors called them, didn't run during the day. However, one never knew. Should nothing be sighted, then there was no harm done. In a worst-case scenario, the Zeroes could drop their depth bombs and act as additional air cover for the daily bombing missions from Rabaul and Bougainville to Guadalcanal.

As soon as possible, however, Sato desired to put to sea again. If necessary, he'd go unescorted. His aircraft were certainly sufficient to cover his ship along with her own AA emplacements. Further, as the carrier was equipped with ASW gear and weaponry, she could act as a destroyer as well. Her depth charge racks, though only holding a small number, were ready to attack, and her sonar combined with the speed and maneuverability of her cruiser's hull made *Sakai* a formidable weapons platform indeed. More than a match for a lumbering submarine, no matter how aggressive her captain.

"I see Omata has thrown himself into his new duties, Sato san," Ryu Osaka said as he exited the navigation bridge and came to stand beside Sato to watch the flight operations.

"Indeed," Sato said. "I have been most pleased thus far. I believe he's even more efficient than Konteki was, poor fellow."

"Yes…" Osaka mused, mostly to himself. "Omata has always loved flying above all else."

They watched for a moment as the flight deck officer clipped in at the bow and readied his flags. Although *Sakai* was equipped with two steam catapults, the ship's beam didn't allow two aircraft to be set up side by side. Instead, the planes were staggered, with one catapult being slightly longer to allow the aircraft to be positioned with one slightly forward. This allowed the wingtips to cross one another and necessitated one catapult to be fired and then the other in succession. It reminded Osaka of the setup aboard the doomed *Leviathan*. Only much larger, of course.

"But you, Osaka san," Sato mused. "I think while you enjoy flying, your heart lies perhaps below the sea?".

Osaka shrugged indifferently, but a ghost of a smile appeared on his lips, "Perhaps."

"Well… with both you and Commander Hideki aboard," Sato went on. "It provides me with additional resources. I have a task for you as well, Commander, if you should accept it."

Osaka cocked an eyebrow at the other man, "Oh?"

Sato felt a surge of inward pleasure. He was certain he'd detected just a glimmer of pique from the slightly younger officer. As if Osaka chafed at being given an assignment… especially by Sato.

"Yes… your submarine experience may prove most valuable," Sato went on pleasantly. "As well as your personal experience with our particular enemy, Captain Turner. I wish you to act as my chief ASW officer and consultant. This is, after all, part of why the great Yamamoto sent you, is it not?"

Osaka nodded, "I suppose it is. I don't know that I have much in the way of expertise that's not already aboard, however."

Sato chuckled good-naturedly, "Come, come, Osaka san! You served aboard submarines, even as executive officer. You faced Turner in combat. You've *met* the man. Your insights are *invaluable*. Do not be modest now."

Osaka once more found himself walking a fine line. No, perhaps a tightrope over a pit of lava was a more apt analogy.

Ryu Osaka opposed the war against the United States. He opposed most of what Japan had done over the past several years, in fact. In his view, shared to some degree by Yamamoto himself, Japan was doomed to lose. Yet the emperor and his prime minister would push the Japanese people until they, as a nation, literally dropped dead. To Osaka's mind, if he could assist America in defeating Japan sooner, it would not only save lives but resources and something of the nation's honor as well.

Men like Art Turner would make this happen all the sooner. Because they pushed the limits of what they, their men and their ships could do. In spite of his aggressive style, Osaka knew Turner to be a good man. A man who fought because he must, but who couldn't hate his enemy so blindly that he'd commit horrific atrocities in the name of nationalism.

Yet here he was, being forced to hunt Turner down. If he balked, or if his efforts were perceived to be lackluster, he, Osaka, might be either removed from active duty or, worse… exposed as a traitor.

So now it was truly Osaka who was pitted against Turner, not the arrogant fool beside him. He'd have to try and hunt the man down, using his knowledge of the submarine service as well as what he knew of Turner to try and corner *Bull Shark*. Could he do so skillfully enough to make it appear that he was giving his all while allowing Turner enough wiggle room to slip through or even take out *Sakai?*

"Is there a problem, Commander?" Sato asked.

No doubt the man would love Osaka to decline. Instead, he simply smiled and said: "Not at all, Captain. Such a duel is both my duty and my pleasure."

"Excellent," Sato said with evident satisfaction.

Both men watched as the flight of Zeroes rumbled down the flight deck and into the air. Both men outwardly calm and both concealing much from the other. Both men also found themselves in a strangely similar predicament. A catch twenty-two, as it were.

Both men secretly wished the other to fail, and yet both men knew that in order for either of them to succeed, the other must as well.

7
COCUMBONA, GUADALCANAL
...HOURS EARLIER

A month ago, if you'd asked Sergeant Charlie Arndt what he thought of killing in general, you would have gotten a rather complex answer. He'd have said that he didn't *like* killing another person, whether there was a war on or not. But he did his duty and understood that in war, it was you or him.

However, he would have also explained that it was easier to pull the trigger on a rifle than it was on a pistol, which itself was easier than using a knife. A rifle, generally speaking, granted you distance. Your target was far away, and somehow, that diminished the target's humanity... making it easier to pull the trigger. With a pistol, you had to be closer by necessity. Fifty yards or less was preferred. But it was still somewhat impersonal... it was the gun that killed; you could tell yourself... not me.

With cold steel, however... there were no illusions. There were no justifications that eased the soul. It was a gritty, up close and personal way to take someone's life. There were few professional soldiers who had the stomach for what was called "wet work."

Now, however... Arndt had a different point of view. He'd been on Guadalcanal less than two weeks, and he'd already seen more than enough to develop a deep-rooted hate for the Japanese. Their fierceness in battle, their savagery and their utter disdain for any race that wasn't their own made them terrible foes indeed. Brutal fighters and vicious captors.

It was easier, therefore, when the Marine stepped up behind the stumbling drunken Japanese Riekusentai with admirable stealth to kill him with his blackened stiletto. Arndt grabbed a handful of the man's sweaty hair, jerked his head back and drove the point of his dagger up and into his skull just behind the right ear. The blade passed through the soft tissues, and the sensation of the tip grinding against the underside of the skull was transferred down to the Marine's hand, accompanied by a gush of warm blood.

Arndt gritted his teeth, finding that his hatred for the Japanese had not entirely muffled his conscience. The thought that this Japanese Marine might have been the very man who put a bullet into Colonel Goettge salved his humanity somewhat, but it was still gruesome when he twisted his blade and scrambled the man's brains. The knife was withdrawn along with a torrent of gore and gray matter, and Arndt let the body crumple bonelessly to the dirt.

He wiped his blade on the dead man's uniform and slid it back into its sheath. He stepped back several paces as an odiferous waft of coppery blood, and oily shit lovingly oozed up his nostrils and nearly turned over his belly.

"Good work," Oaks said, suddenly beside Arndt. He had to admit these Raiders knew how to move quietly. "You and Davie check out the hut. Ted and I will recon the rest of the village. Try to keep things quiet when you frag these sons of bitches if you can."

"Roger that," Arndt said.

"You all right?" Taggart whispered as the other two men moved off into the night.

"They got it comin'," Arndt said sternly.

"Yeah, they do… but it's still hard whackin' a guy out like that," Taggart said.

Arndt looked at him and smiled slightly, "Much as I can't stand these yellow fucks… they're still *men,* y'know? I can do that again, but it does sour your belly a little. That make me a sissy?"

Taggart grinned and squeezed the other man's shoulder, "Nah, Sarge… makes you a human being. You ain't Jack the Ripper. You *should* feel bad ice-pickin' a stranger. Even if he is your enemy. I'm sure that if we survive this shit show, we'll be walking along some street in twenty years and run into some Japanese businessman. You'll say hi to him and have this funny feeling you know him from somewhere… never knowin' that you and he might've exchanged fire back in the war. Funny thing to think about, really."

Arndt snorted, "Maybe that Tregaskis guy will write about that. Or Leckie will put it in his book?"

"That goofy private we met the day you guys came ashore?"

Arndt smiled, "Yeah… says he's keepin' a journal and is gonna write about Guadalcanal someday."

Taggart nodded, "Good. This shit ought to be remembered… even the parts we wanna forget. Let's move in."

"Pistols and blades," Arndt said, pulling out his Colt 1911 and racking the slide. "Yank the door open, and we go in together, splitting up and covering the room. Hut's only fifteen feet on a side, and my guess is Tinkle Tom's buddies are all in a similar state."

"Roger," Taggart said, and the men took their places on the top of the steps.

Arndt yanked the door open, and the two men rushed in, sliding to either side of the doorway and leveling their pistols. Immediately, their senses were assaulted by a heady mixture of sights, sounds and scents.

There was a lantern burning inside the squarish hut, casting the scene in yellowish light and deep shadows. A tinny radio playing some kind of Japanese music, laughter, groans of pleasure and whimpers of displeasure and discomfort washed over the Marines' ears.

Most potent of all, however, were the smells. Heavy bitter Japanese tobacco hovered at the ceiling like an indoor fog. A fog that carried with it the sharp tang of rice wine as well. The ripe testosterone-tinged body odor of three men who hadn't bathed in several days collided with the misty funk of pussy. Yet somehow, that smell, too, was wrong. As if the female scent of a woman taken by force was in some way different than that of consent.

The reason for this was obvious. Three Japanese soldiers and two native women occupied the room. One soldier lounged on a makeshift cot with a bottle in his hands. The man's eyes were half-closed, and a drunken smile plastered on his sweaty face.

One soldier, naked from the waist down, had a dark-skinned native woman bent over a homemade bamboo table and was behind her, happily pumping away, groaning with pleasure as his partner whimpered in pain and discomfort, although she'd been beaten into submission and was not resisting him.

The third soldier, a burly man with a knife scar across his moon-shaped face, was completely naked. He and another native woman, this one a bit plumper than the other and possibly older, were entangled on yet another cot. The soldier was atop her, the woman's legs on his shoulders and pounding away as if trying to drive her through the cot. This woman was growling and occasionally shouting something at the man in Pidgin. She was less cowed by the assault than she was infuriated. No doubt she was hurling some very strong curses at her "lover."

Taggart shot first. He put a .45 slug into the standing man, snapping his head back and coating the palm frond walls behind him in a cascade of gore. The man actually managed to thrust twice more before falling over dead. Arndt didn't bother to shoot, however. He growled, withdrew his KA-Bar and ran at the other fucker… literally. The man had been startled by the report of the heavy caliber pistols and had jerked back off his partner, turning to defend himself, his stubby erect penis gyrating comically and glistening in the firelight. Somehow that sight enraged Arndt further, and he swung his blade in an arc that the Jap tried to defend. With two quick slashes, Arndt batted the man's hands away, slicing both to the bone and drove his blade into the man's windpipe. With a roar of rage and horror, Arndt twisted and sawed, slicing the man's throat and then kicked him over backward to bleed out on the bamboo floor. Another shot roared out, and the sergeant turned to see the man who'd been watching lying flat on the cot, his chest a bloody mess.

Both women began to scream now. As if the sudden violence had roused them from a stupor, and they were now free to descend into madness. Both Marines went to them, securing their weapons and speaking in soothing tones. The two women at first were as frightened of the larger Americans as the Japanese, but this didn't last long.

The older woman must have realized who the two men were and what they'd done. She collected herself first, drew in a deep breath and smiled at Arndt before rushing to the other naked woman and wrapping her in her arms. Only now did Taggart realize the two women, somewhat homely, resembled one another.

"Mother and daughter," he said angrily. "Jesus Christ…"

"They just make it easier to knife their sorry asses," Arndt growled.

Oaks and Entwater split up to do a cursory inspection of the village. There were no sentries posted, which they both thought was odd. There were obviously Japanese here, so why wasn't somebody on guard?

Maybe it was just a small patrol. Other than the drunken soldier who'd come outside, there was no movement and no discernible sound in the village. The huts, although made quickly from local materials that included bamboo, teak, palm fronds and some stones for elevation, were remarkably soundproof. However, when two sharp cracks floated over the quiet village, muffled though they were… it did garner some attention.

From a hut only a few paces from Entwater's position, a door flew open, and a shirtless Japanese soldier bolted out, his Arisaka rifle in hand. He stopped at the bottom of the three steps, his body silhouetted in the rectangle of light from within. The man hadn't been thinking, and he now found himself outside and alone and night blind.

He had little time to contemplate his situation before a .30 caliber rifle shell imploded his skull. Entwater covered the distance in a second and stepped over the dead man. In the process, he'd slung his Springfield and pulled his .45 and clicked off the safety. He crouched low and went up the steps leading with his pistol.

87

The scene inside that greeted him was much like the one that his comrades had found moments earlier. The exception was that there was only one naked Japanese man remaining in this hut. This one had a small Melanesian girl pressed down on her cot, face down, and was joyfully sodomizing her. She cried out and squirmed, but the beefy Jap had one hand pressing on her upper back and the other cupping her small buttock as he thrust.

There were two dead islanders tossed into a corner like old trash. One man and one woman, both probably in relatively early adulthood. Both had ashen gray skin and ominous black holes in their foreheads. The realization of what he was seeing struck Entwater like a freight train... a freight train bearing a load of fury.

Without thinking, he began to squeeze the trigger of his pistol. He hollered in mindless rage as he pumped shot after shot into the Japanese man, making him jerk back and jitterbug grotesquely on his knees before Entwater burned through all eight shots, and the Jap toppled over the edge of the cot, his body a bloody hunk of Swiss cheese.

Entwater holstered his .45 and went to the girl, seeing now that she couldn't be more than twelve years old. She looked up at him, curled into a ball and started to sob uncontrollably. Entwater bent down to comfort her, but the terrorized girl added screams to her sobs and lashed out at him with clawed hands, trying to fend him off.

Entwater leaned back and held up his hands, and spoke to her soothingly. After a moment, she saw that he was dressed in an American uniform and noticed his lightly tanned white skin. She stopped crying suddenly, blinked at him and then threw herself into his arms, letting him hold her naked body close as she once more began to sob, this time in anguish.

At about the same time, fifty yards away, near the largest hut, most likely the headman's house, Philip Oaks also heard Taggart's shots. He thought he saw Entwater disappear behind another hut, and then there was the echoing *crackle* of a high-powered rifle. A few seconds went by, and then the rapid report of somebody emptying an eight-round magazine from a Colt followed. This elicited some surprised exclamations from the hut in front of him, and Oaks was not at all surprised to see the door open. He immediately dropped to his belly and peered at the yellow light within over his iron sights.

The doorway was only ten yards from him, and Oaks entertained the notion of tossing a grenade inside. That would doubtless put down any resistance that might lie within. However, it would also kill any innocent civilians inside as well. Instead, he simply waited in silent darkness.

A silhouette appeared in the rectangle of light. It stood there for a moment, just a black form backlit by firelight of some kind. Oaks didn't fire, though, not sure of the identity of the person.

The man, he could tell by the voice, said: "No savvy nothing 'e no belonga."

Oaks almost chuckled at the thought that he wished Tank Broderick were there. The big navy electrician had picked up on Pidgin very quickly and would understand what the man had said. Of course, it was fairly obvious. Another man's voice, this time clearly Japanese, uttered a harsh command and the native man swung the door closed.

Oaks waited for another few seconds. Nothing happened. There were no sounds from the hut. The door did not open, nor did any windows… if it had windows. Once more, all was quiet in the village. Beyond its limits, in the dense jungle, night birds sang, monkeys chattered, insects added their countless voices to the chorus of immeasurable tropical life… but no human moved outside their dwellings.

"Fuck it," Oaks grumbled.

He rose quietly to his feet, slung his rifle and withdrew his Colt. There was no need to chamber a round; he made it a habit to always keep one in the chamber and then eject the magazine and replace the round. In this way, his pistol had nine rather than eight shots. He only need click off the safety and move in.

At the steps, Oaks put one booted foot on the first, slowly adding more weight to test for creaks or groans that might give him away.

Whoever was inside, at least one Japanese soldier, was playing it cool. Oaks had to assume the man was no fool.

The step supported him, and he tried the next, which also seemed to have settled in. There was no reason to climb the last one; the bamboo pole door was within reach. Oaks could see by the moon's light that there was a sort of handle that turned. Probably a simple bar that kept the door from opening. He gritted his teeth, grasped the handle and turned, yanking the door open and swinging out with it, letting the sturdy door carry him off the steps where he could drop to the ground and crouch beside them.

Immediately, eight shots barked out from within. By the sound, Oaks was certain that an officer was in there firing through the open doorway. Most Japanese officers used the ubiquitous Nambu Type 14 semi-automatic pistol. Like the M1911, it also held eight rounds in its magazine. Unlike the heavy caliber Colt, however, the Nambu used a 7.89mm or .31 caliber round. Poor stopping power and not very accurate over fifty yards.

Oaks heard the distinct clack of the slide locking open and put one foot on the bottom step to lever himself up. He leapt upward, coming to rest half inside the door on his chest, holding his Colt out before him and searching for a target.

He found one.

The Japanese officer stood off to the left, holding his pistol out before him in his right hand. Oaks could see the red sash around his waist, that of it which was exposed at any rate. The man's left arm was wrapped around the middle of an onyx-skinned native man who was easily a head taller than the Jap and fifty pounds heavier.

The native man was dressed in a ragged pair of slacks that had probably been given to him by one of the Protectorate officers eons before. Time and the tropical jungles had reduced the khaki pants to a threadbare and stained relic of better days.

The man wore nothing above the waist, and although his face was deeply lined with age, the torso was still taught with ropey muscle.

Upon seeing Oaks in his camouflage, the islander hollered something unintelligible and thrust out his arms, breaking the hold of the officer. He then turned, grabbed the smaller man by the throat and lifted him off his feet, his two huge and powerful black hands squeezing the life out of the Asian.

The officer kicked and batted, but his strength was no match for the old man. However, when he dropped his pistol and tried to pull something from his belt, Oaks surged up and into the room. He crossed the ten feet or so, put his Colt's barrel against the officer's temple and pulled the trigger. The body jerked, and the man went limp, his brains and blood spraying across the hut's interior.

"Is good done, yank!" the old man said, showing a gap-toothed smile as he let the dead officer fall into a heap at his feet. "You savvy good time belonga my village."

"If by that you mean I showed up in the knick of time… I guess you're right, sir," Oaks said, lowering his pistol. "Sergeant Phil Oaks, United States Marine Corps."

The big old man held out a catcher's mitt of a hand and laughed, "Me headman Tenagao. You welcome, you savvy good-time Charlie!"

Oaks laughed, "Thank you, sir."

A rather pretty, youngish woman popped up from behind a table where she'd been crouching and ran over to the older man. She wrapped him in her arms and began to weep. The old man patted her gently and crooned soothingly. Oaks thought that he must be her father.

"This is wife, Mungevu," he explained. "We thank you savvy much."

"Sarge!" came Entwater's voice from outside. "You in there?"

"Yeah, Ted," Oaks called back. "What's goin' on out there?"

"I found a couple of Japs, and so did the others," Entwater explained unnecessarily.

"Okay… the three of you secure the village," Oaks said. "Hut by hut search and then stand watch. I want to talk to the chief, and then we'll move."

"Aye-aye," said the young man.

Oaks spent several minutes speaking with the headman. It turned out that there were no more Japanese in the village. There had only been a small patrol, a Lieutenant, a Sergeant and five soldiers. Tenagao explained that a large number of men had passed through several days before and had taken up position between the village and the Matanikau. He wasn't sure how many, perhaps a hundred, although his grasp of numbers was less precise. Oaks had to deduce from descriptions such as five, much and many added up to about a hundred. At least a couple of platoons.

Although the man still spoke Pidgin, there was a lot more English in it, and it made communication easier. The headman offered for the men to stay, to take whatever they wanted from the Japanese and hinted that there were several women in the village who would be most grateful. Oaks thanked him but said they had a timetable to keep.

"You keep whatever the Naponapo brought," Oaks said. "After what they did… it's the least you deserve."

Tenagao bowed and smiled, "Is good. But you savvy 'e come, and you kill and protect. I give you gift."

The headman's young wife had been methodically stripping the dead officer of his clothes and gear while they spoke. She stepped forward and handed Oaks a baldrick with a sword sheathed in its scabbard. She smiled and fastened the sword belt across Oaks' right shoulder, and sinched the buckle down tight. Oaks smiled at her.

"Is savvy good sword," the headman explained. "Naponapo headman 'e use, 'e cut in half. You savvy easy-peasy-Japanesie."

Oaks laughed and thanked them both before heading out into the night. They had much to do and miles to go. The Marines hoped that the gunshots hadn't alerted anyone nearby or further on their path.

EAST OF THE TENERU

Joe Treadway knew he was going to die.

The Japanese soldier was so close that Treadway could smell the man's bitter body funk. When he uttered that single word… *Banzai*… Treadway said a quick prayer. Everybody knew what that meant. A vicious Japanese charge with swords and bayonets.

When the attack came, however, it was not preceded by a yell. Nor did it come in the form of a sharp point driven into his belly.

No, there was the sound of a zipper, the rustling of cloth, and then a warm stream of something that stank of ammonia began to rain down on Treadway's head and back.

The fucking Jap was *pissing* on him!

The soldier let out a satisfied "Aahhhh…" and then said something softly in Japanese that was probably the equivalent of, "Oh yeah… that's got it…." Finally, after what seemed like an eternity, the urine stopped, the man put his junk away, zipped up and left the bushes to rejoin his patrol.

Treadway lay there, soaking in another man's piss, lying face down in moldy jungle and seethed. When the sound of soft footfalls disappeared along the road, he let out a string of filthy but quiet oaths.

The muffled laughter from both Clayton and Vousa did not improve his mood any. Treadway rose up on his knees and tried not to vomit.

"Damn, Treadway," Clayton couldn't resist saying. "Talk about fortitude. Don't know I could've stayed still for that."

"Maybe next time *you* give it a try, then," Treadway cranked, rising to his feet.

Vousa grinned, "Good work, private. I thought they had us for sure."

"Me too," Treadway said. "I'm glad to be alive… but I ain't happy about it."

"Don't worry, there's a stream not far you can wash off in," Vousa said. "Need to get that stink off you."

"Yeah, we're not trying to *attract* them after all, Joe," Clayton teased.

"Anybody ever tell you that you're a laugh riot, Clayton?" Treadway grumbled.

Clayton chuckled, "Hey… that's twice now you didn't call me, sir. Guess we figured out what it takes to get you to stop, huh?"

"Just let a Jap pee on him," Vousa said.

"How'd you two funny men like a size eleven USMC issue right in the keister?"

"Okay, okay," Clayton said, clapping Treadway on the shoulder. "We're sorry, Joe. Come on, let's find that stream."

"We're proud of you, Joe," Vousa seconded. "You probably saved our bacon."

Treadway allowed a small smile, "Well… okay."

"Good, now we can be friends and drop all the formality, right, Joe?" Clayton asked as Vousa began to push deeper into the jungle toward where he said a small game trail should be.

"Yes sir," said Treadway.

8

USS BULL SHARK – THE SLOT
AUGUST 19, 1942 – 1230 SHIP'S TIME

Paul "Buck" Rogers sat with Mike Duncan at the unofficial chief's table scarfing down a bowl of franks and beans. The staple meal had been kicked up a little by Henrie Martin, the ship's ranking mess specialist. There were chunks of bacon and a hint of cayenne to add something to the usually plain-Jane fare.

Rogers was pleased to see both torpedo rooms leading Petties grabbing a tray of beanie-weenies, coffee and freshly baked French bread and heading for the table. However, when both chiefs saw the reserved looks on Walter "Sparky" Sparks' and Walter "Murph" Murphy's faces, they knew this would likely be a working lunch.

"Take a load off, fellas," the COB said. "How's life on the edge?"

Murph sat beside Duncan and Sparky beside Rogers. Both men were brawny and took up most of the limited space.

"Christ, Sparky," Rogers teased. "Why the hell didn't you sit next to Mikey? Feel like a blivit over here."

Duncan guffawed, and Sparky grinned, "Not my fault I'm built sexy, Buck. Good genes."

Murph scoffed, "What the hell's a *blivit*, Buck?"

Duncan shook his head, "You never heard that one? A blivit,

young torpedoman's mate, is five pounds of shit stuffed into a four-pound bag."

Murph threw his head back and roared, "Goddamn! Yeah, that about sums you up, huh, Buck?"

"Up yours, Murph," Rogers glared but couldn't suppress a grin. "So, what's on you boys' minds. You look like you been suckin' lemons the whole forenoon."

"Naw…" Sparky drawled. "It's only… well… it's that it's high fuckin' noon, and we're runnin' on top for cryin' out loud. In the middle of The Slot."

"Yeah… the guys are jumpy," Murph said. "With all the Japs flyin' back and forth to Guadalcanal from Rabaul and whatever… why the hell are we hangin' our asses out right in their flight paths?"

Duncan smirked but said nothing, allowing the Chief of the Boat to field that one. His recent experiences in the jungles of Guadalcanal gave him a new perspective on danger and a new appreciation for his nice clean boat. A boat that had no crocodiles, tarantulas, fire ants, poisonous centipedes or grody leeches. Hell, the boat was kept so meticulously clean they didn't even have roaches aboard.

Chief Mike Duncan was *not* a fan of creepy-crawlies.

"Maybe you fellas ain't heard the news," Rogers said, "but we got one of them aggressive-type skippers aboard. Anvil Art Turner… ever hear of him? Submariner and Marine Raider…? Hero of tale and song?"

Duncan snorted.

"Yeah, but come on, Buck!" Sparky insisted. "He's got us roarin' along, all Ack-acks manned, plus extra dudes with Ma Deuces up there… and extra lookouts and all. That always means torpedomen."

"Yeah, our guys gotta climb the sheers, man the guns and wrestle pickles," Murph complained. "Which means that the torpedo gangs spend more time in dangerous jobs than do the juice jerkers or engine snipes."

"Yeah, the navy really shoulda warned us that war would be hazardous," Duncan said bemusedly.

"Look, we ain't bitchin'," Sparky said, holding up a hand. "It just seems that with so much risk-taking… why, it feels a bit like the pickle handlers on this boat are pulling more'n their fair share."

Murph nodded in agreement. Rogers dredged a slice of crusty toasted French bread into his bowl and took a bite. He took the time to think while he chewed.

"Okay," he finally said. "I'll go over the watch and quarter bills. If it looks like there's some imbalance, I'll talk to the skipper and Mr. Williams."

Murph nodded and smiled, "Thanks, Buck. Hell, we ain't whinin' about the captain's methods. Look how much this boat has done just in the past six months. Probably not another boat in the fleet can match our record."

"Yeah, it's just that we want to make sure the work is split fair, y'know, Buck?" Sparky went on. "Sides, we got our own chores to do, too."

"I'll look into it," The COB promised.

The compartment's AM radio set was on, and something by Arty Shaw was just finishing when a sultry, smooth female voice seemed to fill the mess.

"*Well now, all you brave sailors and G.I.'s out there in radio land, this is your loving friend Tokyo Rose coming at you once more over the ether,*" the traitorous DJ crooned. "*I'd like to dedicate this next tune to a special bunch of guys out there… the men of USS* Bull Shark *and the bloodthirsty but well-intentioned First Marine Division on Guadalcanal….*"

"Oh, here we go…." Somebody grumped.

"*…I just thought you should all know how just last night, your brave friends in the submarine service sank a ship loaded with medical supplies and nurses on a mission of mercy to Guadalcanal. A ship loaded with supplies to help aid the poor natives who have been tortured and especially the* poor *young native women who have been* sooo *used… but now I guess the brave Marines will get to keep beating and raping. Thanks U.S. Navy… thanks U.S. Marine Corps. All that sexual assault sort of makes me think of this next tune… so here's The Glen Miller orchestra with… In the Mood.*"

"Fuck you, bitch!" somebody, Rogers thought maybe Tank

Broderick, shouted. A hunk of French bread sailed across the mess and bounced off the speaker.

The men ate for a few more minutes. They'd just polished off their lunch when the gonging alarm of general quarters sounded. Clancy Weiss, who was chief of the watch, came over the 1MC and announced all hands to battle stations surface and to standby for a hard dive. The four men looked at one another and grinned.

"Told ya'," Sparky said and sprang to his feet.

Joe Dutch had the deck. As per captain's orders, the ship was running on top on three-engine speed with number one on charge duty. *Bull Shark* was making fifteen knots headed up The Slot. She'd gone down as far as the Sealark Channel during the night and was now making her way northwest to position herself to intercept another line of Tokyo Express destroyers on their way down from Rabaul and Shortland Island.

After sinking that destroyer the previous night, Art Turner had announced that the boat would be upping her game. He said that until S-52 arrived off The Canal, *Bull Shark* was on her own and had to do the work of two boats. Which meant, as he'd said, that she'd have to primarily be a surface ship that only occasionally dove.

"On top, we can run quickly and work into good attack positions," Turner had explained to his officers. "This is a no-brainer at night. We don't dive at night unless directly attacked. Period. It's my opinion, backed by our experiences and updates in the morning and evening foxes, that the Japs don't have surface-search radar. Most of them don't even have air-search, which in itself is virtually useless for tracking shipping."

"We know the *Sakai* has it, sir," Frank Nichols had pointed out.

"Yeah, and as we all know, the only thing our own sugar dog says is that something's out there somewhere and is a certain distance away," Turner rebutted. "No direction, nothing. And for a high-platform unit to spot us is harder, and even if they do... so what? They have no idea where we are, just *that* we are. Nope, we're not gonna slink away from Jap radar. By day, we're gonna be more vigilant. Post more lookouts for plane spotting, and I want crews on all AA guns, including a couple of fifty cals. Unless it's more than one plane, we shoot at them rather than the other way around. During the day, we keep the SD going every couple of minutes. Switch her on, give it a few seconds and switch it off. That plus our eyes, we should be fine. Even if we spot a Zeke skimming the surface, it's still gonna take him over a minute to reach us from the time he comes over the hill and spots us, if he does. We can clear the bridge in that time, if not get below. It's risky, but that's what we're out here for. We'll evaluate as we go. If it gets too hairy, then we'll pull back to a more conservative approach."

So here was Joe Dutch, standing on the bridge beside Wendel Freeman with four lookouts in the sheers, a man at the bow and one at the stern with binoculars. Two hands stood to either side of the cigarette deck with their Browning M2 machine guns mounted. No ammo servers, though. Should anybody spot aircraft the boat thinks it can handle, then the two bow and stern lookouts run to the raised deck to assist the machine gunners. There were also men assigned to the big Bofors 40mm Pom-pom, a trainer, a pointer and an ammo server. Behind the bridge, the 20mm Oerlikon had two men, a gunner and a server. All in all, there were fifteen men on deck. However, the after engine hatch, mess hatch and forward torpedo room hatch were open, both allowing fresh air into the boat and a multitude of escape routes for the men.

The skipper's orders were clear. Outside the Sealark Channel, where American planes from Henderson Field operated, it was SOP to shoot on sight. As soon as an aircraft was spotted, whatever gun was assigned to that sector would open up, except the M2s, of course, as their range didn't go out to the horizon like the big anti-aircraft cannons. Their jobs were to start plinking at any birds that made it past the screen thrown up by the two heavy cannons.

Of course, Art wasn't totally reckless. Thankfully the Japs were nothing if not predictable. Every day, at around 0800, they lifted off from their airfield at Rabaul to make the five-hundred-plus-mile flight to Guadalcanal. The flights generally consisted of several squadrons of Betty level bombers, sometimes a few Val dive bombers and of course escorting Zekes. They tended to fly high, conserving fuel and avoiding any potential threats from the surface. The likelihood of even a couple of Zeroes diving down to strafe a lone submarine and leave their charges was low. At least on the way *down* The Slot. On the way back, however, it would be a different story. Although the planes, or what was left of them, would be lower on fuel, they'd also be free of heavy ordnance and wouldn't think twice about dropping down, and running past said lone submarine and giving her the old Hirohito how-do.

Thus, *Bull Shark* would boldly defy the Nips during the morning watch, the men on deck watching the dozens of aircraft soaring by high overhead. In that instance, they were not to attack unless any of the birds were low. But at twenty-thousand feet or more, it simply wasn't worth wasting the ammo. However, it took about three hours for the Japs to cruise down to Guadalcanal, another fifteen or twenty minutes to drop their loads, and then they'd start heading back. It was this time, from around noon to sixteen hundred that things could get dicey.

"*Bridge, radar! We have contact! Range three-zero triple-zero yards… close rate is one-seven-five knots,*" came the voice of Eugene Parker, torpedoman first-class who was taking his trick at the gear for his sub quals.

Dutch did a quick calculation in his head. If the plane or planes… the damned SD couldn't really tell you… stayed at that speed, it'd take five minutes for them to cover the fifteen miles or so. Plenty of time to make a decision.

"Radar, Bridge, very well… give me a full sweep on the sugar jig," Dutch said into the speaker. "Assistant officer of the deck, sound the general quarters alarm and announce battle stations gun action."

In truth, there wasn't any need to announce battle stations gun action. The AA stations were already manned, and the two big five-inch deck guns wouldn't be used against aircraft. However, it would get men to their action stations and in a ready position. Men would be hauling up anti-aircraft and machine-gun ammunition from the locker and standing by at the gun service hatches. It also meant that men could be quickly redirected to torpedo action stations should that need arise.

"*Bridge, radar, sugar jig sweep contacts!*" Parker replied. He was obviously getting excited. "*Six contacts bearing three-five-zero, altitude indeterminant.*"

"From the northwest…." Wendel Freeman, acting quartermaster, muttered.

"Yeah… interesting," Dutch said and raised his voice. "Keep a sharp eye, lookouts! We got Jap birds off the nose! Coming in high!"

"I got eyes on 'em, sir!" Fred Swooping Hawk reported. The young Navaho had just about the best vision on the boat. "Look like Zekes, sir! Can't quite tell if they got anything hangin'… but they're flying in a double-column damn near straight for us!"

Dutch had two options. He could maintain course, lowering the boat's profile and making her a harder target. This would only allow the quad-barrel Pom-pom to fire, however. On the other hand, if he turned thirty degrees off course, then Danny Pentakkus could swing his Oerlikon around and add its two barrels to the submarine's attack. This would, of course, make her a wider target for the fighters.

"Wendel, give me hard right rudder," Dutch decided. He felt more than heard another presence appear behind him from the open hatch. He knew without looking that it was the captain.

"Gonna pull our pants down, Joe?" Turner asked calmly.

"Got time to throw up some flack before we either dive or point our nose back at 'em, sir," Dutch said, casting a quick glance at his friend to see his reaction.

Turner was known for allowing his officers to shoulder the responsibility of the watch, even during an attack. He felt this made them better submariners, better combat officers and better men. It was a strategy that he and Dudley "Mush" Morton had spent many an hour discussing when Turner was his student at PXO school.

Everyone could see the Japanese planes now. Two lines of three black specs that appeared, thanks to perspective, to be climbing up from the sea, their bellies exposed. This was a trick of the eye, of course. The curvature of the Earth accounted for it, and soon, the aircraft would appear more level… and then head-on as they dove down toward the submarine to strafe her.

"Ack-ack, weapons free!" Dutch announced, and almost before the words were out of his mouth, the big Pom-pom began to thump, the sound of its rounds giving it the colloquial name. The Oerlikon clattered as well, its twin barrels just free of the periscope sheers and masts.

"I was gonna ask if you thought they might not attack, thinking we was a Jap sub, sir," Freeman said. "But I guess that cat's outta the bag now, huh?"

Dutch grinned, and Turner chuckled, "This mission isn't about stealth, Wendel. It's about giving the Jap pause. Making him aware of the fact that we're out here gunning for him. That if he wants Guadalcanal so bad, then he's gonna pay for it every inch of the way."

Red tracers zipped through the air; every few shells of the cannons being loaded with them to help guide the gunners. Turner watched as slowly but surely, the lances of fire closed in on the incoming Zeroes. One was hit and bloomed into a black ball of smoke with a brilliant cherry-red flower of flame at its center. Although fast and maneuverable, Zeroes lacked any kind of armor. When struck, their wing fuel tanks tended to explode.

"Suck on that you slant-eyed son of a whore!" Pentakkus railed in his heavy Maine drawl. He pronounced it ho-wuh.

"We've stirred 'em up now," Turner stated.

Everyone watched as the tight formation broke apart as fighters angled off in every direction, arcing away from the deadly tracers. Soon, though, they began to regroup, forming up into a line of two and a line of three, each one separating and turning to make a run at the submarine's flanks.

"Pom-pom go right, Oerlikon go left!" Turner shouted, letting Dutch give helm orders. "Ma deuces, time to get into the show!"

The metallic *rat-tat-tat* of the machine guns added to the chorus of cannon fire and the distant but growing roar of radial engines. Turner was pleased to note that the two deck lookouts had already stationed themselves near the machine gunners, hundred-round belts of fifty-caliber ammunition in their arms. Without strict fire discipline, the M2 could burn through a full belt in about fifteen seconds on full auto.

Pat Jarvis had been drilling the machine gunners to use a low rate of fire selection for more distant targets. They just had to hold down the butterfly trigger and aim the gun. The weapon would emit five-round bursts every six seconds or so automatically, allowing for easier aiming. As the M2 had a max effective range of about a mile, they would maintain this rate of fire until the target came to within half of that and then switch to the higher firing rate.

"Lookouts below!" Turner ordered.

The planes were angling toward them now, beginning to fire their own smaller 7.62mm nose cannons as they approached. The idea was to walk their rounds along the surface and up to the ship, then switch to heavier 20mm wing cannons when they were close to maximize damage.

"Splash two!" somebody shouted to starboard.

Turner watched as the three-plane formation was suddenly reduced to one. That single plane, in light of the combined machine gun flak and cannon fire, thought better of its attack run and angled away.

"*Bridge, radar!*" Parker all but squealed in alarm. "*Multiple surface contacts on sugar jig! Bearing three-zero-five, range twenty-three-thousand yards... can't tell how many exactly, but at least two, sir! Speed is thirty-three knots!*"

Another Zero erupted into flame off to port. Unlike the other flight, this pilot was either suicidal or brave. He continued his run, walking his rounds across the waves and straight for the submarine's foredeck.

"Clear the bridge!" Turner ordered and pulled the diving alarm twice. "Wendel, alert control to prepare for emergency deep!"

Already the machine gunners and their assistants were dismounting the five-foot machine guns and hustling them down the after hatches. Pentakkus and Perry Wilkes, the gunner on the Pom-pom, were centering their pieces and securing the ammunition. Pat's relentless drills were paying off.

The Zeroes' bullets just missed the deck, only a couple of heavy rounds chewing into the boat's bullnose and throwing up small clouds of splinters. This, thanks to Freeman's quick order to port the helm hard over and reverse the port engine.

The deck hatches were closed, and Turner followed Dutch and

Freeman down the hatch which was secured by the quartermaster. Dutch looked to Turner, who only shook his head and stood by the ladder.

"Diving officer, rig ship for deep submergence," Dutch ordered. "All ahead flank, rig out bow planes, close main induction."

The order had already been sent back to maneuvering to switch to batteries. Yet the boat still held onto some of her diesel-powered way and was yet making fourteen knots. With the electrical motors now on battery power, they could only make about nine at emergency speed, but even at flank, which was just shy of the ultimate limit, they would reduce the deceleration so that the big submarine could break the surface suction and dive all the faster.

"Green Christmas tree! Pressure in the boat," Nichols called out.

"Open main ballast vents," Dutch ordered, struggling to keep the excitement and fear from his own voice. "Flood bow buoyancy, flood negative, flood safety. Full dive angle on bow and stern planes. Get us in the cellar smartly, Frank!"

The boat angled steeply down at a thirty-degree angle. Anyone not seated had to brace themselves to keep from stumbling or sliding forward. Anything loose on a table or shelf was likely underway, and headed for the deck.

"Forty-five feet!" Nichols called.

"Close main vents," Dutch said. "Anything on sonar, Chet?"

With the ship at general quarters, Chet Rivers had come back on watch to take his usual position at the sonar gear.

"Bad sound profile, sir," Rivers reported. "Contacts are at least fifteen thousand yards off, and our screw noise is interfering."

"Very well," Dutch said.

"One-zero-zero feet," Nichols intoned.

"Helm, all ahead two-thirds," Dutch ordered. "Make turns for five knots. Left standard rudder."

Dick "Mug" Vigliano was seated at his customary station as well, "Maneuverin' answiz five knots, sir. My rudduh is standid' left."

"Steady up on two-seven-zero," Dutch said more calmly. Now that there were more than a hundred feet of seawater over their heads, the adrenaline rush of a few moments before was fading.

"Contacts," Rivers reported. "Two... no three... no *four* sets of fast, light screws, Mr. Dutch. Turn rate still indicates three-three knots as indicated by radar."

"Very well," Dutch said. "Track them and let me know what they're doing, Chet... Think this is a supply run, Art?"

Turner frowned, "Probably, although, at that speed, they'll be in the channel in five hours. Way too soon."

A few moments passed before Chet reported, "Aspect changes on targets... turn rates decreasing... sounds like they're splitting up, sir... assess twenty knots and individual targets are separating... active echo ranging, sir! Low energy search freq!"

"Here we go...." Dutch muttered. "They're forming a cordon."

"Yeah, sweeping for us," Turner said. "Rig for silent running, rig for depth charge!"

"Now passing two-zero-zero feet," Nichols said. "Should I blow negative, sir?"

Dutch bit his lip in thought. With the ship heavy, she'd sink faster, yet if they needed to restore neutral buoyancy with destroyers overhead, the roaring air or working pumps could give *Bull Shark's* position away. He glanced over at the captain, who nodded imperceptibly. Turner was letting Dutch run the show and giving him hints when needed.

"Blow negative to the mark," Dutch ordered down to Nichols below. "Pump auxiliary to sea. Get us neutral, Frank. But keep us headed down and try and find me a layer."

"Assess four destroyers," Rivers said. "Currently bearing... zero-two-zero, zero-four-zero, zero-six-zero and zero-eight-zero. Range is seven thousand on first and nine thousand on the fourth."

That was as much for Dutch as the plotting party below and for Freeman at the chart desk in the conning tower, "Very well, sonar. Let's label them Able, Baker, Charlie and Dog."

A minute or so went past, and Rivers reported again, "All four seem to be on course one-six-five, sir...."

Turner uttered a soft chuckle and pulled his pack of Lucky Strikes from his blouse pocket and lit one, "They're gonna zig-zag across their baseline of southeast and ping the hell outta the sea as they do. How much you want to bet, Joe?"

Dutch snorted, 'Not on your life, Art. Probably go no more than ten or twenty miles and then turn around and come back up The Slot. Figuring we can't get any further than that down here."

"Then once it's dark," Turner opined, "they'll put the pedal to the metal and head down to the island."

"Now passing three-zero-zero feet," Nichols called out.

They heard it then, a barely audible ghostly wail from out of the depths as if some restless spirits were stirring in the darkness. It was the eerie whine of low-frequency sonar beams probing the depths for their prey.

"Helm, reduce to all ahead one-third," Dutch said quietly.

Joining the faint *ooo-eee* of the sound beams came a gentle swishing. Yet with each passing second, both sounds grew in volume, which meant only one thing.

"I think Able is gonna pass close overhead, sir," Rivers hissed.

"Bathythermograph going active," Elmer Williams' disembodied voice floated up from below. He was leading the plotting party at the master gyrocompass table. "I think we're entering a layer…."

"Not a moment too soon," Dutch said. "What's our depth, Frank?"

"Three-six-zero, Joe."

"Okay… make your depth four-hundred and level us off," Dutch said. "Mug, come left to course two-five-five. Let's do a nice ninety-degree course from our buddy up there."

"He's switched to high-energy attack mode!" Rivers suddenly announced. "It's breaking up, but…."

As *Bull Shark* passed through a layer of greater salinity and thus a temperature differential, the density of the seawater acted as a reflector to sound beams. However, she wasn't quite below the sound layer when the hard pinging began. It was remarkably close, almost drowned out by the rapid whooshing of screws, and even as the sounds became attenuated by the thermal layer, there was an audible gong as the sonar beam just kissed the submarine's hull.

"Shit…" Freeman muttered. "You think they got that?"

There was no way to tell as the boat dropped into the halocline. However, Rivers scrunched up his face and frowned.

"I think... think I might have heard splashes, Mr. Dutch."

While a halocline acted as a protective shield for the submarine, preventing an enemy from hearing all but the loudest and lowest-frequency sounds, it was a two-edged sword. If you couldn't be heard, you also couldn't hear, or at least not well.

The screw noises of the destroyer were still audible, but they seemed to come from everywhere at once and were much reduced in volume. All the crew of *Bull Shark* could do was wait. They would wait between forty and fifty seconds if the Japanese depth charges were set at their current depth.

Click,click... click,click...

The ocean around them erupted into volcanic thunder and fury.

9
USS BULL SHARK – THE SLOT

A heart-pounding crackle of thunder surged through the sea, pushing thousands of tons of seawater in a pressure wave that tumbled over the fragile human-engineered machine with raw, mindless power. The three-hundred and eleven foot, twenty-six-hundred-ton steel air bubble rolled to port, sending men and loose objects tumbling.

The Japanese depth charges had been set deep, at least four-hundred feet. They'd gone off fairly close as well. Not within fatal proximity, but close enough to remind everyone aboard *Bull Shark* of why they were called tooth shakers.

"Jesus Christ!" Mug Vigliano griped as he fought with his wheel, now on manual power only.

"How'd they find us, sir?" Wendel Freeman, who'd plunged across the width of the conning tower and ended up sitting in Joe Dutch's lap, asked in pale-faced fright.

"Got lucky," Dutch opined.

"Or those two Zekes were keeping an eye on us and giving the tin cans some direction," Turner cranked. "Stupid tropical water… Captain has the deck! Mug, if you think you can hack it, give me hard right rudder and dial up a two-thirds bell. Frank, you still with me down there?"

"Yes sir," Nichols said, although he didn't sound entirely pleased about it."

Take us deep, diving officer," Turner ordered. "Six bills. Let's get under these assholes and tip-toe outta here. Guess I pushed it a little far this time."

There were scoffs, dismissive sounds and a variety of cavalier negative responses. The men were blowing it off, as they always did, and Turner was pleased by this.

Williams' head popped up through the hatch, "What we've come to expect, Art. Besides, we all know the drill."

"That's true, Elmer," Turner said. "We'll hunker down and clear the area, and then once the sun slips below the rim of the world… we shall see who has the last laugh!"

"Nyehehehehehe!" Buck Rogers laughed evilly from below. That broke everybody up, but they quickly covered their mouths and snickered into their shirt sleeves. The boat *was* rigged for silent running, after all.

As the *Balao*-class submarine planed down into the depths, another dozen depth charges exploded behind her. These, though, were not close, and the only effect they delivered to the submarine was a series of low-thumps and some slight turbulence.

"Now passing five-hundred feet," Nichols reported.

"Mug, all ahead one-third," Turner ordered. "Steady up on three-one-five."

"You don't think those planes can see us this deep, do you, sir?" Ted Balkley asked.

"No way," Turner replied. "A buck… buck and a half, sure. But not way down here. Anything from your gear, sonar?"

"Just ashcans going off, sir," Rivers announced. "I think if one of them DDs crosses overhead, I should be able to pick them up in spite of the halocline… but it doesn't sound like anybody's close now."

"Just a heads up, sir," Freeman stated from his position back at the chart desk. "If we hold this course for another three miles, we'll hit the hundred-fathom curve off Isla de Martinez. Then it shoals up pretty fast from there. The hundred-fathom curve is only a mile from the beach there."

"Plus, there's a coral reef on the inside," Williams added.

"Very well," Turner said.

"Another concern is that there's no guarantee this layer we're under will still be up there if we go too far," Williams advised.

"I know that, Elmer," Turner said. "I'm gonna put some distance behind us, and then we'll plane up and have ourselves a listen."

A tense but quiet half-hour passed. All through the boat, men sat, stood and even lounged at their various action stations awaiting orders. It has been said that military service and war, in particular, was simply a long stretch of boredom occasionally interrupted by brief moments of terror.

Perhaps nowhere was this more poignant than in a submarine at depth where seventy men were trapped together inside a pipe with a limited supply of air, where they had to avoid making any loud noise that they might invite the wrath of their enemy... and where, all around them at every single point, hundreds of pounds per square inch of seawater pressed in on them. The unrelenting and merciless forces of nature continually probing for even the slightest imperfection that might offer a way inside.

In the after torpedo room, Murph sat on the deck between tubes nine and ten with his back up against the bulkhead and pulled a pouch of tobacco and some papers from his blue work shirt. He skillfully began rolling a homemade cigarette with a rich leaf grown on his parents' farm in western Virginia.

Although Murph didn't speak with any discernable accent, he'd grown up in rural Virginia and came from a long line of tobacco farmers whose roots in America went all the way back to the earliest days of Jamestown. However, not wishing to be taken for some slack-jawed country yokel, Walter had long ago mastered his tobacco farmer's drawl.

In the maneuvering room, Danny Pentakkus was sitting at the control cubicle. With Brannigan off with Mr. Jarvis aboard S-52, Pentakkus was now acting chief electrician. In his down-east Mainer's drawl, Pentakkus was quietly telling Doug Ingram, who sat beside him, about an old legend known as the Alamagooselum. Apparently Mainahs had been scarin' their yowans with it since as fah back as anybody could rememah. In his relaxed drawl, Pentakkus wove a rather good campfire story that drew in everyone in the room.

Below them in the motor room, Sherman "Tank" Broderick and Chief Duncan squatted over the bilgeway between the four General Electric motors examining a heavy-duty pipe that acted as a main cooling conduit delivering seawater to the four engines' water-cooling systems. Between motors two and four, on the port side of the bilgeway, there was a branch fitting that broke off to starboard to feed number three. This T-split junction had developed a severe leak and was far more corroded than it should have been. The boat had only been in commission since March.

"Galvanic corrosion," Tank stated.

They didn't need to be very quiet, as the sound of the reduction gearing that drove the propellor shafts masked their voices.

"Yep..." Duncan grumbled. "Got a broke-dick circuit someplace bleedin' into the bilges."

"Need to replace that fitting," Tank continued. "It's already leakin' a gallon a minute from them threads and seams."

Duncan pursed his lips and blew a soft raspberry, "True enough, but we sure ain't doin' it at two-hundred and fifty PSI, that's for goddamned sure, buddy."

Tank chuckled, "Gonna need to either be on the surface or at periscope depth with the motors shut down."

"We could do it down here," Duncan stated. "There's a cutoff valve up ahead... problem is that we gotta shut these beauties down, like you say."

Duncan reached out and patted the housing on one of the big electric motors. A discussion then ensued regarding procedures and possible workarounds.

In the after battery room, Andy Post stood by one of the mess tables where Henry Hoffman, the boat's pharmacist's mate, had laid out some supplies from his medicine locker. Henrie Martin and Bill Borshowski, the ship's cooks, were there as well. As their station was in the galley, their battle station during a torpedo attack or when rigged for depth charge was as Hoffman's assistants.

Post himself was now acting DCO since Joe Dutch was acting

torpedo officer. As Post quietly notated numbers and condition of various medical supplies on his clipboard, he marveled at the variety of duties even an officer had to perform aboard a fleet submarine.

There hadn't been a single patrol yet where anything aboard *Bull Shark* had been the same way twice. New officers had come and gone, promotions, TAD leaving people to have to shift around… and now more of the same. If a man didn't like change, then he should stay the hell out of the boats.

In forward torpedo, Sparky had set up a folding lawn chair between the bunks and was stretched out with a Winston dangling negligently between his lips. Despite this outward appearance of nonchalance, he was carefully observing his torpedo gang going over each tube and the settings for each fish. There were more men up there than usual, as with the boat being submerged, the engine snipes had little to do. In such circumstances, the enginemen and firemen were dispersed throughout the boat. Many went forward and aft to act as extra muscle in the torpedo reload gangs. Some were tasked with helm or planes duty, and others were sent to operate equipment that was no longer on hydraulic power when running silent.

Martin Janslotter, the boatswain, was standing beneath the JP sound head manual wheel, spinning it back and forth or taking direction passed along from Rivers by the room's phone talker. Below the grating were Fred Swooping Hawk and Horris Eckhart, the two men spinning the JK and WCA sound head wheels. These two additional sonar systems were extended below the keel and could be retracted when not in use.

Other men laid in their bunks, either reading a comic book, a paperback or writing letters. No one slept, and not because they were all on duty at battle stations. No one slept because there were four Jap destroyers somewhere out there who wanted to cave in their small metal world around their ears. It was simply that with the men in their racks until needed, they were both out of the way and relatively protected when the ship bucked and broncoed.

The control room was equally silent, although with occasional quiet orders passed down from the conning tower or information passed up to the skipper. The room was extra crowded with men standing by to relieve certain positions, making it hotter and more humid than any other compartment.

At the gyro table, Elmer Williams, Hotrod Hernandez and Clancy Weiss continually updated the plot. Two men sat on the bench in front of the bow and stern plane wheels with two more to either side, ready to take over every twenty minutes. Frank Nichols stood forward of the ladder to the bridge, dividing his attention between the planesmen and the men at the air manifolds on the starboard side. The COB, as duty chief, split his time between making notes at his tiny desk as well as supervising the men all around him. Arnie Brasher sat in the radio room, continually translating the duty log into code for broadcast upon reaching the surface or radio depth with time to transmit and receive.

The quiet was finally broken by the skipper's reassuring voice, "Diving officer, take us up above the thermal… if we're even still below it. Chet isn't hearing anything, so odds are we're still under the blanket."

Although no one would admit it, leaving six hundred feet and heading up to about half that depth was a welcome notice. The nearly incessant groaning of the hull and the occasional pop or ting as metal surfaces heated and cooled or adjusted to pressure could grate on even the most seasoned submariner's nerves. It was a constant reminder of just what they were truly doing.

"Now passing five-five-zero," Nichols reported. "Stern, maintain ten degree up bubble."

"Are you gonna try for one of those DDs, Art?" Dutch asked quietly.

Turner sighed, "No, Joe… not with four of them up there hunting us, plus possibly those two remaining Zeroes. Not to mention that by now, the Jap bombing mission's probably on their way back to Rabaul. No, I just want to find out where they are, so we make sure to stay away from there."

It was when Nichols reported passing three-hundred and sixty feet that Rivers reached up and pressed his earphones to his head with both hands. Turner noticed and moved to lean over the back of the sonarman's chair.

"I've got light fast screws, sir...." Rivers reported quietly. "The sound is still attenuated by the salt layer... guess we're still partly in it... but the sound is fairly close. And sir... there's... there's something else, too... I can't explain it...."

"Put it on the loudspeaker," Turner ordered. "Joe, lend an ear here."

The sonar loudspeaker crackled and filled with a distant and oddly stretched sound. It reminded Turner of a cross between boiling water and falling rain. No doubt the sound of the tin cans' propellors beating the water. Then there was something else, so faint that Turner wasn't even sure he'd heard it. By the look on Dutch's face, though, he knew it *hadn't* been his imagination.

"What the hell was that?" Turner asked.

Dutch and Rivers exchanged confused glances before Dutch said: "You know what it reminds me of... Jacob Marley."

Rivers blinked, "sir?"

"You know," Dutch said. "*A Christmas Carol.* When Scrooge is walking home through the snow and hears the rattling of chains but doesn't see anybody?"

"Well, I'll be dipped...." Turner muttered. "It does sound like that...."

"Now passing three-four-zero feet," Nichols intoned. "Skipper, it looks like we're headed into isothermal water again."

It was as if somebody had unwrapped a scarf from around the submariner's ears. Through the loudspeaker, the more distinct sound of destroyer screws churning the water came through, along with the occasional rattle. Joining this was the soft sound of several low-energy sonar beams probing the sea as well.

"Dogged bastards, ain't they?" Turner asked. "Okay, Chet, get back on the phones and give the plotting party some updated bearings and headings. Frank hold us at three-hundred."

"It's crazy up there...." Rivers said. "I've got four distinct ships... but they're all moving erratically."

"What's that rattling?" Turner asked.

"I have no idea...." Rivers said. "It's almost like one of the Japs' anchors is rattling against the hull... but that can't be."

Dutch took up the headphones and listened as well. On the loudspeaker, there was no sense of direction. However, the headphones output sound in stereo, and the operator could get a sense of direction through his ears. Also, the magic-eye display assisted with this, giving a visual representation of the sound profile around the ship. Additionally, the operator could aim the sound heads and home in on a particular signal. However, with hydraulic power shut down, the only way to do this was to pass orders to the forward torpedo room through a sound-powered telephone.

Dutch, as torpedo officer, had a set that he used to speak directly to the rooms. If necessary, the 1MC circuit could be activated, and orders could be passed out over the general announcement circuit. However, this was a one-way communication only and not exactly keeping with silent running.

Dutch pushed one earcup away from his right ear and held the phone set up so he could speak and listen, "Forward room, conning… Have the JK and JP heads sweep from zero-three-zero to one-five-zero."

The order was acknowledged, and Dutch slid the headphone cup back over his ear. After a moment, the two sonar operators, with their almost preternatural hearing, looked at one another with wide eyes.

"Sir!" Rivers reported. "Able through Dog bearing one-one-five… range two-thousand to three-thousand yards… headings are… I think two are headed about two-five-zero and two more are headed zero-seven-zero… ranges opening…."

"Okay, good, then they're off our starboard quarter and headed south of west and north of east… weird. How about that rattling?"

Dutch turned to look at Turner with a frown on his face, "It's faint, but we keep getting it… it's definitely a metallic rattle, and there seems to be multiple sources."

"Like the cops draggin' the East River for some stiff," Vigliano muttered. Turner looked to the New Yorker's back and saw the man stiffen and turn. "Skipper… they're draggin' for us!"

"Those crafty yellow bastards…." Turner muttered.

"Art, we're approaching the fifty-fathom curve," Williams warned from below. "Recommend we make a turn of zero-six-zero degrees either way to stay in deeper water."

"Well, that tears *that*," Turner stated. "Can't go left, or we'll sail right into the DDs path. If I had to guess, I'd say they're zigging back and forth across The Slot, hoping to find us. Two groups of two on diverging courses… Mug, right rudder. Come to course zero-two-zero."

"Sir, my rudduh is right standid'," Mug reported. "Steadyin' up on course zero-two-zero."

"Aspect change on all targets!" Rivers bleated in alarm. "The closer group is turning… Jesus! Almost right for us, sir! The other group is coming north as well."

"Do they know where we are?" Dutch asked rhetorically.

Williams popped up through the hatchway, "Give me updates every minute or so, Chet. Art, I think this closer group is following the fifty-fathom curve. The other one might just be doing the same but in deeper water."

"Concur, XO," Turner said confidently, although his innards felt a bit watery. "They're *guessing* where we might be and where we probably won't go. Bet those Zekes are still up there and that DD task force commander figures we won't go any shallower than two-hundred for fear of being spotted. Clever, whoever's in charge up there. Mug, all ahead two-thirds. Make turns for five knots. Elmer, Wendel, you fellas keep good track. I want to try and slip between those two groups. I have a feeling those chains they're dragging are more than long enough to reach us. What's their speed, Chet?"

"Turn rates indicate fifteen knots, sir," Rivers stated.

"Kinda slow for DDs on a search and destroy," Dutch opined.

"Yeah… but if they run too fast, they'll be dragging their chains shallower," Turner said. "Probably finding a balance between speed and effectiveness. After all… their prey can only do nine knots at best, and that not for long."

Presently, Rivers turned toward his captain, "Sir, both groups are converging… group Able is running almost straight at us! Group Baker is headed three-four-zero…"

Freeman made some quick notes on his maneuvering board and

looked up, "They'll cross our bow less than two hundred yards ahead, skipper."

"Concur," came the disembodied voice of Elmer Williams.

Turner went to the chart desk and examined Freeman's plot, "Hmm… if we come to course zero-six-zero, we should pass in front of the group Baker ships before they reach us. Then we can continue due east and get past them. Go for it, Mug."

"Comin' right…" Vigliano reported.

Oooo-eeee… oooo-eeee…

The sound of low-frequency search sonar echoed faintly through the hull. The beam was heavily dopplered and not close, yet just the fact that it could be heard *at all* was reason for worry. With the boat turning more northeasterly, they were moving out of the path of the Able group, but active sound beams had a long range, especially on low frequency. Also, with the destroyers moving somewhat slower, their passive listening gear might detect *Bull Shark's* machinery signature if they got close enough.

The sound beams grew slightly loud but also seemed to be coming from astern now as opposed to the port quarter. However, there was another set of echolocation wails now coming from the starboard beam, or just forward of it.

"It's gonna be close," Williams reported. "Recommend we go deeper, sir."

A wise precaution. However, for the time being, Turner had an advantage. He knew where his enemy was, and they didn't know where he was. If they went back down below the protection of the salt layer, that advantage would be lost.

"Not just yet, XO," Turner said. "I want to keep an ear on these—"

"Sir!" Rivers exclaimed. "Screw turn rate increase on group Baker! Indicates… twenty-five knots!"

"Shit…" Turner cursed. "Frank, emergency deep! Flood bow buoyancy! Flood negative, get us down fast! Give me a fathometer reading now!"

A low but audible ping. The fathometer was a low-powered sonar, but it was possible for the pulse to be heard by a nearby enemy ship.

"Seven-eight-six feet," Hotrod's voice said.

"Get us down to seven hundred, Frank," Turner said. "I've got a bad feeling about this! Mug, all ahead full."

The good news was that with the destroyers running so fast, their passive listening would be garbage. Even their active pings would be all but useless except on high power. But high-powered beams were narrower as a result.

"Passing back through the layer," Frank said.

In spite of this, the chilling sound of fast screws began to fill the boat. Faint at first, almost like the soft patter of a spring rain… but the sound grew in intensity and proximity with alarming speed. Even on a full-speed bell, *Bull Shark* was only making seven knots. The boat was angled down steeply, driving herself deep while being negatively buoyant. Turner only hoped it'd be enough.

Chu,chu,chu,chu…

"Here they come!" Rivers announced loudly over the swishing. "They're passing overhead."

Salt layer or not, the sound of a ship's propellers tearing through the water directly overhead was enormously loud.

"Five hundred feet!" Nichols reported.

Then from forward, something clunked and scraped along the wooden deck near the bow. The sound was odd, transmitted through the ship's hull with eerie clarity.

"Oh, shit…" Turner groaned almost inaudibly.

"Maybe they won't notice," Dutch hissed. "At that speed, a chain should—"

He was interrupted by a loud clanging and thunking followed by a heavy silence. Something heavy had been attached to the end of the chain. Probably an anchor. Fortunately, it hadn't snagged on anything. There was plenty to catch on the submarine's upper works. Deck guns, AA cannon, periscopes and masts, cigarette deck railing… but forward of the gun, there was little to snag an anchor unless it happened to jam into a limber hole.

"Phew…" Ted Balkley breathed and smiled.

"We're not out of the woods yet," Turner said. "Mug, hard right rudder!"

Click-click… click-click…

The sea around *Bull Shark* roared and heaved and throbbed with concussive energy. The Japanese had dropped depth charges after sensing that their drogue had contacted something. Although the charges were not very close, they were deep. They'd gone off at five-hundred feet.

The boat was shaken badly. Cork insulation fluttered, light bulbs popped and sprinkled bits of glass about each compartment and men were jangled in mind and body.

"Mug, dial us back to four knots," Turner ordered.

"Now passing six hundred feet," Frank reported. 'No way their charges can reach us now, right, Skipper?"

Turner sighed, "We don't' really know, boys. Intelligence says they don't go deeper than four hundred feet… although those last ones sounded deeper to me. As far as the Japs know, none of our boats go deeper than that. Even the *Gato*-class has a test depth of three hundred. But we've been down to eight."

"Yeah, but the Jap doesn't know that," Dutch said.

Turner frowned, "Mug, steady up on one-eight zero… they might, though, Joe. Remember, when we first met *Leviathan* in June, we went deep. There were ships above us to take note that we disappeared below a salt layer at seven hundred feet. And it's known by now that *Bull Shark* is still out here…."

"So the Japanese know that we've got a boat that can run as deep as any German U-boat," Williams added glumly.

As if to punctuate this, several more ghostly clicks were heard outside the hull. The gut-wrenching telltale that a depth charges hydrostatic pistol mechanism had fired. Every man aboard could have sworn the click came from *below* the boat.

When the ocean heaved again, this was confirmed as great thunderclaps of power exploded behind and just below the submarine. She was kicked in the ass by an enormous mule, surging forward and tilting past her already steep thirty-degree angle by the bow.

The ship pitched and rolled and swayed, her steel screaming in agonized protest to the tortures visited on her by pressure and compression waves.

"Seven hundred!" Nichols gulped.

"Keep us here for now," Turner ordered. "Blow negative to the mark, blow bow tank. Frank, get me a battery sitch."

A moment passed, and then more explosions roared astern of the ship. Slightly more distant now, but Turner knew that Baker group would be calling for their friends to lay down a pattern. He doubted the drogues they were using could reach so far down. Even at minimum headway, the chains would have to be near a thousand feet long.

"We're sitting at forty percent, skipper," Nichols called up. "All this maneuvering and time at depth has taken its toll."

Turner frowned at that and glanced at his watch. To his astonishment, it was nearly seven-thirty p.m. They'd been down for well over six hours now. Strangely, it was only this realization that brought home just how hot and humid it had become in the ship.

With ventilation and air conditioning shut down, the heat from men and machines quickly drove the air temperature in the boat upward. Humidity from exhaled breath and condensation made the air, which was probably approaching ninety, tropical and heavy with moisture. Aside from being uncomfortable, this could also be a problem for the boat's electrical system, as moisture formed where it shouldn't be and created electrical shorts.

Luckily, *Bull Shark* was new, and her insulation and waterproofing were of high quality... yet mother nature would exert her will despite the best human efforts. The great pressure, broken lighting and heavy humidity were already working to stymie Turner's efforts.

"Art, Mr. Pentakkus reports moderate flooding in the motor room," Williams reported. "There's an electrical fire in after battery, too... Andy's on it."

Again, the sea was disrupted by ashcans. Again, though, it was further away and little more than an annoyance. Turner bit his lip and began down the ladder, "Mug, all stop."

Bull Shark would drift for a time, hovering silently at seven-hundred feet. It was getting dark far above, and no doubt the four destroyers would be moving off soon. Unless their task was to simply hound the submarine, they would likely continue on toward Guadalcanal.

In the meantime, Art Turner had other problems to deal with. He had water coming into his submarine, being impelled by two-hundred and ninety-five pounds per square inch of pressure. Somewhere in the after battery compartment… hopefully not the battery well itself… there was an electrical fire. All around him, his submarine creaked and groaned and crackled in protest of this inhuman treatment.

Her captain whispered a silent prayer and a silent apology to his ship and went about seeing to her needs.

10

S-52 – 200 MILES S, SW OF GUADALCANAL

"This here's a little game from my neck of the woods," Captain Waters was saying as he shuffled the deck of cards. "Before I joined up, I was a shrimper outta Galveston. We used to play poker all the time on the boat. Good way to pass the time. Good way to get to know a man, too. Over a game where there's some real stakes. Wouldn't you agree, Chris?"

"Yes sir," Savage stated.

Jarvis wasn't the least bit surprised that the torpedo officer agreed with Waters. He couldn't recall that not being the case in the days he'd been aboard the old boat.

"I used to fish too," Jarvis added. "My family's been fishin' for generations. My dad still runs a longliner outta Narragansett."

"You ever play Texas Hold'em up in Yankee land?" Waters asked with a gleam in his eyes.

Jarvis smiled thinly, "A few times. Lot of High Low Jack up there. We play a lot of cribbage on *Bull Shark*."

"Yeah, we'll break out the board once in a while, too," Tony Skaggs said. "Sometimes the skipper even gets his chess set out. But... well, I don't think I've ever played Hold'em before."

"Well, I guess you're about to get schooled then," Savage jeered. "Hope you got plenty of dough-ray-me to lose, Tony."

"Now, Chris," Waters chastised gently. "This is just for fun. It's not a high-stakes game. Two bucks buy-in and nickel blinds. It's easy to learn, and you'll pick it up as we go. I'll act as button for this first round."

"Blinds?" Savage asked.

"Yeah, like an ante in other poker hands," Savage explained curtly. "In Hold'em, though, there's a small blind and big blind. In our case, that's a nickel and a dime. Gets money in the pot pre-flop."

Waters nodded, "It goes clockwise. So, in this case, Chris is little blind, and you're big, Tony. Every player gets two hold cards. Then there are five community cards laid out on the table. You can use any three of them plus what's in your hand. There's the flop, the first three cards, then the turn, and then the final card is the river. Gives you up to four chances to bet. Now I'll deal us out a hand here…."

Waters went around the table, putting one card face down in front of each man, including himself and then again until everyone had two. They each picked up their cards and inspected them.

"Now Tony," Waters went on, "here it's time for everybody to get into the game or fold. Since it's our Exec's turn, he has three choices. Call, which is to match the big blind, fold if he doesn't like his cards, or he can raise if he's feelin' a bit confident."

Jarvis grinned, "It's Tony's first hand, so I'll just call the blind."

Jarvis threw in his ten-cent chip. Waters nodded and did the same.

"Now, as the small blind, Chris here can either fold, or he's got to put in at least a nickel if he doesn't want to raise."

Savage tossed in a chip and then looked at Skaggs. Skaggs frowned at his hand and looked to the captain.

"You're big blind, Tony, so you can raise or check," Waters explained. "Since you already paid in, even if you don't like your cards, nobody raised, so there's no point in folding now. To check means to continue the play without raising."

"I'll do that, I think," Skaggs said.

"Okay, so here comes the flop," Waters said.

He first laid one card face down and then laid three cards face up in the center of the table—a ten of hearts, a queen of hearts and a three of clubs.

"Why'd you lay that one face down?" Skaggs asked.

"That's a burn card," Savage explained. "You burn one before each new community card is dealt. Now, as the player to the button's left, I get to go first. I can either check or bet here… and I choose to bet. A quarter to play, boys."

Jarvis whistled, "Look at the big spender over here. Must have a pocket queen, huh?"

Savage grinned wickedly, "Cost you all two bits to find out, big man."

Skaggs frowned at the table, lifted his hold cards, frowned again and then sighed. He tossed a twenty-five-cent chip into the pot.

"Uh-oh, young Mr. Skaggs is takin' the bait," Waters said with a chuckle. He cocked an eyebrow at Jarvis. "How bout you, Exec? You as bold at the card table as in the connin' tower?"

Jarvis grinned, "Well, skipper… there's almost a buck in that pot… would be *foolish* not to see what's next. I'm in."

Jarvis tossed in his quarter and smiled at Savage. Waters chuckled to himself as if he'd heard a private joke to which only he'd been privy.

"I'll see Mr. Savage's quarter and raise another," Waters intoned. "Let's see which of you boys got the cajones to face off against your high and mighty skipper."

The ship took a heavy lee lurch just then, and the table tilted fifteen degrees to starboard. Everyone's hands went instinctively to his coffee mug.

"Seas are getting up," Savage noted. "Looks like that squall is turning into a major blow, sir."

"Yup," Waters said nonchalantly. "Poor old Mr. Lutz is up on the bridge with the lookouts getting' soaked. Luck of the draw, I'm afraid. But since we had to dive and stay down to avoid that Jap… we gotta run on top to charge up. This storm lets us take advantage of some daylight and make way. So what's it gonna be, Chris?"

Savage frowned, glanced at his cards, frowned again and then laid them down, "I'm afraid it's the old foldareno for this guy."

Jarvis schooled his features. He'd been paying close attention to

Savage's face, and he'd seen the sour look pass. It was an interesting tell. He watched the captain and Skaggs as well. The skipper was, as to be expected, thus far totally inscrutable. Skaggs, on the other hand, seemed to wear his emotions on his sleeve… and yet Jarvis couldn't be sure he had an accurate read on him.

This was confirmed when he said: "Call."

Jarvis followed suit, much to the captain's amusement, and the turn was placed. A queen of diamonds.

"Uh-oh," Waters said. He pulled a cigar from his blouse pocket, snipped the end with a cutter and applied his gold zippo. "Whatcha gonna do, JG?"

Skaggs puffed out his lower lip for a long moment and then shrugged, "Over two bucks in there… guess I'm committed. Or should be… dime."

Jarvis called, and the captain smiled and called as well. He then burned another card and dropped the river card—a three of spades.

"Damn…" Savage muttered, thumping the table lightly and snatching up his coffee mug as the boat heaved her bulk over to port.

"Two pair showin' on the board," Waters chuckled. "Now remember Tony, you gotta use *both* your hold cards. So if you got a queen or a three but not both, you don't have a full boat."

"Yes sir… hmm… check," Savage said after a moment's consideration.

"Fifty cents," Jarvis said immediately, tossing two chips into the pile.

The steward had laid a green felt cloth over the wardroom table, which kept the chips from sliding with the ship's sickening rolls.

Savage scoffed, "Typical meathead tough guy, huh Jarvis? Gotta try and force your way? Think you can muscle the skipper outta the hand with fifty cents?"

"It's a game, Savage," Jarvis said pleasantly.

Savage harrumphed and snorted derisively, "If you say so…."

"Well, Exec," Waters intoned. "I suspect you got something up your sleeve. You play cards like you live. Aggressively. Wonder what Art Turner would do now?"

"Probably raise," Skaggs chuckled.

"Yeah… go for broke no matter what happens," Waters mused. "Well… I'm not quite so filled with youthful exuberance as you and Anvil Art, Pat… as a man gets older, he learns to take his time about things… however, that bein' said… call. Time for the showdown, boys… let's see what you got, Tony."

Savage laughed and lit a cigarette. Skaggs narrowed his eyes at him and laid down his hold cards.

"Oh! Pocket threes!" Waters whooped, slapping the table. "God damn, son! Four of a kind! Exec?"

Jarvis grinned and laid down a pair of tens. Waters laughed again. He laid down a queen and a deuce.

"You only had a queen, sir?" Savage asked incredulously.

"Yup," Waters said. "Don't blame you for that last bet, Tony. Well played. You'd have had the pot, Pat, with that boat… nice hand, gents. I thought I had you on the turn, Tony. Got yourself almost four bucks there on your first hand. Nice job."

"Pfft…" Savage muttered. "Beginner's luck."

"My first Hold'em hand, Chris," Skaggs said, grinning evilly at the other man. "But it weren't my first rodeo, cowboy. Been playin' poker all my life."

"Never trust them sweet innocent types, Christopher," Waters stated. "Good way to burn through your eatin' money."

"Let's try that again," said Savage, who was now the dealer.

As they played on, alternating between different poker games as was the dealer's choice, Jarvis began to suspect that this was more to the captain than what it appeared. More than simple off-watch recreation or a way to spend some time getting to know his officers. Jarvis sensed that Waters was using the contest to compile personality profiles on his men. Savage he already knew, of course. But Skaggs and Jarvis were new to the ship, Jarvis the newest of all. Waters wanted to see for himself how his Exec would act and react.

Upon discovering this, Jarvis would randomly change his tactics. One hand, he'd be aggressive almost to the point of foolishness; on another, he'd play conservative and fold even though he held good cards. On yet other occasions, he'd blend the two styles. This was especially easy with Hold'em when there were so many bets.

"Well, fellas," the captain said after nearly two hours of play, "looks like it's about that time. Our Exec is headed up to take his watch in a few. Enjoyed playin' with you all. Maybe after supper… and if this storm lets up… we can do it again. Crawford is a helluva player."

"Almost as hard to read as the skipper," Savage said wryly.

Jarvis stood and had to brace himself against the bulkhead. He frowned at the feel of the ship.

"Skipper… it's been building out there since the forenoon," the Exec stated. "Feels like fifteen to twenty footers out there. I'll go up and have a look-see… but we may want to dive. Batteries ought to be topped off by now."

"Dive?" Waters gently rebuked. "I saw the look on your face last night when we dunked to avoid that Jap destroyer. Now you want to run from a little weather?"

Jarvis frowned, "We don't *know* it was a Jap, sir."

"Hey, does it matter?" Savage asked. "We're supposed to high-tail it to Guadalcanal regardless, not mix it up with every ship we see."

Jarvis frowned and leaned over the table, "I don't recall asking your opinion, gunner."

"He makes a point though, Exec," Waters went on calmly. "We'll have plenty to do in The Slot. We only got fifteen pickles aboard, and they're meant for the Tokyo Express. Hell, if you got your way, why, we'd have nothin' left when we got there."

Jarvis pulled in a calming breath before saying: "Sir, I wasn't suggesting we *attacked* that ship. Only that we lost a good sixty miles when we most likely wouldn't have been detected on the surface at all."

Waters eyed him, and there was a certain coldness evident in the brown eyes, "You questioning my decision, Mr. Jarvis? Or maybe something else?"

Jarvis stiffened, "Not at all, sir. Only clarifying my thought process

Waters nodded slowly, and Savage failed to conceal a smirk. Skaggs said nothing but both of his eyebrows went up as he looked from Waters to Jarvis.

"Good," Waters said. "Then keep that headpiece goin' on watch, Lieutenant. In my opinion, the weather isn't severe enough yet to dive under. If it's nasty for us, it'll be nasty for any Japs that might be out here. So, we cruise on top until and unless things worsen."

"Aye-aye sir," Jarvis said. "With your permission, I'll assume my duties."

The captain nodded, and Jarvis slipped out into the passageway, fuming. He made his usual turn through the boat, observing the men at work and at rest. When he re-entered the control room, Jarvis was pleased to find Jack Cleghorn waiting there, already dressed in foul weather gear and holding out a set for the executive officer.

"Expecting to get damp, Jack?" Jarvis asked as he slid into the overalls and then the jacket.

"Well, it sure ain't smooth sailing up there," Cleghorn said, grinning wickedly at the three lookouts who stood by in their own foulies.

The three men scowled at the leading petty officer. Jarvis noticed that all three were older men, not one of whom was younger than himself. As he thought about it, it suddenly occurred to him that this was the case for most of the men aboard S-52. Yes, there were a handful of young guys… yet at least half the enlisted crew was in their thirties or older. He wasn't sure why he thought this was strange, but it bothered the exec.

On the surface of it, this was unusual in a wartime navy. With war breaking out with Japan, hordes of young men had swarmed to join up. On the heels of these, there were draftees being conscripted into the Army, mostly. Generally, however, as the majority of any military branch's personnel were on the lowest rungs, it also followed that they'd be young.

Aboard S-52, however, there were mates in their thirties, E3s nearly there and a disproportionate number of men over forty, not counting the chiefs. Either many of them had come in late, or there were other reasons why the crew of the old boat seemed to match her own age.

"All right, listen up, men," Jarvis said. "It's gettin' nasty up top. Might be worse; we'll have to see. I want everybody clipped in and being extra careful. Depending on how bad it is, we'll relieve the lookouts every hour."

"Mr. Lutz has been relieving them every two," Cleghorn stated.

"Well, it seems to me that the sea's gotten up over the watch, so we might need to tighten that up," Jarvis stated. "A man exhausted isn't doing the boat any good and is a danger to himself. Okay, it's that time, boys… once more unto the breach."

The first officer led the way up the conning tower ladder and stood by as the hatch was opened, and three lookouts came tumbling down, their yellow slickers glistening with rain and spray. They went down again into the control room to remove their gear, life vests and harnesses and place them into the pump room to drip-dry.

Jarvis and his three men were similarly garbed. Inflatable Mae West life jackets over their safety harnesses which were themselves fastened over the foul weather gear. The new lookouts took the binoculars from the off-watch men and went up the swaying ladder and out into the storm. Jarvis and Cleghorn followed and were immediately shocked by the violence of the weather.

The sky above the boat was a low blanket of sooty gray that stretched from horizon to horizon. Or what could be seen of the horizon. Torrential tropical rain hammered the boat and the sea around it, making it impossible to determine the true distance to the horizon. All around the ship, a leaden sea heaved and surged into a roiling mass of hills capped with foam. White horses rose as high as the bridge fairing and more than a few as high as the lookout perch in the periscope sheers. A roaring wind tore across the face of the angry sea, howling through the masts and limber holes and giving one the impression of a host of lost souls wailing and calling for the sailors to join them.

"I relieve you sir!" Jarvis shouted to be heard over the howling blow.

Lutz stood with Chief Brannigan; the two men huddled into the small bridge space in a futile attempt to take shelter. Both men looked back, their faces streaming and pale.

"You're a welcome relief, XO," Lutz said impassively as if he wasn't riding a steel bobber. "Batteries are topped, running on one and two with an eighty / ninety split. FBTs one Charlie and one dog online."

"We're on course zero-two-five at all ahead standard," Brannigan reported. "Making eight knots in this slop, sir."

"Ship rigged for surface, no enemies sighted," Lutz finished.

Cleghorn scoffed, "Could you see any in this soup?"

"We haven't, Jack," Lutz stated.

"Well, you fellas get below," Jarvis said, exchanging places with Lutz and clipping in. "There's plenty of hot coffee down there."

"How'd the poker game go?" Lutz asked coolly.

Jarvis shrugged, "Broke even. Skipper did, too. Maybe made a buck. Tony made out, and Savage done his dough dirty. Lost it all."

Lutz nodded. The man never went too far from equilibrium, "Very well. Well, have at 'er."

The two went below, and Brannigan closed the hatch. It opened again, and Jarvis looked back, thinking that one or the other had forgotten something. Brannigan's eyes met Jarvis' from the narrow slit. Jarvis thought there was worry in them. He nodded at the chief to let him know he'd gotten the message... although, in truth, he wasn't sure he had. The hatch clanked closed and was dogged.

"Well, this is a fine mess you got me into, sir," Cleghorn shouted as he wiped a fresh burst of spray from his eyes.

"Hey, don't blame me for this, pal!" Jarvis jibed. "*I* wanted to go to Palm Springs... but *you* just *had* to go to the Solomons!"

Both men laughed and coughed as the S-52's bow smashed through the upper face of a big roller and sent seawater surging along the upper deck to break into a solid sheet of foam and spray against the conning tower's fairwater. Once through, the boat's bullnose plunged fifteen feet downward into the trough just in time to smash into another cross-sea.

"What do you think the wind is?" Cleghorn asked.

"Gotta be force ten or eleven!" Jarvis hollered. "Christ, this might be a tropical storm for all we know."

"It don't seem to be gettin' better, sir."

"Yeah, no shit, Jack!"

"Why don't we fuckin' dive then!?"

Jarvis laughed, "You tell me, quartermaster! We got enough juice; we can get down below these seas and ride this out for a while... but the skipper seems to want us to suffer. Doesn't that seem strange to you? After last night?"

Cleghorn pursed his lips and appeared as if he might clam up again. Jarvis scowled at this. He needed somebody on this barge to level with him. Frustrated, he grabbed Cleghorn's arm and leaned in close.

"Goddammit, Jack! There ain't nobody here but us chickens! Level with me, for Christ's sake."

Cleghorn worked his jaw muscles for a moment and then slapped a hand on the wet bridge rail, "I think it's you, sir."

"Me?" Jarvis asked incredulously. "What the hell did I do?"

"It's not what you done," Cleghorn said. "It's… it's more what you represent."

"I'm just here to do a job, Jack, not compete with the skipper," Jarvis grumbled.

"Yeah… but that ain't how he sees it, I think," Cleghorn stated, opening up now. It seemed as if he really wanted to but was having a crisis of conscience over it. "You're this hotshot guy from this hotshot boat with a hotshot skipper. He's pushing forty and still an O4 and still on this old tub. The only shot he's had so far this war was that last patrol."

"Where he sunk three ships," Jarvis pointed out. "Any skipper'd be proud of that. What I don't get is why this heller suddenly wants to dive at the first sign of a light in the dark, but he'll keep us all up here in this friggin' blow until every man aboard pitches his guts up! What gives?"

"You keep this between us?" Cleghorn asked after nearly a minute of silence.

"If you want… and if it doesn't endanger the boat," Jarvis said. "I can keep a confidence good as the next man, Jack… but I also keep my priorities straight. My mission and my men. If you tell me something that puts that in jeopardy, I can't keep it quiet."

Cleghorn stared out at the miserable weather for a long moment. Even when a gout of water thrown up by a side sea dashed him in the face, he didn't even flinch. Finally, he turned to face Jarvis.

"Not a lotta guys would be honest like that, sir. Most folks would just make a promise with no intent to keep it. Just so's they could hear what they wanted to know."

"I don't make promises I don't keep, Jack."

Cleghorn nodded, "I can see that, sir… I think the skipper's lost his nerve. That patrol… it did somethin' to him… broke somethin' inside. You know he was the only one left up top when that Jap opened up? When Mr. Daniels, Kafflen and our boys bought it… only the skipper was left alive. Now I don't know what happened up there… but the man who climbed down that hatch wasn't the same man who climbed up it that night."

Jarvis was silent for a moment and then somberly asked: "You sayin' he's afraid? His nerve's gone?"

Cleghorn nodded, "I think so, sir. Then you come along and sort of… hold a mirror up to him. Savage, he's always been in the skipper's court, so he'll piss down his back and defend him no matter what. You'll never win him over. Not like young Skaggs, who thinks the sun shines outta your ass, beggin' your pardon… but here's the skipper with one big thing on his record. Then you come along with your stars and combat pins and your sea stories about Krauts and Japs and all that…."

"It's not like I go around braggin'," Jarvis said.

"No sir… and that's why most of the new guys respect you," Cleghorn went on. "But you've gone through more than any of us, and that includes the skipper. You're still confident and gung-ho, and he's scared."

"He doesn't mind us facing down this slop," Jarvis indicated the weather with an expansive arm wave.

Cleghorn nodded grimly.

"So, what… he'll drive us into a fuckin' hurricane just to prove he's not scared of the Japs?"

"That's my concern, sir," Cleghorn said. "He might go either way, and it might be dangerous."

Jarvis coughed on a mist of spray and clenched his fists, "You mean he might balk when the time comes to attack the japs… or he might go the other way and rush straight into the fire just to prove he's not a coward?"

Cleghorn nodded, "I wish I knew which… but in either case, you're gonna be on the hook when he does it, I fear. You might have to step in for all of our sakes, sir."

"Jesus…" Jarvis moaned, fearing that Cleghorn's analysis was all too apt.

Ahead of the boat, a mountain of slate gray rose. As it grew, like the hump of some impossibly enormous beast, the howling wind blew its top into a flying mist of spindrift even as the crest toppled over onto itself, turning the entire face of the wave into roiling white. Yet the wave still grew, higher and higher, until it appeared as a mountain before the ship.

"Hang on!" Jarvis roared, turning back to look up at the lookouts. "Hold on and hold your breaths!"

The fifty-foot-high wall of water crashed over the submarine, her bullnose only rising halfway up the face before punching through. In an instant, Jarvis and Cleghorn were slammed by tons of seawater that pushed them off their feet and flowed over their heads.

One instant, Jarvis' ears were assaulted by wailing gale-force wind, roaring seas and the continuous booming thumps as the submarine pounded through the waves. In the next, the world was nearly silent. A warm, wet darkness that was at once tranquil and terrifying.

The XO was suddenly taken back to his childhood. He, his father, uncle Mike and a hand named Paul had been out fishing when a bad nor'easter had come up. They'd run for Block Island Sound under one engine and had to anchor in the lee of the island. The storm had shifted in the middle of the night, and the fishing boat had been slammed by high wind and seas. One wave rolled over the work deck, nearly taking Pat with it over the side. Only the rail saved him… but Paul hadn't been so lucky. It had been pitch black, and there was no sign of him.

That was how it went sometimes. One moment you were there, and the next… the sea had you in her bosom for all eternity.

Then he was back in the world of the living. The water rolled away, and he and Cleghorn were picking themselves up and gagging on seawater. Their cable tethers had kept them safe. In the next instant, Jarvis became aware that the lookouts were shouting in alarm.

"Sir! Sir!" one man was saying, gesticulating wildly and pointing behind him. "It's Kintner!"

Jarvis saw with horror that the aft lookout electrician Jimmy Kintner was no longer on the aft lookout perch. For a heart-stopping moment, the XO was afraid that the sea had claimed the man. Then he saw the cable and the figure dangling just above the deck, flailing its arms.

"There he is, sir!" Cleghorn said unnecessarily.

"Can you fellas haul him up?" Jarvis asked the remaining lookouts.

They were already turning to grab the safety line and try and pull. However, they weren't wearing gloves, and the cable was slick. They did manage to haul Kintner up a foot or two, but the man cried out in obvious pain.

"Shit! I think he's injured, sir!" Cleghorn said.

"I've got to grab him," Jarvis said, glancing forward. "After the next roller!"

Cleghorn's eyes went wide, "You'll have to untether, sir!"

Jarvis nodded grimly, "Give us some rudder, Jack. Try and shoulder the next ones while I grab Jimmy!"

"You'll be swept over, sir!" Cleghorn shouted urgently, even as he thumbed the bridge transmitter and ordered right standard rudder.

"Then come back and get me," Jarvis quipped, trying to ignore the sickening fear manifesting as nausea. "Get ready… here she comes.…"

Once more, the bow rose to meet a wave. This time, though, it wasn't dead on, and the corkscrew motion was slightly gentler. As the bow crested the twenty-five-foot wave, Jarvis unsnapped his tether and darted aft until he could seize Kintner's line. Jarvis planted his feet and began to haul, putting his considerable strength to work.

Above him, the men in the sheers added their strength and Kintner was hauled up to where Jarvis could wrap an arm under his armpit and slide another beneath the man's crotch.

"I got you, Jimmy!" the XO shouted. "Are you hurt?"

"My leg, sir!" Kintner cried out. His face was pale and twisted with pain and fright.

"Hang on back there!" Cleghorn shouted as the ship began a ponderous climb skyward again.

Jarvis gritted his teeth and heaved, getting Kintner up and over the rail just as another wave rolled over the main deck and foamed into the bridge. Jarvis had one arm around Kintner's chest and the other around the periscope sheers and clung for all he was worth as foaming seawater rose to his waist. The surge tried to yank his feet out from under him, but he managed to hang on until the water began to drain.

"Think my shoulder's outta whack, too…." Kintner groaned.

"We'll get you below in a jiffy, Jim, don't worry," Jarvis said as he unclipped the man and helped him forward to where Cleghorn was spinning the hatch wheel. The hatch popped open, spilling water into the conning tower to be met by curses and angry questions from below.

"Belay that shit!" Jarvis roared down. "Help me with this man and pass the word for the pharmacist's mate! *Move it*, damn your eyes!"

Several hands appeared and gently guided the lookout below, not without several grunts and cries of pain. As soon as they were clear, Cleghorn slammed the hatch shut, and Jarvis fumbled with his carabiner and clipped himself in.

The boat rose once more to meet a wave, and Cleghorn glanced over at the XO, "You must be outta your gourd, sir."

"Yeah… I must be," Jarvis said.

"*Bridge, Captain… what's your status?*"

Jarvis had to bite back the angry retort that begged to be given voice. He clenched his teeth, took a breath and then pushed the button, "Captain, bridge… It's a shit show up here, skipper. Kintner's been sent down with an injury. We almost lost him in a big swell. Permission to dive, sir!"

A pause, "*Bridge, we* didn't *lose him. Let's not get your nerves in an uproar up there. It's just a storm… this is a submarine, for Christ's sake.*"

Jarvis and Cleghorn exchanged a what are you shitting me glance before Jarvis thumbed the button once more, "Captain, bridge… with respect, sir… we're seeing fifty footers up here. Assess it's not worth the trouble. Helm reports we're only at six knots anyway. Advise we dunk until the worst blows over."

There was yet another long pause, and then the skipper replied, sounding as if he were humoring Jarvis, "*All right, bridge… if you don't think you can handle it, we'll go ahead and dive the ship. Heaven forbid you fellas were uncomfortable up there. Not during a war and all.*"

Jarvis felt the heat of anger flood his wet face, "Son of a...."

"Don't let him rattle you, sir," Cleghorn advised. "He's just showboatin' for the troops."

Jarvis spat and raised his voice even as he pulled the diving alarm twice, "Clear the bridge! We're gettin' outta this washing machine."

"Yeah... great timing," one of the two lookouts was overheard to jeer. Under the circumstances, Jarvis couldn't blame the man and pretended not to notice. He only wondered who the man was really angry with... the captain or the XO.

11

GOETTGE'S REVENGE – FIRST BATTLE OF THE MATANIKAU, PART 1

AUGUST 19, 1942 – 0515 LOCAL TIME

"How the hell we s'posed to get past *this*," Ted Entwater hissed into Oaks' ear.

The two Marine Raiders lay on their bellies beneath a tangle of ferns and vines at the edge of Matanikau village. After leaving Cocumbona several hours earlier, the four scouts had followed the stream and the road east toward the Matanikau River. It became quite evident, even before they came within sight of the village they now scoped, that the Japanese were in the area in moderate force.

There was an observation post outside the village facing down the road. The post consisted of a tent, a Nambu machine gun nest fortified behind sandbags as well as a pair of type 38 75mm howitzers. An entire Jap platoon manned this post, indicating clearly how important they felt the route was, as well as the strategic importance of Matanikau village.

It was then that Charlie Arndt suggested that the scouts split up. One team to skirt the OP and continue on to Matanikau and the other to head northeast toward the mouth of the river. In this way, they could at least cover the two most likely approaches of the Fifth Marines when they came later that day. Also, it would give at least one scouting team a better chance of crossing the river and reporting to command.

Oaks didn't like it, but he also couldn't find any real flaw in the plan. The four men were stronger together, but whether it was four men or two, they were vastly outnumbered and outgunned by the enemy. Two men could move more stealthily in the darkness, Arndt had insisted, and they needed to scout both locations anyway.

So, Arndt and Taggart had vanished into the brush. Oaks and Entwater also veered off into the jungle, moving carefully to skirt the Japanese OP and hoping that nobody was out for a stroll in the wee hours of the morning. After several hours and a few false turns, the pair found themselves on a low ridge overlooking the river and the village named for it. It took some effort to push through the brush in order to get a visual on the village, but this made them feel more confident that no Japanese night patrol would sneak up on them.

Matanikau was much like Cocumbona, and much like the other Guadalcanal villages the Raiders had visited since debarking from *Bull Shark*. Small, thatched huts raised off the ground in a semi-organized pattern. There was a central communal area and larger structure near the center as well as a few storehouses, or so it appeared. A variety of crops were grown behind the village. Probably yams and taro. The heavy scent of burnt wood hung over the village from the previous evening's cooking. Pulled up along the riverbank were several homemade canoes and a couple of modern-looking skiffs that were no doubt the property of the Japanese.

That there were more of them in the village, there could be no doubt. Aside from the boats, there was a pair of what appeared to be the Japanese equivalent of Deuce and a Half trucks. Set up along the rear of the village were two rigid lines of bivouac tents. At least half a dozen Japanese soldiers or Marines walked patrols in and around the village as well.

"Very quietly, I'd imagine," Oaks whispered back. "Based on those tents… I'd say they got a whole company based here."

"Wonder what's down at the beach then?" Entwater pondered unhappily.

"Nothin' good…" Oaks grumbled. "Okay, I've seen enough. We

need to get outta here and across the river. Captain Spurlock needs to know what he's up against."

"And just how do we do that, Sarge?" Entwater asked. "We can't just swim for it… don't forget about the damned crocs."

Oaks pondered that for a long moment, "Well, the sandbar at the mouth is about two klicks… and if I recall, there's a log bridge about two klicks to the south. I think the coast road crosses there… I also recall that there's a ford right around here. No more than chest deep at worst."

Entwater groaned, "How deep you gotta go before the crocs grab you?"

"You and your crocs…," Oaks muttered. "It's nighttime still. I'm sure they're all tucked into their beds… their croc beds."

"Side-splitting."

Oaks snickered, "Hey, kid… you shoulda finished college and been an electrical engineer like you planned. Who told you to join the fuckin' Marines?"

Entwater chuffed, "I didn't just join the Corps… I had to pick the *crazy* unit on top of it all…."

"Takes a special man to be a Raider," Oaks pointed out.

"Yeah… and if we're anything, Sarge… it's special."

Oaks squeezed his shoulder, "We'll figure it out. Let's get to the river out of sight of Tojo, and then we'll see what we can do. If one of your crocs does get too nosey… we'll make him into a couple of nice pairs of boots."

"Well, when you put it that way…," Entwater said and began to quietly back away from the edge of the ridge.

There was a game trail about a hundred yards back, and the two men began moving more or less east toward the river. Both were glad of the cover of darkness, as there was no doubt that the entire area would be crawling with nips in the daytime.

ARNDT AND TAGGART

"Well, this don't look promising…," Taggart cranked as he and his teammate crouched between a haphazard row of palms and a thick copse of birds of paradise. Beyond their hiding spot, the two men could see the beach and the mouth of the Matanikau River. The river, like many on the island, didn't flow smoothly into the sea. A sandbar had formed at the mouth as a semi-barrier between the ocean and the inland water. In some cases, Guadalcanal's many rivers emptied into large mangrove swamps, although this seemed less common on the northern coast.

The position was somewhat fortified. Two large communal tents, probably acting as bunkrooms, were set up among the densely packed palm trees and hardwoods just behind this. No less than three type 38 howitzers were aimed to cover the sandbar and would doubtless rain down explosive hell on any hapless round eyes that attempted a crossing there.

One particularly worrisome Japanese setup was the high observation tower that had been constructed using three sturdy palms as pillars. Set up some forty feet in the air, a wooden platform had been constructed with a ladder giving access from the ground. On top of this platform, at least what the two Marines could see from the ground, were two men and what appeared to be a Nambu machine gun.

"That's a helluva nest for a machine gun," Arndt stated. "Good elevation but also easy to pick off, I'd imagine."

"Yeah…" Taggart said with a frown. "But I don't think that's its primary purpose, Sarge. That elevation gives them a pretty good observation range."

Arndt scowled, "An OP for directing fire then? For those mortars?"

"Yeah… and maybe for naval gunnery," Taggart opined. "They could direct fire from out to sea for quite a ways around here."

"What I wouldn't give for a grenade launcher right now…." Arndt said darkly.

In his mind's eye, he saw the day that Colonel Goettge and his patrol had been ambushed how Arndt had been ordered to get back to the Marine perimeter and report and request assistance. It was a terrible thing, having been one of only a tiny handful of men who'd made it back. Arndt could still remember looking back as he paddled his stolen canoe into the surf and seeing the gleaming flashes of samurai swords as the Japanese cut his comrades to pieces.

It was a visual that Arndt knew he could never forget, even if he lived to be a hundred.

"The Fifth is gonna have their work cut out for them," Taggart said softly.

"Well, if we can get a company across that bar," Arndt reasoned. "They should be able to overrun this position. There's probably no more than a Jap platoon here, maybe a little more… fifty or sixty men at most. But them guns are well-hidden… and if the Nips get cute and send in a naval vessel… that sandbar could be a death trap."

"Roger that," Taggart said. "Probably is… how the hell *we* get across it."

"I say we got three choices," Arndt said. "We go out in the surf and swim along the coast for a mile or so, then come back onto the beach on our side. Or we can go upriver and cross someplace… Probably what Oaks and Entwater are doin' now…."

"Or we book it across the bar and hope the Japs don't see us in the moonlight," Taggart grumped. "So, we can brave sharks in the ocean, crocodiles in the river or angry Japs on this narrow spit of land."

"Least we got choices."

"Funny."

The men were quiet for a long moment, studying the encampment. Other than the two men on the platform, there were only two more guards stationed. One walked back and forth along the half-hidden line of field guns and the other near the far eastern edge of the position. It was clear that this man was watching the sandbar and could see a little way upriver as well.

"I got an idea," Taggart finally said. "But I bet you ain't gonna like it."

Arndt snorted, "I hope it's not something dangerous… or scary. I'm afraid of stuff what's scary… and dangerous."

Taggart grinned, "Then you're gonna crap your skivvies on this one, Sarge… okay, so the OP is to our left, the beach ahead and the river to our right. That OP is a good hundred yards from the other end of the position, where that guy is posted."

"Yeah, I got eyes."

"We work our way through the brush as close as we can to that Jap near the river," Taggart said. "One of us takes him out, and the other plugs that one by the pieces. Then we haul ass across the bar. By the time those two up on the tower figure out what's going on, we're at least two, maybe three hundred yards away."

Arndt groaned, "I'll bet you a fin they got Arisakas up there. Them things are awfully accurate, even out to three hundred yards."

"Yeah… but in the dark?"

"Two camo-clad assholes running through knee-deep water?" Arndt said. "Easy targets."

Taggart sighed, "Well… what've you got?"

Arndt pursed his lips, "Nothin' much better… except that we plug those two up high and *then* beat feet across the bar."

Taggart nodded, "Yeah, but that's gonna take a few more seconds. Our first shot is gonna turn this encampment into a hornet's nest. I figure we got ten, fifteen seconds max before the Japs get up, grab their rifles and come pouring out of their tents and start plinking at us."

"So, what if we can take out that guy to the east quietly," Arndt said. "With a knife? You get him, then shoot the one by the pieces. I'll take out the two on the tower as soon as I see you get the first guy."

Taggart drew in a breath, "Okay, I guess it's the only option we got. We gotta leave the packs, though. Too much weight will slow us down, especially on the bar where some of it is underwater."

Arndt nodded and immediately slipped from his ruck. He reached inside and pulled out a can of Spam and began to open it, "I suggest you eat something then. Gonna need the fuel. Then kill your canteen and leave that, too. Just take our weapons and ammo."

Taggart followed suit, keying open his own can of Spam and sliding the can-shaped hunk of food product out and began to eat. Although the spiced processed meat was hardly what anyone would call gourmet, it did contain a fair number of calories, fats and salt. All things that men engaging in strenuous activity in a tropical environment sorely needed. The men washed down the Spam with what remained in their canteens and hid their packs in the underbrush.

It took the two Marines nearly an hour to move just over a hundred yards from their original observation position and to get as close to the further guard as possible. Although the sound of surf crashing ashore and the cacophony of the island's nocturnal life helped to mask their noise, movement was by necessity slow and careful.

Taggart slung his rifle and pulled the long black blade of his KA-Bar from its sheath. The Japanese guard was pacing back and forth, coming within a few yards of where he hid and then turning and strolling down toward the shore. The Raider watched the man go through this routine three times before readying himself to act.

Taggart was not fond of this plan. It was reckless and extremely risky. Even as he watched the guard pace, he noticed that the sky in the east was beginning to turn from a deep black to a deep indigo. The moon, thankfully, was low to the western horizon. This meant that light would be poor for long-range shooting, and it also meant the tide would be low for crossing the mouth of the river.

But he had to move now, or that advantage would slip away. In the tropics, dawn came as quickly as dusk, and he and Arndt might have five minutes of good dark cover left. He gritted his teeth, watched the guard turn his back and sprang.

Perhaps the guard was nervous or keyed up. Perhaps he was particularly tuned in to his environment, but whatever the reason, the little bastard was on the ball. As soon as Taggart broke free from cover, the soldier whipped around to face the noise. He brought his Arisaka rifle to bear and shouted.

"*Shinnyusha!*"

Taggart cursed. He didn't speak Japanese, or not much, but he did know a few words, and he knew that one meant intruder.

Although an accurate weapon, the Arisaka rifle was not a small weapon. It had a long barrel made even longer with a bayonet attached. This meant that it took the man about a half-second too long to zero in on the mystery figure that had burst from the jungle less than four paces away.

With his left hand, Taggart beat aside the barrel of the gun, and with his right, he plunged the blade of his knife beneath the soldier's chin and into his Adam's apple. The upward arc of Taggart's thrust carried the thick, razor-sharp blade through the man's soft pallet and tongue and up into his braincase.

The soldier's eyes bulged, and his body began to spasm, dancing grotesquely for a moment before crumpling to the ground. However, his last nervous impulse was to close his finger on the trigger of his rifle, sending a round off into the foliage.

Although the bullet hadn't hit anything, the boom of the 7.7mm round seemed to echo for miles. As if the man's shout hadn't already alerted the camp as it was.

"Fuck me…," Taggart cranked as he yanked the Japanese rifle from the dead soldier's grasp and shouldered the weapon. He worked the action, levering in another round and searched for the remaining guard near the field guns.

"Nice job," Arndt cranked from a few paces away as he shouldered his own Springfield. "Real stealthy like."

Arndt began firing up at the men on the tower, who by then had begun to shout and were trying to find cover. From the communal barracks tent, angry Japanese voices began to swear and shout and bark orders.

"Hornet's nest…," Taggart muttered.

An angry bee zipped past his head just as he sighted his man. The soldier had dived behind one of the guns and was pointing his own Arisaka at the Americans.

"Fucker…," Taggart grumbled.

He sighted along the weapon's iron sights, found a portion of the soldier's torso that wasn't hidden behind the howitzer and gently squeezed the trigger. There was a scream of pain, and the khaki-clad Jap vanished.

"Did you get the guys on the tower?" Taggart asked.

"Maybe one…," Arndt replied, backpedaling toward his comrade. "But they're lying flat, and the elevation isn't clear for a shot."

"Screw it, let's bolt!" Taggart said.

The two Marines ran hell for leather. For the first fifty yards or so, the sandbar was above the waterline—nice hard-packed sand on which to run. Then, as they drew further from the eastern side, the river and sea began to encroach. At first, the water was hardly more than an inch or two deep. After a few more seconds, though, it became ankle-deep. Then shin deep.

There were shouts and, even worse, crackles of rifle fire from the Japanese position behind them. Taggart threw a quick glance over his shoulder and felt that he and Arndt had gone a good hundred yards.

"Come on!" Taggart implored. "Get the lead out, taile-end Charlie!"

It had appeared that Arndt was beginning to lag just a bit behind Taggart. However, when the water around the two men erupted in half a dozen little geysers, the other Marine suddenly found a higher gear.

Of course, the water was still growing deeper. It was easily over their knees now, and their flat-out run had become a comical high-step that wasn't a third as fast.

"Argh!" Taggart cried out as a lance of fire streaked across his left arm. "Shit! I'm hit!"

Arndt's pale face glanced over at him, and through his gasps, he managed to ask: "Bad?"

"No… just winged me the yellow pricks!" Taggart said.

"Let's put a couple over the shoulder," Arndt suggested.

He hefted his rifle and pointed it over his right shoulder in the general direction of the camp. Taggart did the same with the Japanese weapon, and the two fired. They had no illusions that they'd hit anything, but it might give the enemy a moment's pause.

They were more than halfway across now, and the sandbar was beginning to grow shallower again. Even as the two exhausted Marines increased their speed, they saw several dark shapes silhouetted against the forest on the western side of the river mouth.

'Oh… Christ…," Taggart gasped. "Not more… Japs…."

"No…," Arndt heaved, "I think… think they're ours… God…"

"Identify yourselves!" somebody shouted from a hundred yards off.

"Laurel and Hardy!" Taggart yelled.

He and Arndt slowed to a fast walk, gulping hot, humid air and sweating profusely. With the sky growing bluer by the second, the fourteen Marines on the opposite shore began to grow distinct. It was a squad complete with officer and sergeant.

"Fifth Marines," Arndt called out when he had enough breath.

"Sergeant Charlie Arndt, and this is Corporal Dave Taggart, First Raiders, sir."

"Looks like you fellas have been playin' on the wrong side of the tracks," said the squad's L T, a baby-faced man who couldn't be more than twenty-two.

"Part of a scouting party, sir," Taggart said as the two bedraggled men secured their weapons and approached the squad. "You part of Captain Spurlock's assault team?"

"Lieutenant Harry Birch," the officer said. "We're one of the advanced patrols. The push is scheduled for a couple of hours from now. You boys got info for us?"

"Yes sir," Arndt said. "We've also got two more men who were up by the Matanikau village. Hope they make it across too. Can we be taken to the captain, sir?"

"Sure thing," Birch replied. "We got a temporary CP set up about half a klick from here. No vehicle nearby, but you can shoe leather it in about ten. Sorry, you won't have any chance to crumb up… but the skipper'll understand. I'll detail a man to show you the way… Leckie, front and center!"

A private even younger than the squad commander stepped forward and grinned at Taggart, "Still in the game, eh Corporal?"

"Hey Bobby," Taggart grinned back. "Good to see you still on your get-alongs."

"Right this way, gents… allow me to show you to your table," Leckie jibed and began moving toward the jungle.

PHIL AND TED

"Well, if this don't beat the band…." Oaks grumbled.

He and Entwater lay on their bellies beneath heavy cover along a narrow trail that followed the river. They'd gone south, following the river's path around a sharp bend just out of sight of the village. The Matanikau narrowed here to only about fifty yards across. There were several rocks sprinkled in the river, and each one trailed a finger of froth.

That, however, was not what Oaks was complaining about. Not

more than ten yards from the men, a Japanese patrol was picking its way up the path and following the river south. It was a small patrol, only five men. Probably a fire team. Still, it was five to two, which was not good odds without automatic weapons.

"We could take 'em out, Sarge," Entwater whispered, his lips nearly touching Oaks' ear. "We could both get two at this range before they knew what hit 'em…."

Oaks shook his head. For although Entwater was probably right, there were other factors to consider. In truth, from concealment, both men could take down two Japs with their first volley. It was only a matter of chambering another round and hitting the next two. Even should the fifth start firing, he wouldn't be able to locate the two Marines in time, or at least it was unlikely.

However, once the shooting started, it would alert others. There was no way to know if this team was alone or if there was another directly behind them or further upriver. Also, the range was short. Any of the Japs could draw their Nambu pistols and start firing into the brush. Oaks and Entwater didn't have the protection of range.

Of course… both men had .45s. They too, could plug the enemy from close range and then make a dash into the water. The question was… could they get across before more Japanese showed up? Were there salt-water crocodiles in this river?

The sky was beginning to lighten. Time was short, and a decision had to be made. Oaks held up his left hand and made it into a gun in front of Entwater's face. The PFC nodded in understanding.

The decision, however, was made for them. From the north, perhaps a mile, two shots cracked. They were distant but still audible. It was as if somebody had hit the panic button. The Japanese patrol spun around in all directions, weapons up and looking for targets. The two shots had been far away, it was true, but their effect was to put the Japs on high alert. When several more rang out, the fire team leader shouted something, and the men began to fire at random.

Rather undisciplined, Oaks thought. There was no immediate visible threat, and they'd just given their position away. He shrugged, yanked his 1911 from its holster and snapped off a quick shot at the closest soldier.

The man yelped, spun halfway around and tumbled over, a gout of blood spurting from his shoulder. The man dropped his rifle and tumbled down an embankment and into the water.

Two more shots rang out, and two more Japanese soldiers went down. Entwater was as good a pistol shot as he was with a rifle. Without saying a word, the two men separated, crawling apart and away from where they'd fired. As they did, a pair of rifle shots boomed out, and two rounds hissed through the brush very close to where they'd been.

Oaks popped up three yards from where he'd fired and sighted in. As he did so, the Jap caught sight of him and swung his rifle around. His head exploded in a horrific cloud of blood and brain. Oaks shifted targets and put two rounds into the chest of the final man, who was swinging his rifle back and forth and looking shocked and frightened.

"Come on!" Oaks called out. "We gotta—"

Entwater had just stood up and taken a single step when the river at the bottom of the embankment erupted into a huge splash. As the two Americans watched in fascinated horror, a huge dark shape arced its body half out of the water, two jaws filled with hideous fangs clamped down on the wounded Japanese soldier. In the next instant, the reptile jerked sideways, dragging its meal back into and below the foaming surface of the Matanikau. The horrified scream of the soldier was sharply cut off with hideous finality. The entire terrifying scene had not lasted more than three-seconds.

"Jesus God all mighty...," Entwater breathed, a hand going to his heart.

"Jesus... guess *swimming* ain't the way to go...," Oaks managed to say.

From down the river in the direction of the village, a chorus of Japanese voices rose in anger and alarm. Entwater looked to Oaks, who spoke passable Japanese.

"That's our cue to beat a hasty withdrawal," Oaks said, waving Entwater after him. "They're sending out a squad to investigate. We'll follow this path upriver a ways and make our way back into the rainforest."

"What about reporting, Sarge?" Entwater asked as the two men jogged away from the scene of their kills.

"Let's hope Dave and Charlie made it," Oaks said. "I don't think we can get back in time. Worst case… we'll do what we can to support them from the rear."

12

GOETTGE'S REVENGE – FIRST BATTLE OF THE MATANIKAU, PART 2
AUGUST 19, 1942 – 0815 LOCAL TIME

"Glad to see you boys," Porter Hazard said when Arndt and Taggart wandered into the mess, looking bleary-eyed and disheveled.

After making their report to Captain Spurlock, the two men had been driven back to Henderson Field, where they'd been allowed to get a few hours shuteye. The captain had relieved them of all duty for the day, but both Marines requested to go in with the assault. Spurlock had smiled and agreed, ordering the two to get several hours of sleep first.

"Mornin' L T," Taggart said as he set a tray down with coffee and a powdered egg and spam omelet. "How's the wounds?"

"Swell," Hazard grumped. "Still ache, but I think I'm good. Hardly even limping today."

"You gonna try and take part in the action, Lieutenant?" Arndt asked, a twinkle in his eye. "Take advantage of the shore leave before they send you back to your nice comfy sub and good chow?"

Hazard smiled tightly at Arndt and removed his BDU blouse, which he wore unbuttoned in a vain attempt at dealing with the heat. He then rolled up the right sleeve of his skivvy shirt and pointed to a tattoo on his bicep.

"You see that, Sarge?" Hazard asked with a cocked eyebrow.

The tattoo was the eagle, globe and anchor emblem of the U.S. Marine Corps. Taggart snickered but said nothing.

"You were in the Corps?" Arndt asked.

"Got that while serving in the Banana Wars," Hazard said. "Did a couple of tours. Even served under Chesty Puller himself. I got out and went to college and was just starting to work for Fairbanks Morse when the Japs bombed Pearl. I rushed to the nearest recruiter and asked to come back in as a retread. He convinced me that if I really wanted to get into the action, I ought to join the Navy and use my mechanical engineering degree in the boats… so I did, and they made me a J.G. But don't think I've forgotten what it's like to slog through a tropical hellhole, Sergeant. How many tours you done?"

Taggart was chuckling now and paying rapt attention to his repast. Arndt flushed beet red and cleared his throat.

"Sir, I… I didn't mean to, y'know… was just kiddin' around…."

Hazard locked eyes with him for a long moment and then let his features relax and even smiled thinly, "Okay, Sarge… well, you'd better watch that shit. Never know who you're gonna piss off."

Taggart laughed aloud now, "Told ya, Charlie. Tried that shit with Entwater too. Still, though, Mr. Hazard, he's a good egg."

"Any guy who lived through the Goettge patrol and then volunteers to go back into that same spot… twice… is okay in my book," Hazard said and grinned. "By the way… any word from Oaks and Entwater?"

Taggart frowned and shook his head. Hazard sighed and sipped his coffee quietly. He felt a sense of responsibility for Al Decker's men. Since Decker had to be shipped off to recover from his wounds, Hazard had been the only officer left from their original mission. He found himself splitting his worry between the Raiders he'd come ashore with and his friends aboard *Bull Shark*.

The men ate in silence for several minutes until their introspection was broken. Somewhere on the base, a siren had been hooked up to replace the old dinner pot bell that had been pulling duty as an air raid warning. Now, the long wail of the siren jolted everyone to attention.

"It's Tojo Time," Hazard groaned. "And that's our cue to move, boys. You ready to head back out into the bush?"

"Yes sir," Taggart said without hesitation. "You joining us, L T?"

Hazard grinned crookedly as the three men hurried out of the mess, "Yeah, but only to act as support at the CP. Doc's not yet cleared me for active… still a little slow on the old gams."

As the three men jogged along the field to a Deuce and a Half being loaded near the Fifth Marine encampment, Taggart thought that for a man who was hobbled, Hazard seemed to be doing pretty well.

"Where you fellas s'posed to be?" A gunnery sergeant asked as Hazard, and the two Marines shoved their way through to get into the truck.

"Hazard, Taggart and Arndt," Hazard said. "Headed for Captain Spurlock's CP, Gunny. We've been personally requested."

The lantern-jawed gunnery sergeant gave Hazard and the other two a quick once over and nodded, "Boswell! Cheever's! Smitty! You take the next ride; these fellas are special delivery! Let's *move out!*"

The truck roared to life amid a chorus of Oo-rahs, and the gunny hardly had time to jump onto the runner before the big vehicle began to accelerate west toward the coast road. In spite of the accelerating diesel engine, the men in the canvas-covered bed heard the drone begin to grow ever louder. That all-too-familiar and sickening sound of Japanese bombers coming in to make their lives miserable.

Of course, the sound of Wildcats revving up and lifting off the airstrip was equally heartening. Ever since Henderson Field opened and the navy began ferrying in fighters and dive bombers, the daily air raids, colloquially known as "Tojo Time" by the Marines, had lost some of their terror and ferocity. Bombs almost always fell, and there were times when naval vessels joined in the fun and bombarded the field from the Sealark Channel, but with the Marine pilots and their aircraft growing in numbers and honing their skills, the volume of destruction had begun to diminish.

Still, sitting in the back of a truck with twenty men all crammed together and only a small opening in the rear to see out of was mentally daunting. The roar of a billion enraged hornets grew overhead and was soon joined by the terrible whistle of descending death. Soon the ground shook, and concussion waves pounded across the open landscape; the area around Henderson Field flattened and cleared of most vegetation. That and the new bomb craters that were opened up each day, the base had the appearance more of something you might find on the moon rather than on a tropical island.

Soon the discomfort of their truck being rocked by nearby bombs exploding was replaced with the discomfort of the vehicle racing along pitted and rutted tracks that were laughably called roads. The Marines in the rear, loaded with rucks and rifles and squeezed together to get as many of them to the front line as possible, all swayed and bumped and jostled each other in a jarring and disharmonious jumble.

Thankfully, the Matanikau was only a few miles away, and the ride lasted only a few minutes. The Deuce and a Half jerked to a stop, and the gunny began bawling orders. The men began to pile out of the truck, weapons held at the ready and their stomachs in knots. For some of them, this would be their first real taste of combat. Other than the occasional patrol, this was the first organized offensive on Guadalcanal. Three companies of the Fifth Marines, nearly four hundred men, were going to cross the Matanikau and engage the enemy in force.

Up until that day, the Matanikau, like the Teneru to the east, had been a sort of no-man's land. The boundary between the Marine perimeter and the rest of the island.

Although the Marines did send out feelers each day… small patrols consisting of single squads or even as few as one or two fire teams, their mission was more recon than anything else, their job was to locate and identify Japanese units and their positions and to prepare the airfield for potential attacks. Thus far, these attacks had been few, as the Japanese were now severely outnumbered and split up with Henderson Field breaking them into at least two distinct groups.

The Command Post was set up just within sight of the river, about half the distance from the village of the same name and the sandbar at the ocean's edge. Several more trucks, one or two with red crosses on them, were parked along the coast road. Several hundred Marines were being organized, and Hazard and his two men were rushed past all of this hubbub to an open-sided tent surrounded by Jeeps, two Indian motorcycles and a handful of bicycles.

Inside the tent, Major General Alexander Vandegrift stood by a table with several officers surrounding him. A major, three captains and a host of lieutenants.

The general was studying a large map tacked down to the table and tapping a pen on several points. Hazard stepped inside and found a spot where he could see. Taggart and Arndt stood behind him, not sure what to do.

"Lieutenant Hazard," Vandegrift said. "How's the leg? Glad you could join the party."

"It's decent, sir, thank you," Hazard said.

"I see you brought a couple of our scouts with you… good," Vandegrift went on. "Have them fall in with Captain Spurlock here. This is his op, so Major Evans has agreed to let him have operational command. Lyman?"

"Thank you, sir," Spurlock said, coming to stand beside the general. "As you all know, the Japs have been clinging onto their positions across the Matanikau since before day one. They hold Matanikau village, the far side of the mouth and Cocumbona a bit to the east. From these three positions, they are well-placed to keep us bottled in or launch their own offensives. Also, as you know. Colonel Goettge was sent to Cocumbona last week based on a report that a Japanese platoon wished to surrender. We now know that this was either a trap or somebody mistook a Jap meatball flag for a white one. In any event, thanks to a recon patrol sent out last night, we have a pretty good idea of what the Japs have waiting for us across the river. Unfortunately, half our patrol has yet to report in, so we're in the dark as far as Matanikau village. However, previous missions and overflights have routinely shown a large number of Nip units there… so we're just gonna assume it's a rat's nest."

That got a round of muted laughs from the men. Even the general grinned.

"I'll be going into the village with L company," Spurlock was saying. "Captain Leadhousen takes B company across the sandbar and takes out that Jap position. We know that they've got men there and a couple of field pieces, so it'll be a bit tricky."

"We'll show 'em," Leadhousen, Hazard assumed it was him, said. He'd never actually met the man.

"I like your spirit, Dale," Vandegrift added. "But this isn't the charge of the Light Brigade. If it looks like you can't take that position without losing too many men, pull back. We can always arrange something else."

"Finally," Spurlock said, "I company is even now loading up on four Higgins boats. They'll be going ashore near Cocumbona and taking that village, then moving along the coast road to join me at Matanikau. Based on the info of Sergeant Arndt and Corporal Taggart, the village may be empty of all Jap units."

"Sir..." Taggart hissed into Hazard's ear.

Hazard cleared his throat, "Excuse me, Captain... but Corporal Taggart is with me and has something he'd like to add."

"Certainly," Spurlock said. "Corporal?"

"Uhm..." Taggart was a little thrown off by all the brass gathered together. He stepped up next to Hazard. "We took down a Jap fire team, sir, that's true... but it was twelve hours ago. I'd have to assume that the nips have discovered their men were killed or haven't reported in. They also know we were at that gun position... it might be good to assume that Cocumbona is better defended now."

Spurlock nodded, "Fair enough. I company is well-armed, and they're bringing pineapple throwers and a couple of Ma Deuces. Anything else? Any questions? Good, then let's move out. We've got boats for my team and a decent rally point to assemble across the river. We'll have a few machine guns posted along our side and ambulances standing by.... Hope we don't need 'em. General?"

Vandegrift shook his head, "that about covers it. Let's move out."

I COMPANY – 1330 LOCAL TIME

The four Higgins boats plowed through rolling seas westward along the northern coast of Guadalcanal. The sky was rapidly clouding up, and it was clear that in just a few hours, some severe weather would be rolling in. The good news was that the Japs knew it too, had already broken off their daily harassment of the airfield as well as the Raider's positions on Tulagi and the other Florida Islands. The *bad* news was that The Slot was becoming a washing machine. Big rolling swells were headed straight down the long passage that ran through the Solomon Islands archipelago.

Even as the wooden boats made their sluggish way along the coast, six-foot rollers were coming in over their starboard bows. This was the best way to take waves, but the Higgins boats were built for landing men and equipment and not for seaworthiness. Their flat bows and slow speeds meant that each swell lifted the bows high and rolled sickeningly under the boat, first heeling her far to port and then back to starboard again in long, swooping arcs that were doing a fine job of making the hundred-odd Marines deeply regret their powdered, fatty and sugary breakfasts.

"We're almost there, boys," the coxswain of boat number one said with a cheerfulness that was most certainly not making him any new friends. "Ten more minutes, and we'll nose up onto the beach. Be thankful you ain't gotta ride back with us. Think this is bad…."

"You ain't helpin', Mac," Captain Arlus Blanch grumbled from his position near the pilot and engineer.

"You gotta forgive him, sir," the engineer stated with a wry grin. "He's got a big mouth. Never knows when to close his yapper."

Almost as one, Lieutenant John Douglas and Gunnery Sergeant Arlo Jenkins stood, leaned out over the starboard gunwale and began to heave. As if they'd thrown a switch, at least half of the thirty Marines in the boat turned from green to pale, and they too launched what remained of their morning rations onto the deck at their and their comrades' feet.

"Now there's some boys what need to learn to keep their mouths shut! Ha-ha-ha!" Mac guffawed, wiping spray from his eyes. "Now, who's gonna clean that up?"

"And you wonder why Marines always talk bad about you squids," Blanch said with a head shake, doing his best to retain the contents of his own stomach against the heaving boat and the stench of the heaving men.

"Uh-oh…," the engineer said, looking out to sea toward Savo Island. "I think we're gonna have company soon, skipper."

Both Blanch and Mac looked out to where the petty officer was pointing. There, on the horizon, was a faint line of smoke visible against the darkening sky. Blanch frowned and worked his binoculars free of the straps and glassed the spot.

"Can't tell yet… looks like a mast, though," he said. "Think it's one of ours?"

Mac stood up on his seat and squinted. "I dunno, sir… somethin' tells me it ain't, though."

"Maybe we oughta put in now," Blanch suggested.

"We're still a mile from the LZ," Mac said.

"How about angling in?" Blanch asked.

Mac frowned, "All funnin' aside, Captain… if I do that, we'll be taking these seas beam-on. The boat can handle that… but the roll will be way worse. You might not have a man can stand up when we'd get to the shore. The course I'm takin' gets us parallel to the beachhead, and then I can head straight in. That way the sea is off my quarter and ain't no worse than now. Plus, it'll be easier to back off. Sorry, sir."

"Better call it in, then," Blanch said. The engineer handed him the radio mic. "Mother, Mother, this is Big Kahuna, do you copy?"

A crackle of static and then: "*Big Kahuna, Mother… we read you five by five, over.*"

"Roger, Mother… have sighted possible enemy surface ship in direction of Savo… appears headed our way, over."

A pause, "*Understood, Kahuna… ETA to LZ, over?*"

Blanch looked at Mac, who held up five and then two fingers. The Marine depressed the switch, "*Coxswain indicates seven, Mother. Request air support, over.*"

Another long pause in which Blanch had to clench his teeth. If they were right, then there might be a Jap destroyer bearing down on them and was no more than eight miles off. At thirty knots, it could be in firing range of the beach in minutes. It already was, technically, but without line-of-sight direction to aim their guns, it wouldn't do much good. Still, by the time the Marines got off-loaded and were making their way up the dunes, a surface ship could easily take them under fire.

"*Kahuna, Kahuna, Mother… have a flight of Wildcats readying for takeoff now. They should be over your position in ten, over.*"

"Understood, Kahuna out," Blanch said tightly and handed the mic back. "Let's hope we're still *here* when they arrive... push this thing for all she's got, Mac."

Unfortunately, the coxswain had already had the throttle pegged for quite some time. The Higgins boats were made for a very specific purpose. They were called LCVPs for a reason. Landing craft vehicle personnel. They had a good engine, but the engine was geared to sacrifice speed for power. Nine knots was just about the limit of what the boxy craft could manage.

Even this speed was reduced with each swell. A big wave would roll in, lifting the starboard bow up toward its crest, simultaneously tilting the boat to the left. Then, as the wave crest rolled beneath the keel, the boat would stagger slightly, its speed reduced to less than seven knots, and then ponderously right herself, heel to starboard and then race down the backside of the wave, picking up speed until she reached her maximum hull speed of about ten knots. As she did so, however, her flat bow plowed up a wall of spray that surged around the high sides and sent sheets of foam cascading over the open decks. Every man aboard was now nearly soaked to the bone, and the sea state was only getting worse.

Finally, though, Mac sighted his landing zone and put his helm to port in the trough between two seven-footers. He brought the sea around to their quarter, which would actually provide more speed. Not a moment too soon, either, as from over the starboard quarter, far off in the distance, a regular *boom, boom, boom* of thunder rolled across the sea.

Yet every man aboard the boats knew it wasn't thunder. No thunderclaps sounded that regularly spaced and precisely timed. That sound had been the man-made thunder of one-hundred and twenty-seven millimeter to the Japanese, or five-inch to the Americans, naval guns. This was confirmed five seconds later when three towering geysers exploded from the waves not a quarter of a mile behind the last boat in line. On the top of each wave, the angular gray shape of a destroyer was clearly visible, making a nearly direct course for the small group of boats.

Then came another set of booms—three from the direction of the destroyer and a fourth. The fourth was slightly off time and sounded as if it'd come from further east.

Number one boat's radio crackled, *"Kahuna one, Kahuna one! This is Kahuna four! Have sighted additional enemy vessel… think possible submarine bearing two-one-zero, over!"*

"Oh, for Christ's sake…." Blanch cranked and grabbed for the mic. "Kahuna four, Kahuna one. Understood. Standby to rush the beach! Get all your men ready, and we head to the dune as fast as we can. Repeat, we head for the dune, no foxholes before, do all copy?"

The other boats acknowledged, and Blanch called for his men to be ready. He was pleased to see that even the seasick men were straightening their packs and double-checking their Springfields. He knew they'd be all right almost immediately upon setting foot on the sand, but for the moment, he felt for them. He'd been seasick plenty to know how debilitating it could be.

"Standby!" Mac yelled, throttling back.

"Get 'em ready, Guns!" Blanch called to his gunnery sergeant.

The Higgins boat nosed her bow up onto the shallow sand, burying her nose in two feet of water. Blanch's gunny started shouting for men to go, go, go!

Marines began leaping over the bow and the sides near it. Behind them, naval guns boomed, and the super-sonic scream of shells soaring through the air motivated even the sickest. Blanch was again pleased to see the unaffected men standing by to give the sick men a hand out of the boat.

"Good luck, sir,"

Mac said as he threw the engine into reverse.

"You too, Mac… stay shallow and watch for those guns," Blanch said and ran forward.

He leapt over the bow even as the Higgins boat pulled herself away from the shore. He hadn't taken more than three steps when, to his right, a pair of five-inch shells slammed into the beach just at the high-tide line, exploding and sending up a gout of sand and tossing shells in every direction. Marines were already beating it up the dunes, forming themselves into their platoons and being shouted at and directed by officers and sergeants.

The only saving grace, and it was a back-handed benefit at best, of having the Japs shell the LZ was that there wasn't a bunch of them hiding in the palms and jungle just ahead.

Blanch ran, his head swiveling back and forth and searching the tree line for any sign of attackers. He had to get his men out of sight of the naval ships, or they'd be blown to bits. Soon enough the destroyer and the submarine might be able to work in close enough to open up with their ack-ack as well.

Blanch reached the peak of the dune and was met by the three lieutenants of first, second and third platoons. He turned quickly back to see what was happening out to sea and wished he hadn't.

The four Higgins boats had backed away from the beach and were making their way east in a line as close to shore as they could. They all knew by now that there were a number of shoals and reefs on this part of the coast, and getting in tight to the beach was problematic. As Blanch watched in fascinated horror, the third boat in line was struck by a shell. There was a white flash replaced by an angry orange fireball ringed in greasy black smoke. Even from half a mile, Blanch could see bits of burning debris soaring high into the air as the boat was blasted into less than her constituent parts.

"God help us all...," he muttered even as several more shells blasted craters on the beach where his Marines had come ashore not two minutes earlier.

"Sir?" one of the L Ts asked.

"Spread out," Blanch said. "We make our way into the jungle and don't stop until we reach the village. The shelling ought to stop when we vanish... but there's no guarantee of that. Make sure you follow your procedures and keep scouts out ahead. It won't do to get jumped by a Nip patrol. Let's double-time it, men!"

From off to the east, a dull roaring could be heard. It rapidly grew as a flight of F4F Wildcats vectored in from Henderson. Blanch said a quick prayer, and he and the officers began to move their platoons. From his right, a lucky shell struck the tree line only fifty yards from third, and when the roar of the explosion died, Blanch's guts were twisted as more than one man began to scream in agony and terror.

He ran toward them, waving at the other two units to get moving.

As he did, the radio on his gunny's belt began to squawk. The man was right beside his captain, not letting more than two yards get between them for even a second.

"Big Kahuna, Big Kahuna, Flyball one, do you copy?"

"For Christ's sake… go see to the wounded and get that platoon off this beach, Gunny!" Blanch ordered as he took the radio. "I'm right behind ya'!"

More shells thundered behind Blanch. The concussion waves lifted him off his feet, and he was aware of flying through the air for what seemed like an eternity. So intent was he on his goal that his legs still pumped, and by some miracle, he landed and kept on going with hardly a stumble.

"I read you, Flyball!"

"You boys get inland, Captain… we're gonna give these Japs somethin' else to worry about."

"Roger that, Flyball, thanks!"

Four Wildcats wheeled overhead, so large that they must have only been skimming the treetops. They angled out toward the destroyer and submarine while a group of four Dauntlesses zoomed in behind them, much higher up. Blanch couldn't take the time to watch the fight, too busy was he inspecting the condition of third platoon and helping to carry a wounded man into the jungle.

Three men were dead. The shell having sent shrapnel and bits of palm trunk flying. One look was enough to know there was no chance. One man's head was gone, another had been torn in half, and still, another had a hole in his chest large enough to pass a soccer ball through.

As I company moved away from the beach and into the dubious cover of Guadalcanal's rainforests, Blanch hoped the pilots fared well. Ever since they'd flown overhead, the shelling had stopped. Yet even from several miles away, the staccato chatter of machine-gun fire and the repetitious popping of anti-aircraft cannon was unmistakable. He asked the good Lord to protect them and to protect his men as well.

13

GOETTGE'S REVENGE – FIRST BATTLE OF THE MATANIKAU, PART 3

AUGUST 19, 1942 – 1315 LOCAL TIME

Getting L company across the river was not exactly the sort of carefully planned and executed evolution that Captain Lyman Spurlock hoped it would be. Not that he was in any way surprised, of course. After all, what resources were available to the Marines on The Canal were spare as compared to their numbers.

Admiral Richmond Turner had withdrawn his transports on the ninth of August after the fateful battle of Savo Island. Afraid that his ships were too vulnerable to the aggressive Japanese air attacks by day and warship attacks by night, the Admiral had pulled out with less than half the Marines' supplies sent ashore. Admiral Frank Jack Fletcher and his carrier task force had done the same thing. And although carriers and supply ships had returned, the latter was only a fraction of what was needed. After only twelve days in the Solomons, the nineteen-thousand Marines comprising the FirstMarDiv spread out across Guadalcanal, Tulagi, Gavutu and Tanambogo, and Florida Island were showing the consequences of reduced rations and hard work. Most of the men, from General Vandegrift down to the lowliest private, had lost between three and six pounds.

However, the Marines weren't entirely without resources. Aside from the Cactus Airforce, and perhaps most important as the campaign dragged on, was the First Amphib Tractor Battalion and the First Tank Battalion. The latter backing up B company on their push across the mouth of the Matanikau and the former assisting Spurlock with getting his L company across.

Even so, the resources were spread thin. Currently, he had two AmTraks, a DUKW amphibious flatbed truck and a couple of canoes and skiffs hastily assembled from local supporters. It had been enough to get himself and First Platoon across, which was enough men to set up a perimeter around the staging area.

As Spurlock watched the big AmTraks plow across the river, he couldn't help but keep one eye on the jungle around him and his men. There was no way by now that the Japanese didn't know the Americans were on the move and coming across the Matanikau for them. Even as his men were ferried across, Spurlock could hear the rumbling of heavy weapons fire from the north. B company was either beginning their push, or the Japs were pushing back. Spurlock could only do what he could to secure his rally point before all of his men were ready.

"Skipper, I've got reports from B and I companies," Porter Hazard said as he idled up to Spurlock with his heavy-duty field communications set.

Spurlock had taken a liking to Hazard immediately upon meeting the man. Aside from the fact that they were the same age, Hazard's heavy Georgia accent, which he was often kidded with because it sounded a lot like Foghorn Leghorn, the Hanna-Barbera rooster, was open and friendly. His service with the Marine Corps and in the Navy made him an invaluable resource. Also, the fact that he'd been taken and abused by the Japs, lived to talk about it, and on top of that, was ready and willing to get back into the fighting was undeniably admirable.

Hazard stood with the heavy radio pack on and holding what looked like an oversized telephone handset to his ear. He nodded and looked expectantly at the captain.

"Go ahead, Porter."

"I company made it ashore," Hazard reported. "They were shelled by a Jap destroyer and submarine. Four men wounded, three dead. They're making their way in to Cocumbona now."

Spurlock sighed, "Jesus... in broad daylight... and B company?"

"Havin' a rough time of it, sir," Hazard stated. "First Tank can't get their machines within visual range of the Jap position. According to Dave and Charlie, that sandbar is too mushy to get tanks across anyway. So our boys are trading shots with the Jap field pieces... but so far, the Japs own that sandbar."

"We should ask Henderson to pay those bastards a visit," Spurlock said. "Little fire from the sky will fix their wagon."

"Yes sir..." Hazard stated. "They've got a flight out harassing the Jap ships, but heavy weather is coming in, maybe tropical storm level stuff, so the field isn't keen on sending up any more birds right now."

"Then it's up to the good old infantry," Spurlock decided.

"Oh, sir... Lieutenant Georgio of the second requests permission to load his platoon into a couple of trucks and head south," Hazard finished. "There's a heavy log bridge across the Matanikau about five klicks south they can drive across and come at the village from the other side."

It was a good idea, but Spurlock dismissed it out of hand, "Negative. We don't have any intel on that area and have no idea what could be lurking down there. Two trucks could be tempting targets, and they could be overwhelmed. Nope... we need everybody we can, here."

"Aye-aye, sir," Hazard said and moved off a few paces to make the calls.

Corporal Dave Taggart of the Raiders appeared next. He came to attention and saluted smartly, "Corporal Taggart reporting as ordered, sir."

"You up for a little forward recon, Corporal?" Spurlock asked, not unkindly. Taggart had done his fair share of work over the past twenty-four hours.

"Yes sir."

Spurlock grinned, "Are you sure you're up for it or just toughing it out to uphold the reputation of Colonel Edson's Raiders, corporal?"

Taggart grinned back, "Little column A, little column B, sir. Either way, I'm ready for whatever you need, sir."

"Good man," Spurlock said. "Put together a fire team from First

Platoon. You and three men only. The L T will tell you who's best suited. I'd like you to try and work your way west and to the northwest of the village. Give me a visual report on what you see there. We're almost ready to go here and should be on the move in fifteen. We've already scouted the route, and we'll be hitting the village from the northeast quadrant, so your observation could prove invaluable."

"Yes sir," Taggart said. "Permission to request heavy weapons for when the show starts?"

Spurlock nodded, "Granted. Take a couple of grenade launchers. Also, I think they've got a couple of BARs. Take at least one."

Taggart snapped to and saluted again, "Aye-aye, sir. I'll call it in as soon as we're in position."

OAKS AND ENTWATER

The two Marines stranded on the west side of the Matanikau had collected the rifles, ammo and grenades from the Japanese they'd killed and had melted back into the jungle to the southwest. They worked their way around to their original observation position atop the ridge that overlooked the village. They were silently making their way along the same narrow path they'd used hours earlier when they had a nasty surprise.

From either side of the trail, and without making a sound, half a dozen men suddenly appeared as if by magic. They weren't Japanese soldiers, however. The men wore only breechcloths and necklaces, and their skin was the color of dark coffee.

One man, a tall, lanky figure, stepped up, held a long spear at his side and gave Oaks what might be called a salute, "I Cantu of Cocumbona. Headman 'e savvy you friend. You kill Naponapo in village, 'e makum belonga find savvy you be your men."

Oaks' mastery of Pidgin was far from complete, but he understood the gist of what the man said. The headman of Cocumbona, whom he'd met only the previous night, had sent these six men to act as warriors to assist Oaks in his attack on the Japanese.

"Can any of you men shoot?" Entwater asked, aiming his

Springfield at nothing and making shooting noises in an attempt to explain.

Cantu grinned, "I shootum. All shootum. Belonga three or two guns savvy Cocumbona… but they not bang now times."

"I think that means they've got some old weapons," Entwater explained to Oaks. "Probably old British jobs that have rusted out."

Oaks nodded, "Yeah, that's what I figure. Well, since we're luggin' around these Jap sticks, let's pass them out and see if these fellas can shoot."

The Japanese weapons and ammo were given to the men Cantu indicated were the best shots, including himself. Both Marines elected to keep the grenades themselves, as they weren't sure the islanders would know what to do with them. Oaks explained, twice, that they were going to spy on the village and were waiting for a large number of Marines to attack. When they did, he indicated that the eight of them would assault the Japanese from their flank.

Although Cantu's mastery of English was about as good as either American's mastery of Pidgin, the man seemed quite intelligent and picked up on things quickly. He also indicated that he knew of a better path to where Oaks wanted to go. The Marines were impressed at how easily the native men moved through the dense jungle. Their bare feet were no doubt hardened to the chore and were sensitive to the ground. They moved fast and silent with the two Americans in their midst.

Cantu brought the team out on top of the same ridge, not more than two hundred yards from the place Oaks had chosen. However, the hunter indicated that where they were, the stream that ran between the ridge and the village was only knee-deep and could be crossed quickly and with some cover from a small patch of teaks.

It became painfully clear almost immediately that the Japanese stationed in and around the village were ready for an attack. The men, numbering perhaps over a hundred, were arranged in firing lines at several points. There were at least a dozen who were set up near the field with the type 89 knee mortar as if they were an artillery train. The vehicles had been moved, and in at least three places, the Japanese had established Nambu machine gun nests with fairly decent cover.

The reason was obvious. The Marines were readying themselves not far from the village, and the sounds of machinery could be heard even up on the ridge. Oaks felt no small amount of guilt over the fact that after their heroics in Cocumbona earlier that morning and after taking down the Jap fire team hours earlier, they had certainly given away the fact that Americans were operating on this side of the river. A clever Japanese officer would simply assume that this was the prelude for something bigger and prepare.

"We gotta do somethin' Sarge," Entwater almost pleaded.

Oaks bit his lip. There *was* something they could do, but it would expose them to the wrath of a Japanese unit far larger and better armed. He shrugged and waved Cantu over into a huddle with himself and Oaks.

"Okay, boys, we're gonna open up on them," Oaks said. "That machine gun nest there on the other side of the stream should be in range. We spread out, five yards apart, and when I give a whistle, we all open up on those three nips manning it."

"You know they'll turn that thing on us," Entwater said.

"Yeah… but if we take those three out, it'll be a little while before they get their shit together again," Oaks opined. "In that time, we all shift to the west. The Japs'll send a patrol out for us… but maybe by then, Captain Spurlock will be ready for his push."

The two Marines and their four shooters arranged themselves. To Oaks' surprise, Cantu said some rapid words in the native language of the island and two of the men, two without firearms, began to make their way down the ridge to cross the stream. Oaks looked to Cantu, who was to his right, and the Melanesian man only smiled.

The natives were impressive. Oaks could hardly see them among the brush as they made their way to the edge of the narrow stream. He figured he only saw them at all because he knew where to look. Quickly, the men slid into the water, moving like crocodiles with only enough of their heads showing to breathe. They then low-crawled out of the water and into the stand of hardwoods. They vanished into the trees no more than twenty yards from the Japanese machine gun nest. The soldiers never even turned to look, so focused were they on the area in front of the village that would soon become a battlefield.

Oaks wasn't sure what orders Cantu had given the men, but he couldn't worry about it now. He didn't know when the assault was to come, but he sensed it was soon. The growling of distant diesel engines had died down all of a sudden and from far away to the north, perhaps two or three klicks, the rumble of big guns exchanging volleys was unmistakable. He'd also heard the roar of aircraft flying overhead between the village and the beach several minutes before. That and the rapidly darkening sky overhead made it clear that the balloon was about to go up.

He raised his fingers to his lips and blew a shrill horse whistle that seemed to echo for miles. More than one group of Japs looked in the direction, and quite a few voices began to shout in alarm.

Almost as one, five bolt-action rifles crackled. Oaks' own shot came late as he'd given the signal. He sighted along the barrel of his M1903 and was surprised to find that the three Japs on the Nambu had all been taken down. Certainly, one kill had been Entwater's. The kid could knock stink off a monkey from three hundred yards. The machine gun wasn't quite that far. Yet, at least two of the natives had hit their targets, too. Damned impressive for untrained shooters.

"Shift!" Oaks called out.

The village erupted into chaos. Japanese voices began shouting by the dozens, and more than one weapon was pointed at the area of the ridge. Arisaka rifles crackled, and a group of men began to make their way toward the now unmanned Nambu nest.

As Oaks and his men shifted fifty yards to the west, he thought he saw a pair of dark blurs moving between the hardwoods below him and the machine gun nest. He wanted to shout out a warning. To tell the natives not to risk their lives and be spotted. As soon as the Japanese saw them, they'd be shot.

However, from a quarter-mile away to the north, another disturbance caught the attention of the Japs. At least some of them. Several weapons fired, and two grenades exploded near a truck, turning it into a greasy flaming wreck and killing three Riekusentai.

Then, from out of the rainforest in the direction of the river came L company. First a dozen, then two dozen and then more than a hundred men seemed to explode from the foliage. Men took up position and began firing even as multiple M1 grenade launchers sent pineapples soaring into the village.

Oaks saw that the two Melanesians who'd gone down were going to make it to the Nambu at about the same time as four Jap soldiers. If he wanted to get into the fighting, it'd be now or never.

"Go, go, go!" Oaks jumped to his feet and began waving his arm, pointing down to the stream.

He should have kept at least three men back to provide covering fire until the other half made it to a decent position where they could then cover the others' move. However, there were only six of them, and things were happening fast.

At the Nambu nest, the two Melanesians sent their long spears flying straight at the onrushing Japanese Marines. The four men were startled to see the natives, and their moment's hesitation was all it took. Two of the men were impaled on the long shafts and went down screaming in agony and clutching at their bellies.

The other two brought up their rifles and shouted in anger, pulling the triggers and then racing forward, leading with their bayonets.

Miraculously, neither shot hit. The two Melanesians, both fast and light on their feet in spite of being burly men, charged full-tilt at the enemy. At the last instant, both men dove and rolled, causing the two marines to pitch forward ass over tea kettle as they plowed into the men with their knees and shins. In a lightning-fast move, the two islanders rolled to their feet, yanked wicked knives from sheaths around their waists, and plunged the blades into the back of the necks of the two soldiers.

Oaks saw all of this peripherally as he half ran, half stumbled down the embankment and into the stream. By the time he got across, the two islanders had gotten to the machine gun and were opening fire, sending heavy-caliber rounds into the village. Oaks was surprised that they could even operate the gun, although the soldiers had probably had it ready to fire. It became clear that the islanders weren't familiar with its intricacies when the machine gun burned through its ammo and the bolt locked open. He also saw out of the corner of his left eye a couple of the men in the Japanese knee mortar line take notice and train their launchers in the direction of the captured nest.

"Run!" Oaks shouted. "Get out of there!"

Cantu added his voice to Oaks', and the two islanders looked back and then lurched away from the gun emplacement. Oaks could have sworn he heard the tell-tale *thump* of a grenade launcher seconds before a trio of type 89 launched 50mm mortars exploded almost on top of the Nambu. The position burst into a great cloud of dust, dirt, debris and blasted sandbags. By the time the explosion cleared, it was evident that that particular gun would never be used again.

Out of the dust, the two islanders appeared, staggering but on their feet and moving to retrieve their spears and the rifles of their vanquished enemies. The islanders around Oaks whooped, and he and Entwater joined in, elated that the two brave men had gotten out of the blast zone.

From the other side of the village, Taggart and his fire team were spread out just within the boundary between the viney, leafy jungle and the edge of Matanikau's fields. Unlike Oaks, who'd had the high ground, Taggert found that the approach to the village from the northwest quadrant was from a gently sloping decline. No doubt helping to drain the village during heavy rains or flooding. Somebody had chosen the spot very well whenever they'd settled there.

Unfortunately, it left Taggart's team somewhat vulnerable. They'd come out not far from the line of Japanese knee mortars. And although Taggart had two M1 grenade launchers mounted to his and another man's rifles, their range was only about a quarter that of the deadly type 89. It meant that in order to bring his own small artillery to bear, he'd have to be well within the easy kill zone of the Jap weapons.

They'd done it, though. Using the cover of the jungle to work in close enough that the BAR could hit something. Taggart had activated his walkie-talkie to report in.

"Bugs, this is Tweety bird… Bugs, Tweety bird, do you copy, over?" Taggart said quietly into his radio.

A crackle and then Hazard replied: "*This is Bugs, I read you Tweety. Go ahead.*"

"There's some activity to the south," Taggart stated. "I heard half a dozen shots… line of knee mortars about three hundred yards from the east end of village… couple of them are re-aiming… assess Sergeant Oaks and Entwater are still out there, Bugs."

A pause and then, *"Roger that, Tweety. Can you do any damage to the mortar line?"*

"Affirmative, Bugs… but we're a bit vulnerable," Taggart explained. "Once we open up, it's gonna get hot, over."

"Understood, Tweety… we'll provide distraction. Out."

And they had. The entire L company burst from the jungle and began sending rounds downrange along with thrown and launched grenades. Taggart saw something happening several hundred yards away on the other side of the village. One of the Nambu machine guns began to open up on the lines of Japanese soldiers. The weapon quickly burned through its ammo belt, and three of the knee mortars took it out.

"Take them out!" Taggart shouted to his men, all four ten yards apart. "M1s and rifles. Our targets are those bastards with the type 89s!"

The world was a battlefield now. Hundreds of rifles crackled and popped. Machine guns growled their throaty growl as they sent 12.5mm rounds spraying toward the Marine lines. Grenades soared through the air, and flashes and roars peppered across the village, turning the area into one dusty, cordite-scented madhouse.

Thus far, the Japanese were getting the worst of it. From somewhere in the Marines' rear, a fire team with bazookas was targeting the Nambu nests. The big anti-tank weapons didn't take long to home in and blast the sandbagged machine guns and their crews into horrible clouds of debris, roiling sand and gory lumps of flesh.

It became clear to the Japanese that more aggression was required. From somewhere in the village, a voice was raised, and the word Banzai was shouted. Well over a hundred Japs raised their voices and took up the call. Even the remaining mortar men abandoned their weapons and screamed out the war cry as they rushed into the teeth of the Marine assault.

"Go!" Taggart shouted. "Bayonets!"

The Marine line and the Japanese line met in a screaming, roaring melee of pure insanity. Taggart led his small team toward the fray from its left flank just as Oaks led his seven men from the right. There was so much dust in the air that it wasn't until the two small teams got within spitting distance that they could tell friend from foe.

Overhead, a tremendous thunderclap exploded over the land, almost simultaneously with an enormous flash of lightning. As the Americans and the Japanese met, it was as if the Gods themselves had arranged the most dramatic scene possible. The first real land engagement of Guadalcanal was in full swing, complete with a dramatic stormy backdrop.

Marines were taking down Japs as they rushed in, but the ground was quickly closed. Captain Lyman Spurlock was in the center of his men, his rifle held before him as a Japanese officer, and two soldiers rushed him, their own bayonets flashing in the lightning and cries of Banzai tearing from their throats.

The captain was dimly aware of another man beside him as he moved forward to meet the charge. It was his gunnery sergeant, rifle held like a club and ready to swipe away the thrusts of the enemy blades. To his surprise, Spurlock also noticed another man to his right. A burly figure that moved with just a slight limp but still nimbly without the bulk of his radio pack.

Porter Hazard had his own war cry. He bellowed in rage and let fly with an impressive number of curses and epithets, some so fueled by fury they were hardly more than animal growls. The three men met their foes, and blades and rifles clashed.

The gunny beat aside the bayonet of a big Jap soldier, and the two men fell to smashing each other with fists. Spurlock twisted to his side, avoiding the thrust of the officer's blade and the two men twisted by one another, having to spin around in order to come back together. By the time they did, Spurlock saw that the officer had abandoned his gun for a Katana that he'd unsheathed.

With another cry of anger, the Nip came in, arcing his blade from high up in order to cleave Spurlock's head from his body. The Marine went to his knees, ducking and bringing up his weapon in defense. There was a cry of pain, a string of Japanese curses and a small spray of something warm and salty on the captain's face.

His bayonet had caught the man's right forearm and plowed it open. In an admirable feat of determination, the officer switched hands, grabbing the hilt of his sword before his nerveless right hand could release it. Even as he lurched forward with a drive toward Spurlock's belly, the captain scrambled back and managed to regain his footing. The officer didn't make it any further, however. The bloody point of the gunny's bayonet burst from the man's chest in a fountain of dark heart's blood.

"Grab the sword, sir!" the gunny said.

Both men turned back to the fighting to see Porter Hazard kneeling on the chest of a disarmed soldier and squeezing his big hands around the man's throat. The Navy Lieutenant was screaming incoherently into the other man's face, which was turning a dark shade of purple.

The gunny moved to help Hazard, but Spurlock put a hand on his shoulder, "Let him go, Gunny. He needs to get his payback for what they did to him."

The two men had their own problems to deal with. Several more soldiers were charging in, and Spurlock saw the gunny flinch back and spin half around. A 7.7mm round had struck him in the shoulder. Surprisingly though, the gunny simply went with the spin, came back around, side-stepped and drove the blade of his bayonet into the throat of the soldier who'd fired at him from almost point-blank range. The man's Banzai shriek was cut short as the steel blade blasted apart his voice box and sent the man tumbling to the dirt, choking and gagging and carrying the gunny's rifle with him.

Spurlock's own man drove in, and the captain swung the unfamiliar weight of the Katana to fend off the blow. There was an audible clang as the steel of the sword met the Arisaka's barrel. The captain thought to throw away the sword, thinking that it must have been damaged by the contact. However, when he side-stepped and swung the sword two-handed, he was both elated and disgusted by the result. With no small amount of awe and horror, Spurlock watched as his blade bit into the soldier's neck, cleaving his head from his body. The arc of the blow continued to drive the blade down and to the left, severing the man's arm at the shoulder before it swung free. Spurlock was splashed with a warm coppery fountain as the mangled body crumpled before him. In stunned surprise, the captain realized that he'd hardly felt any resistance to his powerful swing and that his now crimson-sheathed blade was still perfectly sharp.

This distraction nearly got him killed, however. Another Jap was coming in, intent on taking down an officer. Yet before his bayonet could tear open Spurlock's belly, a burly shape slammed into him and drove its own bayonet into the man's chest. Porter Hazard drove the man to the ground, twisted the rifle back and forth sadistically, and stepped back, gasping and heaving and looking at Spurlock.

"You all right, sir?" Hazard managed.

The captain blinked at the sweaty, bloody and frenzied submariner. The man's eyes were wide and wild with fighting madness.

"Yeah… thanks… how about you?"

Hazard's look of mania dissolved as he grinned crookedly, "Feels good to get a little of my own back, y'know, sir?"

The three men found themselves alone suddenly. In an island of calm as the Japanese line had split and was breaking. The Marines were pounding after them through the mud, and their leader only then noticed that a moderate rain was falling. He also heard the cries of his own men. Men groaning in pain and calling out for a medic. He wondered how many young boys he'd lost. How many of his young Marines would go home with a sleeve pinned to their jackets or in one boot… or who wouldn't go home at all, except perhaps in a coffin.

Once the Japanese line broke, the battle quickly faded. Some of them got away; some cut down as they ran. Taggart and his team moved out and fell upon the soldiers who'd retreated to take up their knee mortars again. The men were slaughtered to a man, and the Marines collected as many mortars and as much ammo as they could.

On the other side of the fields, Oaks, Entwater and their six islanders found themselves in something of a brouhaha with a dozen Japs. The fighting fell to hand to hand, and when it was done, nine Japanese soldiers were killed and three taken prisoner. Cantu lost one man after two Riekusentai spitted him on their blades. They were then summarily impaled by primitive wooden spears that went clear through their torsos.

In the process, Oaks was able to capture a small Japanese truck, and he and his team piled in, driving across the village toward the Marines. Entwater stood on the runner beside the driver's side, shouting that they were Marines and that Betty Grable was one hot tomata.

"Nice job, boys!" Captain Spurlock met the truck as Oaks pulled to a stop near a collection of wounded men. "We can use this to get back across the river to the south."

"I thought you didn't want to risk that, sir," Hazard said as he shook Oaks' hand.

"We've got a couple of guys here who can't wait for a boat ride, I'm afraid," a Navy Corpsman said as he approached, his camos and hands covered in blood despite the rain. "Still faster by road going the long way around."

"Think you can get 'em back, Leng?" Spurlock asked.

Petty Officer William Leng nodded, "Larry Wescott is the worst, sir. Belly wound. I think if I can get a Marine to ride shotgun, I can get us back to base in under a half-hour, sir."

It was then that Taggart and his team trotted up, arms loaded with captured type 89 grenade launchers and mortar shells. Taggart shook hands with Oaks and Entwater, and Hazard. Spurlock explained the situation, and Porter Hazard was voluntold to ride with Leng.

"Sir, I…" the submariner began to protest.

"No arguments, Port," Spurlock said. "I can see you've overdone it. Ride back with Leng here, and you can give the general our initial report. We've lost four men and eleven wounded. I just heard we got at least sixty-five Japs. Leng, get your worst cases in the truck. Who's got an automatic weapon?"

"Sir!" one of Taggart's men stepped forward and held out his big BAR.

"Give it to Hazard," Spurlock said. "Good work, everyone."

Hazard helped Leng load PFC Larry Wescott into the open bed of the small Nissan truck. The man's lower belly and upper thighs were soaked with blood. He'd taken a bayonet to the belly that had torn it open but not deep enough to disembowel him… although it was close. The soldier who'd done it had also jabbed the man repeatedly in the thighs before he'd been shot.

"You're gonna be okay, Larry," Leng was saying as he and Hazard made the man as comfortable as possible.

It was clear to the officer that Leng and the Marine were friends. Wescott, in spite of his pain, grinned at Leng, "Think Jeanie will be impressed, Billy?"

Leng gave the man a shot of morphine and patted him on the shoulder, "She'll probably marry you soon as you get back to Pearl, buddy. Rest easy now."

Leng and Hazard climbed onto the small cab, both grateful to be out of the heavy rain. Although it certainly felt good after the heat of the battle.

Leng took the wheel and Hazard the other seat. He rested the barrel of the Browning automatic rifle on the window frame, ready to unload heavy fire at anything moving that wasn't wearing Marine green.

As Leng drove out of the village toward the coast road, Hazard noticed that there were several Japanese soldiers huddled together near the steps of a hut. Hazard found that odd. He couldn't say why, but there was something about the way the men lay that didn't seem right. If they'd been killed, they wouldn't be lined up so neatly. They were bloody, it was true, but...

"Bill... step on it, turn quick!" Hazard shouted in sudden alarm.

As he did so, one of the Japs sat up, smiled at the oncoming truck and swung his arm. Too late, both Americans realized what the man had done. The grenade landed between the right side front and rear tires and exploded.

The truck tilted crazily, actually going up on two wheels for a moment before jouncing down hard just as another grenade exploded. This one went high and over the truck and burst in the air.

Leng slammed on the brakes, the truck fishtailing in the mud. Hazard jumped out, bringing up his heavy BAR and began spraying the wounded Japs with .3006 rounds. He emptied the entire magazine into the four men, ensuring that they were, in fact, dead.

"L T!" Leng's voice called out in obvious fright from the other side of the truck.

Hazard ran around, glancing into the bed to see that two of the four men that had been lying there were gone. As he rounded the truck, he saw that they'd been thrown out and were lying in the mud. One man was groaning, and the other, PFC Wescott, was lying face up, his belly now torn open and leaking ropey intestine. Hazard felt his bile rise as he moved closer.

"Billy…" Wescott said to his friend, his voice sounding like that of a drunk's. The morphine shot was making him loopy and masking most of the horrifying pain the man would otherwise be in. "Am… am I gonna die?"

"Don't talk like that, pal," Leng said with a smile. Even in the rain, however, Hazard could see tears brimming in the Corpsman's eyes. "You're gonna be okay, Larry. You're gonna be okay…."

Hazard knelt down, and it was clear to him that Wescott wouldn't be okay. His wounds before had been bad enough, but now his guts were spread out over his legs and the ground around him, and his crotch was thick with blood.

Leng met Hazard's eyes and then laid his head on his friend's chest, sobbing. There was nothing to be done. Hazard put an arm around Leng's shoulders and was surprised to feel another's there. Wescott had reached up to offer his friend comfort in his grief. Grief over his own death. Hazard looked down to see Wescott's eyes glaze over. His own vision blurred then, the emotion of the moment overwhelming him.

The first battle of the Matanikau had been a success. Yet it had come, as others would later, with a price. Death would not be denied, even in victory.

14

USS BULL SHARK – THE SOLOMON SEA

AUGUST 19, 1942 – 2130 LOCAL TIME

It was raining heavily when Art Turner threw open the bridge hatch and climbed out of the conning tower. The rain felt good, so good in fact that he hadn't donned his rain gear. He'd simply removed his blouse and undershirt and came up on deck bare-chested. It was August, and the rain and air were warm and felt fantastic on a body that had been hot, sweaty and coated in unpleasant odors for most of the day.

"Little rough tonight, skipper," the COB said as he joined his captain.

"Yeah, this is a pretty hearty storm," Turner observed, wishing he could light up a smoke. "From the looks of it, though, I'd say the worst of it must be to the south a ways. Not even that windy here. Just a rolling six-to-eight-foot swell."

"Think we could let the guys come on deck with soap and shampoo and take advantage of this free shower?" Buck Rogers asked.

"Yeah, I think it's all right," Turner said. "Might do the same myself. In shifts, though. Ten men at a time on the after deck. It is a bit sporty up here. Also, let's open up the torpedo room hatches and take a suction through the boat. Damned fire stink is still floating down there."

Rogers grinned, "Dunno, skipper… almost prefer it to the diesel fumes and B.O."

Turner laughed, "Yeah, well… once we get the lads scrubbed up, there won't be any more dude funk… well, no *fresh* dude funk."

Rogers laughed and went below to see to organizing the men. Almost immediately, Elmer Williams's face appeared to take his place in the hatch.

"Permission to come up to the bridge, Captain?"

Turner smiled down, "If you don't mind getting wet, Elmer. You're always welcome."

The XO climbed up and closed the hatch. He wore a rain jacket and sou'wester. He grinned at Art and his somewhat pale bare chest, "Not gonna get much of a tan tonight, Art."

"Hell, Elmer, we're all so pale the moon might give us a burn," Turner grinned. "Whatcha got for me."

"Frank and Joe have completed their report," Williams said. "First, Frank has asked if we can charge on three engines for a while. Battery number two needs some extra love."

Turner nodded and thumbed the bridge speaker, "Maneuvering, bridge, put one, two and three on charge and four on propulsion. Maintain heading at all ahead standard."

There was a momentary pause. Turner wasn't able to communicate with any part of the ship from the single speaker. In truth, his message was transmitted to the conning tower and control room. There, one of the phone talkers would relay his messages to any other part of the ship. After a moment, Andy Post, who was officer of the watch, came back.

"*Bridge, conning. Maneuvering acknowledges, and helm reports Bendix log indicates five knots.*"

"Very well," Turner replied and looked back to Williams expectantly.

It was past sunset, and the iron-gray sky was rapidly darkening. Williams was already little more than a silhouette against the leaden backdrop of sky and sea.

"Electrical fire was due to a saltwater short," Elmer reported. "As we figured. Frank reports that Tank and Mike found a cooling line leak in the motor room. Cracked weld or corroded threads on an elbow. They think it's galvanic corrosion. Seawater was leaking in pretty good on that last deep dive and made its way forward, etc."

Turner sighed, "Which means we've got some loose juice someplace back there."

"Yeah, and Chief Duncan would like permission to cut out that fitting and replace it, or at least weld a patch," Williams went on. "But he needs a stable platform."

Turner frowned, "Which we don't exactly have right now. It's not terrible, but certainly the pitching and rolling will make their jobs difficult. Is that why Joe wants to charge so fast? To go back down to a couple of hundred feet where it's nice and still?"

"Aye sir."

"Okay, makes sense… and I assume that our juice jerkers also drained the affected cells on battery number two just to get rid of any seawater," Turner said.

"As per your orders, sir," Williams replied. "They actually did them all. Drained all one-hundred and twenty-six cells, and they're refilling them with good fresh now."

Turner frowned, "Better safe than sorry. I swear I sniffed a little chlorine before we opened up. Okay, what else?"

Williams shrugged, "That's it for the big stuff. Obviously, we've got broken bulbs being replaced, gauge glass, some insulation… the usual round during an Art Turner ash canning."

"Oh, so now it's *my* fault?" Turner pretended to whine. "I didn't *ask* the Japs to drop tooth shakers on us, y'know."

"Well, Art… you did run on the surface in broad daylight and shoot down four of their planes," Williams chastised. "Those Zekes are expensive, you know."

The two men laughed and were joined by the lookouts who'd overheard. It felt good to laugh. To sluff off the tension of a battle as the rain washed away the grime.

Buck Rogers appeared again with a bowl. In it was a bar of Ivory soap, a razor and a bottle of Brek shampoo. Turner grinned at the collection.

"Figured since you're up here, sir, might as well get gussied up,"

The COB said straight-faced. "Get you lookin' as cute as the Brek girl in no time."

"Nix," Turner said and then laughed. "Is this just a ploy to get me naked and see my naughty bits?"

"Of course," Williams dead-panned.

"Well… okay… but no laughing," Turner said.

"No sir!" Rogers replied snappily. "Never make fun of the captain's wedding tackle. First thing we learned in sub school, sir."

That broke everyone up. Turner quickly doffed his shorts, skivvies and sandals and began washing and shaving. Aft of the conning tower and the after five-inch, men were doing the same. Coming up through the engine room and after torpedo room hatch carrying nothing but soap and shampoo. On a freshwater poor ship, any lasting rain was a chance to really give the body a going over.

There was little chance of being caught as well. On a rainy evening where the visibility was poor, it was unlikely that any Japanese ships would happen upon them. Also, as the boat needed a little TLC, Turner had ordered *Bull Shark* to head west by south and out of the Solomon Chain and just into the Solomon Sea.

"How long do our boys need to put everything to right, XO?" Turner asked as his razor rasped over his cheeks.

"We've used most of our reserve water to refill the cells," Williams stated. "Couple of hours to recharge and check the electrolyte balances… then Chief Duncan says no more than an hour to repair that elbow."

"All right, tell you what we do," Turner said, swishing the razor in the now nearly full bowl. "Let's get the batteries topped off, and then we'll dive. Let the Chief do his thing and feed the men without the boat jittering. Then we'll come back up and run back into The Slot and go find us some Japs. We can crank up the water evaporators to full too. I've got no doubt that we've missed out on quite a few Tokyo Express runs already."

"Think those four DDs are still out there lookin' for us?" Rogers asked.

Turner shrugged, "Maybe, maybe not. But at night… we've got all the advantages, especially in a storm. With our SJ, we can get right up on top of them before they'll even know we're there. I intend to extract a pound of flesh from those yellow bastards, gentlemen."

"Yes sir," Rogers grinned.

Williams sighed, "Wish we could count on S-52 to backstop us."

"Yeah…" Turner said. "But they probably won't be in the area until tomorrow night at the earliest. Still… once they are, I'd sure like to station them right in the middle of the channel. We give the Japs a good pasting halfway up to Rabaul and then when they get by, as some of them must… and think they're in the clear… wham!"

"S-52 kicks them right up the ass in sight of land, ha-ha-HA!" Rogers enthused.

Williams chuckled, "That'll learn 'em… although, aren't we forgetting something, Art?"

"Sato and the *Sakai*," Turner said less jovially. "No, Elmer, I haven't forgotten. Trouble is that while that lunatic might be out there thinking that he and I are in some kind of goddamned… contest… I'm out here to do my duty. We got a job to do, and that's gotta come first. If we run into *Sakai* and can work in, we'll sink her, plain and simple. But we're here to derail the Tokyo Express, and that's what I intend to do… or at least do our part in it."

"You think maybe those four tin cans that busted our balls earlier were from this Sato guy, sir?" Rogers asked.

"Yeah, good question," Williams noted. "Dragging those chains and anchors wasn't just routine. Those four ships were *looking* for a submarine. No doubt about it."

"True," Turner agreed. "Of course, we sunk a destroyer not far from there the night before, so it's not really a surprise they'd up their game… still, you fellas have a point. That might've been Sato's doing. But he failed, so now it's our turn, one way or another. In my view, we can do as much harm to him personally by not taking it personally."

Both men looked bewildered, and the XO said so.

"What I mean is… the more ships the Japs lose to us, and lose them under Sato's nose, the worse light it puts him in," The Captain explained. "We don't have to go after *Sakai*, necessarily; we just have to make Sato look foolish, I think. And there's always Osaka to think about... I wonder if he's aboard that carrier or went back to Yamamoto."

IJN CARRIER *SAKAI* – SHORTLAND HARBOR, SHORTLAND ISLAND

Standing around the large chart table in the strike carrier's Combat Information Center reminded Ryu Osaka of the large situation table that Admiral Yamamoto had set up aboard *Yamato*. Although the admiral's table was larger and he used model ships to visually represent battle theaters, it was still a close enough situation to make Osaka wistful. He enjoyed working with the admiral and had learned much. On the other hand, working with Sato was a vastly different and much less pleasant experience.

Where the venerable admiral was modest, consistently downplaying his genius and tactical abilities, Sato was arrogant to the point of nausea. The man had never done anything particularly noteworthy that Osaka knew of. His career had been an adequate one but hardly distinguished. Now, due to a tragic twist of fortune, this nondescript commander had been made captain, even temporarily, of one of the Empire's carriers. Even a small one.

Yet was it tragic, this situation in which fortune had worked so well in Sato's favor? Osaka had his doubts. Based on what he knew of Sato's nature... his temper, his arrogance and his ambition... he began to wonder if captain Igawa's ritual suicide was, in fact, just that. What Osaka knew of *that* man didn't quite dovetail with his actions, either.

Unlike Sato, Igawa did have a rather distinguished career. Graduated high in his class at the Naval Academy, served on surface ships since the early thirties and distinguished himself as both a pilot and officer during the Seino-Japanese War. He'd been given command of the new *Sakai* because of his record and his proven levelheadedness. Not a man to lose such confidence in himself after what amounted to a rather minor setback.

It wasn't even a defeat. Simply that the carrier had been damaged and a destroyer lost. Hardly worth killing oneself over. After all, had Yamamoto committed Seppuku after Midway? Had Nagumo, who in truth most certainly should feel shame, done so? If a man like Nagumo, who was notorious for his hesitancy at times, didn't feel enough shame over losing half the Kido Butai… then was it truly possible that a jovial, confident and intelligent man like Igawa would've thrown himself into the sea simply because his ship needed a drydock?

This line of thought naturally led to an even more unpleasant conclusion. If Igawa didn't kill himself… then he must have been murdered. And there could be only one suspect for such an evil deed. The man who had so easily slid into Igawa's place once it became conveniently available. Unfortunately, no one else aboard seemed to hold this suspicion. Or at least had wisely not shown it. Even Omata Hideki hadn't said anything of the kind. He'd been recovering from his wounds on the night that Igawa went missing, and so had no real opinion on the matter… yet even Hideki hadn't made any open statement along the lines of thought down which Osaka now traveled.

"You seem contemplative, Osaka san," Sato said, breaking a long few moments of silence.

"He does that," Hideki, who was on his feet and declared fit for duty, added with a wry smile. "It makes us think he's devious."

"Let's hope he is," Sato said with a small but genuine smile. "Your idea of combining an air search with a squadron of destroyers dragging for the submarine was quite interesting, Commander."

"We did lose four good pilots," Osaka lamented. "And we did not, to my knowledge, sink the *Bull Shark*."

"If the submarine sighted *was* the *Bull Shark*," Hideki pointed out.

"Oh… I think we can assume it was," Sato said thoughtfully. "Running on the surface in broad daylight? Two deck guns mounted? I'm certain that was our man. The real question, perhaps, is, after this aggressive move on our part, what will Turner do? Dare we risk sending a convoy this evening?"

"I don't believe we have a choice," Osaka said. "Is not Colonel Ichiki and over nine hundred of his men due to arrive at Taivu Point this evening?"

Sato nodded, "Six destroyers full of gear and men. It may be prudent for us to accompany them. Perhaps if we time this just so, we might be able to achieve several things upon the morrow...."

"Such as launch a pre-dawn scouting mission to proceed south of Guadalcanal and locate the American carrier group?" Hideki asked eagerly. "I would personally like to lead such a mission, if so."

"We're already down four aircraft," Sato said hesitantly. "I would hate to lose more on a scouting mission."

Osaka found that a bit strange. Generally, Sato was the first one to propose leaping in where angels feared to tread. Now he was suddenly cautious? Why?

"It could be timed just so," Hideki insisted. "Such that if we do a two-hundred-kilometer sweep south and east of the island's weather coast, we could head back and rendezvous with *Sakai* right about the time the daily bombing mission from Rabaul reaches the American position. Perhaps we might even come in early and assault the airfield just after dawn when they least expect it. Should we find Fletcher's group, we will then be able to report their position to Admiral Yamamoto, who can then perhaps intercept them with Nagumo's fleet."

"Ambitious," Osaka admitted and surreptitiously glanced at Sato.

The new captain nodded sagely, and yet there was still that in his carriage that indicated hesitation. Osaka wondered if perhaps the man had what the Americans would call a "streak of yellow" running through him. Was he afraid? And if so… of what? It wasn't as if it were he, Sato, flying off the carrier in the pre-dawn darkness and coming back over American-held territory in daylight with only a handful of planes.

"A good idea," Sato said finally. "Yet I fear it will take more resources away from our primary mission."

"And that is?" Hideki asked.

"To find and to *sink* Arthur Turner's submarine," Sato said sternly.

Osaka raised an eyebrow, "Indeed? Have we received new orders about which I am unaware, Captain?"

Sato's face stiffened and then flushed ever so slightly before he drew in a breath and answered evenly, "It is true, Commander, that we are to ensure the success of the nightly supply runs down New Georgia

Sound. However, it has been made clear to me in our last coded update that this would be best achieved by ridding the sea lane of *all* American submarines. It is known that this *Bull Shark* is operating in our theater; thus, our mission is to sink her."

Now Osaka understood. Now he saw what was truly behind Sato's hesitation. It wasn't that the man was concerned for his pilots or for spreading his resources too thin. No... it was more about letting himself get distracted from his ultimate goal of *besting* Art Turner.

What Sato did not know, nor even did Hideki, was that Turner had confided this to Osaka before turning him back over to his countrymen. Sato was obsessed with Turner for reasons that Osaka couldn't fathom.

"He *has* proven most irritating," Hideki admitted with a wry smile. "As we have seen firsthand."

"Well then," Sato said, "the question which must occupy us next, Commanders... is what will Turner's counter move be? How will he react to Commander Osaka's bold plan to drag the sound for him?"

For all his grandiose talk when speaking to Turner and his obvious obsession with his own game, Sato didn't seem to be displaying a great deal of imagination. It seemed more to Osaka that since agreeing to help Sato, it was he doing the thinking. It made him uncomfortable, to say the least.

Aside from his patriotic views... which were admittedly contradictory at times... Osaka *liked* Turner. He'd found the man to be intelligent, thoughtful and open-minded. On the other hand, he did *not* like Sato. The man seemed egotistical and so eager to prove himself that he'd go to any lengths... even murder?

"No thoughts, Osaka san?" Sato prodded gently.

Osaka thought he might test at least one of his hypotheses, "I shall have to put some thought into it, sir. What does your tactical mind suggest?"

Sato frowned at this. It was clear even to Hideki that Sato had come to rely on Osaka's suggestions more than he would probably wish to acknowledge. Hideki did not know Sato well, but he did know Ryu very well. He could sense that his friend was testing the captain to see what he'd do.

"We will join the convoy," Sato said after a moment's reflection. "We will escort the six destroyers to Guadalcanal and launch our recon flight before dawn, as Commander Hideki suggests. Excuse me, gentlemen, I must get the ship underway and radio the convoy. During the night, commander Osaka, please put your mind to the problem of Turner. I'm sure that together, we can formulate a plan to trap him."

Sakai's captain strode out of the CIC, leaving the two friends alone. Hideki opened his mouth to speak, but Osaka put a finger to his lips. He led the two of them down the companionway and then out onto the flight deck, where they huddled beneath an overhang on the forward end of the island.

"What's going on, Ryu?" Hideki asked finally when the men had lit cigarettes.

"He's a fool, Omata," Osaka grumbled. "He has gotten it into his head that he and Turner are personal adversaries. Yet he wishes for *me* to do his thinking for him."

"You do have experience," Hideki admitted. "We both do."

Osaka scoffed, "Indeed, Omata… indeed. We have experience enough to know treachery when it's right in front of our faces as well."

Hideki looked surprised, even in the darkness, "You think… think he's a traitor?"

Osaka began to pace. He so wanted to explain everything to his friend. To explain his own feelings on the war and his part in providing intelligence to the Americans. Yet Hideki was a loyal officer. He believed in Japan and her glory. Mostly, though, he believed in Yamamoto and in his friend Osaka. Would that trust and friendship survive such revelations?

Osaka drew in a deep drag and then let the smoke out slowly, stretching the moment out dramatically, although unintentionally, "I don't believe he's a traitor to the emperor, in the sense you mean… but I think the man has developed an unhealthy obsession with Turner. Turner himself told me of the radio conversation he had with Sato. The man talked as if he and the American were duelists on some bizarre field of honor, and it is their ships that they choose to wield against one another."

Hideki narrowed his eyes, "Turner… told you this? Why? And you believed the American?"

"I think he's an honorable man, Omata," Sato said. "And I think our captain is not."

Hideki was confused and did not try to hide it, "I don't understand…."

Osaka stopped pacing and faced him, "Don't you find it suspicious that Captain Igawa committed Seppuku over what amounts to such a minor setback?"

"Yes… I do suppose it seems an extreme reaction."

"And did you get the impression in the time we've known the captain that he was so prone to such extremes?"

"I… no, I can't say that I did," Hideki admitted. "But we've only known the man for a fortnight."

"Yes…" Osaka said, half to himself. "And in that fortnight, what have you observed about Sato?"

Hideki almost smiled, "That he's an arrogant ass who has an over-inflated opinion of himself and his abilities."

"Exactly," Osaka said. "I don't believe an experienced and well-seasoned man like Igawa would kill himself just because his ship received minor damage."

Hideki suddenly realized what his friend was implying, "You aren't suggesting… suggesting that Sato *murdered* the captain!"

Osaka walked a few paces away and flicked his ash. Once more he drew deeply on the harsh tobacco of the Golden Bat. He rather wished he had a pack of those Lucky Strikes Turner smoked. He felt like a man adrift at sea. All alone with only his limited resources to help him. He needed more.

Osaka turned back and strode up to his friend. He drew in a deep breath, coming to a decision that would likely change the course of his life, "Yes, Omata. I believe he did. And there's more… there's something I have been wanting to tell you for some time… because I may need your help."

"You have it, Ryu."

Osaka emitted a soft and bitter chuckle, "Don't be so eager, my friend. For once, I tell you what I must tell you… you're going to be faced with a very difficult choice. It might make us closer, or it might make us enemies."

Hideki couldn't imagine what his friend was driving at. However, he did trust Osaka. He decided that whatever it was his friend had to say, he'd listen and keep an open mind.

"I'm listening, Ryu."

Osaka sighed, "There is an American intelligence man named Webster Clayton of the Office of Strategic Services. He came aboard *Leviathan* the night she was sunk."

"Yes, I remember…."

"Clayton has been receiving intelligence from a Japanese officer with the code name Shadow," Osaka explained.

"My god…" Hideki breathed.

Osaka smiled thinly, "This Shadow has been funneling information to Clayton in order to assist the Americans in defeating our Empire all the more quickly. He believes that this war is wrong and that Hirohito and Tojo will stop at nothing, including the deaths of millions of young men, until our enemies drive them to their knees. Admiral Yamamoto shares this view as well."

Hideki's mouth dropped open, "You're not suggesting that Admiral Isoroku Yamamoto—"

Osaka actually laughed, "No, Omata… he's too much a creature of duty ever to think of such a thing. No, Yamamoto is not Shadow… I am."

Had Osaka struck out with his foot and crushed Hideki's testicles, he could not have been more surprised nor flabbergasted. His mouth still hung open, and he stared at his friend in abject bewilderment and disbelief.

"No, I am not joking, Omata."

"But… but *you*… you of all people, Ryu?"

"I am no traitor," Osaka suddenly flared, his eyes flashing. "I do what I've done because Japan *cannot* win this war. We will lose. It is inevitable. It is not that I wish the Americans to win, per se… it's that I don't wish Japan to lose so badly that we fall back into the dark ages and become so crippled as a nation that we must spend the next century as some third-rate vassal."

"Is it not better to die free than to live a slave?" Hideki asked.

Osaka laughed bitterly, "Is it? Are we not already slaves to our leader's ego and pride? Don't believe the propaganda, Omata. You've seen for yourself that the Americans are not fighting to conquer us or to take territory. *We* attacked *them*. One can make all the excuses in the world about trade embargos and the like… but the United States isn't out to take over Japan. Yet if… *when*… we lose to them, they'll doubtless assist us in rebuilding. They'll no doubt insist on establishing naval bases on the home islands. And we'd need that. Because do you think that if Russia or China comes out of this war intact that they won't burn with a desire to exact revenge on us?"

The widespread implications of what Osaka was saying were quite disturbing and held the unmistakable ring of truth. However, like most Japanese, Hideki could not help but cling to the idea that his people were chosen by the Gods to be victorious.

As if reading this in his eyes, Osaka went on, "We can't beat them, Omata. Yes, we have some advantages now. We have an edge in technology and a jump on things, as they say. Yet the Americans have industrial might and resources that we can only dream of. They have something else, too, Omata. They adapt. Do you know why we lost at Midway? It wasn't simply that Nagumo made a series of strategic errors. It was that he cannot adapt. He believes in the foolishness of our divine power. So, it never occurred to him that the Americans would find his carriers. Just as it never occurred to anyone else that a huge fleet would land thousands of men on Guadalcanal. This war is already *lost*, Omata! Certainly, we're better at surface warfare at night. Certainly, our Zeroes are faster and nimbler than anything anyone else has. Certainly, our soldiers are dedicated to the point of brutality because they see every other race as inferior… but all this is a paper tiger, my friend. The United States was caught with their pants down, but they have more men, more factories, more oil, more food… they'll keep coming and coming at us. Relentlessly wearing us down until their Marines come ashore at Honshu and storm the palace!"

Hideki drew in a shuddering breath. He didn't want to believe what his friend was saying, but, in his heart, he knew it to be true.

He'd already seen several things for himself that lent credence to Osaka's belief.

"When we do lose," Osaka said, hammering home his point. "We'll have made mortal enemies of China, Russia, India, Britain, Australia, the Dutch West Indies… The Philippines Islands… in short, we'll be surrounded, Omata. And who will be the only ones to keep our people safe?"

"The Americans…" Hideki had to admit.

"Help them to win sooner, and perhaps this war will only go on until 1945 or 1946… sit back and do nothing. Continue to act as men like Sato act, and it may go on into the 1950s. Until Japan and her people are a land of the dead, who wander aimlessly through a wasteland of our own making. Now you know my secret, Omata. You must make a choice. A hard choice, and for that, I am truly sorry. You can turn me in, do your duty as a good citizen of the empire… or help me."

Hideki didn't hesitate for more than a second. He reached out and laid his hands on Osaka's shoulders, "There is no choice, Ryu. I'm with you. You have my trust and support."

Osaka smiled and embraced him briefly, "I am grateful, my friend. Now we must help a man I despise to hunt down and kill a man I admire and even like… or at least we must make it *appear* that way."

"All the while finding a way to allow Turner to come out victorious?"

Osaka nodded, "Just so."

15
TAIVU POINT, GUADALCANAL
AUGUST 20, 1942 – 0330 LOCAL TIME

Colonel Kiyonao Ichiki hated improvised night landings. That there was a raging storm churning up the Sealark Channel and turning the night as black, wet and discordant as possible was not improving his mood any.

It wasn't even a proper landing, for that matter. He and his nine-hundred and seventeen men had ridden down from Rabaul on half a dozen destroyers. Ships designed for surface combat and not for the transport of soldiers and equipment, let alone their comfort. They had no proper landing craft, only a pair of motor launches from each ship that could hold only a handful of men. Much of their important gear had been sealed in large aluminum canisters that were pushed over the side to be washed ashore or dragged in by boats.

The only positive thing that could be said for this operation was that if he could barely see his hand in front of his face, then certainly no Americans ashore would notice his unit coming ashore and assembling for their assault. He was told that there was one more positive element… that the most violent part of this storm was far to the south, and because of that, the ships were somewhat in the lee. Even so, the channel was roiling with heavy sea making it a misery to climb down the cargo nets and into the small bobbing boats.

"Perhaps this weather will keep the American carriers busy for the next day or two, sir," said Major Aki Kinjo, his adjutant.

Ichiki had just fumbled his way down the side of the destroyer and had nearly been pitched into the angry black sea by the violent motion of the small launch. Only by the quick action of several of his men, who grabbed him and eased him into the lively craft, was he spared. This had succeeded only in further blackening his already irascible mood.

"It also means *Sakai* will not be able to launch her planes, Major," Ichiki cranked as he settled in and tried to ignore his heaving belly.

The strike carrier had joined up with the six destroyers only a hundred kilometers from Savo Island. Her purpose, as Ichiki was told, was additional ASW support and air cover in the morning. She'd launch a flight of fighters and bombers to try and locate Fletcher's carriers so that Yamamoto could send the combined fleet to intercept them. If possible, the aircraft would harass the airfield on Guadalcanal as well.

After the thirteen hours of transit that he and his men had endured in the cramped destroyers, Ichiki had insisted that after dropping him and his men off, the ships would bombard Guadalcanal and Tulagi. He'd suggested to the task force commander that this was to soften up the Americans for his own ground push… but the truth was that Ichiki was simply pissed off and wanted to punish somebody for his misery.

After this day and night, the army colonel would be quite grateful to set foot on solid ground again. Before transferring to the destroyer at Rabaul, he and his men had been aboard transports that had carried them from Guam. For several weeks now, it seemed, they'd been at sea and had grown quite tired of it. Even in good weather, a ship rocked and heaved and pitched and was always in motion. When the weather got bad, and the seas got up… it could be an exercise in utter wretchedness.

Ichiki had to hand it to the Imperial Japanese Navy, however. The men aboard ship and in the boats seemed to know their business. Ichiki himself, who was known for his excellent night vision, could see nothing… absolutely nothing… other than the vague shapes in the boat. Even the side of the destroyer was more felt than seen. The only exception was a small point of light. A lamp or beacon ashore with a red filter over it to preserve night vision. It was this single point in the darkness that the launches had to aim for.

In spite of the pounding rain, the inky blackness and the choppy sea, the thing was eventually done. Ichiki's detachment was met by a small unit of Riekusentai who were stationed at Taivu Point. They assisted the men in retrieving the barrels of supplies, which included clothing and weapons for the army as well as additional food for the Naval infantry.

"Shall I organize a bivouac for the men, sir?" Major Kinjo asked.

Ichiki stood beneath a tent dripping and trying to review his maps and intelligence reports without getting them wet. At least the weather was warm enough that he wasn't shivering in his saturated clothing.

"Yes, let the men rest for a few hours," Ichiki said tersely. "Let them and their stomachs get used to land once again. However, we will be moving out after dawn. It is thirty-six kilometers to the Teneru River and the eastern American perimeter. I wish to cover the distance quickly without fatiguing the men before we attack."

"*Hai*," said Kinjo and bowed slightly.

"However," Ichiki raised a finger and met his assistant's eyes. "Alert Lieutenant Oshika to get *his* platoon ready to move. They may eat a light meal, and then I want them to march westward along the shoreline until dawn. They shall act as advanced observers and can radio back their findings."

Kinjo hesitated for a moment, not wishing to incur Ichiki's wrath, "Sir… Oshika and his men are fatigued as well."

"Are they?" Ichiki asked wryly. "Because from what I have observed over the past few days, they've seemed quite conspicuous for their *lack* of activity. Oshika is a spoiled brat, major. He comes from a wealthy family and is used to privilege and ease. The rest of the battalion knows this. It will be good for them to see Oshika and his men put to work… for once. See that it is done and tell him I expect that he makes at least twenty kilometers by sunup. He is, after all, marching along a *beach* with no obstruction. Unlike the rest of us."

Kinjo bowed again, "*Hai*."

Ichiki returned to his intelligence.

Not more than a hundred yards away, on a slight rise topped by a dense copse of vine-covered hardwoods and huge ferns, three men lay on their bellies and watched the camp. Or tried to watch it. Like the Japanese, their eyes were having no more luck with the dark and stormy night.

"Can't see a darned thing," Joe Treadway grumped. "And I swear something's crawling up my leg…."

"Least you don't smell like pee anymore, Joe," Webster Clayton teased.

"No, just B.O. and jungle rot," Jacob Vousa added with a snicker.

"Oh… I thought that was Old Spice," Clayton added.

"You guys suck… sirs," said Treadway.

Both of the other two men reached out and squeezed the young Marine's shoulder. They'd spent the last day moving east through the jungles, and Treadway had long since completely rinsed off his fatigues. Of course, the heavy downpour was keeping them moist and uncomfortable.

"They must have come ashore," Vousa said after a few more minutes. "Although I can't see anything. I swear I heard waves slapping against a hull a little while ago."

"Yeah…" Clayton said. "I'm sure you're right. I wish this damned rain would stop… least then we could *hear,* if not see something."

"This the romantic adventure you dreamed about while lounging behind your desk in Washington, sir?" Treadway jibed.

"Most definitely, Joe," Clayton said. "This and being aboard a submarine during a battle and going down way past test depth and almost suffocating. Oh, and Joe?"

"Yes sir?"

"Quit calling me sir."

"Yes sir."

Vousa chuckled and was about to make a comment when a heavy roll of thunder broke in on their conversation. They thought that was strange because even though the storm was fairly intense, there hadn't been any lightning in several hours.

From off toward the west and north, several flashes lit up the low clouds, and more thunderclaps rolled. A regular sort of staccato drumroll accompanied by bright orange-white flashes that partially lit up the Japanese camp before them.

"That's naval gunfire," Treadway stated. "Those damned DDs must be shelling Henderson and maybe Tulagi on their way back. Yellow bastards…"

"Why waste the ships, I guess…." Clayton muttered. "Do you fellas see that… are those men forming up on the beach?"

In the intermittent flashes, enough light reached Taivu Point to silhouette a group of perhaps thirty or forty men clumped together down by the water's edge. After a few minutes, the men appeared to line up in several columns and begin walking at a moderate pace westward along the shoreline.

Then, from the west, a huge and brilliant flash that outshone all that had come before it cast a pale moonlight glow over the entire camp before them. The flash seemed to pulse, darkened to orange and then red and fade away. Even as it did, a stupendous *booom* rolled over the sea, bringing with it a wind that briefly slackened the rainfall.

"What the hell was *that?*" Vousa asked in hushed awe.

"I'd say somebody wasn't pleased with the Japs bombarding them," Clayton said.

"Wonder what hit them?" Treadway asked.

Clayton grinned and couldn't help but chuckle, "Unless I miss my guess… something tells me that a Jap ship just got torpedoed by a certain submarine I know."

"We must report this," Vousa said after a moment's consideration.

"Radio's not strong enough from twenty-two miles, sir," Treadway advised.

"My home village isn't far from here," Vousa explained. "My wife has been keeping Martin's teleradio safe. Since we came down, he hasn't had a use for it, so he thought it'd be good to put it someplace where it might come in handy."

"How far is your village?" Clayton asked hopefully.

"Just a few miles," Vousa said. "We can rest for a few hours, get some hot food and then pursue the Japs."

SEALARK CHANNEL – 10 MINUTES EARLIER...

"Chet, what can you tell me?" Art Turner asked the sleepy sonarman.

The general alarm had gonged almost as soon as *Bull Shark* had passed between Savo and Florida Islands. The SJ radar, which had been sweeping constantly since the boat re-surfaced after her motor room repairs, had detected several ships in the Sealark Channel. Turner had known even as he rushed to the control room that they were probably too late to prevent a Japanese landing. The destroyers could travel at over thirty knots to his maximum of twenty-two.

Better late than never, however, the submarine had picked out no less than eight surface contacts on the distant horizon. Williams' tracking party had determined that the ships were probably close to Taivu Point. This required no great leap or feat of navigational legerdemain, as that seemed to be the Japs' preferred drop-off spot.

Once within ten miles or so, Turner had ordered the boat down to periscope depth and to proceed at one-third. In this way, the sonar technician could build a good sound profile and identify each ship. Turner then could determine which ones to hit, if any at all.

"I'd say they're all tin cans except one, sir," Rivers said. "Fast light screws, two apiece… but one ship has three."

"A cruiser," Joe Dutch opined from his place at the TDC.

"Or a modified cruiser," Turner said with a predatory gleam in his eye. "A strike carrier, perhaps."

"Are we gonna go after him, sir?" Hotrod Hernandez asked from the chart desk.

"Turner grinned, "Let me guess, Hotrod… it's customary in your primitive village of Long Beach for a lone submarine to attack no less than *eight* vessels with anti-submarine capability?"

"It does make all the *chicas* go *loco, señor capitan*."

Everyone laughed, and Turner only shook his head, "Smartassin'est boat in the goddamned Navy... and I'd agree with you, Hotrod... but we ain't got any girls around."

"Maybe Mr. Post can requisition us a few, hah?" Vigliano asked, getting another round of laughs.

"All right, children," Turner tried but didn't quite manage to sound stern. "Let's lock it up. We gotta take this seriously. There's supposed to be some kinda war on er somethin'."

On almost any other type of ship, and certainly in other navies, the casual banter that went on aboard a submarine and on *Bull Shark, in particular,* might seem not just unseemly but downright undisciplined. However, Art Turner had learned early on, thanks to a few hints from his friend and former instructor Dudley "Mush" Morton, that a happy sub was an effective sub. Letting the men joke around and blow off steam helped to take the edge off the tension and fear that, if left unchecked, could rapidly infect a crew. The men needed to be irreverent and puff out their chests a bit when going into battle. It helped them to survive.

Submarine warfare was, in some ways, unlike any other kind. Each type of fighting, be it air to air combat, large infantry clashes, hand to hand fighting or big surface ships lobbing massive shells at one another, had its unique aspects, but they also had something in common. Most types of warfare allowed men to take an active role in fighting back.

While it was certainly true that in an offensive evolution, every man on a boat took an active role. This was true for a torpedo or gun action. However, a submarine was also subject to depth charge attacks. This was a completely defensive evolution.

During such attacks, the men had no choice but to sit quietly below the surface of the sea and take a beating. They remained still, often in the dark, while the sea pressed in on them and the enemy dropped bombs all around their ears. The fear during such operations was perhaps no greater than that faced by a pilot or soldier... yet it was unique unto itself.

The psychological trauma from underwater attacks could and had turned even the strongest men into blubbering piles of terror. So many elements combined in the mind to induce a horror such as no other warrior faced.

"I've got some numbers, Captain," Chet Rivers said. "I believe I've identified several groups of ships. Looks like they're underway now."

"Very well, Chet, give the XO what you've got," Turner said.

Rivers explained that there were three distinct groups of vessels. Although from the distance of just over eight miles away, it was hard to make out individual ships when close together, he could hear three different groups. One was moving north by northwest in the direction of Tulagi. Another seemed to be hugging the Guadalcanal coast, and the third was moving slowly eastward and would either pass between Guadalcanal and San Christabel or just north of San Christabel Island.

"That last one consists of a single DD and the three-blader, sir," Rivers reported. "Moving off at eight knots."

'Hmm... we'll never catch them unless we surface or they turn around," Turner mused. "Wonder why those other DDs are... Chet, which group is closer?"

"The Guadalcanal group," Rivers said. "Four ships, all DDs and making twenty-five knots."

"Designate that as Able group," Turner said. "Give me an intercept course."

Rivers listened for a moment, "Able is bearing... three-five zero... headed two-eight-five... range fourteen thousand yards, sir."

Hotrod jotted the numbers down, "Course one-five-five is good intercept, sir, if we kick it up to five knots."

"You heard it from the horse's mouth, Mug," Turner said, forcing his voice to remain cool and calm. He always seemed to get a jolt of energy when conning an approach and attack. Yet he also knew that it was important for the men to see him as cool and collected. "Come right to course one-five-five. All ahead two-thirds, make turns for five knots."

"Maneuvering answerin' two-thirds," Mug replied. "Sir, my rudduh is right full... comin' round to one-five-five."

"Maneuvering acknowledges five knots," Dutch said. He had a sound-powered telephone around his neck and could also act as conning tower phone talker.

"Very well," Turner said casually and reached into his shirt pocket for a pack of smokes. In a pique of embarrassment, he realized that he didn't even *have* a shirt pocket, as he'd come to the conning tower in his skivvies and undershirt.

Dutch noticed and flashed him a grin. The temporary torpedo officer held out a pack of Lucky Strikes and a lighter, "Brought these from the wardroom on my way up, Art."

"God bless you, Joseph," Turner said sheepishly and lit up. "And if you tell anybody ashore that I keep misplacing my butts, I'll bust you down to Lieutenant so fast you'll wish your father had never met your mother."

The men around snickered and muffled their laughter. Dutch grinned, "I ain't no stoolie, Art."

"Okay then," Turner said and puffed. "Joe, alert both rooms to open outer doors. Not sure if we'll need the after room, but with so many targets, one never knows. Have them set the depth on all fish to four feet, speed fast."

It was an admirably short amount of time before Sparky and Murph both had their phone talkers report ready. Joe reported this even as the ten ready-fire indicator lights glowed on the torpedo fire control board.

"That's some good work, Joe," Turner said. "You keep that up, and you'll make Lieutenant in no time."

The men all laughed again. They were in high spirits and were excited. No evident fear, no trepidation. Just eager and ready to do their duty. This in spite of the fact that the boat wasn't going up against some tankers or freighters.

They were attacking fellow predators. Destroyers. Ships specially designed as offensive weapons. Both to hunt down and sink surface targets, as well as persecute submarines.

Generally speaking, a submarine's job was to locate merchant shipping convoys and sink them. To deprive the enemy of vital supplies. A single oil tanker or cargo ship was, to the Navy, worth half a dozen warships. It was common doctrine for submarines to actually *avoid* engaging warships simply because their limited weaponry could be deployed in far more effective ways.

It was common, however, for convoys to be escorted by destroyers or light cruisers. Even in these cases, though, the submarine's job was to take out as many merchant ships as possible and then run away. This sometimes resulted in heavy depth-charging by the escorts.

Now, though, *Bull Shark* was *intentionally* going after ships designed to sink her. On one hand, it was a satisfying bit of payback… yet on the other, the dangers were all too clear. If it was hard to evade a single DD or perhaps two tin cans working in tandem… how hard would it be to escape from six or eight of them?

Although not rigged for silence, the boat was quiet. So, when the sea seemed to thrum around them repeatedly, it did not go unnoticed. Turner frowned for a moment and then cursed.

"Up scope," he said and snapped the handles of the search scope down to confirm what his ears were telling him. "Dammit! They're shelling the island! Probably the airfield… son of a bitch. Mug, all ahead full. Ten degrees left. One good thing is that the bastards are making it easy to spot them. Down search, up attack, Radar."

Ted Balkley was acting periscope assistant. He hit the appropriate buttons, and Turner peered through the attack scope's eyepiece.

"Okay… he looks fairly close," Turner said. "And those gun flashes are lighting him up… no flashless powder tonight… what've you got, Chet?"

"Muddy sound profile at this speed, sir," Rivers said. "But I think about three-thousand yards. Speed appears down to six knots, though."

Turner cursed as he watched the scene before him. Four tin cans, all in a line, slowly cruising along the beach and lobbing five-inch shells at Henderson Field. And as it was dark, there was little the airfield could do to defend themselves. Too dark to get aircraft up, and although they had anti-aircraft batteries, they didn't have any significant shore-defense guns to speak of. Certainly, nothing that compared to the combined twenty guns of the destroyers.

"Art, why not use the snorkel?" Williams' head said as it popped up through the control room hatch.

Turner snapped his fingers. He often dismissed the super-secret, nobody else has it, and nobody will for years device that had been clandestinely installed aboard his boat. It seemed so alien to use the diesels while submerged. And the thing was so often useless under certain combat or weather conditions.

"Right you are, Elmer," Turner said. "Frank, open main induction, start the rock crushers. Also, get me to radar depth. Can't risk running on top with so many DDs about... but we're gonna take a few down."

There was a clang as the main induction valve, which was connected to the telescoping snorkel, opened and allowed fresh air to be drawn into the boat. Soon after, four rumbles fired off in quick succession, and the entire submarine vibrated with the strength of over five-thousand horsepower, generating more than five *million* watts of electricity.

"Mug, maintain ahead full," Turner said. "Ted, get Joe some numbers on that leading tin can. Let's see if we cut the head off, the snake will die."

"Bendix log indicates eighteen knots," Vigliano said.

"That's more like it!" Turner announced.

"Range to first target is two-six-zero-zero yards," Balkley said as he studied his SJ surface search radar screens. "Bearing three-four-three."

"What's our preferred shooting range, sir?" Dutch asked as he began to crank values into the torpedo data computer.

"Better make it close," Turner said. "Eight hundred yards. We'll give him tubes one and two, pivot around to the north and floor it. Maybe we can catch those other Nips giving Tulagi a hard time."

As he spoke, Turner spun completely around and searched the black night. To their north, he could see gun flashes from the vicinity of Tulagi. They were probably fifteen miles away, at least. Even at emergency speed, which was even slightly faster than flank and the most that the boat's propulsion system could give, it'd take *Bull Shark* forty minutes to cover that distance. A helluva lot could happen in forty minutes.

"Think they'll see us running like this?" Dutch asked his friend and captain.

"Doubt it," Turner said. "In this soup? Even if they do... it'd be a brave and foolhardy Jap indeed who went up against the mighty Joe Dutch and his *evil* TDC."

Dutch chuckled, "Evil? Nah, that's Pat's deal. I'm a kinder and gentler torpedo officer."

"What's the difference, sir?" Hotrod asked wryly.

"I'll still blow you outta the water," Dutch said. "But I'll smile when I do it."

"Well, get your chompers ready then, Joe," Turner said. "We've got about two minutes until we're in range. Take your data from radar, and I'll backstop Teddy with an asparagus stick observation."

The two minutes seemed to creep by as if it were hours. Finally, however, the range reached a thousand yards, and Turner ordered Vigliano to slow to one-third. Balkley gave Dutch another set of readings, and Turner focused his targeting reticule on the destroyer's foremast.

"Looks like a *Fubuki*," the Captain reported. "Final bearing… mark."

"Three-five-five,' Hotrod said.

"Angle on the bow is starboard eighty-five," Turner reported and adjusted his stadimeter knob. "Range… eight-five-zero yards."

"Matches with radar," Dutch said. "Set. Shoot anytime, sir!"

"Fire one!" Turner said, unable to keep the excitement from his voice now. After six seconds, he said: "Fire two!"

The boat juddered as the two ton-and-a-half, twenty-foot-long torpedoes were ejected from inside her by a column of high-pressure air. As the fish moved out of the tubes, their steam engines were started, and they quickly accelerated to their maximum speed of forty-six knots.

Inside the boat, the men worked their jaws, having to clear their ears from the small but significant pressure of the impulse air being gulped back inside the pressure hull by the torpedo tubes' poppet valves.

"Hard right rudder, helm… all ahead flank!" Turner ordered.

The ship heeled slightly to the port side as she swung her bow to the right. The powerful diesels once again revving up as they spun the generators that drove the massive currents of energy into the four GE electric motors.

"Seventy-five seconds to impact," Dutch reported.

"Both fish running hot, straight and normal, sir," Rivers added.

"Mug, bring us around to zero-one-zero," Turner stated.

"We're not gonna set up on another one?" Duch asked.

Williams was once again half-visible in the hatchway. He met Turner's gaze and nodded. He understood the captain's motivation, and Turner was giving him permission to explain while he observed the kill.

"We're just trying to scare them off now, Joe," Williams stated. "We need to save our limited number of weapons to sink these ships when they're *on the way* here, not leaving the area."

Dutch nodded grimly, "Right… we're here to kill soldiers, not sailors."

"As grim as that sounds… it's true," Turner said. "I'd rather sink a ship full of soldiers and supplies. That's what we're here to do. Okay, here she comes…."

There was an audible *thwack-boom* as the torpedo struck the leading destroyer just under the focs'l. The nearly seven-hundred-pound Torpex warhead ignited and blasted the ship's bow into a raging angry red-orange fireball. As Turner watched, awed as always by the destruction, the second torpedo struck amidships, and the entire ship lurched, heeling to port and then heaved upward in the middle as if being bent by a giant's hand. This was, in fact, accurate. The giant being brutal physics. The ship's starboard boiler had been hit and exploded in a tremendous thundering blast that vibrated all the way through the fleeing submarine. Within a minute, no more, the ship was gone, leaving only a few bits of flaming debris in the sea and perhaps some dying men.

The attack did have its desired effect. The remaining vessels, even those off by Tulagi, broke off their shore bombardment. They went to flank speed and ran up to thirty-four knots, rapidly heading back in the direction of Rabaul.

"Mug, all ahead-one-third," Turner ordered, both elated and humbled by the destruction his orders had wrought. "Frank, put number one on charge and let's prowl around here for a bit. I'd like to see what the *Sakai,* if that was her, is up to. When the DDs run out of radar range, we'll rig for surface and follow the last known course of the eastern group. Stand down from battle stations, Elmer. Smoking lamp is lit and have the galley serve the men up some coffee, and let's see about getting the morning meal underway. Something tells me that Sato isn't going to hang around and wait for us… not this time."

16

NEW GEORGIA SOUND – NORTHEAST OF SAN CHRISTABEL ISLAND
AUGUST 20, 1942 – 1130 LOCAL TIME

Lieutenant Pat Jarvis and Chief Harry Brannigan ducked into the maneuvering room and were immediately assaulted by the smells of burnt rubber, melted wiring and hydraulic fluid. The room was in something of a shambles as the electrical crew worked to repair storm damage and set the boat back to rights.

"Welcome to the show, Mr. Jarvis," Chief Paul Cantone said from his customary perch at the control cubicle. "Come to help mop up, have ya', sir?"

"Looks like you've got it in hand, Chief," Jarvis said pleasantly. The smart-mouthed SOB bugged him, but Jarvis was determined not to let it show. "How we doin' back here anyway? Ready to take on the Japs or what?"

"Oh yes sir," Cantone replied cheerfully. "You gonna go up on deck and take 'em on all by yourself, XO?"

"What's that crack supposed to mean?" Brannigan asked with narrowed eyes.

Cantone grinned, "Way I keep hearin' it, our XO here is a one-man wreckin' machine, Chief. Probably wants to lay alongside a Jap tin can and carry her by boarding, eh sir?"

Jarvis grinned back, but Brannigan could see that the humor was not reflected in his eyes. They were flinty, "I'm not opposed to it, Chief. You in?"

"I'll go where I'm needed, sir," Cantone hedged.

"Uh-huh," Jarvis needled. "Accept up on deck during a gun action, huh, Chief? Leave that to other guys, right?"

Brannigan had to school his face. This was the first time he'd seen Jarvis' cool crack. The first time the lieutenant let some of his pique show at this crew's disdain and nearly open insubordination. Brannigan admired how the XO had elected to let the wrinkles iron themselves out, but he could see that Jarvis' patience had just about reached its limit.

Cantone flushed, and his own eyes turned to steel, "Not sure what you mean, *sir*."

"Oh, just think it's kinda funny, is all," Jarvis said. "How your XO, your COB and even your *former* leading petty from the torpedo room went up on deck to help out… but you were back here the whole time."

There were half a dozen men in the room or down in the motor room who overheard this, and to a man, they snickered. Even the ones that were in the S-52 boys club who didn't like the new XO or his COB.

"Why do I feel like you're implying something, *sir?*" Cantone asked with barely contained anger. "Somebody's got to be back here to drive the boat, sir."

"Yeah, that's right, Chief," Jarvis said with superficial good humor. "You stay back here and drive the boat. But be ready because we're about to enter The Slot, and I can tell you from *experience* that it's awfully lively out here."

"We're always ready, sir," Cantone said stiffly.

"Good," Jarvis said cheerfully. "Because I intend to take this boat into harm's way, Chief. Into battle, that is. Not into a goddamned hurricane just for fun. We're goin' after Jap tin cans. It's dangerous, fast work. I hope you're up for it."

Everyone who heard understood perfectly what the comment about the storm meant. Cantone, as one of Waters' staunchest supporters, did not take it well. His face was now bright crimson with rage, and he stood to attention.

"That's up to the *captain*, sir," Cantone said tersely. "I don't think I like what you're gettin' at, sir."

Jarvis met his eyes, "I'm not getting at anything, Chief. Just that we all need to be ready for what's comin'. Ain't that right, COB?"

Brannigan grinned as well, "Yes sir, Mr. Jarvis. We've both been through some shit out here. Took down a Jap freighter and big *Fubuki*, played cat and mouse with another *Fubuki*... and hell, went up against a damned carrier task force and came out intact. Including being stuck on the bottom for over a day after being ashcanned by a couple of pretty pissed-off Nip DDs, huh Mr. Jarvis?"

Jarvis nodded, "It's dicey out here, that's for sure, COB. But a good boat and a good crew can do wonders. That sound like you fellas?"

All the men either cheered or made some form of affirmation. Most of the crew aboard S-52 had been with her a long time and were firmly in the captain's camp. They admired him. Yet this new officer and Chief of the Boat were already war heroes, and their enthusiasm and their abilities intrigued the men.

That Mr. Jarvis had risked his neck to save a lookout's life the day before had not gone unnoticed. Although the hard-liners still looked at the new officer and COB with a wary eye, their respect for Jarvis had gone up a point or two. Of course, certain holdouts like Cantone would probably never come around, but that was life.

"All right, carry on then," Jarvis said and turned to leave. "Oh, and one more thing, Chief."

Cantone had just taken his seat again, and he looked up at the XO with a face of stone. Brannigan got the impression that the chief electrician's mate didn't trust himself to speak.

"When's the last time those fish were routined?" Jarvis asked, pointing at the two reloads for the boat's single stern tube.

"Day after we left port, sir," Cantone said defensively. "As per your *orders*, sir."

Jarvis nodded, "Good... how about the one in the tube?"

Cantone flushed again. He cleared his throat. He was well aware of how spit and polish Jarvis was when it came to the ship's weapons. Being a torpedo officer, that was his usual job, after all.

"Not since it were loaded in, sir," the Chief admitted. "Probably been a week now."

"It should've been routined along with the others, Chief," Jarvis chided gently. "Gooch and his boys did all of theirs."

Although the rebuke was delivered without rancor, it still stung Cantone. It stung because he'd gotten caught out in being derelict in his duties. He knew damned well that the loaded pickle should've been pulled and routine checks and maintenance performed. Yet he'd failed to have it done, hoping that he wouldn't be asked. His former captain and XO never bothered to double-check him. Even Mr. Savage, the boat's torpedo officer, left such details up to the men in the rooms.

"Yes sir," was all Cantone could say. "It's just we got busy with other jobs...."

"I hear ya', chief... but I'm sure you can find the time now. Let's see that done now then," Jarvis stated. "Have that fish pulled, re-lubed, re-fueled, the whole bit. After that storm, I want to make sure we're ship-shape. Wouldn't want a dud fish, would we, Chief?"

"No sir," Cantone said.

"Good," Jarvis stated. "I'll let you get to it then."

The XO ducked through the hatch and into the engine room, leaving behind a seething Cantone. As soon as Jarvis and the COB had gone, Cantone all but exploded.

"Fuckin' prick..." Cantone seethed.

"He likes shit done right," torpedoman's mate third-class Jack Branson commented as he began checking the tube's pressure in preparation to open it. "Ain't that right, Jimmy?"

Jimmy Kintner chuckled, "Sure as hell did something right yesterday. Saved my ass plain and simple."

Cantone scoffed, "You two are new here. So I get why you'd think our new XO is a big wheel. But this boat's been through a lot, and she's got a lot of water under her keel. I do things the way my *captain* wants them done."

"Now you do them the way your new XO wants them done," said

Harry Brannigan's voice as he ducked back into the room. "You got a lotta balls, Chief, talkin' to him that way."

Cantone felt freer to talk now that there was no officer present, "Hey, I been on this boat for years, Chief. Frankly, I been a *chief* longer'n you have. So, I don't need no jumped up fuckin—"

In three quick strides, Brannigan crossed the deck, grabbed Cantone by his dungaree shirt and yanked him off the bench. He pivoted and slammed him up against the frame that surrounded the control cubicle. Brannigan was just under six feet and had a medium build, although plenty of defined muscle. He glared into the other electrician's eyes for a long moment.

"I don't' know who the *fuck* you think you are, Chief," Brannigan snarled. "You're damned lucky that that man up forward has some self-control. He might not kick your ass for ya', but I will. You *ever* talk to him like that again, and you and me are gonna tangle. And after I beat the snot outta ya', I'm gonna bring you up for a captain's mast on insubordination charges. You *got* that?"

"Hey, I don't need this guy comin' into my room and bustin' my balls," Cantone flared back unwisely. Although Brannigan had twenty pounds on Cantone, the latter grew up on the streets and had confidence in his ability to fight. Of course, Brannigan was the COB, and it wouldn't do to mix it up with him.

"He wouldn't need to bust your little nuts if you'd do your fuckin' job *right*," Brannigan pressed. "You knew that fish wasn't maintained. You ignored the order and left it untouched on purpose. That cuz you're just lazy, or did you do it out of spite?"

"You two assholes think you're hot shits, dontcha?" Cantone shot back, his temper fraying. "You come onto our boat and start makin' changes, alterin' routines and tryin' to show us up. Just cuz your skipper gets a few lucky breaks don't mean you're such hot shit. No matter what that wet behind the ears ninety-day wonder Skaggs thinks."

"Oh yeah?" Brannigan pushed. "You got it all figured out, huh? Then how come your skipper went out on three patrols, and this boat didn't bag so much as a sampan? And on that last one, you got lucky. Had to fight topside cuz you couldn't run away fast enough."

"Hey fuck you, Brannigan!" Cantone said, seeing red now.

Brannigan knew he was pushing the man too far, but he didn't care. He needed to hear the truth, and Brannigan wanted to see what he'd do, "Yeah, fuck me… but least my boat ain't loaded with cowards. Yeah, you heard me. I heard what happened that night your XO was taken out. Heard how he fucked up and was warned about the Japs but didn't pay no attention. I also heard that you guys could've taken down that DD had you only acted faster. Word is that *somebody* froze up when showtime arrived."

"You mother *fucker!*" Cantone brought up his hands to smash them into Brannigan's gut.

The COB saw it coming, of course. Knew that he was pushing Cantone into folly. He simply stepped back and sideways to avoid the short blow and rammed one of his own hard fists into the man's gut. Cantone doubled over and groaned, trying to gasp for air. The rest of the men in the room simply froze, waiting and watching to see what would happen next.

"You been warned, Cantone," Brannigan said dangerously. "One more smart-ass remark, one more insubordinate crack, and you're on report. I'll have that chief's hat stripped off and bust you back down to apprentice, you understand me?"

"You ain't gonna report this now?" Branson asked.

"Nah, I know I rode him too hard," Brannigan said. "But he had it comin'. Mr. Jarvis don't back down, boys. He don't run from a fight or hesitate. And he sure as shit expects all of us to do our jobs and then some. Why… you get with the program, and this boat might not just come back; it *might* come back with the kind of reputation you want. You don't get with the program… well, God help ya'."

Pat Jarvis had a few quick words with Chief Lockner in the engine room. Lockner, although one of the old S-52s, had a more circumspect attitude. He preferred to judge a man by what he saw, not by reputation or the opinions of others. Jarvis and he seemed able to work together smoothly without the kind of tension that crackled between himself and Cantone.

As the XO moved forward, he noticed Brannigan duck away and move aft again. The XO smiled to himself, knowing full well what the COB was about. He'd personally wanted to smack the mouthy bastard upside his head but thought that in this case, such measures were best handled by the Chief of the Boat.

In the torpedo room, Jarvis found Chris Savage speaking with Harvey Gooch, the leading petty who ran the room. The two men stood between the four torpedo tubes talking in low tones. Around them, the men who lived there lounged in their bunks while those on duty inspected loading gear and were in the process of inspecting one torpedo's tail assembly.

"Attention on deck," Gooch called out when he saw the XO come through the hatch.

"As you were," Jarvis said, holding up a hand. "Don't let me interrupt anything, Gooch. Just makin the rounds before taking my trick at the wheel. How're things up here?"

"You can see for yourself, sir," Savage said, just a hint of irritation in his voice. "Room's ready for action."

Jarvis sighed slightly. Here was another hard case he'd never win over. He missed *Bull Shark*.

"Never had any doubt of it," Jarvis said. "What's with number fifteen there?"

Gooch, who didn't seem to mind Jarvis' appearance, smiled thinly. Like Skaggs and Kintner and a few other men, Gooch was new to S-52. He'd replaced John Kench, who'd been killed on the last patrol by the Jap survivors. Gooch had actually served with Jarvis on the old S-33 when she was in the Med. That was nearly eight years earlier, though. Jarvis had been a wet behind the ears ensign and Gooch a torpedoman second-class. Yet even then, Gooch had seen the makings of a fine officer and knew Jarvis to be a top-notch sailor.

"Last routine I didn't like the looks of the props," Gooch said. "Last routine, we swapped out the fish in the tubes with those in the racks. That way, we could make sure every one of these pickles was 4-O, sir."

"Good thinkin'," Jarvis grinned. "Glad Mr. Savage here is on top of you boys. I got a feeling we're gonna be calling for your talents, fellas. We're just about to—"

Jarvis's pronouncement was interrupted by the click and hiss of the 1MC general address channel opening. The captain's voice echoed through the ship.

"*Attention all hands,*" Waters announced. "*This is the captain. We have just officially entered New Georgia Sound. We're just to the northeast of San Christabel Island. Some of you may know that San Christabel is the next one down from Guadalcanal. We're going to head up The Slot until dark and hopefully either meet up with* Bull Shark *or catch a couple of Japs between us. We got a good boat and a good crew. Focus on your jobs, and we'll get through this and maybe even come back with a couple of Tojo's scalps on our belts. God bless. That is all.*"

A round of applause and muted cheers rose up through the boat. They were good words. Jarvis only hoped that they weren't just that… that Waters hadn't really lost his nerve as the rumors had it.

"Well, glad we're all set up here," Jarvis continued. "As I was about to say, we're in Indian country now. Thanks for all your efforts, boys."

Jarvis ducked out and headed aft. It was nearly time for him to assume the watch.

"Stand by for hourly observation," Jarvis said.

He was standing by the periscopes in S-52's cramped conning tower. Chief Brannigan, acting quartermaster of the watch, stood at the DRT repeater with a maneuvering board. Every few minutes, he'd go below and cross-check his notes with the master plot on the gyrocompass table and the master dead reckoning tracer. He would also spend half his time below in the control room at the duty chief's desk, updating logs and taking care of other issues related to ship operations and personnel issues.

Jarvis would have preferred to run on top. Generally, this wasn't done aboard a submarine on patrol. The boat was too easy to spot during the day. A submarine usually operated on the surface during night hours where she could get more speed from her diesels and recharge her batteries. During the day, the boat stayed below and out of sight. Should she detect a target, of course, she'd work up to it submerged, or if possible, surface and get out in front of a convoy and then re-submerge for an attack.

However, the waters around the Sealark Channel were primarily controlled by the Allies during the daytime. Japanese ships operated in and dominated the area by night. The only exception was during the almost daily Tojo Time air raids on Tulagi and Henderson Field. Then, a surfaced submarine could be vulnerable to attack. However, S-52 was currently fifty miles from Lunga Point and making only three knots. Far to the east of the hot zone. Jarvis did not expect to make any contacts this far out and by day.

"Diving officer, bring us to periscope depth," Jarvis ordered. "Minimal rise on the planes. Sonar, anything out there?"

Bobby Gaines fiddled with his gear. Unfortunately, S-52's sonar systems weren't quite up to *Bull Shark's* standard. Although they'd been upgraded more than once, the gear was still a few years old and didn't quite have the range or power as newer equipment.

"Uhm…" Gaines frowned and fiddled with his directional knob.

Jarvis stepped over to lean over his shoulder and look at the magic eye display, "Something, sonar?"

"Can't quite tell, sir…." Gaines muttered, still fiddling. "I think there *might* be something out there… but it's really faint."

"Can you get a direction on it, at least?" Jarvis asked.

Gaines turned up the volume on his headphones as far as it would go and used the direction knob to rotate the JP sound head through a complete rotation, "Whatever it is, it's somewhere between one-two-zero and one-six-zero relative, sir. Best I can do now. It *sort of* sounds like machinery…."

"Okay, then let's see what we can do about that," Jarvis said. "Harry, bring us around to starboard by one-four-zero degrees. Increase speed to four knots. Let's see if we can't edge a little closer to this, whatever it is."

Brannigan met Jarvis' eye, "Skipper's order book states we're to maintain two-eight-five, sir."

Jarvis smiled ever so slightly, "Yeah, I know, Harry. But we're also supposed to locate Japs."

Brannigan nodded and turned forward, "Helmsman, right standard rudder. Come to course zero-six-five. All ahead two-thirds. Phone talker… maneuvering, conning. Make turns for four knots."

Orders were acknowledged, and charts were marked. The ship turned slowly toward the northeast and slightly increased her speed. After another ten minutes or so, Gaines spun around in his chair excitedly.

"Contact!" he exclaimed. "Definite surface contacts bearing zero-one-zero, sir! Range… sixteen thousand yards, possible multiples. Screw noise is garbled so far, but at least one, maybe two ships out there, sir!"

Brannigan laid a hand on the young man's shoulder, "Take it easy, kid. No need to get excited. Just routine."

"Yes Chief…" Gaines said, but he was obviously keyed up.

"All right then," Jarvis said calmly. He slipped on a rain jacket that hung from a peg on the bulkhead and pulled a floppy rain hat on as well. "COB, give me the search scope if you please."

Brannigan hit the button that raised the search scope. As it rose, Jarvis snapped the handles down, and Brannigan stopped it just when the eyepiece was at the right level for a man six-feet two inches in height. From above, water began to drip around the edges of the periscope barrel. Rather a lot of water, the COB thought.

Jarvis stepped up and pressed his eye to the rubberized viewer, reaching up to make sure the brim of the rain hat was turned up so that water would at least flow down and away.

"Humid today," the XO muttered absently as a trickle of seawater dripped onto his head and flowed down his back and shoulders. He rotated the scope slightly to starboard and cursed. "God *dammit*… it's fogged! Well… it's not a total gray out… I can kind of see… I might have smoke on the horizon… ought to see at least a stick by now… Lutz, get the plotting party assigned if you please."

"Are we going to battle stations, Exec?" Lutz asked in his odd semi-detached way.

"Not sure yet, Crawford," Jarvis said, shaking his head to help the water along. "Need to identify what's out there… wait, I see something… looks like a mast just peeking over the hill. Christ…

down scope, Harry. Let's give it a few minutes and try the attack scope."

"Shall I alert the skipper, Mr. Jarvis?" Lutz asked as he poked his head through the hatchway. "If enemy ships are in sight…."

"Let's wait to be sure, engineer," Jarvis replied. "I'd hate to bug him for nothing."

"Sound profile is getting better, XO," Gaines said. He was in the habit of younger sailors who referred to the first officer as XO rather than Exec. "Range now fourteen thousand yards, turn rate indicates four knots. That's weird. Awfully slow…"

"Yeah…" Jarvis mumbled. "Hmm… let's try the attack scope, COB."

The slimmer attack scope rose, and Jarvis stepped up to it. Like the search scope, this one leaked. It leaked even more profusely than its sibling. By the time Jarvis looked through the eyepiece and adjusted his focus, there was a visible puddle around his sandals.

"That's better,' he said. "Thing leaks worse, but the optics are clean… Okay, definite mast, and I see a bow coming up over the… wait a *minute*… that's a square bow… holy hell! It's a flat top! There's a damned carrier out there, and I think he's got an escort DD. Yup, there he is; might be an *Asashio!* What've you got, sonar?"

"Definite multiples," Gaines said, trying to rein in his ebullience. Jarvis wondered if this might be the first time the kid had ever been in combat or been tracking a real enemy. "I've got twin light screws, that's the tin can for sure… and three heavier screws. Gotta be the carrier… weird, though. I thought carriers all had four props."

Jarvis chuckled and rubbed his hands together. He looked over at the COB to see that realization had dawned on Brannigan as well, "They do, sonar… except for strike carriers built on cruiser hulls. I'll bet dollars to navy beans that's *Sakai* out there."

"Wow…" Brannigan said. "Wonder why she's out here all alone?"

"Might be trying to find our carriers or just biding her time, like before," Jarvis said. "But it appears as if the angle on the bow is port three-three-zero. She's gonna cut right across our path. COB, plotting party, give me a good intercept course. I want to get within a thousand yards. They're serving themselves up on a silver platter, boys. Walking straight into our jaws. S-52 is about to bag a flattop! Mr. Lutz, sound the general alarm. Chief of the watch, on the 1MC… battle stations torpedo!"

The sound of the cathedral bells began to gong through the ship. Brannigan grabbed for the communications handset slung from the overhead and selected the general alert circuit.

"Chief of the watch on the 1MC," he intoned loudly so as to be heard over the alarm. "All hands to battle stations! All hands to battle stations! This is not a drill. Battle stations torpedo. Have sighted Japanese carrier and escort!"

"Down scope," Jarvis said. "Messenger of the watch, please alert the captain… as if he doesn't already know."

That got a round of laughs from the men in the conning tower. The energy around Jarvis had rapidly gone from quiet professionalism to tense excitement. Their boat was about to attack a major target, and the man currently at the con not only had experience but had faced off with this very ship before.

Something nagged at Jarvis, though. Something about the speed of the ships. He was about to make a note of it when Salty Waters ascended the ladder from the control room.

"You ordering an attack on your own authority, Exec?" Waters asked tensely.

"Got *Sakai* and her escort in our sights, sir," Jarvis reported, stepping back from the scope. "See for yourself. It's your call, of course, but I figured better ready than not."

"Sir, that course is zero-four-five," Brannigan said after checking his notes.

"Concur," said a man from below. Jarvis thought it was the chief yeoman.

"Sir?" the helmsman turned to look at the captain, his face clearly beaming with eagerness.

"Just a moment, boys," Waters said. "What's their course and speed, Mr. Jarvis?"

"Four knots, headed about three-hundred sir," Jarvis reported.

"Why so slow?" Waters asked. "Doesn't that seem suspicious?"

Jarvis snapped his fingers, "Yes it does… when we first sighted them back in early August, sir, they were doing the same shtick. Moving slow during the day. Turned out that a Jap submarine was hovering below their keels."

"And knowing this, you're just going to take us into battle under potentially the same conditions?" Waters asked incredulously. "Work us in nice and close so that a Jap sub can send *her* fish at us?"

"Sir... it's a high-value target of opportunity," Jarvis said. "We should easily be able to evade any Japanese fish and the reward—"

"Let me have a look," Waters snapped. "Up attack scope, COB."

Jarvis slipped out of the rain gear and handed it over to the captain. Waters slipped it on and took his position behind the scope. He looked through the eyepiece for a long few seconds and then stepped back.

"Down scope," he said. "I don't like it. Smells a lot like a trap to me."

"They can't know we're out here, sir," Jarvis protested.

"Your own reports say she's got ASW capability," Waters argued. "She's probably hearing our engines right now. Who's to say her submarine escort isn't even now calculating a firing solution on *us*. Those two surface ships would mask her screw noise nicely. No... no, Exec. I know you're hot for blood, but we're not gonna put the ship in jeopardy just to satisfy your thirst for glory."

"Sir!" Jarvis snapped to full attention. "I must protest that! It sounds a great deal like a personal character assassination."

Waters frowned at him, "Can't take a little criticism, Exec, then you're in the wrong business. I've seen guys like you all my career. So gung-ho. So ready to rush in, and so often, it gets other men killed. Maybe you ought to open yourself up to a little advice now and then from people with more experience. I've been in this game ten more years than you have, Exec. I know a few things, too. And I know when one of my officers is a little too eager and isn't looking at all the facts."

Jarvis felt rage bubbling up inside him, and it was taking a mighty effort to maintain some semblance of professional calm, "Sir, again, I protest. I'm simply trying to do my duty. I'm not glory-hunting. That is a high-value target specifically listed as one we should be on the lookout for. The setup is easy, and I felt it was appropriate to take offensive action, *sir*."

"I do not concur, Exec," Waters said. "COB, stand down from battle stations. Captain has the con. If it'll soothe you, Exec, we'll dive down and pass under them. That way, Gaines here can hear if a sub is using the carrier as a hat or not. Once we *know* the situation, we can then make an *intelligent* decision based on *facts*."

Jarvis' face was hot with anger and humiliation, "Aye-aye, sir. Permission to assist the plotting party as I'm not needed here, sir."

"Granted," Waters said, stepping back and removing the rain gear. Just before Jarvis' head disappeared below the rim of the hatch, the captain said: "Oh, and by the way, Mr. Jarvis… I'd expect that a man who's willing to criticize my chiefs would at least be open to a little advice himself."

Jarvis didn't trust himself to speak. He only continued down the ladder. Just before going below the hatch combing, he met Brannigan's eyes, and the look in them appeared as angry as Jarvis himself felt.

17
NORAMBAO VILLAGE, GUADALCANAL – BETWEEN TAIVU AND COLI POINTS
AUGUST 20, 1942 – 1715 LOCAL TIME

Webster Clayton awoke feeling as if he'd gone a dozen rounds with Willie Pep. His whole body ached, and he was drenched in sweat. He groaned and rolled to a sitting position, surprised to find himself on a pallet of pleasantly soft coir, covered in a blanket.

He rubbed his eyes and glanced at his watch, shocked to find that it was well after five in the afternoon! Upon reflection, however, it shouldn't have surprised him. He, Vousa and Treadway had been going almost non-stop for several days. What little sleep they'd had was caught in brief snatches between taking turns watching over one another.

After seeing the night naval battle and the Japanese platoon heading west along the beach, Vousa had led the three of them to his new home village of Norambao. The village was located about halfway between Taivu Point and Coli Point and only a few miles from Aola. Set up somewhat inland on a gently rolling hill at the edge of the northern plains, Norambao, like so many villages, had direct access to a small, swift-running stream. The fast water meant no crocodiles and that the water was good to drink.

The village was of a fairly large size for Guadalcanal. Perhaps a hundred people lived there in something better than average conditions. There was no electricity, of course, except for a small generator that stood outside the headman's house to be used for a radio on occasion. The homes were of typical thatched-roof Guadalcanal style, raised off the ground on stout hardwood pillars with bamboo and palm wood walls. Unlike some villages they'd seen, however, these homes often had more than one room, shuttered windows, and almost every one had a front or back porch, depending on their position, on which people could sit in the evenings when it was cooler.

The hut in which Clayton currently found himself was a simple one-room affair with two cots and a small table. It was used as a guest cottage, Vousa had said. As the OSS man rubbed the heavy sleep from his eyes, he took note that Treadway's cot was already empty. He also noted that some rather delicious smells were wafting in through his partially open door, and his stomach was rumbling in anticipation.

He stepped out into the open and blinked in the bright sunshine. The heavy storm of the night and early morning had passed, leaving in its wake a cloudless sky and pleasant breeze. Clayton began to walk around the village, searching for the only two people he knew.

Norambao was arranged in a roughly circular fashion, with private homes encircling a communal area complete with a large firepit and a sort of pavilion for gatherings. The stream gurgled past on the eastern side of the village, and to the south and west were a variety of crops being grown. There was even a penned-in area comprising several acres in which pigs and even a few sheep grazed and ambled about. Fresh water, fresh vegetables and even livestock… Clayton thought that Norambao was probably an upper-class community for Guadalcanal.

"Over here, sir!" Joe Treadway called from the porch of a large house. The headman's house. Clayton waved at several islanders as he went, including a trio of women who seemed to take an unusually attentive interest in him. One was older, perhaps forty or so and a bit homely. However, the two youngers of the trio were rather attractive. One in particular, perhaps in her middle twenties, stood out for her slim, lithe figure and large dark eyes.

"Good morning, sir," Treadway joked as Clayton mounted the steps to the porch.

"Morning, my eye," Clayton said. "It's after five, for Christ's sake. What've I missed?"

"Not much, sir," Treadway admitted. "I only got up about a half-hour ago."

"There you are, Web," Vousa said, stepping out of the house. "Hungry?"

"Famished," Clayton replied. "Don't suppose you got any coffee brewing in there?"

Vousa grinned, "Coffee? It's got to be ninety-five, Web. How about a glass of cool tea?"

"Sounds divine," Clayton said, following Treadway inside.

The house was, by Guadalcanal standards, a mansion. It had no less than three sleeping rooms and one large communal room that was a sort of combination living room and kitchen. There was a large table with several chairs around it and even a sort of bamboo-framed sofa stuffed with coconut husk. On the sofa sat a teenage boy of perhaps fifteen or sixteen and two girls who weren't quite in their teens yet. A pretty and slightly plump coffee-skinned woman worked at something in the cooking area.

"The chief has gone off to the weather coast for a few days," Vousa explained. "He left word that if I arrived that I could use his hut. Mine is pretty full, so this one is better for entertaining. By the way, this is my wife, Irene, our two daughters Janie and Becky and my son Samuel."

Introductions made and hellos exchanged; Clayton took a seat at the table with Treadway. He glanced around in confusion, slightly distracted by the smells of roasting pork, "Uhm… I'm kind of surprised, Jake… you all have English names."

"We converted to Christianity before leaving Malaita," Irene explained in her Melanesian accent. "We had to leave because of the… unpleasantness."

Clayton noticed the quick look she darted in Samuel's direction. No doubt there was a story here, but Clayton knew better than to pry.

"I was targeted by a murder gang," Vousa explained. "Before I retired last year. Malaita is… in bad shape. A lot of crime. Lot of brutality. Samuel's mother and father were killed by this same gang. I've known him all of his life, and Irene and I adopted him."

"I'm sorry to hear that, sir," Treadway said empathetically. "I'm sorry for the fact that this war has brought so much pain to these peaceful islands."

"How often is it so?" Irene asked, something of anger creeping into her voice. "When the first world goes to war, it's often the third world that pays the price."

Treadway nodded and lowered his eyes. Even Clayton was taken aback by her sharp but perfectly understandable words. Vousa reached out and patted the young Marine's arm.

"I'm sorry," Irene said. "I don't blame you two… and you Americans are at least here to help us. We appreciate it, it's just…."

"I understand, ma'am," Clayton offered. "The only consolation I can offer is that we're committed to throwing as much manpower and resources at driving the Japanese from this land and these islands as it takes. And once gone, your land and homes will still be yours."

A meal of roasted pork, yams and coconut rice was served. For their part, Clayton and Treadway filled up, glad not to be eating canned rations. With the word of a large number of Japanese soldiers joining those already ashore, the islanders took the opportunity to over-indulge as well. They never knew when their food stores might be looted.

"Bad news about the radio, Web," Vousa said. "With so much Japanese activity, the teleradio gear was taken away a few days back. The chief thought that if the Nips came here and found it… it would implicate everyone here as collaborators."

Treadway scoffed, "Collaborators… it's the people on this island who side with the Japs that are collaborators, sir."

Vousa nodded, "Yes, Joe… but these are simple people. They see others such as white men and even the Japanese as… it's hard to explain… as higher up the food chain than themselves? More advanced, you might say. Although many are learning that the Japs are certainly not acting very admirably."

"On the other hand, the amount of intel the islanders who are disposed toward us provide is invaluable," Clayton said. "Not just here on Guadalcanal, but for the rest of the war. That's why I'm here. To see how things are going and to sort of… build a model of what we can expect as we leapfrog across the Pacific."

"For the time being, I think we should report back to the line," Treadway said. "The Japs are massing for an attack, and our guys need to know they're coming, sir."

"I agree," Clayton said.

"As do I," Vousa added, "But I think we need to take a closer look. All those men that came ashore aren't here to lie on the beach. Something tells me they might already be on the move."

"So we should follow them back toward the perimeter?" Clayton asked.

"I think so," Vousa said. "Track their movements and progress and then get ahead of them in time to warn the Marines at Alligator Creek. That has to be where they'll attack."

"Well, we're rested and fed," Treadway said. "I say let's scram out, sirs."

Vousa grinned, and Clayton chuckled, "Put the brakes on there, Joe. Let's not run off half-cocked just yet. What do you think, Jacob?"

Vousa tapped his chin, "Those Naponapo came ashore a few hours before dawn… and they probably needed a few hours rest. If they're marching west… the main force, I mean, not the scouting party we saw during the battle… they've got to cover twenty-two miles or so."

Treadway nodded, "And if they have any heavy gear like artillery pieces, it'll slow them down, I bet."

"Making what… two miles in an hour?" Clayton asked.

"If that much," Vousa said. "My guess is they haven't made it much past Coli Point. And by now, they must be camped. You just can't march men twelve hours a day in full gear and dragging a couple of mortars. Not in this tropical sauna anyway."

"Agreed," Treadway said. "So that's why I'm sayin' we go now and try and get *ahead* of them, sir."

"I think we've got time for that, Joe," Vousa said. "If they're encamped now, which I bet they are, then we can wait until dark and move both closer to them and around them with less chances of being detected."

Clayton nodded, "All we need is for some Japanese patrol to stumble on us. We'd be wiped out for sure."

"So, we leave after sundown?" Treadway asked.

Vousa nodded, "And we'll take Samuel with us. He knows this side of the islands well as I do, and we can use him to run messages if need be. The Japanese won't suspect a couple of islanders even if they see us. But you two...."

Clayton grinned, "Understood. Well, let's eat up and get ready for another wonderful evening stroll, fellas."

"Don't worry, sir, it'll be a real *gas!*" Treadway enthused.

"Joe..." Clayton began, frowned and thought better of it.

Treadway grinned broadly, and his eyes glittered, "Yes sir."

LUNGA POINT – JUST OFF THE SHORE OF HENDERSON FIELD

The Higgins boat nosed up to *Bull Shark's* hull bow first. With the built-in gangway extended, Art Turner, Paul "Buck" Rogers and Elmer Williams could drop down into the open boat. The sea had calmed considerably, and in the semi-protected little bay, hardly a hand was needed to help the men down. Turner turned back to Joe Dutch and waved, grinning wryly.

"Take care of my ship, Joe," Turner said. "No wild parties and no joy riding, y'hear?"

Dutch chuckled, "Awww... gee whiz, dad."

"Welcome aboard, sir," the boat's coxswain said. "Petty officer third-class Eugene McCarthy, sir. Everybody just calls me Mac. This here is my engineer, engineman first-class Brad Rigger."

"Thanks for the pickup, Mac," Turner said. "Glad the sea's laid down, or I'd have had to flood down to get into this contraption."

Mac grinned, "Shoulda been with us yesterday, Captain. Me and three other boats brought a company of Jarheads over to Point Cruz. Was six and seven-footers rollin' in. Poor fellas lost half their lunch...

we even got shelled by a Jap tin can and sewer pipe, if you can believe that."

"Damn," Rogers said. "How'd you come through?"

Rigger lowered his eyes, and Mac frowned, "We lost our third boat, Chief. Thankfully it were empty, havin' already dropped off the Marines... but lost two good men."

"I'm sorry to hear that, skipper," Williams said.

Mac frowned, "Well... it's a war, ain't' it? We headed over to the S-boat now, sir?"

Turner nodded, "Yeah, got another load of VIPs for you, Mac."

Two boat lengths away, S-52 sat at idle, bobbing slightly in the mild waves. Evidently, her captain didn't want to take any chances and had the boat flooded down by the bow. Mac eased the Higgins boat gently up against the submarine's pressure hull, and three men climbed off the angled deck and over the square bow of the LCVP. One was Bernard Waters, of course. The other was Pat Jarvis, and the final man was Harry Brannigan. The *Bull Sharks* all smiled and shook each other's hands. Turner extended his to Waters.

"Good to see you made it, Captain," Turner said. "Hope your trip was uneventful."

Waters chuckled softly as he puffed on a cigar, "Had some nasty weather day before yesterday. Not much else to speak of."

"We did sight *Sakai* this morning, sir," Jarvis said, a half-smile playing at his lips. There was something in his eyes Turner couldn't quite identify. As if Jarvis were trying to communicate something.

"That right?" Williams asked. "Did you guys take her out?"

Waters smirked, "We deemed it an unacceptable risk under the circumstances, Mr. Williams. Remembering how in your own report, I read that the strike carrier was acting as a lid for a Jap submarine... I felt that getting in close might expose us."

"You think they were doing that again, sir?" Rogers asked.

"They were moving at four knots, Chief," Brannigan said. Turner thought there was something in his eyes, too.

"Well, I'm sure you made the right call," Turner said. "Mac, a nice beach, if you please."

The Higgins boat moved toward what appeared to be a partially completed wharf. Mac explained that it had been started by the Japanese, and as soon as the Navy CBs arrived, whenever that would be, they'd get the project going again. He also explained that while the Marines had their own engineering battalion, they were busy repairing the airfield each day after the Japanese air raids.

Soon enough, Mac guided the boat up to a small dock, and the six submariners exited. As Turner looked back toward his submarine, he noticed that she was already gone. Both of them were, in fact. While it was late in the day and the likelihood of a Japanese bombing raid was low, it was decided that two surfaced submarines were simply too easy a target.

The guests were met at the foot of the dock by Porter Hazard, Dave Taggart, Phil Oaks and Ted Entwater. Everyone shook hands, and the greeting between the Marines and Turner was particularly warm, as was his hug with Hazard.

"Glad to see you fellas are getting' around on your own landing gear," Turner said, beaming. "How is it with you, Port? Phil?"

"I'm back to a hundred percent, sir," Oaks said and then glanced at Hazard.

"I'm nearly there," Hazard said. "We just had a little dust-up with the Japs yesterday… but came out of that unscathed."

Taggart scoffed, "Yeah, and the L T here killed two of the yellow bastards with his bare hands, sir!"

Turner met Hazard's eyes. In them, he saw the pain and stress of his recent ordeal. Yet he thought he also saw resolve. Almost as if to confirm this, Hazard nodded.

"Felt good to get some payback, Captain."

"Well, we've got duties, sir," Oaks said, saluting the officers.

"Thanks for meeting us, Phil," Turner said.

The Marines fast-walked off across the field, and Hazard turned to guide the submariners, "General Vandegrift is waiting at the Pagoda for you, sirs. He's interested to hear what you've seen out there and what your plans are to be."

"That depends on our leader here, Lieutenant," Waters said, indicating Turner with a nod.

"I vote we sink some Jap ships," Williams said.

"Here, here!" Jarvis rejoined, giving a thumbs up to his friend.

"Lord save us from eager beavers," Waters said with a world-weary sigh.

Nothing more was said until the seven men stepped into Vandegrift's office. It was really a small conference room in one corner of the administration building. The general stood as his guests were announced by an adjutant. He grinned at Turner.

"Well, if it's not Anvil Art himself. How do, Captain?"

"I'm still vertical, sir," Turner said. "How about yourself?"

"Busy," Vandegrift stated. "Take seats, gents. Sorry I can't offer you any coffee… supplies here are thinner than Tokyo Rose's claptrap."

Buck Rogers grinned and set a can of Nescafe down on the table, "Little housewarming gift, General."

Vandegrift chuckled, "I'll be. Awful kind of you, Chief. Navy chiefs… like gunnery sergeants, they always stay one step ahead."

Williams set a can of non-dairy creamer and a small box of sugar next to the gift, "All the COB's idea, sir."

Introductions were made, and hot water was ordered. After the pot was brought in and the men mixed themselves a cup of instant coffee and doctored it, Vandegrift got right down to brass tacks.

"Here's where we are, skippers," the general began. "Yesterday, I sent three companies of the Fifth Reg across the Matanikau to discover what happened to a patrol sent out a week before. Nasty business, but we took out at least sixty-five Japs. B company got repulsed trying to cross the sandbar, and I company found Cocumbona empty, thanks to your Raiders, Art."

"*My* Raiders, sir?"

"With Al Decker out of the theater, they're still attached to you," Vandegrift said. "Although I received notice that Decker and Lider are both en route from New Caledonia aboard a destroyer. Anyway, I also sent Captain Charles Brush out this morning with A company from the First Reg. he's already reported in that he ran into a Jap patrol. He wiped them out as they were backed up against the beach marching west."

"From Taivu Point, no doubt," Waters interjected.

Vandegrift nodded, "Just so, Captain. Couple of things. First, they were Jap regulars. *Not* Riekusentai. They had detailed maps of our perimeter, well-marked with Marine positions. They also had some ship-to-shore codes, which may be of interest to you gents."

Turner and Williams exchanged glances before the captain said: "Sir... we ran into a rather large convoy of tin cans last night, or early this morning more like. Anyway, there were six of them and possibly an additional two."

"Yeah, we know," Vandegrift grumbled. "Lousy squinty-eyed sons of bitches shelled us for over twenty minutes... although, in the dark, they didn't do too much damage. I assume that was one or both of you fellas who took one out and chased them off?"

"Yes sir," Williams said.

Vandegrift looked to Waters, "Did you take note of this action, Captain?"

"No sir, we had yet to arrive in the channel," Waters said, perhaps a tiny bit defensively. "We only rounded the eastern tip of Guadalcanal after sunup."

Vandegrift nodded, "I see. Well, Captain Brush suspects that there are more japs headed our way. Marching from Taivu and will probably hit our eastern lines tomorrow sometime. No doubt this is the first of many such pushes, as they land more men and supplies by night. I could wish that Mr. Clayton was here to fill in some gaps, but...."

"Webster Clayton?" Turner asked. "He's here?"

Vandegrift snorted, "Yes... went out with Jacob Vousa and a new Marine on a recon patrol. Haven't heard from them in a couple of days, but it's twenty-two miles to Taivu, and they're moving by stealth and at night."

"What can S-52 and *Bull Shark* do to help, General?" Waters asked.

"You can start by derailing this damned Tokyo Express," Vandegrift grumbled, fixing himself another cup of coffee. "As if that's our only problem... command thinks that Yamamoto is up to something. The Kido Butai is out in the Pacific, they think. Somewhere between Truk and the Eastern Solomons. Admiral Fletcher's three carriers and their escorts are south and east of us...

the thought is that sooner rather than later, those two fleets are gonna mix it up. Way I hear it, Admiral Nimitz is damn near to flipping his wig over the whole thing. Not much *we* can do about a major flattop battle… but if you two fellas can kick the Japs up the ass by night, my Cactus Airforce will do it by day. Maybe if we can't plug the dike entirely, we can at least slow down the Jap troops movements."

"We'll do our best, sir," Waters said confidently.

From Turner's seat, he could just see Jarvis' expression. At Waters' last declaration, Turner swore he saw something dark cross Jarvis' face. Possibly Brannigan's, too, for that matter.

"What's your plan, Art?" Vandegrift asked.

Turner drew in a breath, "Since *Bull Shark* is faster and can dive deeper, my thinking is to station S-52 in Sealark Channel. Captain Waters will be our goalie, sir. I'll go up The Slot and position my boat between here and Rabaul. What ships I don't get; Captain Waters can pounce on when they get by me."

"Then, if they manage to drop off supplies, we can get them afterward," Water stated.

"I'd rather we not do that," Turner said. "For obvious reasons."

Waters appeared to bristle at Turner's statement. Vandegrift took notice and was curious. Turner had been placed in command, that much he knew. Was Waters tweaked at having a man eight years his junior giving the orders?

"Not obvious to a simple ground-pounder like me," the general tried to mollify Waters a bit. "Captain Waters' would appear to be correct… what's your thought, Art?"

"No offense intended to Captain Waters, sir," Turner said, smiling disarmingly, "but to sink empty ships is something of a waste of our limited supply of weapons, I fear. Better to let them load back up and *then* hit them. It's a bit… ruthless to say it like this, but… we're more effective on this mission if we kill as many *soldiers* as we can, not just ships. Usually, small military ships like destroyers are low-value targets for a submarine."

"Although there is one warship, I think we should prioritize," Jarvis put in.

233

Waters chuckled softly, "My temporary Exec has a bit of a thing for a certain Japanese strike carrier, I'm afraid."

"Probably a good idea, Captain," Turner said. "The XO of that ship made some rather personal threats aimed my way. He seems to be obsessed with engaging me in some kind of duel."

Hazard piped up with evident tension in his voice, "And he means it, sir. All the bastard could do the whole time I was his… *guest*… was to brag and boast and practically slather over the idea of taking down Anvil Art Turner."

Waters snorted derisively before he could catch himself. Turner saw the angry expression hardened Jarvis' face and spoke quickly to avoid an incident.

"I know, Bernard… it's ridiculous to me too… but that's the straight goods nonetheless," Turner said. "So, the sooner he's out of the game, the better, I think. One or both of us must nail *Sakai* at some point."

Waters flushed slightly, taking Turner's concession, not as an olive branch as intended but rather a criticism. He cleared his throat in an attempt to maintain calm, "And when and *if* the situation is right… we will, Captain."

"Good. And I'm not suggesting taking any crazy risks," Turner went even further in hopes of smoothing the ruffled feathers. By Waters' expression, he knew he hadn't quite hit the mark.

"All right, gents," Vandegrift said. "We've all got our jobs to do. Lieutenant Hazard, since your ship has returned, I'm releasing you to return to her. I think you're more than fit for duty. Thank you for your efforts ashore."

Turner could see that Hazard was torn. Part of him wanted to go back to his boat, and the other wanted to stay and slog it out with the Marines. Finally, though, he smiled and stood with everyone else, "Thank you, sir."

Outside the Pagoda, Hazard stopped everyone, "Captain, there are a few folks here who'd like to say hello, sir."

Turner grinned, "All right… it's about an hour to dusk. We'll be headed back out then. Captain Waters, why don't you come with us.

Pat, Elmer, you two can catch up, and the Chiefs here can do the same. Landing beach at 1930 gents."

Jarvis' and Tirner's eyes met for a brief moment. Turner could tell that Pat Jarvis was simply itching to get him alone, but he could also see that Waters suspected this. It would be impolitic, not to mention blatantly obvious, so he simply held Pat's gaze and ever so slightly shook his head.

18

THE SLOT – 90 MILES NW OF SAVO ISLAND

AUGUST 21, 1942 – 0022 GUADALCANAL TIME

Frank Nichols was officer of the deck, and Porter Hazard his assistant. The two men had spent several hours talking about Hazard's time on Guadalcanal, along with Post, Turner and Dutch. That night's supper had been a lively affair, and Turner had even broken out his half-empty bottle of old Scotch so the men could celebrate.

Before turning in, Williams had gone with Turner to his stateroom for a private conversation. Total privacy aboard a submarine was nearly impossible, even in officer's country. Men were constantly moving back and forth through the passageway, and the officer's staterooms were only closed off by a hanging baize curtain. However, all the men aboard knew better than to eavesdrop. It was an unspoken rule, especially when it came to the captain's cabin.

"What's on your mind, Elmer?" Turner asked as he sat on his bunk and removed his sandals.

Williams sat behind Turner's small desk and lounged as best he could against the bulkhead, "I had a little chat with Pat before we shoved off, Art. He had some… interesting things to say. He wanted to tell you himself, but…."

Turner nodded, "Yeah, I sensed that. Old Salty Waters was

running interference on his play, though. I take it there's trouble in paradise?"

Williams chuckled, "You could say that. Pat thinks Waters has lost his nerve. Thinks that last patrol and the surface fight with the destroyer broke something inside him."

Turner frowned slightly. He sensed something going on with Waters as well. However, the man was a seasoned and decorated sub captain. It rankled a little hearing a junior officer playing armchair shrink.

"He didn't make these claims lightly, Art," Williams said, sensing Turner's feelings. "He backed it up with some pretty damning evidence."

Turner sighed and shrugged, "Pat's got a good headpiece... so what's he think?"

Williams explained about S-52 not going after *Sakai* when they had just about the perfect setup. He explained how Waters had kept the boat on the surface during what amounted to a tropical storm south of Guadalcanal. Only after nearly losing a man did Jarvis convince the captain to submerge. He touched on a few other points and items Jarvis had noticed aboard as well.

Turner leaned back against the bulkhead and blew out his breath, "I was afraid of something like this. I feel bad for Pat... he's got himself a bad mojo situation on that boat. Like we had here when you selfishly abandoned us to Begley and Pendergast."

Williams opened his mouth to protest, smiled and then shrugged, "Let that be a lesson to you, then."

Turner chuckled and then got serious once more, "Not much we can do for Pat and Chief Brannigan on this. Let's just hope things work themselves out and that Waters doesn't choke up in a situation where we might need him."

"Think that's likely?"

"Who knows? Everything Pat reported to you *can* be explained... we'll know for sure when the time comes to set him up for a kill," Turner said. "Which, I hope, will be sometime before dawn."

Now it was just after midnight, and a crescent moon hung high overhead. Porter Hazard stood on the bridge with Nichols while the two men shared a smoke. The early morning was warm, of course, and a light breeze blew across a sea with hardly more than a ripple upon its glittering surface.

"How's it feel to be back aboard, Port?" Nichols asked quietly. "Gotta be a bit confining after being in the open for almost three weeks, huh?"

"Yeah, it's gonna take some gettin' used to," Hazard admitted. "But it's also a good feelin', Frank. Lookin' forward to sending a few Japs down to meet old Davy Jones, you know?"

Nichols nodded, "Still angry about the treatment they gave you ashore?"

Hazard chuffed, "Well, it sure as hell wasn't what you might call neighborly."

"Yeah… well, if it's any consolation, we know how to find 'em on this boat," Nichols said a bit more cheerfully. He suspected that Hazard's experience had left a deep mark on him and didn't want to pry. Either his friend would talk about it, or he wouldn't.

"I heard that," Hazard said and grinned at Nichols. "I heard a certain engineer I know bagged himself a Jap tin can."

Nichols shrugged modestly, "Well… it was a team effort."

Hazard nodded, "What I like about the boats, Frank. What I liked about bein' a Marine, too. Bein' part of a team… well, it's gettin' on, I'd better go handle the combat sweeps."

On the heels of that statement, the bridge speaker crackled, and Doug Ingram's voice emitted from the tinny speaker, *"Bridge, sonar… distant contacts. Very faint, bearing one-three-five… range maybe twenty-thousand yards."*

"And there ya' go," Porter said, vanishing down the hatchway.

Nichols drew in a deep breath. This was what they were waiting for. At that time of night, and at their position, they should encounter Tokyo Express ships headed down The Slot for Guadalcanal. At thirty knots, it would only take the destroyers three hours to reach Taivu Point, and that would give them several hours of darkness to unload and exfiltrate the area.

Nichols pressed the button, "Sonar, bridge… home in and give me course and speed asap."

"*Bridge, conning,*" Hazard spoke next. "*Permission to do sugar jig combat sweep.*"

"Conning, bridge… granted," Nichols replied. "Get with Dougie on sound; I suspect that at ten miles, you should be able to pick up those Japs, Port."

There was a pregnant pause while the men worked their gear before Fred Swooping Hawk, the radarman of the watch, came over the speaker, "*Bridge, radar, confirmed. Detecting three faint targets, bearing one-five-eight, range nine-eight-zero-zero. Speed is… thirty knots. Heading appears to be one-six-five. Assess destroyers zigzagging, sir.*"

"*Jives with sonar,*" Came Ingram's voice next. "*Detecting fast light screws.*"

"What's your call, OOD?" Hazard asked from the hatchway.

"Captain's night book makes it clear, Port," Nichols said. "Sound general quarters and open all torpedo doors. Battle stations torpedo."

Beside Nichols, Ralph "Hotrod" Hernandez appeared, having returned from a trip to the head. As quartermaster of the watch, he stood by, waiting for orders. Nichols could see the look of excitement in the swarthy man's eye and his white teeth gleaming in the moonlight.

"Hotrod, ring me up a full speed bell and bring us full left rudder to…." Nichols thought for a moment, picturing his boat and the three tin cans moving southeast. "To let's say… zero-seven-five."

Hotrod rubbed his hands together, "Once more, the mighty *Tiburon* circles to the attack!"

"Sometimes I think you enjoy this just a little too much, Hotrod," Nichols said.

"I am but a simple yet excitable peasant, *señor* Nichols," Hernandez replied in an exaggerated Mexican accent. "The people of my village relish the hunt… be it for an enemy, a nice pair of *chichis,* or a quality attorney."

Nichols laughed in spite of the situation, "Sometimes you're such a drip, Hotrod."

"*Si,*" said Hotrod.

After the fourteen gongs of the general quarters bell subsided, Hernandez gave his helm orders. The submarine began a turn to port, swinging around onto her new course and then accelerating. With a full battery bank, all four diesels were on propulsion duty. At full speed, the ship was making a good eighteen knots.

"What's the story, Frank?" Turner's head asked from the hatchway.

Nichols explained the situation, although he had no doubt Turner had gotten the details on his way up. The captain smiled and nodded.

"Should we dive, sir?" Frank asked.

"Nope, not at night and not at their speeds," Turner replied. "I'm on the plotting party and the approach. Once we have their base course, I'll work us in for an attack. I know you're OOD, Frank, but if it's all the same, I'd like to let Porter handle the attack. He's the only one of us who hasn't bagged himself a Jap ship, and I think he wouldn't mind the opportunity."

Nichols grinned, "Of course, sir. Would you like to take the deck, Captain?"

"Nah, you guys stay up here," Turner said. "I'll grab a phone and relay my helm orders. My thinking is to get out ahead of the convoy and run before them to diminish their approach speed. Then give at least two of them all four stern tubes. Probably have to dive after that."

"Aye-aye, sir," Nichols replied. "Lookouts, keep a sharp eye open."

Down in the control room, Turner, Williams and Clancy Weiss worked at the master gyrocompass table on the big plot. Assisting them was Martin Janslotter, the ship's new boatswain. Like every man aboard, Janslotter needed to know how to do every job on a submarine in order to qualify for his silver dolphins, which he had nearly done in just a short time with *Bull Shark*.

"Okay, we're gonna close the range fast," Turner said. "Once we're where I want us to be, we'll head along the same parallel course as the three tin cans."

"But we don't know yet what that is, sir," Chief Weiss stated as he worked a pair of dividers on the chart.

"Well… it's a safe bet they're headed to Guadalcanal and Taivu Point," Turner said. "It's not exactly a mystery."

"They *could* angle off and go around the outside of the Florida Islands," Williams suggested. "Or do an end-around to the weather coast of The Canal and come in from the eastern end."

Turner shook his head, "If it were twenty-hundred or so, Elmer, I'd agree. But it's too late for them to take such a circuitous route and still make it to Taivu in the dark, let alone get out of the area before Fletcher's planes and the Cactus Airforce gets their birds aloft. Nope, they can zig and zag to their yellow heart's content… but in the end, their base course is gonna be around one-three-five or so. So, you can stick that in your pipe and smoke it, boatswain."

Janslotter looked up from his maneuvering board and smiled, "I don't have a pipe,

"Well… you're the boatswain," Turner said. "Requisition yourself a pipe."

"And then you can stuff the Jap's heading in it," Weiss teased.

"And smoke it," the XO finished.

Anybody ever tell you guys that you're mean?" Janslotter asked.

"Only jerks," Turner said, and the four of them laughed.

"Aspect change on targets," Ingram called down from the conning tower. "They're altering course to port, sir."

"Mark that, Elmer," Turner said. "Radar?"

"Concur," Swooping Hawk said. "Targets appear to be in phalanx formation… speed is constant, still thirty… new heading is… one sec… dammit… ah! New heading is one-zero-five degrees true, sir."

Turner made a pencil mark on the chart and drew a line, "Uh… huh… as I suspected, gents. What's the range up there?"

Both sonar and radar agreed closely on a range of six thousand yards and opening slightly. Turner nodded and adjusted his sound-powered telephone.

"Bridge, control… come right to new course one-three-five," Turner said. "Have maneuvering make turns for fifteen knots."

The acknowledgment came, and Turner could hear the order relayed down from Hernandez to Wendel Freeman, who was taking his trick at the wheel. No doubt Freeman had heard Turner, as he was just below and astern of his helm, but the naval custom of orders given, repeated and confirmed went through proper channels for a reason.

"Okay, Port," Turner said. "If I'm right and their base course is the same, they should pass us to port at about a thousand yards. I doubt we'll get more than two ships, if that. But I figure let's set them up for a stern shot. Give them the tubes at an oblique angle and let their speed work against them."

"Roger that, skipper," Hazard said. "What range do you want?"

"You're the attack officer, Port; I'll leave that up to you," Turner replied, winking at Williams. "Just remember their DDs and nimbler than a boogie-woogie girl in hot pants."

That received a hearty laugh from the men in the conning tower as well as the control room. It was one of the things his crew loved about their captain. Even in a tense situation, he knew how to ease that tension and pull them all together. Turner had found, perhaps through instinct, the right balance between comradery while still maintaining the solid, almost God-like command presence that tradition demanded of every ship's captain.

"Buck," Turner said, stepping away from the chart table and over to the diving station, where Paul Rogers was acting as diving officer.

With Nichols on the bridge and Hazard in the con... not to mention Andy Post acting as DCO, there was no other officer to man the station. Usually, the diving officer would have the COB backstopping him. Nichols controlled the planesmen and gave orders to the COB or chief of the watch, who then handled the men at the various air manifold systems.

"Sir?" Rogers asked.

"We may need to dunk fast," Turner said. "Be ready for a hard dive."

Rogers nodded, his attitude and his stance exuding the hard-won confidence of a man who'd spent sixteen years in the Navy, seventy percent of which was spent serving aboard submarines. He knew his job; he knew everybody else's job, and he understood how to lead men.

"Yes sir," The COB said and smiled wryly. "I'll keep her in one piece until Mr. Nichols comes down, don't you worry."

Turner grinned, "I never worry when you're around, COB."

This last was said loud enough for all the men to hear. By using his title, Turner was also solidifying his faith in the chief which in turn solidified the men's faith in him. A bit stagey, perhaps. Even melodramatic to Turner's mind... yet sometimes that was a skipper's job. He had not only to manage the working of his ship and the working of his men… he also had to manage souls. It was something he was very good at and was fortunate to have quite a few men aboard who were as well.

"Got them on attack scope," Hazard called down. "Definitely three tin cans… I think a *Fubuki* and two *Asashios*. Phalanx formation, nice bones in their teeth… uh-oh…."

Turner met Williams' eyes before tilting his upward, "What's on, Porter?"

"Not quite sure, sir… something's…."

The engineer was cut off by a low but audible boom. At first, it sounded like distant thunder. Yet everyone knew that there was no storm that night. The single boom was then followed by five more.

"Is that… gunfire?" Williams asked.

"Porter, what's in your scope?" Turner asked tensely. "Muzzle flashes?"

"Negative… got splashes, though!" Hazard replied excitedly. "Short and somewhat astern… but I swear I didn't see flashes, sir."

"Christ…" Turner said, moving toward the ladder. "The Japs have some kind of flashless powder… the real concern is how the hell do they *see* us? We're three miles off in the dark…."

"Radar!" Williams and Swooping Hawk shouted the word in such perfect unison it was almost as if they'd rehearsed it.

Turner was confused momentarily until the gears clicked into place in his mind, "You detecting radar, Freddy?"

"Yes sir, broadband fuzz!" the Navaho said tightly. "No sweep, just a constant background…."

"Sugar dog," Hazard muttered. "One of them ships has an air search set."

"And it's enough to tell them *something* is out there in the dark six thousand meters off," Turner cranked. "And they must have spotted our wake."

"Confirmed!" Hazard just managed not to shout as he watched through the scope. "Lead ship is peeling off… turning to starboard."

"Confirmed," Swooping Hawk added. "One target is now CBDR, sir! Speed increasing to thirty-five knots!"

"Frank!" Turner bellowed up the hatch.

The diving alarm sounded even before the name was out of Turner's throat. In the next instant, men began practically falling down the bridge hatch.

"Hard dive, Buck!" Turner said. "Make it snappy! Wendel, hard left rudder, all ahead emergency!"

The enunciator dials that telegraphed engine settings to and from the maneuvering room had only five primary settings. Stop, one-third, two-thirds, standard and full. In order to get a flank speed setting, the helmsman would ring up full speed twice, thereby ringing the bells in the maneuvering room twice. This would tell the operator at the control cubicle to pour on extra power. He would then do the same to alert the helm that this order had been received and the setting initiated.

There was, in extreme cases, a seventh speed setting known as emergency. In this case, the helmsman would ring up full speed *three* times. In short, this told the maneuvering room and engine rooms to go beyond maximum limits. To exceed the diesels maximum engine pressure or MEPs and/or exceed the TVGs for the batteries, which would overload their output. On the surface, running diesels, this generally meant that the engines would emit visible smoke from their exhausts. It also meant an extra knot or even a knot and a half past flank. In *Bull Shark's* case, nearly twenty-three knots.

"Want me to start a solution?" Dutch asked from his place at the TDC.

"Not yet, Joe," Turner said. "They're on to us now. Better we get deep and figure our next move that way... damnit... since when do the Japs have radar on their destroyers?"

"Probably slapped one on in response to our hijinks," Williams opined. "Maybe Sato's doing, sir."

Art swore under his breath, "Stand by, Buck... we're gonna get every ounce of speed outta her and then take the plunge."

"All hull openings secure except main induction," Rogers said.

Frank had been the last one down the ladder, and Hotrod had dogged it for him. The lead engineer and diving officer hurried below to assist the COB.

"Bendix log indicates twenty-three knots, sir!" Wendel said excitedly.

"Phone talker, alert maneuvering to standby to answer bells on batteries!" Turner said. "In five-seconds, kill the rock crushers, close main induction and switch to motors only… mark! Rig out dive planes! Open main vents, flood all tanks, Frank! Full dive on the planes!"

Even as Turner called out these orders in rapid succession, Hazard took one last look through the periscope and called for it to be lowered. There was a sudden cessation of vibration as the four big diesels shut down, and it was replaced by a dozen staccato thunderclaps that echoed above and below the waterline.

"Dive, dive, dive!" Turner said.

There was a roar as all vents were opened, and hundreds of tons of seawater rushed into the main ballast tanks, auxiliary tanks, negative tank, safety tank and bow buoyancy tank. The submarine angled alarmingly forward as her bow planes bit and forced her bullnose down, shoving her beneath the waves at over twenty knots. Although her electric motors couldn't push her nearly that fast on batteries alone, her massive inertia helped to keep the way on.

"Fathometer reading!" Turner ordered.

A low ping, and then Paul Rogers reported, "Two-two-five fathoms, Captain."

"Plenty of water," Hazard said.

"Yeah, plenty to die in…." Ingram muttered from the sonar set.

"Belay that shit, Mister!" Turner snapped, startling the younger man. "Mind your fuckin' panel! Get me data on those tin cans, pronto!"

"Aye sir… sorry sir…." Ingram replied meekly, his face flushing with shame. He felt a hand squeeze his shoulder and knew without seeing that it was his captain. He focused on his audio output to try and hide his embarrassment.

"Helm, all ahead-two-thirds," Turner said. "Reverse your turn."

"Now passing seven-five feet," Nichols called out. "Thirty-degree down, sir."

"Rig ship for depth charge," Turner ordered. "Let's hope they're too intent on getting to the island to spend too much time spanking us... what've you got, sonar?"

In combat situations, Turner liked to get his A-team in their positions. Yet he knew that his other men needed this kind of experience to improve them. Ingram had made a natural comment, but his captain had to nip it in the bud. Such negativity couldn't be allowed to thrive, or it would spread like wildfire. It was amazing how quickly confidence and bravado could mutate into fear and self-doubt. Such emotions simply didn't serve in combat. At least not as prime movers.

"I've got all three, sir," Ingram reported. "Two are still on course, I think. The other guy... he's closing in fast! Thirty-five knots and range is now one-one-five-zero yards... active pinging, attack freq!"

They could all hear it. Over the sound of the rapidly churning screws came the unmistakable metallic pinging of echolocation. It was slightly off the port quarter now. Turner had ordered the ship on a perpendicular course when they'd dived and then had reversed the turn in order to zigzag. However, the tin can was just too close to evade. The submarine simply didn't have the speed or maneuverability underwater to evade a DD moving at six times her speed.

"Helm, maintain your turn on full left rudder," Turner ordered. "Bring her around to zero-four-five true."

Ping... ping... ping...

Shoom... shoom... shoom...

The sounds of impending attack were clear to every man aboard the boat. They'd all been through it now, some of the plank owners more times than they could accurately count. Both pinging and screw noise grew intensely loud with gut-wrenching swiftness.

Shoom,shoom,shoom,shoom...

Ping,ping,ping,PONG!

"She's passing overhead," Ingram said with eerie calm. "They've found us... turn rate is decreasing, too."

"Yeah, thirty-five knots is too fast to hear anything that's not right under their keel...." Hazard mused.

"Now passing one-two-zero feet," Nichols said.

"Rig ship for silent running," Turner called. "Hang on, boys!"

"Splashes…" Ingram said. "Six of them…."

They'd be set shallow. The Jap commander would know the submarine couldn't have gone too deep that quickly. It would only be a matter of fifteen or twenty seconds now.

Click,click… click,click…

The ocean thundered as first two, then four and then finally six in total depth charges imploded and then exploded at one-hundred and forty feet. *Bull Shark* was heaved forward and rolled to starboard as her long, slim hull was twisted and battered by pressure waves. Outside the hull, the sea roared and pulsed and throbbed with power.

Inside the hull, loose objects and people were sent skittering across the decks. There was the popping of incandescent bulbs bursting and the hiss of air escaping from someplace. Steel groaned, something clanked, and more than one man cried out in terror without even realizing he'd done so.

"He's *definitely* slowing, sir!" Ingram was no longer calm. His face was glistening with sweat in the red lighting. "Oh Jesus… the other two are altering course… headed this way…."

"Two-zero-zero feet!" Nichols reported.

"Snap it up, diving officer!" Turner said.

"We're max down!" Nichols reported. "Another couple good ones like that and…"

He didn't finish. He didn't have to. The boat was heavy and negatively buoyant. By now, neutral buoyancy would have been established, and they'd simply be planing down. Turner had to decide between sinking as well as driving deeper more quickly or rigging his ship to maintain trim and depth should something be damaged.

"Helm, all ahead full," Turner ordered. "Frank, blow bow buoyancy, blow negative to the mark. Bring us to neutral buoyancy."

The increased speed would help the ship drive down, but it could also make them easier to detect on passive sonar gear. Of course, as they'd already been detected on active, and now two more ships were joining the party, it made little difference.

"Here they come!" Ingram cried out.

"Helm, full left rudder!" Turner ordered.

"My rudder is left full, sir!" Freeman declared.

The world above their heads was a cacophony of spinning propellers and pinging sonars as three ships crossed close to each other, and through one another's wakes.

"Splashes... four... eight... fourteen sirs!" Ingram said, yanking his headphones off.

"Hold on!" Turner called out, wrapping his arms through the bridge ladder. He and Hazard were practically entwined together.

"Oh boy..." Dutch moaned.

Wha-boom... boom, boom, boom... boom-badda-boom-boom!

The lights all over the ship went dark suddenly. A New England blizzard of cork insulation flew through the air. Sounds of shattering, smashing, tearing and shouting reverberated through the ship

Joe Dutch, in spite of pressing himself into the chair at the TDC, was flung sideways, hit the deck on his shoulder and tumbled through the open hatch, falling to the control room floor unconscious and bloody. From below, a sound that reminded Turner of snapping logs made his stomach churn.

It wasn't logs being broken, of course... it was the sound of thousands of volts jumping across circuits and going where they were not supposed to go. They had, unfortunately, the proper medium for such jumps as there were no less than a dozen small leaks throughout the ship. Some were spraying a fine mist of seawater across compartments, some gurgling into the bilge and others spraying pressurized water in a steady stream from broken pipe fittings.

Worst of all, seawater was filling the battery compartment in the after battery room and had already gotten into the electrolyte of a number of the one-hundred and twenty-six individual cells. Electrolysis had already begun, and soon chlorine gas would begin to fill the submarine.

"Frank!" Turner called down, clinging desperately to the ladder and to Hazard.

"Mr. Nichols is unconscious, sir!" Rogers called. "I'm at the dive station!"

"What's our depth, Buck?"

"Two-eight-zero feet and dropping, sir," Rogers said. "Although we've lost main power... still got propulsion, thank God!"

The ship wasn't quiet, however. Not entirely quiet. Even running silent, there was a noticeable vibration from the four powerful GE electric motors. Even when running at slower speeds. For whatever reason, the electrical failures they were experiencing didn't prevent the motors from driving the ship.

For now.

"Wendel, you okay?" Turner asked the helmsman, who was slumped in his chair.

"Think I might've busted my nose, sir…." Freeman said a bit unsteadily.

"Can you steer?"

"I… I think so, sir…."

Turner looked around. The other men in the compartment were at their stations, each one rubbing at a particular bruise or pain. He met Hazard's eyes at the same time he realized that he *could* meet them. There was a single emergency bulb burning yet, casting the compartment in a hellish crimson glow.

"Layer!" Chief Weiss called up from below. "Bathythermograph is jigging, skipper!"

"Thank Christ…" Hazard muttered.

"Porter, take the wheel," Turner said. "Clance, get the compartments open. Secure from depth charge. We need Hoffman in here! How's Joe? Porter, head us northeast. One-third speed."

Turner helped Freeman down the ladder and into inky blackness. It immediately pissed him off for some reason.

"Get a goddamned battle lantern on down here!" he all but roared. "What the *hell* are you men about! Let's look alive, for Christ's sake."

Somebody had been retrieving it, and a dim light filled the compartment. Turner sat Freeman at the chief's desk and went to where Rogers and Weiss were kneeling over two bodies. One was Nichols, who'd somehow been knocked off his feet when Dutch had plummeted down the hatchway. This had mercifully broken Dutch's fall but had caused Nichols to clunk his head on something and knocked him out. The side of his head was bloody. Knowing how much head wounds bled, though, Turner guessed it wasn't too bad.

Joe Dutch, on the other hand, lay on his back. Turner could see that his left shoulder had been dislocated, and his face was a red mask of glistening blood. A three-inch split along his hairline was still trickling.

"What's our depth?" Turner barked.

"Three-two-zero, sir," Leroy Potts, the ship's baker and one of the only three black men aboard, had been taking a trick at the bow planes. He looked back at Turner with reassuring confidence, his thick arms steady on the wheel before him, hydraulic power having been shut down for silent running.

Beside him, Horris Eckhart, one of the boat's engine snipes, held his hands steady on the stern plane controls as well, "Should we keep her going down, sir?"

Good question. Turner needed to think, to focus. He was worried for his men, his boat and his friend who lay on the deck before him. He had to broaden his mindset to encompass everything at once.

He had to think like a captain.

"Hold her at three-fifty, fellas," Turner said. "Let's see what our friends on the roof do next."

With main power down, the sonar gear was inoperable. There was some sound, though. Sounds of fast light screws chewing up seawater as destroyers maneuvered above their heads. Yet it didn't sound as if it was *directly* overhead. That could be due in part to the salt layer, but Turner didn't think so.

He listened for a long minute before deciding, "They're buggin' out. Probably don't have time to screw around with us all night. Good thing… they certainly did enough damage."

There was an audible sigh of relief from the men around him and above in the conning tower. It was temporary, however. Turner knew, in that way that all captains tuned into their ships knew, that *Bull Shark* had been hit hard, and there were casualties to deal with that had yet to be located. Casualties to the boat and to the men.

"Phone talker, all compartments from aft forward," Turner ordered. "Complete damage and situation report to the XO."

Williams was removing his duty blouse to make a pillow for Dutch's head. As he did so, Turner noticed him wince.

"You okay, Elmer?"

"Wrist hurts like a bastard," Williams groaned. "Otherwise, I'm okay. You?"

"Swell," Turner grumped. Something tickled at the back of his mind. "Buck… I think we need to get the batteries offline. There's a lot of water coming in, and I'm not sure…."

Rogers nodded, "I'll take care of it, sir."

Bull Shark may have taken a couple of good punches, but she wasn't out of the fight yet. With good men like Williams and Rogers and Hazard and the others, Turner knew they'd pull through. He hoped, however, and the thought came surging up into his consciousness like a raging tornado that S-52 would be ready to jump those three Nip sons of bitches up there and give them a nasty surprise.

19

S-52 – SEALARK CHANNEL
AUGUST 21, 1942 – 0330 GUADALCANAL TIME

"Contact!"

The sharply declaimed announcement jolted Chris Savage out of a daydream he'd been having. It was just after three in the morning, and the duty shift was quiet. In spite of the fact that a naval vessel ran twenty-four hours a day, there was still a certain unconscious respect for the nighttime. As if the men awake and working in the middle of the night had made some unspoken agreement to walk, act and talk quieter than during the day.

Ironically, Savage had been daydreaming… well, nearly *actually* dreaming if he were honest with himself… about attacking a Jap convoy and winning himself a silver star. When Bobby Gaines broke into the quiet of the control room, it sent a surge of adrenaline through Savage. He covered his surprise by casually lighting a Marlboro before turning to face the sonarman.

"What've we got, Bobby?" he asked in his best officer of the deck tone.

"Sounds like multiple surface contacts coming into the channel," Gaines reported, fiddling with his gear. "Possibly… three, sir. Light, fast screws, range sixteen thousand yards… turn rate indicates… thirty knots. Assess Japanese tin cans headed for Guadalcanal."

"Well, well..." Savage replied calmly, although his innards were churning in an uncomfortable mix of excitement and fear. "Step into my parlor, said the spider to the fly...."

Tony Skaggs's beaming face appeared in the hatchway to the control room, "Shall I sound the general alarm, Mr. Savage? Want I should get the plotting party stationed?"

"Keep your pants on, Tony," Savage said indulgently. "They're still eight miles off yet. Inquire in the radio shack if there's any transmissions from *Bull Shark* again. They're *supposed* to radio ahead when they let DDs slip past them."

Skaggs frowned, "I've had Pete Vasquez in the radio room all night, sir. He's reported nothing."

"Well, have him check again while I grab a look," Savage said tersely.

Skaggs vanished before Savage could see him roll his eyes. He was JOOD and had no choice but to follow orders. He knew what *he'd* do right then, but it wasn't his call.

S-52 was running submerged at radio depth. After charging her batteries, the boat had been dived and allowed to drift at thirty feet. Just shallow enough to allow her radio mast to transmit and receive. It also allowed for a semi-high look from the periscopes, as their heads would be twenty-three feet above the water at that depth.

With that height, Savage would have a nearly six-mile horizon. At night and with a low moon, it wouldn't let him see the destroyers from eight miles off, not even their masts yet. However, that would change soon.

"No contact on radio," Skaggs reported as Savage peered through the search scope's eyepiece.

"Very well," Savage said. "I think I *might* have a mast, but it's hard to tell yet. Bobby, can you give me a baseline course and target count yet?"

Gaines was making notes on a scratch pad, and he turned to Savage, "Course appears to be one-two-zero, sir. No zigging detected."

"Ballsy..." Steve Marx, the duty helmsman, muttered to himself.

"That's your Jap for you," Savage said wisely. "All right, Tony, sound the bells. Send the messenger of the watch to notify the captain personally."

"And the XO, sir?" Skaggs inquired.

Savage scoffed, "He'll hear the alarm. The skipper will decide where he wants Jarvis."

Ever since the boat failed to attack the *Sakai* the previous morning, there had been a dramatic increase in tension in the boat. Waters' dressing down of Jarvis in public had created a ripple effect that had further divided the crew along the fractured lines of their loyalties.

The Waters camp had been smugly satisfied that the uppity and *temporary* XO had been put in his place. The Jarvis faction, naturally, had expressed their displeasure at this, and there had even been whisperings that the captain was perhaps not quite as bold as he might be.

What was more distressing, or should have been, was the fact that there were a few Waters' supporters who leaned in this direction as well. While they might not know quite what to make of Jarvis, they had to admit that the man was competent and possessed more than his fair share of grit. The contrast between the two top men aboard S-52 was shining a rather harsh light on things. And in that bare-bulb illumination, the skipper wasn't quite showing up as well as his crew would like.

Even Savage was beginning to have his doubts. He told himself that Jarvis was just a blowhard with a big head. He told himself that Waters was a great man. Well-seasoned and experienced. Yet a niggling part of his mind kept asking the same questions over and over again.

Why hadn't the captain attacked that carrier? She had only one escort and was lined up perfectly. Some bunk about a possible hidden submarine notwithstanding. As much as Savage hated to admit it, the XO had been right in his assertion that even if there *was* a sub under the carrier, S-52 should have taken the shot and could have evaded.

Also, Savage was bothered by the fact that the skipper had kept the boat on the surface during that nasty storm three days back. It was needless, too. Even if they'd *spotted* a Jap ship where no Jap ship should be, it was so rough the ship wouldn't have been able to attack. S-52 wouldn't either. Any fish fired off in those big seas would've run wild anyway. And on top of that, they'd almost lost a lookout.

Savage had tried to get Lutz's opinion on the matter. The two men shared a berth, after all. Lutz, however, in his stubbornly clam-like way, had refused to offer any opinion on the matter. That in itself was both strange and galling. Lutz hadn't always been so tight-lipped. Before that last patrol, he'd been an outgoing and cheerful sort. Now he was as closed off as a bank vault.

The general alarm gonged, and Savage could only shrug as the periscope was lowered. In a minute or so, the captain would arrive and take over. He wasn't from the Mush Morton or Art Turner school. Waters believed that it was the captain's job to run an attack, no bones about it.

It was Jarvis who appeared first. The XO popped up through the hatch and finished buttoning his duty blouse, "What's the scoop, Mr. Savage?"

Savage had to force down his distaste. No matter what he might think of Jarvis, the man *was* the senior officer, "Three DDs headed down toward Taivu Point, we think."

"Wonder how many left Rabaul?" Jarvis asked with a crooked grin.

"What do you mean?" Savage inquired.

Jarvis chuckled softly, "Wonder how many *Bull Shark* took down further up The Slot."

"Well, since we didn't get any radio transmission warning us that these Nips were on the way," Savage said a little peevishly. "My guess is none... sir."

"Uh-huh," Jarvis said noncommittally.

Captain Waters came up the hatch next and cast a quick glance around, "Report, officer of the deck."

Savage gave Waters the run down thus far. The captain nodded coolly and reached for the raincoat and hat hanging on their pegs, "Very well. A bit crowded up here, Exec. Maybe you can find something useful to do?"

Jarvis managed to school his face before saying: "I can take charge of the plotting party, sir."

"Good," Waters said. "Keep a *very* careful track of them tin cans."

"Aye-aye sir," Jarvis said as he began down the ladder. "I'll get you a good intercept course in a minute."

"Did I say we were gonna attack?" Waters asked archly.

Jarvis just managed not to sigh or roll his eyes, "Well sir, as our orders are to sit here and take out any Tokyo Express ships that come our way *before* they drop off… I assumed that was your intent, sir."

"I'll let you know my intent when I'm damned good and ready, son," Waters replied coldly.

"Aye-aye, sir," Jarvis said and dropped into the control room before his temper could get the better of him.

Savage sat down at the TDC and waited. He found that his inner voice was whispering to him again, and he didn't like it. Almost as if he'd sensed it, Waters turned from his place at the scopes to regard Savage with lidded eyes.

"What do you think, OOD?" the captain asked. "Think we should set up for an attack?"

Savage blinked in surprise and was suddenly unsure of himself, "I… I'm ready to support whatever decision you make, sir."

Waters' mouth twitched up in a near-smile, "Spoken like a good subordinate, Christopher. But I didn't ask you if you were gonna back me up… I was askin' you if you thought we should attack, as Mr. Jarvis is so eager to do."

Was the skipper testing him? Savage couldn't help but feel a vague sense of unease. It appeared as if the captain were baiting him or setting him up somehow. Although Savage wasn't quite sure what the right answer was, he was certain he had to say something.

"Well sir… Mr. Jarvis is correct in stating that our job *is* to sink these destroyers before they can offload," Savage stated firmly, although he knew he was still prevaricating.

"That's true," Waters said. "But we're one S-boat with five torpedo tubes against three destroyers armed with ASW equipment and weaponry. If we were hunting a convoy with three escorts, would we attack? Certainly, we might… but we'd know that three DDs would come after us. Those are long odds. Now there isn't even a couple of civvy ships to distract them."

Savage couldn't believe he was about to do it, but he said: "I agree with Mr. Jarvis, sir. I think it's our duty to attack. They don't know we're here, and we can send at least four fish at two tin cans before they know we're out here. Then we can dive or give the third our stern tube. I think at night, and with the element of surprise, we have a chance."

Waters frowned, "Do you? And this is based on your vast experience, is it?"

Savage felt his cheeks burn with embarrassment, "Sir… you did ask. As I say, I'll follow whatever orders you give."

Waters considered him for a long moment and then turned away, "Helmsman, all ahead one-third. What's the current bearing, sonar?"

"Targets bear zero-five-zero, sir," Gaines said.

"Very well… helm, full right rudder," Waters ordered. "Make your course zero-seven-five. That will at least get us started. Whenever our Exec finishes his calculations, we'll see how far off I am. Make it official, Mr. Savage. On the 1MC… battle stations torpedo. Order the torpedo room to open outer doors. Order maneuvering to open their stern door, too. How about it, Exec?"

After Savage had made his announcement and passed his orders through his sound-powered telephone set, Jarvis' head popped up through the hatchway, "Recommend increasing to two-thirds and heading zero-eight-five Captain. Those DDs are making a helluva lot of way."

"You heard the man, Marx," said Waters. "Up attack scope. Range, Bobby?"

"Ten thousand yards, sir," Gaines reported.

Jimmy Kintner had been taking his turn at radar, which was virtually useless as the S-52 had only the old SD set. He acted as periscope assistant and pressed the button to raise the slim attack periscope. Waters adjusted his raingear and stepped up to peer through the lens.

"I got 'em now," Waters said. "They're hull up and got bones in their teeth… Okay, down scope. Crawford, you down there?"

"Yes sir," came the engineer/diving officer's reply.

"Take us down to periscope depth," Waters said. "Chris, alert the forward torpedo room and maneuvering to set their speed to high on all fish and their depth to twelve feet."

"Uhm… sir?" Savage interjected, nervous now about offering any opinion, even though it was his job.

"Something to add, torpedo officer?" Waters asked tersely.

"Yes sir… as we now know, the Mark 14 runs deep… recommend depth of four feet for these targets, sir."

"When I want a recommendation, I'll ask for one, Lieutenant," Waters snapped.

I just had to open my yapper, Savage thought. *Was in the Old Man's good graces until I was stupid enough to agree with Jarvis…*

"Captain, with respect," Jarvis' head and shoulders appeared in the hatchway as if conjured by Savage's thought. "I can personally attest to that. The magnetic exploder mechanism is defective, but even when it does work, practical experience shows that the torpedoes are running at least ten feet too deep."

"This ain't no debating society!" Waters barked. "I didn't ask for advice, goddammit!"

Jarvis met Savage's eye, and for the first time, the younger officer felt a twinge of empathy with Jarvis. Waters seemed oddly out of sorts. He was usually so cool and collected but now was as prickly as a desert cactus. Savage quickly passed along the orders while Jarvis met the captain's gaze.

"Sir, it's my *job* to provide accurate information," Jarvis said firmly.

"It's not your job to be deliberately insubordinate!" Waters snapped. "I don't need an Exec who second guesses me. This is *my* boat, son. I told you when you came aboard that I had my way of doin' things."

"Yes sir," Jarvis said flatly. "And the captain requires accurate data. I was only attempting to provide it and to back up Mr. Savage."

"Well, the *Captain* don't need your advice right now," Waters said. "I'm tryin' to run an attack here, now get below and do your *fuckin'* job!"

Jarvis gritted his teeth and vanished. Strangely, Savage didn't take any pleasure in the other man's second chastising as he'd done the day before. He couldn't quite figure it, but this time he actually felt a bit bad for Jarvis. Perhaps it was because the XO had been defending him, of all people.

"What range do you wish to attack at, sir?" Savage asked warily.

"Better find a balance between caution and boldness, Chris," the captain replied, suddenly sounding comradely. "Let's say… eight hundred yards."

"Eight hundred, aye," Savage said.

"Time to firing range?" Waters asked.

"Seven minutes, Captain," Jack Cleghorn replied. He was posted to the plotting party and figured the captain would respond to his information better than Jarvis'.

The XO had made this clear when the question was asked by pointing at Cleghorn. The quartermaster opened his mouth to say something, but Jarvis shook his head no and cut his eyes to Archie Lockner and Dennis Saunders, the chief yeoman. Both chiefs were working on the plot, and both were men who were pretty firmly in Waters' camp. At least as far as anyone knew. Fortunately, they were both bent over the master gyro table and missed the looks.

"Sonar, can you give us more detail on target positions?" Jarvis asked.

A pause and then, "Three ships, sir… based on sound profile, I'd say they're traveling in a phalanx formation… maybe five hundred yards apart."

"Matches with observation," the Captain said.

Notes were made, and the men waited. Time passes with excruciating sluggishness when something extraordinary is anticipated. And an impending attack with the potentially deadly consequences that came with it was just about the most extraordinary event of all.

"Aspect change on targets!" Gaines suddenly exclaimed. "They're turning, sir… turning right for us!"

Cleghorn's eyes went wide. He and the two chiefs looked to Jarvis as if for reassurance. The XO saw fear in their eyes. Perhaps less in Cleghorn's for whatever reason.

Jarvis shook his head no. There was no way the Japs had spotted them. Not at night and with the scope down from three miles off. It was most likely just an evasive course deviation now that the convoy was in Guadalcanal waters.

"Hard left rudder!" Waters ordered.

Jarvis frowned and tilted his head upward at the overhead. He wanted to state what he'd tried to convey without words… but he knew he'd only receive another rebuke from his very touchy skipper.

Yet there was something in the captain's voice that Jarvis didn't like. It was just a hint, but he'd swear it was there. Was it panic? No, perhaps that was too strong a word… certainly fear, though, at least to a degree. However it was classified, Jarvis didn't like it. It made *him* nervous. Nervous about a great many things. Things that *could* happen, things that *would* happen… and things that might have to be done.

"Tell him, one of you," Jarvis said quietly to his party. "Tell him that this maneuver screws up our approach."

Lockner chuffed, "Not me, sir. He's already in a bad mood, and I ain't getting in Dutch."

"I'm just a clerk," Saunders said with a shrug.

Jarvis frowned. He knew neither of the men would go against the captain, especially on his behalf. Yet he'd hoped that duty would override their dislike of him.

"Shit…" Cleghorn cursed and glowered at the other two men before raising his voice. "Skipper, advise this course change compromises our approach."

"You got the men doin' your talkin' now, Exec?" Waters sneered.

Jarvis squeezed his fists, "No sir, but I concur. We'll lose them."

"They've spotted us," Waters said in a tone that suggested that Jarvis was the damnedest fool that ever walked on two legs. "Lutz, take us down to one-five-zero feet, smartly! Exec to the conning tower."

Jarvis uttered a foul oath under his breath before going up the ladder. Waters' eyes blazed at him as he emerged from the opening.

"You want to get us killed, is that it?" Waters asked. "No matter what the Japs do, let's just charge in and get another star, right?"

"Sir… I'm only stating that this maneuver robs us of our positional advantage," Jarvis said, hanging onto his temper by fingernails. "Those destroyers *aren't* pinging. We're not on the surface, so even if they *had* radar, we're undetectable. However, at this speed, they *could* detect us if we're making too much noise! Sir, they know these are American controlled waters, at least by day, so they're being cautious. We could *still* get them, sir, if—"

"That'll do!" Waters growled. "I don't want, nor need, *your advice*, Lieutenant. Consider yourself on report!"

"Sir?" Jarvis asked in genuine surprise.

"I think you're an arrogant, insubordinate glory hound who's deliberately putting *my* ship and crew in danger!" Waters exclaimed.

He knew he shouldn't have. He knew that he shouldn't have let Waters get to him, but Pat Jarvis' patience only went so far. As his face flushed in rage, he pointed a finger at the other man, "And *I* think, *sir*, that you've lost your nerve and you're using me as an excuse not to—"

"You're relieved!" Waters roared out in fury. "Confine yourself to your stateroom, or I'll have your pal Brannigan do it for you!"

Jarvis's color went from red to pale in an instant. He squared his jaw and met Waters' wide eyes with his own steely ones, "That won't be necessary, *sir*."

Jarvis stalked aft, ducking through the hatch into the after battery compartment and nearly collided with Chief Brannigan. When the chief saw the barely contained fury written all over Jarvis' face, he actually took a step backward in shock.

"Sorry, Harry…" Jarvis said absently. "I've been sent to my room."

Brannigan looked confused. He'd been aft assisting in the engine room and had just been called to the control room.

"Sir…?"

Jarvis sighed and gave him the edited version. Brannigan sighed and clenched his fists.

"He's gonna get us killed, sir," Brannigan said.

Jarvis scoffed, "Pfft… not if he keeps runnin' away from everything he won't."

Brannigan scowled and shook his head, "I dunno, sir… I've seen this before. Guy loses his nerve, and then he flip-flops between over-caution and recklessness. When I was a kid, we had this buddy, Tommy. Tommy was kind of a shy kid, not too many friends, but an okay kid. Anyways, he was always afraid to do stuff. Wanted to pal around with us and go to the lake and play on the rope swing or whatever… but he always chickened out. Then he turns sixteen, and his pop gets him this old twenty-two Ford, right? And Tommy works on it for a year. Soups it up, turns it into a real hotrod, y'know, sir?"

Jarvis thought he knew where this was headed, "So everybody wants to drag with Tommy, but he's too scared to."

"Yeah, and that's after he goes around braggin' about how great his ride is," Brannigan went on. "Anyways… one day, the captain of our football team, big good-lookin' guy we all called Dozer, on account he was a big old bastard… bigger'n you even, sir. Well, Dozer tells old Tommy he'd better put up or shut up because if he don't, he's a loud-mouthed sissy. So they race and…."

"Yeah," Jarvis sighed. "I think I get the picture. He goes from caution to reckless and totals his hotrod, am I right?"

"Not to mention Loraine Wellman, his sort of lady friend," Brannigan said. "The both of 'em, sir… it was brutal."

"I get your point, chief," Jarvis said, clapping him on the shoulder. "So I need you to get the message across forward. The Japs ain't hunting us, they're just being cautious, but the skipper's got us runnin' on full power. If they get close…."

"He won't listen to me any more than you, sir."

"No… but maybe the other chiefs will. You gotta *try*, Harry."

Brannigan bit his lip, "Aye-aye, sir."

Jarvis continued on to the tiny doghouse he shared with Skaggs and flopped onto his bunk. As the executive officer, he had a few perks in this cabin. For one, like the skipper's bunk, Jarvis' had a compass repeater as well as a speaker that he could activate to tune into the communications circuits. In this way, like the captain, he could listen to the phone talkers and even the conversations in the control room and conning tower to a degree.

He switched the speaker over to the control room feed. He heard the tinny voices and Lieutenant Lutz saying that the boat was leveling off at one-five-zero feet. Jarvis sighed. He could still feel the vibrations of the electric motors running at high speed. At thirty knots, the destroyers would probably not detect them, but still…

What he heard next, however, chilled his blood. It was faint because the speaker, Bobby Gaines, was in the conning tower, and the control room microphone barely picked him up. But it was loud enough for Jarvis to hear.

"*Aspect change on targets, sir! Screw noise diminishing… they've cut their engines!*"

"Oh hell…" Jarvis muttered. "They're doing a dash and listen… checking to see if any Yanks are lurking in the channel… and Waters is ringing the damned dinner bell!"

Then he heard the unmistakable sound of low-frequency search pings. The captain had ordered a dive and a course change less than three thousand yards away from the Japanese destroyers. If they fanned out and did an active search pattern…

"*They've got us!*" Gaines shouted.

Jarvis closed his eyes and crossed his fingers.

20

S-52 – SEALARK CHANNEL

"Sir… they might be able to hear our screws," Gaines warned.

"I didn't ask for suggestions, sonarman," Waters replied tightly. "Confine your comments to giving me accurate data on the Japs, if you please."

Gaines flushed, "Aye sir… Bearing is now one-zero-zero and opening slowly… range two-thousand yards."

S-52 was still running at a full speed setting, giving her six knots of way. Unfortunately, the reduction gearing of her electric motors and propellor shafts allowed enough ambient noise into the water to be detected by a passive sonar set listening carefully.

The three destroyers were already on high alert, having encountered and either chased off or sunk an American submarine hours earlier. Now, being in Sealark Channel, they were certain that there *must* be an American submarine stationed there. Especially after losing a destroyer just the night before.

So they had radically changed course and then went to all stop, allowing their thirty knots of momentum to carry them a ways while their sonar technicians could listen to the now quiet ocean.

Waters, in his haste to put distance between his boat and the approaching surface ships, was allowing enough engine noise out into the environment to be picked up. His reasoning had its merits, as the boat was now crossing directly through the DDs line of travel. However, had he not changed course at all, or gone right, the gap would have widened more quickly.

He knew he needed to reduce speed and probably go deeper in an attempt to find a halocline. Yet his fear, a monstrous thing that had risen up like a terrible force that would not be denied, glowed white-hot and brilliant in his soul. Such abject terror was a new experience for Bernard "Salty" Waters… but it was hardly the first time.

That night… that terrible night…

Something had broken inside him. Something he didn't even know was there, nor that *could* be broken. Now he stood between his periscopes, looking to all outward appearances as calm and collected as ever… except for the sweat beading on his face and running down in cold rivulets from his armpits. Yet the boat was warm, so that was at least not an obvious sign. However, he wasn't simply standing tall and aloof… he was rigid with fright.

Savage knew. Somehow, in some way, he knew. He'd sensed it even before S-52 had put into Brisbane, yet he didn't want to face reality. He had sensed that the captain had gone through something and that his confidence had been shaken badly. The torpedo officer hoped that it was temporary… and perhaps it was. Perhaps, in time, Waters would regain his self-assurance and come to grips with the loss of his men and his friend, the former XO.

Yet right now, his problems were putting the entire ship in mortal jeopardy. Savage was surprised to find that he wished Jarvis were here. Surprised but not entirely shocked. However he felt about the interloper, Jarvis *was* a rock, and he knew his business.

Savage had been resentful in the extreme when Jarvis had come aboard and been put in the first officer's slot. Savage felt that this should have been his place as the next senior man aboard. Now, though… maybe it was a blessing. Because after how Waters had treated Jarvis and had sent him packing… Savage was glad it wasn't him.

Then again… now he was here, and Jarvis wasn't. *Somebody* had to do something for the sake of the ship; the captain's wrath be damned.

But he couldn't nerve himself to do so. The captain's blood was up, and he was not in the mood for interference.

Ooooo-eeeee… ooooo-eeeee…

They were coming.

Aboard the *Fubuki*-class destroyer leader *Viper's Fang*, Kaigun Daisa Hitake Yamata stood at the plotting table with his hands clasped behind his back. A full captain, not the usual less senior officer who would command a destroyer, Yamata had been specially assigned to oversee the success of what the men were calling the "rat cargo" runs. Personally asked by Yamamoto himself, Yamata, of course, could not refuse.

Until recently, Yamata had been teaching at the Naval Academy. A twenty-five-year naval veteran, Yamata was arguably the nation's most seasoned and most brilliant anti-submarine warfare expert. Known to his students colloquially and affectionately as "The Sensei," Yamata had been charged with creating a special program specifically designed for destroyer captains.

His students were among the best of the best destroyer captains in the fleet, and with good reason. Yamata's intense thirty-day course focused not on such things as operating echolocation gear or the deployment of depth charges. By the time captains were placed into Yamata's classroom, they were expected to have mastered these operations already.

No, The Sensei's curriculum was centered around cleverness. How to think in three dimensions and how to get into the mind of a submarine commander. Yamata's students were taught the tenants of Sun Tzu, and how knowing one's enemy was the key to defeating him. Destroyer captains were trained on how to read not just the ocean but how to judge a submarine skipper's character and personality by his actions.

When the idea came to utilize destroyers to ferry men and equipment to Guadalcanal by night, the venerable Yamamoto had contacted The Sensei. He wanted him to personally oversee the operation. He would be given the *Fang*, which had recently been fitted with an air search radar system. Ironically primitive by American standards... ironic because in so many ways Japan was ahead of the technology curve... the radar would at least give Yamata an edge.

He'd also been informed that there was a very good possibility that a dogged and wily American named Turner and his new submarine would be lurking in New Georgia Sound. A submarine with extraordinary depth capability as well as speed and excellent sound and radar equipment. Further, Yamata had been contacted by an officer in temporary command of a strike carrier who had much the same things to say about Turner and his *Bull Shark*. This officer, Sato by name, admitted that he'd met Turner, as had one of his officers. It was Sato's belief that Turner must be hunted and destroyed if the operations on Guadalcanal were ever to succeed.

Yamata had thought Sato a bit of an odd duck. Perhaps even somewhat obsessive about this American. As if he was taking things personally. Although Sato's ship had ASW capability, the man had not gone through The Sensei's class. Otherwise, he might have known better.

Yamata was a tactician. He believed in the concept of stoicism. Your enemy in war was not to be idolized nor villainized. He was simply a man doing a job for his nation, as you were. Empathize with him in order to understand him... but do not ever sympathize with him before his defeat nor hate him personally simply for being on the opposite side of the field.

Yamata had been given a gift earlier that morning. When his radar had detected *something* several kilometers off. The equipment was almost laughably inadequate. It could only detect an object and give its distance. Not even a bearing to go on. However, at night, this was an advantage because this was when, more often than not, submarines operated on the surface in order to charge batteries and take advantage of greater speed.

When the radar tech had announced a contact, Yamata had instructed the lookouts to carefully scan out to the middle distance. One had seen the foamy line of a periscope's wake, glowing faintly with phosphorescence. No doubt the submarine had been angling to attack his convoy.

It was on the way to Guadalcanal from Rabaul that the ships of the rat cargo were most vulnerable. This was when they were prime targets, after all. Their job was to race down what the Americans called "The Slot" and deliver their men and supplies. Once done, the destroyers could exit the theater and circle back to New Britain, or they could go back up the sound, pinging and seeking out targets. They could certainly still be attacked, as was proven the night before when the shore bombardment was interrupted by an exploding destroyer.

Yamata had aggressively attacked the submarine, and it had vanished. He didn't know if it was the *evil* Turner or not. The engagement hadn't lasted long enough for him to determine this. He also didn't know if he'd destroyed the boat. The newer American subs had proven to be deep divers. Turner's own had been shown to have gone down to at least two-hundred and thirty meters in June.

Regardless, however, Yamata had neutralized the threat. There was no way even the newest American fleet submarines could catch a destroyer running at nearly full speed. Now, however, it was logical to assume that yet another boat lay in wait in the American-controlled waters between Guadalcanal, Savo, Tulagi and the other Florida Islands.

And he'd been proven correct. His maneuver to kill the engines on all three ships had revealed... something. His active sonar had yet to locate a submerged contact, but the sharp ears of his own ship's sonar operator *had* detected a mechanical transient within only a few kilometers.

"There is something out there," Yamata told Lieutenant Commander Daki, the ship's operational commander. He tapped a spot on the chart. "Here."

"Sonar is not entirely certain," Daki replied cautiously, not wishing to directly contradict The Sensei. He had been one of his recent students and knew all too well of the instructor's low tolerance for certain things. Unsubstantiated guesses, flights of fancy or a willingness to ignore even insignificant data.

"I am entirely certain, Daki," Yamata said. "There *is* a submarine out there. Even had sonar failed to detect any sound, there is a submarine out there. Have radio inform our two charges to proceed at one-third. As we shall. No more than eight knots. Have them fan out to a thousand meters to either side of us. We shall sweep for this boat. He is near."

"*Hai*," Daki replied and bowed. It was the only response he could make.

"And Daki…" Yamata added while still examining the chart. "Order all ships to go silent. Secure from active pinging."

That nearly brought Daki up short and forced a question from his lips. Wisely, however, he managed to contain himself and simply bowed again and moved to the radio shack.

"The opportunity for his defeat is provided by your enemy…." Yamata said with just a hint of a smile playing at his lips.

"They've stopped pinging," Gaines stated. "I'm detecting increased machinery noise and… screws, sir. They're starting their engines again."

"Sir…" Savage began hesitantly. There was something about the actions of the Jap ships that alarmed him. He couldn't quite say what it was, except that the feeling was vaguely uneasy.

There was something… crafty about the maneuvers that caused his skin to creep.

"You have something to add, torpedo officer?" Waters asked.

"With all due respect, sir… shouldn't we reduce speed, alter course or dive… or all three, sir?" Savage asked tentatively. "Somebody up there *knows* something…."

"Scared, Chris?" Waters needled ever so slightly.

This made Savage's face burn again. Both with humiliation and with real anger toward Waters. Humiliation because the captain was right. Chris *was* afraid. And that the man had so blithely exposed this to the men around them angered Savage.

Savage had always struggled with his ego. He was young, a bit cocky and blessed with good looks. A part of him knew that he probably let his ego run a little wild sometimes. Yet he was learning, if slowly, that there were times when you *had* to put that aside.

"Yes sir," Savage admitted openly.

Hell, who wasn't scared? Acting like you weren't scared didn't mean shit. Men got scared. Submarine battles could be scary, especially when you were on the receiving end. If the men were scared, it might make them feel a little better to know that the officers were human, too. At least the junior officers.

The captain, of course, was expected to be the rock at all times. A ship's captain was a mighty figure. A towering pillar of terrible strength.

Yeah, if only...

"Well, if it'll make you feel better, Chris," Waters joked. "We'll go ahead and take evasive action. Helm, reduce to all ahead one-third. Alert maneuvering, I want four knots. Crawford, fifteen degree down bubble. Let's see if we can't find ourselves a halocline. Helm, right standard rudder."

The orders were given sensibly and acknowledged. Savage didn't like the jokes at his expense, however. Up until recently, that had not been Waters' way.

"Now passing one-eight-zero...."

"... heading now three-three-zero...."

"Range closing... fifteen hundred yards...."

Pat Jarvis was beside himself. He lounged on his bunk and watched the gyrocompass repeater slowly swing toward the north. He knew that Waters was trying to slip between the center DD and the one to her left, or he thought so.

He also knew that the boat had reduced speed, thus becoming quieter, thank God. Yet sitting in his dog box cabin with nothing to do but listen to his fate unfold around him was driving him bananas. Pat Jarvis' temperament was ill-suited for passivity.

The hull creaked and groaned around him, and without having a depth gauge to read, Jarvis knew they were planing down. The obvious down angle on the bow would've been a dead giveaway in any case. He wondered how deep Waters would go.

The S-class boats had a test depth of two hundred feet by design. However, as all submariners knew, that was not the maximum. Every submarine, in fact, after completing her sea trials, would engage in a test dive to find out exactly what her test depth was. It was generally considered to be that point when leaks began to appear.

Aboard *Bull Shark,* the depth gauge glass had been marked at six-hundred and thirty-five feet on her initial dive trials. Of course, the submarine was built to a spec of four hundred, so it wasn't much of a surprise. However, after that dive and after finding the issues, the mark had been updated. It had been re-marked in early June when the boat had gone down to eight-hundred and five feet without losing the integrity of the pressure hull. To be conservative, Turner had the official test-depth mark on the gauge set somewhere in between to seven-hundred feet.

The crew of *Bull Shark* had yet to find her crush depth, thank God…

In S-52's control room, the gauge had been marked to three-hundred and fifteen. Pretty damned impressive for a boat rated to only two-hundred, and that had come off the ways in 1922. Yet unless there was a halocline above that limit, the depth made little difference. If the boat couldn't hide, it was only a matter of time before the three destroyers found her out.

When the eerie echo location began again, Jarvis could sense that this was probably about to happen. The low-frequency search beams wailed mournfully around him. Their spectral voices probing the blackness of the early morning waters like lost souls longing for refuge.

No, not refuge… more like lost souls calling for others to join them in the cold embrace of a watery grave…

They seemed to be coming from port and starboard… and when they ramped up to attack frequency and began to grow louder, the XO closed his eyes and said a quick prayer. The sonar beams were joined by the churning of steel blades through seawater and then…

"*All hands! All hands! Rig for depth charge!*"

Ping… ping… Ping… PONG…

Then silence. Jarvis stood, clutching at the bunk support and not sure what to do. He wasn't used to this. Wasn't used to having nothing to do when an enemy surface ship was attacking. Should he stand, should he sit, or…

Wha-BOOOOOOM!

He found himself flat on his back with flashing stars circling. Just like that. One moment, Jarvis was standing and the next lying on the deck and not sure how he'd gotten there. The bow was angled even further down. He flexed his muscles, rotated his head... nothing broken... he got to his feet.

"Flooding in the maneuvering room!" somebody called. Not over the PA but just yelled it.

"Fuck this," Jarvis growled and barreled out into the compartment. Waters could only court-martial him once, and he'd be damned if when asked, "Where were you when the ship was battered into razor blades, Jarvis?" if he'd say, "Oh, cowering under my bed like a big sissy as ordered, sir."

He ran aft.

"Now passing two-five-zero feet!" Lutz called up through the conning tower hatch. "We're past official test depth, captain!"

There was no answer. An overhead pipe had split at a fitting, and a fine but insistent mist was spraying down into the control room. More than one man was picking himself up off the deck, nursing bruises or pressing hands against cuts.

Lutz happened to look aft through the hatchway into the after battery compartment in time to see Jarvis exit his stateroom and run aft. The XO leapt through the hatch into the engine room in that weird half-crouched way that kept him from hitting his head.

For the first time since the new officer came aboard, Lutz was truly glad for it. He felt in his gut that the big man could and would handle any emergency that arose.

"Captain!" Lutz called again.

"Captain's out," Savage finally responded, although he didn't exactly sound as if he were in control of his faculties either.

Lutz went up the ladder and peered around. Every bulb but one had been shattered and that single bulb, a red one, cast the conning tower in an infernal pallor that made the scene all the more frightening.

Waters lay sprawled on the deck, blood on his face and his mouth slack in forced unconsciousness. Kneeling over him, Chris Savage's own face was a bloody mask from a cut over his left eye. He looked up, pale and slightly bewildered. Lutz knew instantly that he'd also received a bad bonk on the bean.

Lutz's odd calm, something he'd put in place after the last horrific incident aboard this boat, was beginning to fray. Seeing injured and bleeding men slathered in demonic light was quickly unraveling the stoicism he'd so carefully been wrapping himself in.

Somebody needed to take charge, and do it now… but somebody had to man the diving station, too… and the pharmacist's mate should be called…

"Mr. Lutz," a confident voice called from below and was accompanied by a tug at his shorts leg.

"Jarvis…?" Lutz asked, feeling a bit like he was not quite connected to the world at that moment, too.

"Chief Brannigan, sir," the COB said. "Shall I man the dive station, sir?"

"Yeah… yeah, COB," Lutz said, blinking away his fog. Or trying to. "Call Homer in here, too. What's our depth?"

"Three hundred and going down, sir," Brannigan said.

Lutz was comforted by how calm the chief sounded. Then again, he'd been in the navy a good five years longer than Lutz himself… so that made sense. As he pondered this, the boat spoke out with a series of groans, creeks and pistol shot like cracks that made Lutz's belly jump.

What to do…?

"Orders, Mr. Lutz?" Marx, the helmsman, asked, almost begged, really.

"They're circling around for another run, sir," Gaines said from the after end of the conning tower.

"Oh Jesus…" Lutz muttered. "What do I do now?"

Pat Jarvis undogged the hatch to the maneuvering room and ducked through it and into a watery chaotic hell. Half a dozen men were shouting and screaming at one another over the sound of a rushing waterfall. Several pipes in the overhead had burst, shooting out multiple streams of silvery foaming seawater. Chief Cantone stood in the center, shouting at the men seemingly to no effect.

"Chief!" Jarvis hollered over the din. "What's the story back here!"

Cantone's face went through an odd range of emotions. First resentment and then surprise and then something that might have been relief.

"Two transfer conduits busted open!" Cantone shouted back. "And I think we got water comin' in below, too!"

"Well, then what the Christ are you all doin' back here? Jerkin' it?" Jarvis shouted. He stepped up to two men and grabbed them, each by their collars and spun them around so he could shout in their faces. "At ease! Get ahold of yourselves!"

"Sir! We're takin' on—" one of the men said, almost hysterical with panic.

"No shit, Dick Tracy!" Jarvis barked. "And runnin' around like headless roosters ain't helpin'! You two, get a fuckin' patch on that line! Look alive now, goddammit!"

He pushed the two men to an equipment storage locker and flung the door open, spilling out a variety of gear and tools. This seemed to snap the two men out of their funk. He then ran to Cantone.

"Chief, get into the motor room and figure out what's leaking down there," Jarvis said. "I'll get the other pipe patched. Hurry it up, now! We're still at a down angle, and I think we might have a problem in the conning tower."

Cantone's eyes bulged, "The Skipper? You think…? We're still goin' down? What's our depth?"

"Don't worry about that shit now," Jarvis grabbed the smaller man's shirt in both fists and pulled him close. "Get ahold of yourself, man! You're a fuckin' *chief*, for Christ's sake! These guys are lookin' to you for guidance, and you're flippin' your wig! Just think about sub school and the trainer. This ain't no different! Now take Branson and get below! *Move* it!"

Jarvis could see that the two men he'd grabbed were already wrestling a clamp patch over the transfer line. The patch was essentially two halves of a pipe, about six inches long, with flanges on the outside for bolts to run through. The patch was fitted to the pipe to either side, and then four bolts were cranked down to seal it.

The other pipe that was spewing water was lower down on the port bulkhead. It was an air-transfer line that fed the after main ballast tanks. It had been invaded by seawater and burst at a connection point. Fortunately, there was a seacock aft of the rupture that could cut off the water flow for the time being. Jarvis went to the handle, shoving two sailors aside who were nearly catatonic with terror.

What the hell was wrong with these guys? Jarvis pondered as he wrapped his hands around the handle and began to pull. It didn't budge. Either corroded in place or from the pressure, or both.

All these guys had been through training… so why were they so paralyzed?

He grabbed one of the men and slapped him across the face, "Travis! TRAVIS! Snap out of it, damn you! Help me seal this flow!"

Travis, a nineteen-year-old kid from Missouri whose only experience with water was watching boats move up and down the Mississippi, blinked at Jarvis. The XO slapped him again and shook the kid.

Finally, he saw some light flicker in those wide brown eyes, and the XO put the man's hands on the long red handle. Together they pulled, putting all their weight and muscle into it. Again, the valve wouldn't budge. Jarvis was nearly ready to find another option when there came a shrill squeal and the handle turned ninety degrees.

The silence, or more accurately, the lack of roaring water, was so stark that even Jarvis was temporarily at a loss.

"Patch on, sir!" one of the other men said.

"Okay, good work," Jarvis said and looked down the grating hatchway into the motor room. "Chief?"

"I think we got it, Mr. Jarvis," Cantone said. "Just need to get the pumps workin' to get this water out."

"You okay if I go forward then?"

"Yes sir," Cantone replied. For once, with no sneer or contempt in his voice.

. . .

The scene in the control room and conning tower wasn't much better. When Jarvis arrived, dripping and hot in spite of it, he saw several men laid out on deck, including the captain. Homer Burk, the slightly overweight pharmacist's mate from Cleveland, was bent over them doing what he could.

"Harry?" Jarvis asked Brannigan, who stood splay-legged like a prizefighter in the forward center of the room.

With that one question, Brannigan knew exactly what Jarvis wanted, "Headed zero-zero-zero at all ahead one-third, depth three-four-zero feet. Japs are circling overhead, but they haven't dropped another batch on us yet, sir."

"A layer, do you think?" Jarvis asked.

"No bathy on this boat… but maybe."

"How deep do you think she can go?" Jarvis asked.

Brannigan arched an eyebrow, "All the way to the bottom, sir… but as for staying in one piece… hard to say. She's an old boat, sir."

"Blow some six-hundred-pound air into the pressure hull to counteract," Jarvis said. "And get the drain pump on. Pretty bad leaks aft, but I think we're okay for now. See what you can do about neutralizing our buoyancy. I'll see what I can do about neutralizing the Nips."

Brannigan grinned, "This isn't the relaxing vacation you promised me, Henry."

"Meh," Jarvis said as he went up the ladder. "Least it ain't boring, Martha."

Crawford Lutz was standing by the torpedo tubes, looking lost. Chris Savage sat on the deck, holding a cloth to his head and looking dazed. Jack Cleghorn stood by the dead reckoning indicator repeater and chart desk looking strained. Marx was staring at Jarvis, as was Gaines. They both looked hopeful and in dire need of direction.

"Chris, get below and have Homer look at that head," Jarvis ordered. "Crawford, can you man the TDC?"

Lutz blinked in surprise, "the TDC?"

"Yeah, this thing," Jarvis said, pushing the man into the operator's seat.

Savage struggled to get to his feet, "I should be… up here…."

"Not if you're loopy," Jarvis said. "Can you get down the ladder?"

"I think so…" Savage replied dazedly. "But—"

"But nothin'," Jarvis barked. "I don't have time for this. Get below and get looked at. Helm, all stop. Ring me up a reverse bell, all back two-thirds! Bobby, give me and Jack here some info on our targets! Diving officer, reverse your planes."

"Oh hell…" Jarvis heard Brannigan grumble, and he swore he heard a chuckle.

"Hard to pinpoint," Gaines said. "The sound profile is a bit attenuated, sir… but I think one is just abaft the port beam at about a thousand yards, another is almost astern of us, and the other is five-hundred yards off the bow. If I had to guess, I'd say they're converging."

"Very well," Jarvis said. "Harry, level us off at four bills."

The down angle slowly swiveled from forward to aft as S-52 began to move backward and down. Jarvis had to clear his ears as high-pressure air filled the boat, increasing internal pressure in an attempt to ameliorate the boat's ability to fend off the hundreds of pounds per inch of seawater that probed unceasingly for a way inside.

"What're you doing, sir?" Lutz asked.

"They've been tracking us," Jarvis said. "But based on the lack of tooth shakers and the sound profile, I think we're inside a salt layer. That captain upstairs is calculating where we'll be, and he's going to attack that area. I'm moving us away in the most direct line."

"Are we gonna attack?" Lutz asked.

Jarvis glanced at him, "No, Crawford. We lost that advantage some time ago. I'm just trying to save our asses at the moment. To fix a major screw up, frankly."

"Sir?" Lutz asked.

Jarvis scoffed, "Your brave captain nearly got us killed because he's lost his nerve and isn't introspective enough to realize it. He should've removed himself from command after that last mission. We had a perfect attack where we might have taken out two of these DDs. Instead, he unzipped his fly, and now we're all in mortal peril. Sorry to burst your bubble."

Lutz did not object. He only lowered his eyes. Like it or not, the XO was right.

Down below, Chris Savage heard the comment as well. And although he'd been Waters' most staunch supporter, he couldn't argue with Jarvis. The man was right. Only his quick thinking could save them now. Savage only hoped it wasn't too late.

"I think I hear splashes!" Gaines hissed.

Jarvis drew in a breath, "Everybody cross your fingers and toes… and we're now running silent."

A dozen depth charges thundered in the deep. Yet they weren't close. Close enough to be heard and close enough to rock the boat, but not close enough to damage her.

This happened twice more, each time the sub-surface explosions getting a little quieter with distance. After the third round, Jarvis ordered the engines to all stop in order to save the batteries.

"I think we're okay," he said, removing a soggy pack of Camels from his breast pocket. "Shit… we'll wait it out for a while. They have a delivery to make and should move off in a few minutes. Phone talker, alert all compartments to stand easy at battle stations and the smoking lamp is lit. I don't suppose I can cadge a pill from anybody?"

This drew a chuckle from the men in the tower. Lutz actually smiled as he held out a pack of Chesterfields, "I'd buy you a drink if I could, sir. But this is the best I can do for now."

Jarvis grinned and took a cigarette, "That's okay, Crawford… least this way I'll look cool."

21

GUADALCANAL – WEST OF TAIVU POINT

AUGUST 21, 1942 – 0930 LOCAL TIME

"You think they'll come this way, Jake?" Webster Clayton asked quietly.

"So many men, and with at least one field gun?" Treadway answered. "I'd say so, sir."

"I agree," Vousa added.

Three men crouched low in a stand of rosewoods, birds of paradise and vines on a small rise that overlooked the coast road. One a Melanesian former Solomon Islands Protectorate officer, one an intelligence agent with the Office of Strategic Services and the other a young Marine PFC. Above them, well concealed in the fronds of a betel nut palm, was a fifteen-year-old boy with sharp eyes and remarkably steady nerves.

"We need to get back to the perimeter and report," Treadway insisted. "We know the Japs are here and know that almost a thousand of them are marching for Alligator Creek."

"Yeah, but they should've been here by now, right?" Clayton asked. "I mean, they left their camp at Taivu over twenty-four hours ago, and we're a little more than halfway… so where are they?"

"Twenty-two miles is a long way on this island," Vousa said. "At least with so many men and equipment. Even on this side where the terrain is friendlier."

"Hmm..." Clayton frowned, deep in thought. "Maybe Joe's right... maybe we should high-tail it back regardless. What if they passed us up in the night?"

The men fell silent at this. It had crossed all of their minds, of course. Yet Vousa wanted to be certain. Clayton did as well, naturally. Treadway didn't much care either way, except that he hated the idea of his brother Marines being surprised by a thousand Japs.

"Papa!" Sam called down suddenly. "I see somethin'! I think it's metal a'gleamin' through the trees there."

"Where, lad?" Vousa asked.

"A bit to the right... there's a break in the jungle, and I can see shiny things," the boy replied.

"Come on down, then," Vousa said and grinned. "Sharp eyes, that boy."

There was the sound of scrabbling and scratching of hardened bare feet on rough bark, and Samuel's lean, lithe form appeared. He, too, was smiling.

"Can you describe what you saw, Sam?" Clayton asked.

"Definitely men, sir," Sam said.

"Jesus... you got him doing it now, Joe," Clayton observed wryly.

"Yes sir," said Treadway.

Sam chuckled, "I couldn't really see much... but sun on metal, for sure... and boots."

"Boots?" Treadway asked.

"Yes... they're up on a rise. Maybe the same high as me in that tree... and I could see their feet," Sam explained. "Regular boots, too. Not those funny kind the Naponapo wear."

"Tabis..." Clayton muttered. "So, they might be our guys, then?"

"Maybe," Vousa said. "In that case, we need to make contact. If it is the Marines, then they may be walking right into the jaws of a larger enemy force."

That made all of their stomachs tighten. Treadway's eyes brightened, "Permission to—"

"No, Joe," Vousa said, holding up a hand. "I'll go. I've got my

American flag here to show, and I know the terrain and can guide them."

Treadway frowned, a vague sense of unease flittering across the nerves in his back and belly. Clayton nodded slowly in agreement.

"I'll go and make contact," Vousa said. "Why don't you two start back for the perimeter. Sam, you go with them to show them the best ways. Then when I get to the lines, I'll send you back home to let mama know what's happening. You think you can do that, son?"

Sam puffed out proudly. Not only was he being given a real-life mission in a war, but his adopted father had also called him son. It was a small thing, but to the boy, it meant more than his teenage soul could express.

"You sure, Jake?" Clayton asked.

Vousa nodded, "Not a problem, Web. Hell, even *if* they turn out to be Japs... I'm just an islander out foraging. Can't risk you lads, now can we?"

With that, hands were shaken, and hugs exchanged, and Jacob Vousa vanished into the brush like a spirit. For a long while, the three men stood on their hill and listened. It would be difficult to hear anything over the din of the biomass of Guadalcanal. Although Sam thought the soldiers were no more than a quarter-mile off, the huge amount of active and vocal life effectively drowned out any kind of identifiable noise.

At least for a time. After about fifteen minutes, perhaps twenty, a man-made sound broke through the cacophony. It was the echoing crack of a rifle.

"Probably a warning shot into the air," Treadway said. "SOP..."

And then, in one of those odd lulls that sometimes occurs in nature or at a loud cocktail party, the rainforest quieted, and shouts could be heard, and words called out in anger.

The words were Japanese.

As Jacob Vousa moved through the underbrush, he pondered the irony of his situation. Almost two years ago, he'd retired from the Protectorate and had decided to move his family from Malaita to

Guadalcanal. Part of it was to separate them and himself from the local crime there, of course.

Certainly, staying in the area in which he'd been operating and had made enemies for years was not a good idea. Guadalcanal was an entirely different situation. While there was some small crime on the island, it was a pittance compared to Malaita. Generally speaking, the people were friendly, and there was quite a lot of work on the Lever Brother's plantation and others.

Yet how ironic indeed that not long after settling into their comfortable village, the world war had come right to their doorstep. Vousa had taken Irene and Sam and his two daughters away from the thieves and drug dealers and street gangs of Malaita and plopped them right into the middle of a war zone. A war zone where Japanese soldiers did whatever they felt like in the name of racial superiority.

At least there were men like Marty Clemens to fight back, however. And the American Marines had come to drive the Japanese away. Vousa knew enough about America and Britain to know that once successful, they wouldn't then turn on their Melanesian partners. If anything, the allies would help the people of the Solomons after the war. They'd help rebuild and provide modern services for the education of the children and treatment for the sick.

Vousa smiled at that. He thought of the brave men he'd already met. Marty, of course, whom he'd known for a number of years now. There was that submarine captain, Turner, and his men, and those Marines who'd come to the island at the beginning of the month. Brave, funny and generous men.

Now that he was closer, Vousa could see through the brush and up onto the rise. Samuel had been right. The soldiers there were dressed in standard boots, and their uniforms weren't the light beige or khaki he'd seen so often on the Naponapo. It was hard to really tell from this distance, but Vousa was sure they were U.S. Marines.

He'd been given a small American flag by Al Decker, the officer who'd accompanied Turner. A small gift, just something to hang onto or hang outside his house. Yet now, it was a symbol of friendship.

Vousa pulled the flag from his pocket, unfolded it and held it high as he moved incautiously up the rise and out of the jungle. He called out to a small group of men gathered together beneath the shade of a cluster of teaks.

Too late, he realized his foolish error. Although the men wore darker green, they were not American uniforms. They lacked the camouflage pattern and were a shade lighter. Also, the Japanese wore those funny hats with the cloth hanging down on the sides and in the back to protect them from the sun... as these men did. They were also smaller in stature, and when they turned to see who was calling out... they had the slanted eyes of his enemy.

Shouts rose, weapons were raised, and Vousa knew he was, as Marty would say, totally and completely *fucked*.

Four men surrounded him, directed by what was probably a sergeant. His flag was yanked out of his hands, and his weapon snatched away. Vousa was grateful... sort of... that the gun was an Arisaka rifle and not an American weapon. At least he could try and claim he wasn't working directly with the Yanks.

Harsh words were spoken, and Vousa was shoved forward. He briefly entertained the notion of making a break for it. Lurching off into the rainforest and vanishing. A deadly notion. He wouldn't get more than three paces.

All he could do now was to bide his time. To potentially distract the Japs so that Clayton and Treadway could get back to the Marine lines... and so that his son could get away.

Vousa was marched along a short path and into a larger clearing in which hundreds of men milled about. Some stood by bivouac fires cooking their rations, others were setting up tents, and still, others were inspecting a field gun that had been dragged along with them. Near a large tent, several officers stood and spoke to one another. One of them, a man dressed in the usual light khaki, red sash and hanging sword of an officer, looked toward the group of soldiers with bemusement. Vousa didn't know Japanese rank insignia, but he could tell that this man must be of high rank.

The soldiers pushed Vousa roughly up to the men. The sergeant said some gruff words by way of explanation, and the officer nodded and regarded Vousa coolly. He then spoke in an even tone and seemed to be asking a question. Vousa spoke some Japanese and was able to glean the meaning. The officer wanted to know who he was and why he'd approached his soldiers. Vousa pretended to be ignorant and only blinked at the man and shook his head, a half-smile of blithe stupidity his only response.

The officer said something to one of his aids, and the man hurried off. The officer moved closer to Vousa, pacing to one side and then the other, inspecting the islander as if he were a cut of meat or a new vehicle.

The officer stopped before Vousa, and his black eyes met the Melanesian's and bore into them. The eyes were cold, almost dead, and yet contained in their onyx depths a terrible resolve that made Vousa uneasy. In his mind's eye, Vousa saw the Japanese officer's face morph into that of a ravenous shark. Its huge jaws, overstuffed with razor-sharp teeth opened, ready to consume him… and those eyes, those depthless, soulless and horrible eyes…

A fist shot out and snapped Vousa's head back, replacing the image of the hungry shark with dozens of exploding stars. The officer barked out an order, and hands fell on Vousa then, roughly dragging him to one side of the clearing. There, he was lashed to the trunk of a tree. The sergeant laughed harshly, said something in Japanese that Vousa recognized as rather unfriendly, spat on the islander and then walked away.

It became evident, and rather quickly that Vousa was to be tortured. For one thing, they'd tied him to the northern side of the large tree. The side where sunlight would not be shaded either by morning or afternoon in the summer. Already, after just a few minutes, Vousa felt the unyielding solar radiation flowing over him, heating him and drawing the water from his body as unending rivulets of sweat.

That was not the worst of it, however. It didn't take long before he felt them. The fire ants. There was a nest at the base of the trees, and the little creatures had already homed in on Vousa. Whether out of curiosity or in defense of their nest, the stinging insects began to work their way up the tree and onto his boots and under his trousers. Some disconnected corner of his mind was thankful that he'd chosen to wear nondescript clothing on that day rather than the BDUs he'd been given.

Tiny hot lances of pain prickled up his legs. The ants stung or bit or whatever they did, moving from his calves to his thighs... up his torso, inside the trousers and stung his groin. It was horrific because he could not react. He couldn't swat them away or scratch at the burning pinpricks on his skin.

Mercifully, after perhaps an hour, the ants moved on. For whatever reason, they'd decided they'd made their point and left the creature alone. Left him alone to experience each and every one of the hundreds of painful stings the little army had left. Of course, the sun continued to broil Vousa, and he began to get light-headed.

He couldn't be certain, but he suddenly jerked his head up and thought that he might have slept. He must have... the sun was nearly directly overhead by then. That was a blessing, at least. He could only hope that his friends and adopted son had long since left the area. He prayed that when they heard the Japanese shouts upon his revealing himself, that Clayton or Treadway or Sam hadn't tried something heroic.

Something tepid and wet was thrown in Vousa's face. He coughed and then tried to slurp up as much of the water as he could. A man shouted at him in harsh, guttural Japanese. A hand slapped him, seeming almost gentle in comparison to the fire that throbbed over his lower body.

The ropes were untied, and once more, several pairs of hands grabbed Vousa and half-pushed and half-dragged him across the clearing to the large tent where he was led inside.

An officer sat at a folding table with several maps open before him. Beside the officer was a soldier, appearing pinch-faced and worried. With a shock, Vousa realized that he *recognized* the man! He'd met him the year before, and they'd even spoken a few times. His name was Ishimora, and he'd been a supervisor on the Lever Brothers plantation.

By the surprised look in Ishimora's eyes, Vousa knew that he recognized him, and his heart sank.

The officer said something, and Ishimora bowed slightly and looked to Vousa, "Mr. Vousa... This is Colonel Ichiki of the Imperial Japanese Army. My name is Ishimora, but I believe you remember me, as I remember you."

Vousa nodded but said nothing.

Ishimora continued, "I have told the colonel that you were a Solomon Islands Protectorate officer and have recently retired... although you still associated with and worked with Martin Clemens."

"Of course you did," Vousa croaked, fury rising in him.

"The colonel wishes to know where you got that flag and that rifle," Ishimora asked sourly.

"Go fuck yourself!" Vousa spat. "You traitorous, back-stabbing cowardly little shit. And you can pass that on to your precious *colonel* in the bargain."

Ishimora glared at Vousa. Yet, in his features, there was just a hint of an amber flush. Vousa's barb had gone home, and Ishimora tried to cover his discomfort with anger. He repeated the words exactly, and to Vousa's surprise, Ichiki laughed.

Ichhiki asked another question, sounding almost friendly in his tone. Again, Vousa understood the gist. Even if he'd spoken not a single word of Japanese, it would've been plainly obvious under the circumstances.

"The colonel desires you tell him all you know about the American Marine positions, perimeter and strength of men, type of weapons and so forth," Ishimora said coldly.

Vousa said nothing. He only glared at the man he'd once actually liked. A heavy silence fell, and from nowhere, it seemed, something hard and heavy struck Vousa on the left cheek. An explosion of fireworks lit off in his mind as his head snapped to the right, and waves of dizziness and pain rippled from his head down into his shoulders.

Someone shouted something harsh. The colonel sat behind his table and waited. Ishimora was the only one to look uncomfortable. Vousa hoped it wasn't for his sake but for the man's own. As if failing to get Vousa to talk would somehow reflect badly on Ishimora and bring him to grief as well.

"Tell him, Jacob," Ishimora pressed.

Vousa only stared and sneered at the man.

Another officer, one who'd been standing off to Ichiki's left, cursed and drew his sword. He stepped forward and, with a swift and practiced motion, slashed the blade across Vousa's left arm. So sharp was the blade and so precise the cut that at first, he hardly felt it.

Only when the sensation of warm blood flowing down his arm and oddly soothing his ant bites did the pain of the laceration register.

It hurt, but it was hardly debilitating. It could have been, though. Jacob knew from experience that the Japanese Katana was incredibly sharp and could cleave a man nearly in half from skull to hips if driven home hard enough.

Ichiki met Vousa's eyes. As before, they were endless onyx pools that revealed little… except that perhaps this time, and Vousa half-believed he'd only imagined it, that there was a modicum of respect lurking in those bottomless orbs.

Ichiki said something, and Ishimora grinned with malevolent glee, "The colonel says that if his questions won't avail, then he suggests that perhaps the *ants* will be more persuasive."

Once more, Vousa was dragged to his tree. This time, however, he wasn't tied to the trunk. This time, he was forced down onto his back. His arms and legs were staked down, and his boots removed. There was harsh laughter and disobliging words, and the soldiers walked away.

Once more, the sun beat down relentlessly. Once more, the fire ants marched to the call… and in greater numbers. Now they swarmed over Vousa, biting him, each tiny mouth taking a tiny chunk of him. They were eating him alive… death by a million cuts.

He couldn't tell how long this went on. He simply lay there, his entire body one enormous flaming ball of pain. Sooner than he thought, though, his bonds were released, and he was dragged to his feet, brushed off and then suspended by his arms from a branch. There he was once more shouted at, sworn at and beaten. Soldiers took turns slamming their rifle butts into Vousa's limbs and torso. Ishimora himself delivered several vicious kicks and punches.

At one point, a hard blow to his gut made Vousa gag and vomit. This brought laughter and jeers from the now large crowd of Japanese men around him. Ichiki was there, but he wasn't laughing. He uttered just three words. Harsh and commanding, and everyone went silent.

To his astonishment, someone stepped forward and pushed the

opening of a canteen into Vousa's lips. The canteen was tipped, and Jacob drank. He drank and drank and drank. Although grateful, a part of him was sorry for his own weakness. Ichiki wasn't being kind. He wasn't offering a reprieve for the brave man who wouldn't betray his fellows.

No... Ichiki was only keeping Vousa's body going so that he could receive more tortures.

More than once afterward, Vousa passed out. At one point, he was dimly aware and a little surprised to find that the sun had set. Light still glowed in the sky, but the brutal orb itself had dipped below the treeline. As he was being cut down, he saw Ichiki again, regarding him stoically. Ishimora was beside him, waiting expectantly. The colonel said something that Vousa didn't or couldn't understand. Yet when he saw Ishimora flinch, the sight brought with it a vague sense of satisfaction.

Ishimora said nothing until Ichiki barked at him, "The... the colonel says that if you will not talk, then you will be marched into the jungle and executed. He says... he says that while he respects your dedication, it cannot be allowed. He also says that he respects your courage and that you are not some filthy... filthy cowardly collaborator who turns on his fellows for his own personal gain."

This last was said shamefully, and Ishimora actually hung his head. Jacob somehow found the strength to croak out a bitter and scornful laugh before the soldiers dragged him away.

They moved west, perhaps a few hundred yards until they came to a small clearing. There, the sergeant who'd first captured him smiled cruelly and aimed his rifle. The bayonet was affixed, as were the bayonets of the other five men. They would not shoot him, not wishing to make any noise.

An order was barked, and two soldiers grabbed Vousa's arms and pulled in opposite directions, both holding him erect and keeping the arms out of the way. With adder-like speed, the sergeant drove the point of his blade up beneath Vousa's armpit. Even as the pain burst inside like a red-hot poker, Vousa's mind somehow tracked the sensations. He felt the blade slide inside his body and then out again, just above the collarbone... and then in again, piercing the soft flesh under his chin and actually splitting his tongue.

More blows and thrusts came then. One went in the side and came out his chest, several more just jabbed, puncturing his chest and abdomen. Once, Vousa actually managed to free an arm and ward off a deadly bayonet thrust that would've pierced his heart. This, however, was the last of his resistance. His hands were bound in front of him, and a thunderous crack on the back of his skull turned Vousa's world black, and his body crumpled as if bonelessly to the mold.

When Jacob Vousa returned to consciousness not fifteen minutes later, he was more than a little surprised. His body was one giant wound that stung and throbbed and pulsed. Strangely, he didn't hurt as much as he thought he should have. Probably in shock…

With a force of will that even Hercules would have applauded, Vousa struggled to his feet and began to stumble westward, using the last of the day's light as a guide. As he moved, he began to chew on the ropes that had been used to bind his wrists. It was a long and slow process, yet it gave him something to focus upon. Something to pass the time until he could find the Marines.

He *must* find them… must warn them… he must know what happened to his friends… and his boy…

With this single-minded purpose, Jacob Vousa stumbled into the rainforest. More often than not, he fell to his knees and crawled. Yet, against all odds and all sense, he managed to make progress.

"We gotta go back for him," Treadway was pleading to Captain Brush at the First Battalion CP at Alligator Creek. "Sir…"

"At ease, Treadway," Brush said and glanced at Clayton. "You think he's still alive, sir?"

Clayton and Treadway met one another's eyes. In truth, the odds were small. No, that was a lie… they were all but nil. Yet after hearing those voices, they'd stopped Sam from going after his father. They'd convinced the boy to go back to his village and let them know what was happening, as his father wanted.

Both Treadway and Clayton had argued with each other.

Interestingly, at various points in the argument, they'd each taken the side of yes, let's go get him and no, it'd be suicide.

"I don't know, sir...." Clayton said, "but, we should at least—"

A shout from the sandspit. Alligator Creek was part of the Teneru River. It broke off from the river and became something of a marshy swamp separated from the ocean by a forty-foot wide sandspit. Not unlike the mouth of the Matanikau.

On this spit, a squad of Marines stood guard and watched as, out of the gloom, a lone figure materialized from the jungle, lurching and stumbling toward them. A man raised a shout, and when the figure didn't respond, several men went to accost him.

"What the hell...?" Brush asked.

Soon enough, the mystery was answered. To the utter shock of Treadway and Clayton, the Marines half-carried a bloody and battered Jacob Vousa into the lights. Everyone was horrified by his wounds and by the visible welts of hundreds of red ant bites that covered every exposed inch of his flesh.

"Jake!" Clayton said, tears threatening to overflow. "Oh my God... how... what...?"

"Japs..." Vousa barely managed to say in a voice that sounded as parched and cracked as Death Valley. "Coming..."

"Medic!" Brush hollered. "Water! Now!"

A pair of Navy corpsmen appeared and began to tend to Vousa as best they could. Two canteens of water were poured into the man, and he could barely speak even so, his voice muddy and garbled because of his wounded tongue.

"A thousand men... Colonel Ichiki... marching with gun...." Vousa explained groggily.

"We know, sir," Brush said. "Your friends reported it. You'll be all right, Mr. Vousa. Get him to the clinic, pronto."

"No... close," Vousa pleaded. "An hour, maybe less...."

"We're ready," Brush said, "thanks to you and your men. Mr. Clayton, Treadway, do you wish to accompany him back to base?"

Both men looked at their friend and scowled. They wanted to go with him but knew there was nothing they could do now. Instead, the Marine and the OSS man exchanged a glance.

"We'd like to stay, Captain," Clayton said.

Brush nodded, "Okay… you've certainly earned your stripes… but it could get rough."

"Good," Treadway said and set his jaw. "I hope it gets real rough for Tojo, sir. He's got it comin'."

22

GUADALCANAL – BATTLE OF ALLIGATOR CREEK

AUGUST 22, 1942 – 0217 LOCAL TIME

"This place is green and evil," Robert Leckie said quietly as he lit a cigarette. "Even in the dark… can't you feel it, Teddy?"

PFC Ted Entwater stood beside Leckie, clutching his rifle with a much tighter grip than he would like to acknowledge. He couldn't help but agree with Leckie. The swampy creek before them, black save for a slash of silvery reflected moonlight, was deeply foreboding.

He and his other Raiders had been assigned to several key positions along the line earlier that evening. Once Clayton and Treadway had returned with news of an approaching Jap force, confirmed later by a nearly walking dead Jacob Vousa, Sergeant Oaks had voluntold the remaining men of Decker's team for duty.

As a sharpshooter, Entwater had been assigned to Leckie's machine gun crew to act as security. Somewhere out there in the dark, Taggart and Oaks too were waiting in silence. Private Treadway had gone someplace, and Mr. Clayton was at the CP with Colonel Kates.

The only sounds outside of the ubiquitous noises of Guadalcanal at night were the occasional low voices of orders given and received and the movements of equipment. Entwater could see vague shapes of men on the sandbar that cut Alligator Creek off from the sea. He knew that they were completing a barbed-wire barrier in an attempt to stave off the flood of enemy troops.

Not that the Marines had much in the way of barbed wire, of course. All of theirs was still aboard Admiral Turner's ships, which had abandoned the Marines two weeks earlier. What wire there was had been scrounged from the former coconut plantations. Evidently, Entwater thought bemusedly, them coconuts were apt to try and run off.

Not far from the sand spit, a pair of 37mm guns were set up and loaded with canister shot. Like in the old days of sailing ships, canister contained large numbers of lead balls, essentially turning the pair of guns into huge shotguns. In order that these vital pieces were kept operational and secure, Phil Oaks and Dave Taggart had been assigned to cover them.

Joe Treadway, much to his chagrin, was back at the command post acting as escort to Webster Clayton and the journalist, Richard Tregaskis. The three men clustered around Jacob Vousa, who had yet to be moved back to the airfield and the surgeons there. An ambulance was scheduled but had been delayed.

"How you hanging in there, Jake?" Clayton asked as the three men stood by the man's makeshift stretcher that had been set up in the aid station just beside the main command tent.

"Can't believe… I'm still alive," Vousa mumbled through the pain, drugs and his swollen, split tongue.

The medics had given him a sedative and had done a little patching. At least as much as they could do under the circumstances.

"Can we get you anything, Mr. Vousa?" the journalist inquired, his long tall frame hovering over the islander like some dark scarecrow.

"Can you ask Marty to come?" Vousa inquired. "I'd like to have him take a message to… to my family. At least they'll know…."

Clayton looked to Treadway, who nodded, "I'll radio it in and have him on the next ambulance. You stay with us, sir… you'll make it."

Vousa grinned, the pain of his many injuries, especially his hideous throat wound clearly showing in spite of the morphine, "Thanks, Joe… and one more thing… stop calling me sir."

Treadway's throat suddenly locked up on him, and he barely managed to croak, "Yes sir…."

Vousa smiled and slipped into an uneasy sleep.

As if his consciousness shutting down were the trigger that set off the explosion, the night was torn open by the unmistakable and inevitable sounds of war. From across the creek, several Nambu machine guns began to chatter along with the higher-pitched bark of Arisaka rifles. From the direction of the sandbar, a multitude of voices roared out in cries and shouts of anger and even insults.

"Prepare to die, Yankee!" rose in a chorus heard even at the CP two-hundred yards away.

"Fuck Babe Ruth!" several Japanese soldiers roared out in unison.

It would have been comical if not for the scene at the barbed wire barrier. The charge of the first wave of Japs was stopped, at least temporarily, by the borrowed barbed wire. Dozens of soldiers, then as many as an entire platoon, were snared and snagged and jumbled in a writhing, swearing, snarling… and shooting… heap of humanity.

"Let 'em have it!" the second lieutenant in charge of the 37mm battery roared out.

The two guns under his command thundered just as Taggart and Oaks began firing their weapons. Taggart still held onto the Thompson sub-machine gun brought all the way from *Bull Shark*. And although the barbed wire barrier was about two hundred yards away, beyond the gun's effective range, he opened fire anyway.

The Thompson wasn't pinpoint accurate at that range, but when firing into a hundred men all grouped together, it didn't matter. It was difficult to tell the effect of Oaks' and even Taggart's firing. The 37mm guns, however, had an immediate impact that was clearly visible even in the dark.

Men screamed in pain, and great swaths of them seemed to vanish. Mowed down by the hideous physics of flying lead projectiles. Heads and bodies bobbed and jerked like a herd of cows headed down to feed.

The Marines were grateful for the darkness. For although they could see the *effect* of their gunnery… they couldn't see the details. Couldn't see the limbs being torn from bodies. Couldn't see the fountains of vermillion that soared into the night air and washed over other men like a tropical spray. They couldn't see ropey entrails ripped from guts and flung outward and back, where they wrapped around the arms and necks and faces of other men in a tableau of horror too hideous to contemplate.

And yet more enemies came. Ten, thirty… even fifty men were scythed down, and more came to take their place. It was simultaneously terrible and glorious. This was truly the first real battle on Guadalcanal. Not a few platoons or even companies skirmishing in some village but a knock-down-drag-out between battalions.

Although Ichiki had foolishly sent men straight into their deaths at the sandbar, they were by no means the only combatants. Across the creek, machine gunners and lines of mortars opened up, filling the intervening spaces between the two lines with angry tracers and flashing explosions.

When no less than three knee-mortar propelled grenades landed within fifteen yards of Leckie's machine gun, Entwater was jolted out of a fascinated trance he hadn't even realized he'd fallen into. A cloud of water and mud temporarily blocked out what he could see, and he instantly realized the three men under his charge were in trouble.

"Bobby! We gotta move!" Entwater shouted over the now enormous sound of weapons fire and shouting men. "They're homing in on us!"

"Roger that!" Leckie said. "Shanks! Tommy! Let's move as soon as that belt's gone!"

"Shit, Bobby!" the gunner, Shanks, cranked. "I don't even know what I'm shootin' at. Can't see my own pecker; it's so dark."

"Hell, there ain't enough light at high noon for you to see your own pecker!" Private Tommy Nevvins jibed.

"Just aim for the noises," Leckie said. "Now, let's move! I can't see them either, Shanks, but they can sure as hell see our muzzle flashes!"

"We need backup over here!" Phil Oaks roared over his shoulder as he saw the barbed wire barricade begin to fold under another push from the Japs. "L T! We could use a squad or two RFN!"

"On the way!" the lieutenant, a fresh-faced recent college grad not more than twenty-three, said. "Down! Get down now!"

The air was ripped open as no less than a hundred rifle rounds sizzled through the air, pinging off the two field guns. The fire was being sent across in salvos, and once it began, Oaks, Taggart and the ten other men assigned to them couldn't keep up. They hit the dirt and returned fire as best they could.

"We gotta pull back!" the second looey shouted, almost in Oaks' ear. "We gotta make a break for it, Sarge! They'll overrun us if we don't!"

"With all due respect, sir!" Oaks hollered back, his mind abuzz with the terrifying sounds of ricochets, pings and occasional cries of pain and terror, "we can't abandon this spot! If we do and them Nips get these guns, they'll turn them on us, and we'll lose the left flank!"

"We're pinned down!" The L T insisted, sounding not quite steady.

"Timmins! Oliver! Reload and fire, goddammit!" Oaks shouted.

It was a long shot, and Oaks knew it. But if he could get the two guns firing again, they'd put a halt to the Japanese push. The longer the men were pinned, the more frightened they'd become and less likely to act.

There was no answer. Oaks cursed and began to low-crawl toward the nearest 37mm, "Davie!"

"On it, Sarge!" Taggart shouted from ten yards further toward the beach.

Oaks found his way to the firing control of the gun, and a quick blind feel told him that it'd been loaded. Or at least the breech was closed. His hand also found the unnaturally still form of a man lying partially upright against the gun carriage. The hand came away wet with tacky blood.

Even as he positioned himself to reach the trigger mechanism, Oaks felt the body of the gunner, probably Timmins… it was hard to tell in the dark… begin to jerk as if he were having some kind of fit.

The Sergeant knew what it was, though. The Japs were sending rounds into the corpse. Christ, they had good eyes.

Taggart's gun roared, the brief flash of the muzzle illuminating a scene right out of a Hollywood war picture. Men sprawled on the sandy earth, some cowering, some firing, and some, from their odd positions, dead or wounded.

Screams in the night, a slackening of fire. Oaks lurched upright, found the trigger handle and pulled. The gun bucked and roared, and more Nips cried out.

"Reload!" the L T shouted as, from behind him, the sound of many boots thumped closer, and rifles began to crackle over the Marines' heads.

Help had come just in time.

Colonel Ichiki had been frustrated by the conditions of the battlefield when he'd ordered the first attack. Now, however, after several hours of fighting and with dawn not far away, he was furious. He knew… he could tell simply by counting muzzle flashes and rifle shots that the Americans across the swamp outnumbered his men. Yet that wasn't his biggest concern. His was the superior force, had the superior skill and the superior lineage.

It was well known that the Americans were soft. They were effeminate men who didn't *like* fighting. They'd rather talk and negotiate and wheedle. They complained when the rains came and were said to refuse to fight in such conditions.

Yet… they still had numbers on their side. Ichiki was even willing to go so far as to believe that the *intelligence* about American fighting qualities was at least to some degree propaganda. He'd heard rumors that the Americans had their own propaganda about his people as well. That they were small and weak and had poor vision… especially at night. He'd seen the caricature of prime Minister Tojo they passed around so liberally. The one with the thick glasses and buck teeth.

Regardless of what the truth might be, the Marines would gain an advantage once the sun rose, certainly. It was vital, therefore, that Ichiki get at least a company's worth of men across that damned sand spit. That they seize that position and thus allow more men to come across. Once this was achieved, victory was as certain as the sunrise itself.

"Sir, the sand spit continues to remain a choke point," Major

Kinjo interrupted Ichiki's thoughts as he rushed beneath the hastily erected command post tent.

"I'm aware of this, Major," Ichiki said, a scowl etched into his features. "This is unacceptable. We *must* establish a position on the other side of the river mouth... if one can call it that... in order to funnel our men across and push the Yankees back."

"Yes sir," Kinjo said hesitantly. Even in the near-total darkness, with only a single small lantern burning, the thundercloud that rested on Ichiki's brow was plainly obvious. "I have a suggestion, sir."

Ichiki nearly snapped out that he hadn't *asked* for one but held his tongue. Kinjo was a good officer, and he was only trying to do his duty after all, "And that is?"

"I have spoken with several of our island guides," Kinjo stated. "It seems the Rand McNally company and their mapmakers were not precisely accurate."

Ichiki huffed derisively, "I am not surprised. Go on."

"This is not the Teneru River," Kinjo explained. "Not exactly. It is a part of the river, but the river doesn't flow smoothly into the sea. It ends here at what is called Alligator Creek. The creek is something of an offshoot, and I'm told that approximately two to three kilometers south, the streambed is dry. We could move our men there and go across, attacking the Americans from the south, sir."

Ichiki seemed to consider this, but only for a moment before he shook his head, "No, major, no. It would take nearly two hours to complete such a maneuver, and by then, it would be light. Well after dawn. No, we must attack *here* and now. Perhaps if it were earlier... but no matter."

Kinjo shifted uncomfortably from one foot to the other, "Sir... estimates put the Marine forces as much as twice our number... and that's not counting on reinforcements. There may be many more Americans ashore than we at first thought."

"This is as may be, Kinjo," Ichiki said resignedly. "Alert Lieutenant Ashika to ready his platoon. He's so eager for glory, that one... let him earn it. Have our 75mm crew soften the area up first. Inform him that I wish for him to push across that damned sand spit. Failure is *not* acceptable. Should he fail to achieve this goal, he need not return to us."

Kinjo flinched, but he also knew when his commander's mind was made up. As he bowed and turned to go, there was a huge explosion not far away. It was nearly as violent as the churning in his belly.

Near the middle of the creek, perhaps in three feet of water, a broken-down Amtrak lay rusting. Or it would begin to rust in short order in the heavy tropical climate of Guadalcanal. The track had been abandoned several days earlier when it had become hopelessly bogged down after having engine trouble.

Unfortunately, the tractor was still mostly above water and now, at least for a time, acted as a man-made island. From this island, a trio of Japanese soldiers had set up a Nambu machine gun nest. They'd carried the gun and ammunition through dark waters that were nearly over their heads at one point. Finally, though, after what seemed like an hour, they'd reached the Amtrak and had set up. From that position, the machine gunners were nearly halfway to the Marine lines and were using their machine gun to good effect.

Targets were difficult to see, of course. Yet there were plenty of muzzle flashes and larger spits of flame from American mortars to aim at. Also, the far end of the sand spit where the Americans had reinforced their two 37mm guns with a platoon stood silhouetted against the sea and was in the Nambu's range. The gun opened up just as another group of Japanese soldiers began to make their way toward the Americans across the no-man's land of the spit.

Joe Treadway, having been drafted as a runner by Colonel Kates, was racing behind the lines toward the Marines' 81mm howitzer. His message was simple: take that tractor out.

Private Sid Philips was nearly scared out of his wits when the other young Marine slid to a stop beside him. He didn't recognize the man, but he did recognize that he was nearly out of breath and had probably come from the CP.

"Colonel Kates...." Treadway gasped. "Sent me! PFC... Joe Treadway."

"Sid Philips," the other young man said with a grin that showed white in the dark. "You okay, Joe?"

"Swell..." Treadway huffed. "Tried you on the radio, but...."

"Yeah, got waterlogged when we had to hit the deck," Philips said with a shrug.

"Hit the mud, more like it," said the mortar's loader.

"Stuff it, Herb," Philips said wryly.

"I done stuffed it, Sid," Herb replied, grinning. "Now I'm waitin' for a target."

Treadway managed a chuckle, "See that Amtrak out there, about the middle of the Creek?"

"Yeah, what about...." Philips was asking, and then he saw the bright, rapid flash of a heavy machine gun. "Oh, Christ... you tellin' me the Nips got that tractor?"

"Well, that ain't Cagney and Robinson and their Tommy guns out there!" Treadway quipped.

"Okay, you heard the PFC, boys," Philips said, raising his binoculars. "Gimme... elevation minus five... left fifteen."

The trainer and elevator worked their wheels and brought the light howitzer around to the proper bearing. As the tractor was only a hundred and fifty yards off, there was no need to elevate the gun and lob shots. Philips was going for a straight-on.

"Fire!" he shouted.

The gun thundered and belched a crimson tongue of flame. Amazingly, the first shot went home. The entire upper works of the tractor, including the three Japanese and their machine gun, erupted into a pillar of flame and smoke. Half the tractor was blown into fragments and the remaining portions, that which stuck up above the creek, began to burn. Enough light to provide a little illumination in the immediate area.

Enough light to see nearly three dozen Japanese soldiers wading straight for the mortar's position.

"Oh, shit!" Philips called. "Get down!"

All along the line, small groups of Japs had braved the dark swampy creek and were almost on top of the Marine lines. As they came closer, firing their Arisaka's, a big 75mm howitzer began to thunder from the coconut grove across the creek.

Many Marines had to dive into their shallow holes and pray as grenades began to arc through the air toward the Americans. Dozens of them lit the creek shore with hellish red-white fire. And then the Japs came.

Nearly a hundred in total, they splashed through the shallows, firing and screaming like mad. Most of G company was positioned near Philips' gun and converged, meeting the Japanese bayonet charge with a charge of their own.

Suddenly, Treadway, Philips and Herb found themselves in the middle of a madhouse. Philips' trainer, a young Marine barely out of high school, hadn't moved fast enough during the initial attack and shrapnel from a grenade tore his throat and belly open. He lay on his back and bled to death in less than two minutes. In a way, it was a blessing, as daylight would reveal hideous wounds later on.

"Forget shooting!" Treadway shouted, organizing the two privates as best he could. "Fix bayonets and get ready! Here they come!"

Rifles crackled, and explosions shook the ground, actually causing small waves in the creek. The horrific battle light created a terrifying strobe effect as nearly two hundred men met one another in ferocious and bloody up close and personal fighting.

It was like something out of a horror flick. As Treadway and his two companions emptied their magazines and rose to face the oncoming Japanese, their images flashed and jerked in the light. Dark hair, snarling faces and pounding feet. They met, steel clashing against steel all around Treadway. It was like nothing he could've imagined. Nothing like the sort of orderly firing line warfare he'd expected.

This was more like the old sailing ship days when men would board one another's vessels, and a melee of insanity would erupt. No organization, just man-to-man brutality that defied logic.

A Japanese soldier was charging Treadway, his gleaming blade leveled for the American's belly. Treadway's reflexes took over, and his body moved almost independent of his mind. He side-stepped, actually bumping into Herb and knocking the man out of the line of another charge. As Treadway stepped sideways, he drove the point of his own blade into the chest of the onrushing man even as the other's slid under his left arm but doing no damage.

There was a shocked and strangled cry from the Nip as he paused, looked down and then pitched over backward, gurgling his last. Treadway's rifle was carried with the man, and he found that he couldn't remove it from the man's chest; it had lodged so deeply into the breastbone.

"Watch it!" Philips said as Treadway placed his boot on the dead Jap's belly and yanked.

It was too late, or nearly so. Herb and his man were grappling with one another, and a fourth Nip drove his blade in toward Treadway. The young Marine threw out his right arm to beat the bayonet aside, and the sharp point plunged straight through his forearm. Treadway cried out and threw himself backward, jerking his own weapon free and pulling the Jap off balance, as the man refused to let go of his Arisaka.

The next thing Treadway saw in the kaleidoscopic nightmare of muzzle light was Sid Philips driving his own blade into the Jap's face. The man didn't cry out, only began to caper wildly as if some sadistic puppeteers were jerking and yanking his strings. This show of horror lasted only five or six seconds, although, to the observers, it might have been an eternity.

"Jesus Christ!" Herb goggled. "What the hell is this?"

"A war, numbnuts," Treadway said. "A real gas, ain't it? Now, what say we take out that slope gun across the way?"

Back and forth it went. At one point, just before dawn, a company of Japanese soldiers tried to secure Oaks' position by wading out into the surf and swimming parallel to the beach and then coming ashore from the sea. Circumventing the sand spit altogether.

Unfortunately for them, the Marines still held the position and the two 37mm guns. Taggart was the first to see them.

"What's that... out in the surf?" he asked no one in particular.

"Looks like a bunch of crab buoys or somethin'," the second looey who'd been in charge of the guns muttered in reply.

"Nah... their *heads!*" Taggart exclaimed. "L T, they're Japs!"

And the guns of the men and the canister shot of the 37mm were turned out to sea. The desperate ploy by the Japanese to turn the Marines' left flank failed miserably. Not a single man made it ashore.

Not alive, at any rate. They would come ashore, of course, over the next day or two. Some whole, some with missing limbs or a head… and of these, not all were caused by lead projectiles. For over the next two days, the dark shapes of triangular fins could be seen in the surf line.

As the sun began its journey into the sky, the light revealed a scene that, to most of the Marines, was the most gruesome thing they'd ever witnessed. Little did they know, however, that this was only the preview.

Dead Japanese lay piled all over the creek. From the sandbar at the north end to the shores near the Marine lines and on the opposite side. Here and there, where small sandbars lay just inches below the surface, more men were stacked, almost like cordwood, upon one another. Seagulls wheeled and cawed overhead, screeching their hunger for the rotting flesh below.

Colonel Kates launched two simultaneous attacks to complete the job. He sent Lieutenant Colonel Creswell and two companies from First Battalion south. Creswell crossed the dry stream as the now-dead Major Kinjo had suggested before dawn. He and his men marched toward the coconut grove where Japanese survivors huddled together, seemingly stunned and leaderless.

Across the sandspit rode five light tanks. The growling machines had no choice but to roll over the dead, their metal treads grinding human flesh into hamburger and growing so thick they were clogged with gore.

Robert Leckie watched them, his stomach lurching and his mouth agape. He noted that it looked like a meat grinder, and his vivid imagination could only approach but not truly contemplate what it must be like for the tank crews. To feel their machines riding up and over the dead… to hear the sickening crunch of their bones and the awful… awful… squelching as soft tissue was masticated by the remorseless iron teeth of the war machines.

And the smell… what must it be like…

Although appearing ready to throw down their arms and

surrender, the Japanese rallied at the last moment. Perhaps it was the sight of the tanks, their cannons thundering and their turret-mounted machine guns chattering. Perhaps it was Creswell's men marching down on them. Perhaps it was their indoctrinated Japanese code. Death before dishonor.

Whatever the reason, the surviving soldiers charged the Marines, bayonets flashing and curses on their lips. It was brave… foolishly so. They were outnumbered, and although the men managed to wound and even kill several Marines, it was all for nothing. They fell, one by one or in small groups, to rifle fire and bayonet thrusts.

"A stupid waste of life," Creswell was overheard to say. "What's *wrong* with these people?"

It was a question that would be asked repeatedly, although in different forms, over the course of that long, hot day.

When Treadway made it back to the CP, he was surprised to find Oaks, Taggart and Entwater already there. These men, whom he'd only known a few days, were already becoming closer to the young Marine than he could know. There were smiles and laughs and concerns for Joe's wound. All four of them went to the aid station and were further surprised to find Webster Clayton there with Martin Clemens.

"You lot appear as if you've lost a pound and found two pence," Clemens joked. "You all right?"

"I got tagged," Treadway said, holding up his bloody arm. "Considering how things look out there in daylight… I think I got off light."

"Well, you fellas did fine work out there, sir," Clayton said to Joe, smiling wryly.

Treadway flushed a little, "Don't call me sir, Mr. Clayton… I work for a livin'."

Everyone laughed, and Clayton shrugged, "Any man who gets run through with a Jap bayonet is sir in my book."

"Thanks… but I'd prefer you didn't call me sir," Treadway said absently as a medic began to clean his wound.

"Yes sir," Clayton said, and everyone broke into peals of laughter.

"Well, I think I'd better go have a look for myself. Want to come, Marty?"

"Sure thing, mate," Clemens said. "Would do my heart good to see this."

"How's Jake?" Oaks asked before the two civilians exited the tent.

Clemens smiled, "He dictated his death letter to me… but I think that lad's gonna pull through. Tough as they come, you know. Last word I heard is that he's in surgery, and the doctors are hopeful."

Webster Clayton had come to Guadalcanal to get first-hand field-won knowledge of how the Japanese were conducting themselves on the ground in the Pacific theater. What he saw was shocking. Even more so than what he'd seen in his first few days.

It was as if horror had become a living, breathing entity, and it had been given free rein on Earth. The dead, already beginning to bloat in the mid-morning sun, were strewn over a half-mile area in horrid little piles. Hundreds of birds were lighting on the corpses and plucking at their eyes… and even this was not by any means the most terrible sight.

Private Robert Leckie met the two men and stood by them, having been relieved of his machine gun and asked to stay with the two men he'd already met.

"That sound…" Leckie observed, pointing at a group of six Japanese soldiers lying face down in six inches of muddy creek water. "My God… that sound…."

There was, now that Leckie had pointed it out, a low humming that seemed to come from everywhere. As if there were half a dozen transformer boxes nearby with improper shielding. Yet the sound was not generated by the buzz of high voltage… it was something else, something natural.

As the three men watched, their mouths clamped shut in disgust, cones of black mist appeared at several points over the bodies. No, not random points… over the wounds. With each ghostly appearance and disappearance of these floating funnels, the bodies seemed to grow hazy and dark.

Flies, billions of them, were finding a repast such as they'd never known. The heat, the stink and the rapid decomposition had drawn them in from miles around.

The tall and lanky form of Richard Tregaskis joined the trio and watched in silence as well. All the men kept wondering how much more horror they could witness and still keep whatever was in their stomachs down.

And somehow, the evil presence that hovered over Alligator Creek could still be relied upon to deliver more.

Now it was time for a lesson that the Marines would not be able to forget. One that would change the way they fought their war.

As medics moved among the bodies, searching for wounded, the wounded found them.

In the distance, the tanks still fired, and men still fought behind the barrier of the coconuts. Overhead, a squadron of Wildcats of VM-223 flew over from Henderson Field and began strafing the few remaining Japanese soldiers. Hemmed in on all sides but one, the Japanese ran straight into the sea.

Yet, in the creek, their wounded brethren were still fighting the good fight. Should a medic come close to a wounded man, he would lash out with his bayonet or fire his rifle. More than once, one or two corpsmen would get close to a pile of dead Japanese and be cut down.

In one horrific incident, two medics were alerted to a group of six wounded Japanese. The men moaned and cried out in pain and called for assistance. The medics ran to them, intent on rendering aid in the timeless tradition of war. When they bent down to tend to their enemies' wounds, three of the soldiers set off hand grenades. Eight men were torn to ribbons.

Upon seeing this, Colonel Kates sent out a general order for all Marines to shoot any and all bodies they found. Whether they appeared dead or not. No quarter was to be given.

At last, after a battle that waged for sixteen hours, sometimes teeth-clenchingly fierce and sometimes as just a few random shots, the sun began to slide below the trees. What few prisoners there were had been rounded up and the wounded carted off to Henderson. The First Marines stood watch, still, of course. Not knowing when another Japanese push would come, especially once it got dark.

As the light faded and darkness once again fell on the land, there was indeed another surge. This time, though, it was not the Imperial Japanese Army. These new visitors were far older and had even less pity than those who came before.

In the darkness, throaty grumbles and hissings could be heard. First in ones and twos, and then by the dozens… possibly even more. Large bodies that moved easily through the water and on the land flowed across the field of dead. Like the tiny flies and the birds before them, these creatures found the rotting corpses of men, tasted them, and found them good.

All through that night, in spite of the fact that these creatures were doing them a favor and were even jokingly adopted by the Marines… the fuel for their future nightmares was being stacked like cordwood.

Saltwater crocodiles feasted. The darkness gratefully masked the sight… yet it couldn't mask the sounds. Great grunts of satisfaction… mighty slurps as huge chunks of oily meat were swallowed… and the hideous, never to be forgotten crunching of bones between ivory fangs as old as the oldest dinosaur went on… and on…

…and *on*…

There would be one final casualty of the Battle of Alligator Creek. This last soldier stood by himself on the now moonlit beach not far from the coconut grove. He, too, heard the crocodiles come. He, too, heard their incessant feeding. His mind, too, could visualize the blood-chilling activity in what was now a charnel pit.

Yet this last man, Colonel Ichiki himself, would not suffer nightmares for decades to come. There was no need, for he was living his own. A nightmare of his own making.

He had rushed his men into this battle. He had failed to properly reconnoiter the American position, and now, by last count, eight hundred and thirty-three Japanese sons would never return to their mothers.

Not in this life.

There was but one thing to do. One final prescription that must be taken, no matter how bitter the medicine might be.

Ichiki removed his cigarette lighter from his pocket and flicked it into life. A small flame, flickering in the light breeze, glowed, briefly illuminating a face that was a mask of pure despair.

The flame was applied to the flag of the 128th regiment, and the banner flashed into flickering orange. Ichiki held the honored flag as long as he could before letting the remnants flutter away in the breeze, consumed and turned to ash before they touched the beach.

He then said a silent prayer, bowed in the direction of Japan and his emperor, and pulled his service weapon from its holster. He carefully cleared the weapon, being certain that it would function. He racked the slide, ejected a round and then re-seated the magazine and charged the pistol.

All around him, Guadalcanal sang its eternal song of life. Monkeys chittered, mosquitos hummed, cicadas buzzed, and night birds cawed. Yet that sound… that horrible crunching and grunting …

One more sound was added to the night. A sharp crack that broke through and quieted the insects for a brief moment. Yet that moment passed, and so did the misery of Colonel Ichiki forever.

PART TWO
BATTLE OF THE EASTERN SOLOMONS

"Most of the men died from the concussion… and then were roasted. They were… blackened… but not burned or withered, and they looked like… iron statues of men. Their limbs smooth and whole… their heads rounded with no hair…."

— LIEUTENANT FREDERICK MEARS

23
THE SLOT – 25 MILES NORTH, NORTHWEST OF SAVO
AUGUST 22, 1942 – 1130 GUADALCANAL TIME

"How you fellas doing up here, Sparky?" Captain Art Turner asked as he made his way into the forward torpedo room.

"We ain't leakin', sir, and that's about as good as we can say," Walter Sparks reported as he came to attention.

"At ease, guys," Turner said a little wearily. "I know it's been a long night. I just wanted to see how everything was for myself."

"We got all the leaks plugged, Skipper," Tommy Perkins added in his casual surfer way. "Room's holdin' air nice, but…."

"But we ain't got tubes five and six figured out yet," Sparky said, almost sounding defensive. "That big short might've fried the firing mechanisms, sir. Don't know what all we can do outside a drydock."

Turner frowned, "I was afraid of that. I think we should pull those fish and maybe get a couple of electricians in here to do a more thorough inspection."

Sparky frowned, "Well, sir… it's just then we gotta pull up the gratings and gettin' them fish up and stowed…."

"I know it's a ball breaker," Turner said, his voice sounding a bit tight, "but we've got a shitload of Jap tin cans and an aircraft carrier to plug, Sparky. We gotta try all the tricks we can."

"Sir…" Sparks hesitated and went on anyway, "we been up damn near twenty-four hours cleanin' up the mess up here. And it seems like every time we go up against these Japs—"

"Mr. Sparks," Turner squared off with the leading petty officer. Sparky had maybe twenty pounds on Turner, but the captain had two inches of height and, although not as bulky, had wide shoulders. It gave him an intimidating presence. "This is a ship of war, Mister. And we're *in* a war. Nobody promised that it'd be easy. Nobody promised it'd be a party with pound cake and Shirley Temples all around. This is hard, gritty, gut-wrenching business. How many men has this boat sent to a watery grave, Sparky? Hundreds... maybe thousands? So, if, on occasion, we all gotta pull double duty or bust a gut routining fish or whatever the *hell* is required, then we do so! It's our goddamned *job!* And if in the course of that job, we all have to give up our lives for our country... then that's our goddamned job too. I don't want to hear whining; I don't want to hear my men second-guessing my decisions, understand? What I want to hear are ideas and solutions!"

Sparks came rigidly to attention. His face burned hotly with shame. Inside, he knew that he hadn't been complaining, and he also knew that Turner was simply venting. Under normal circumstances, Art Turner's mild manner invited opinions and even suggestions. However, like the rest of them, he was stressed and tired, and this wasn't the time for anything but strict obedience.

"Yes sir!" Sparks said smartly.

"Very well, Mr. Sparks," Turner said more evenly. "Pull the fish in number five and six, and I'll have Mr. Dutch come forward to help with the inspection. That is all."

Turner turned and stalked out, ducking through the hatchway. When he'd gone, Sparks blew out his breath and relaxed.

"Jesus, Sparky," Perry Wilkes said with a shake of the head and a wry smile. "He's got a bee in his bonnet."

"He's the skipper," Sparks said. "It's his privilege. Hell, Art Turner may be the best sub driver in our fleet... maybe the best captain in the Navy. If he's gotta blow his stack once in a while, then that's what chiefs and LPOs are for. Better me than one of y'all. Now, let's do as we're ordered before one of us has to walk the plank."

That got a round of moderate laughter, and the men went to work.

. . .

Turner stepped around the open hatch in the deck. The hatch led down to the platform over the forward battery where Tank and Doug Ingram were carefully inspecting each individual cell of the giant Sargo bank.

"How's it goin', fellas?" the captain asked.

"So far, so good, sir," Tank called up. "This one didn't get much seawater. Only a dozen cells had to be drained and refilled."

"Good," Turner said, "carry on."

"Shit, Tank," Ingram whispered as the captain's footsteps moved off. "Glad he didn't eat our asses off."

"Sparky had it comin', kid," Tank said. "Sides, we're all tired and tense. Captain is just as human as the rest of us."

Turner ducked into the wardroom and was met by Eddie Carlson holding a mug of steaming coffee, "Thought you might need this, sir."

"You're a prince among men, Eddie," Turner said, gratefully accepting the cup.

Carlson grinned, "My mama always said that there weren't nothin' couldn't be figured out after sittin' down over a nice refreshing glass of iced tea. I figured for Navy men, a cup of Joe works as well."

Turner grinned and slid into a chair on one side of the table. At the end, in Turner's usual seat, Elmer Williams had a mess of papers spread out before him. He was compiling damage and repair reports for the ship's log.

"I see you're hard at it, XO," Turner observed.

"My work is never done," said Williams, not looking up from his writing. "Besides… don't want to get in Dutch with the skipper."

"Ha-ha," Turner mused dryly.

Williams looked up and smiled thinly, "You all right?"

"Sure… why do you ask?"

"Sir… we heard you lay into Sparky," Carlson said. "Sound travels in a sub, y'know."

"You bein' a wiseass, Mr. Carlson?" Turner asked with an arched brow. "Tryin' to get yourself on my shit list."

"Well sir..." Carlson said with a shrug and a bright smile that was hard to resist. "I figure I feed ya... so I'm mostly safe."

Turner laughed, "Good point. Still, Elmer... I shouldn't have snapped at him like that."

Williams scoffed, "You're the skipper, Art. It's good for the men to know that underneath that calm exterior lies the heart of a Breadfruit Bly now and then. They won't love you any less for it, huh Eddie?"

"No sir," Carlson agreed.

Turner finished his mug and set it down. He rose and cracked his back, "Good. Why I joined up, to be loved. Okay... on with the inspection. See how many other supervisors I can lace into. Better have the boatswain rig a grating, Mr. Williams."

In the control room, Turner met with Buck Rogers, who was standing at the master gyrocompass table updating the plot with Hotrod Hernandez. The room was mostly quiet, with men attending to their duties and others finishing up minor repairs from their battle with the Japanese squadron the day before. With Jarvis gone, the boat was still short an officer, even with Hazard having returned. The COB was acting as both chief of the watch and JOOD.

"How's she holding up, Buck?" Turner asked.

"They gave us a wrench but nothing fatal, Captain," Rogers said. "I think we're almost a hundred percent through the boat... or as close as we can come right now anyway."

Turner nodded, "Glad to hear it. And the men?"

"As a fine representative of the crew, *señor*," Hernandez drawled, "I can state unequivocally that we are all ready to visit a terrible vengeance upon our enemies. It is the sole reason for my existence, *tambien*."

"I thought the sole reason for your existence was hot mamas?" The COB asked wryly.

Si," said Hotrod. "Pretty women and avenging myself upon the Japanese... and tequila."

Turner laughed, "Geez... you really are full of tamales, Hotrod."

The quartermaster picked up his maneuvering board and shrugged, "*Es verdad*... now, if you gentlemen will excuse me, I must report to

Mr. Hazard with an accurate position and make sure we don't hit an iceberg."

"That boy must've inhaled a lot of exhaust," Turner mused once Hotrod had vanished up the ladder. He drew in a breath. "Seriously, Buck... how are the boys doing?"

Rogers lit himself a Camel, "Tired, a bit tense... maybe a little worried. We've gotten our asses kicked twice in a row on this patrol, Art. Yeah, we got a tin can and a couple of planes... but the last two outings have been rough."

"You think they're...." Turner tried to frame his question so as to get a true read on his men without giving the impression that he was seeking personal approval.

"No," Rogers said matter-of-factly. "No way have they lost faith in their skipper, Art. And how about you? How's your head and heart?"

This was not a question that an enlisted man, even the chief of the boat, would normally dare ask. Hell, it wasn't a question most officers, even the executive officer, would ask his captain. However, Art wasn't most skippers, and his relationship with Rogers went beyond the usual bounds.

"I'm fantastic, COB," Turner quipped. "Except for blowing my stack with Sparky ten minutes ago."

Rogers looked in question. Turner explained, and the COB only shrugged.

"It's good they see that side of you from time to time," Rogers stated. "Never forget, Art, that no matter how close we all are aboard a boat... you're still the *captain*. A Navy captain is something special, and they need to know he can and will lower the boom when required. And you know something else? It actually makes them respect you more. Feel closer to you, maybe. Because if you can break bad once in a while, it makes you as human as them, and why... it breeds even greater loyalty."

Turner clapped him on the shoulder, "Thanks, Buck. You're a sharp guy for an ignorant sailor man."

"What've I been tellin' you all these years?" Rogers asked and chuckled.

Turner moved aft and ducked his head into the radio shack. He was surprised to find Arnie Brasher at the set along with Andy Post and Chief Weiss. Brasher was tuned into a message, and Turner could hear the coded beeps coming in.

Bull Shark was running on the surface. She had been all night, and in spite of her damage and her inability, at least for a time, to fight anything that came her way… nothing did. The previous night had not delivered more destroyers full of men and supplies to Guadalcanal.

However, early that morning, the submarine received the standard fleet broadcast, and it held news of a battle being waged on the island. Details were scant at zero-eight-hundred, but from all reports, nearly a thousand Japanese were attacking the Marines along their eastern perimeter at a place called Alligator Creek.

"We getting an update, lads?" Turner asked.

"Just collating the transmission now, sir," Brasher said absently.

"It's the repeat," Post said. "We're just confirming. It's from S-52, sir. The chief here is about to decode once we've verified that we've got it right."

"Excellent," Turner said. "I'd like to touch base with Captain Waters again. Let me know when you're done, Chief. I'd like to send a reply. I'll be aft for a few but should be back up here by the time you finish."

"Aye sir," Weiss said.

Turner left them to their work and moved aft again and into the after battery compartment. As with the other battery, men were down in the access inspecting and refilling the individual cells that had been contaminated by seawater or that had any of their elements fried by the large surge that traveled through the boat.

In the galley, Henrie Martin and Bill Borshowski were busy preparing the noon meal. Smells of frying potatoes and something savory permeated every square inch of the compartment. There was a large tray of donuts laid out on the serving counter, and Turner snitched one as he went by.

"You don't ruin dem appetite, Cap'n, you hear?" the Cajun cook said cheerfully. "Got dem french fry and a nice chili a'comin'."

"Don't worry, Henrie, after the day we've had, I'm famished," Turner said and grinned. "Smells good; what's in it?"

"Got four or tree secret regredients you goin' love, sir… and that's for true," Martin said.

"That means it'll be spicey," Borshowski said. "Everything special means spicy down in Louisiana apparently, sir."

"No complaints here," Turner said.

"Well, we gotta use dem canned chili," Martin all but sneered. "On account the cold rooms ain't had power for a bit."

Turner nodded, "Yeah, I hear that. Should be back up by now, though."

"They are, sir," Borshowski said. "Stuff in there should be fine, especially the freezer. But we figured let it lie, and we can work with some of these rations for lunch."

"Carry on, men," Turner said, grabbing another donut as he moved on.

In the forward engine room, Turner found Frank Nichols supervising a party of men who were working to repair the starboard water evaporator. The room was, as it always was, sweltering. Even with the air conditioning, which had thankfully *not* been affected by the surge, operating at full power, the heat generated by the two big GM engines made working in the compartment a sweaty endeavor. Add in two water evaporators boiling hundreds of gallons of seawater to make fresh and the black gang compared it to a tropical summer's day.

With *Bull Shark* running on the surface, the hatches were all open, at least. From the forward torpedo room all the way to the after room, these open hatches pulled in fresh air and created a pleasant wind-tunnel effect through the boat. Unfortunately, it was nearly noon in August, less than six hundred miles south of the equator… so it was hardly a cooling breeze.

"How we comin' along, Frank?" Turner shouted pleasantly over the rattle and rumble of diesels chugging along. "Think you can save her?"

Nichols pursed his lips and tapped the clipboard he held to make notes on absently. Turner had served with the man long enough by then to recognize his moods and gestures for what they were. At that look, he knew that the outcome was doubtful.

"We've got two problems with the unit," Nichols explained. "First, all of the heaters were fried. We have replacements, which we've installed, but we're still short a couple. The second problem is that there isn't enough heat to initiate the boiling process and maintain it without all the heaters."

The compressed vapor distiller, for all its power and usefulness aboard, was a fairly simple device. Some kind soul had also made it easy to maintain. The distiller was mostly comprised of a large water vessel in which a nest of ten cone-shaped tubes filled the center. Seawater was let in, heated, and as it rose toward its boiling point, being hotter toward the top of the tank, it would emit steam, which was collected at the top of the vessel, compressed and then pushed down through the cone-shaped tubing. This cooled the steam and made the cones into heat exchangers.

"Isn't it true that once the process starts," Turner opined, rubbing his chin in thought, "that you almost don't even *need* the heaters?"

Nichols nodded, "Yes sir... once all that compressed steam enters the system, it does most of the work of heating the seawater as it cools... problem is, it takes over an hour to get the seawater to the boiling point. And that's with all six heaters working. We've got three."

Turner sighed, "I see your point... there isn't enough heat to raise the seawater to the boiling point... but... so what you need is additional heat, right? Something to kick-start the thing?"

Nichols nodded, "We're gonna try and machine a couple of new heaters, but...."

"But what about the engines?" Turner asked. "You've got two diesels in here that are freshwater cooled, but that also have a seawater cooling system, too. Could you connect a pipe to one of them, or both, catch the outflowing seawater and redirect some of it to the vessel? Rather than being input at ambient sea temperature, which is about eighty-five, it'd be as hot as the engines get."

"That's not boiling temp, though," Nichols said dubiously, although his mind was beginning to warm up to the idea. "But it doesn't have to be... at regular operating temperatures, the diesels run at about a hundred and forty...."

"Is that enough to let the heaters get a leg up?" Turner asked.

"It might be, sir...." Nichols pondered, almost absently. "Maybe I could even shut down the freshwater system on one of them... yes, I think it might be a workaround, sir. At least for the time being."

Turner grinned and clapped him on the shoulder, "See? I'm not just a great set of legs, Frank... no matter what you guys say."

Turner headed aft, leaving smiles and laughter in his wake. In the after engine room, which was far quieter and cooler, the captain found Chief Mike Duncan overseeing a party of engine snipes doing some routine maintenance on engines three and four and on the fuel separator.

"You keepin' these fellas straight, Mike?" Turner asked.

"Straight as a bent arrow, sir," Duncan said.

"Any problems in here on account of our little run-in with the Japs?" Turner asked.

"Oh, we've got most of the pieces picked up, sir," Duncan said. "Having some trouble with the fuel separators... but it's a matter of doing the work. Got Swooping Hawk and Eckhart on them. Need to fit a new service line and drainpipe to number two, but Freddy'll have that done in two shakes. He's a crackerjack plumber, that kid."

"That so..." Turner mused. "When he's got it licked, Mike, have him report to Frank forward. They're working on a slapdash hot water feed to the number two evap. Maybe Freddy can assist."

"Be glad to, sir," called Swooping Hawk from where he was half-buried in an access hatch in the deck.

"You've got good ears, Freddy," Turner mused.

"Ancient Navaho magic," Swooping Hawk replied.

Turner groaned and shook his head amusedly, "Great... another one. Like I don't get enough of that horse pucky from Hotrod."

The maneuvering room was, perhaps, in the greatest state of disarray. This was to be expected, as it was the heart of the boat's electrical systems. This despite the fact that the two huge Sargo batteries were forward.

Beneath the maneuvering room were the four GE motors. Additionally, there were circuit breakers, switching panels and other gear located in the maneuvering room around the central control cubicle.

When the boat had developed no less than ten independent leaks, seawater had sprayed, flowed, poured and seeped into the boat from a variety of areas. A good deal had come aboard in the maneuvering room and had soaked several electrical panels while simultaneously invading the batteries. There were several open high-voltage circuits, and thanks to the seawater in the bilges, the current was carried throughout the ship and had affected every compartment to some degree.

"Argh! You goddamned son of a whore!" a drawling Maine accented voice cranked loudly from the open deck hatch into the motor room. "For the love of the jumped-up Christ… Hey, Baxta, you up theya?"

"Ayuh!" Paul Baxter, electrician's mate, called down in a very good imitation of a down-easter.

The other half dozen men working in the compartment began to laugh and writhe with mirth. Even Turner had to clamp a hand over his mouth to stifle a guffaw. None of it was disrespectful, though. Everyone liked Danny Pentakkus, who was filling in for Chief Brannigan, and thought his down east Maine accent was the greatest thing they've ever heard.

"If I come up through that hatch and find even one of you sons of whores laughin' at me up theya, I'm gonna break my goddamned foot off in your kiesta!" Pentakkus grumped. "Baxta?"

"Right here, Danny," Baxter called down, his face going red with an effort not to laugh. "Watcha need?"

"I could really use a six-pack and a humma, but I suppose that ain't in the cahds now, is it?" Pentakkus drawled. "Send me down that big ass slotted screwdriva, a new pair of wire strippas and a couple of dry rags… fuckin' coolin' pipe blew the fuckin' patch right offin'n 'er."

Baxter gathered the tools and bent low over the hatch, "Heads up, Danny, Captain's back here."

A moment later, Pentakkus' dour sweaty face appeared above the combing, "Oh, didn't know you was theya, Skippa. Come back to see how we'a'doin', ah ya'?"

It took a remarkable effort for Turner not to answer with a drawn out "Aaaayyyuuuhhh!" Instead, he grinned and said: "Taking a turn through the boat, Danny. How's your end."

"Holdin' it up, sir," Pentakkus said with a wry smile.

"Do that around Chief Hoffman, and you'll get jabbed," Turner joked. "How we doin' after that shock?"

"Most everythin' is set to rights," Pentakkus explained. "We replaced burnt wiya and dried what needs dryin'… only thing, though, skippa… that for Christ sakes patch Tank and Mike put on blew right off. Gonna have to do 'er again."

"Really?' Turner asked in surprise.

"Oh, not from anythin' they done… just a lot of presha, and I think the surge mighta melted the sealant before it set propaly."

"Well, keep at it," Turner said. "Let me know if you need anything."

"Oh, ayuh… but I think we got 'er in hand, I guess," Pentakkus said and grinned.

Turner headed into the after torpedo room chuckling. Not just because of Pentakkus' amusing patterns of speech. It was mostly because *Bull Shark* had taken a good beating not long before, and in less than a day, she was nearly back up to snuff. She was a tough boat, built tougher than any before her… yet it was really her men that made the difference. A set of rough and tumble, smart and funny, hard and kind and all-around dedicated sailors. The kind of men who'd win this war.

They were the kind of men who, in 1987, while sitting on their front porches and smoking their pipes, would tell the documentary filmmaker how it really was back during the war. How it weren't such a big thing, them depth charges and other self-effacing statements. Statements whose genuine humility could never even approach what it took to hide the true heroism and bravery those old men would evince and dismiss so casually.

The kind of men who one day would dandle their grandchildren on their knees and tell them about the time their old skipper traded a couple of roast beefs for a couple hundred pounds of fresh dolphin fish. Or how when that new kid, I forget his name, was dying from a Jap Zero bullet to the guts, how it were Eddie Carlson, the officer's steward who sat up with him and held his hand and told him he'd be okay. How that kid had gone easy on account of old Eddie.

They'd explain how when they were in port, if anybody ever called Eddie or Henrie or Leroy a shine or spook or nigger within earshot of any *Bull Shark,* why they'd drag that guy out and kick his ass around the block for drill. And how them black fellas was some of the finest submariners in the fleet and how not your old granddad or any of his shipmates ever let that sort of foolishness pass.

The men in the after room were in the process of routining their fish. Although they'd done so recently, Murph felt that with so much goings-on lately, that he'd feel better should they check everything over.

"Come to check up on us, Skipper?" Murph asked as Turner entered the room.

"Somebody has to, Murph," Turner said. "Everybody knows you after room fellas are a bunch of tosspots."

"Well, we are now," Murph said, jerking a thumb at Martin Janslotter, who was carefully guiding the number nine fish onto a skid.

"Don't pay any attention to him, sir," Janslotter remarked. "he's just sore because he ain't got any friends on account of his sweet disposition."

"Or lack of one," Smitty jibed.

"Yes sir," Murph explained to the captain. "It's a regular comedy show back here… except that none of these shitbirds is in any way funny."

"Take my Murph, please," torpedoman Milt Zagler quipped as he heaved on a tagle.

"You hear this, sir?" Murph grumped. "Even the new kid thinks he can bust my balls."

"Uneasy lies the head that wears the crown, eh Murph?" Turner asked wryly.

"Ain't it just so, sir… course, I'm the guy what assigns all the shit detail… so… it ain't all bad," Murph said and grinned wickedly. "We're in good shape, though, sir. All our gear is fine, and I've even done some manual tests on the planes and rudder. Stuffing boxes for all the shafts seem okay, too. We had a mildly interesting pounding, but nothin' this lady can't handle."

Turner shook his head, "What's it take to shake you up, Walter?"

Murph scoffed, "Japs, Krauts, tooth shakers… they don't amount to a hilla beans, sir… but get my ex-wife down here, and you'll see this fine fellow running for the hills."

Turner laughed, "I learn something new about you every week, Murph. Well, carry on."

"Carrying on, sir."

The 1MC channel hissed as it was opened, and Andy Post's voice called through the ship, "*Captain Turner, please report to radio. Repeat, Captain to radio. We have an urgent message from S-52. That is all.*"

Turner ducked out and made his way forward. He'd known the message was coming, of course. He'd been waiting for Post and Weiss to decode it. Yet the fact that Post would call him forward and said that it was urgent sent a little shiver of anticipation up Turner's spine.

Even after a hellacious attack from three Japanese destroyers that knocked his boat and his men for a loop, Turner found that he was still raring to go. Perhaps even more so, with the eagerness to get a little payback.

He wondered about himself. Was it only zeal to do his duty, or was he a little touched in the head?

Either way, he was looking forward to the next move.

24

"Seen any sea monsters, Port?" Art Turner asked as he climbed up to the bridge with a message flimsy in his hand.

"Nothin' to write home about, sir," Hazard said. "A Kraken, giant sea serpent… the occasional Megalodon."

"Just another day then," Turner quipped.

"I take it we've got some news, sir," Hazard inquired, casting a glance at the paper.

"We've made contact with S-52," Turner stated. "Long and short of it is that they got banged up by the same three Japs that kicked us in the ass, too. In the process, the captain received a head wound, and Pat is now in temporary command. He's requested a face-to-face and should be hoving into view anytime now."

"*Madre de dios…*" Hotrod muttered.

Turner chuckled, "Not the half of it, Hotrod… he reports sighting *Sakai* again at first light. Off to the east."

"Be nice to get that bastard, sir," Hazard said, a dark expression crossing his features. "I got a *personal* grudge with that son of a bitch, Sato."

"I thought you might," Turner said. "And I'm right there with ya."

"Well, sir, the deck is yours," Hazard began. "Ship is—"

Turner held up a hand, "Hold on there, Port. Once Pat arrives, I'm having him and his second come across, and we're gonna have ourselves a little pow-wow. I'd like you there. Hotrod, you think you can mind the store while we do?"

"Aye-aye, Skipper," Hernandez replied.

Both Hazard and Turner looked at him. The quartermaster looked back innocently.

"That's it?" Turner asked.

"No remarks about your humble peasantry or the customs in your simple village?" Hazard added.

"My wit is to be savored, *señores*... an overindulgence desensitizes one to its quality," Hernandez replied.

"Hotrod," Turner said, clapping him on the shoulder, "you're a weird dude."

"*Si*," said Hotrod.

The men's laughter was interrupted by a shout from one of the lookouts, "Sir! Surface contact bearing three-four-five horizon... possible submarine!"

"What's she doin', Grigsy?" Hazard asked.

A pause and then, "Headed right for us, sir... I'm getting a signal now... it's S-52 requesting permission to close, sir."

"Shall I send for a signal gun, sir?" Hotrod asked Hazard.

Although Turner was there, Hazard was still officer of the deck, and all commands must go through him. He looked back at Turner.

"Have radio send the acknowledgment over the short-range," Turner said.

Hotrod called down, and Hazard had the lookouts come down from the perch. Even though the radio transmitter was above their heads when the radio mast was extended, it was still a wise precaution. A radio on full power generated enough radiation to cause injury if you were too close. Although a low-powered short-range transmission wasn't dangerous, should a short or power surge occur, it could be an issue.

The message was sent, and the men went below to be replaced by the next watch. Hotrod, who had been given the deck at that time, had ordered the ship to come to an all stop once the S-52 was within a half-mile.

Marty Janslotter came up on deck with a party of men carrying boat hooks and several lines. As everyone watched, the older boat came about and heaved to along *Bull Shark's* port beam. Several men came on deck and inflated a rubber raft, which was gently lowered into the mild swell. Turner saw Pat Jarvis and one of the boat's officers… what was his name… Savage? Yes, Savage… clamber down into the boat with two enlisted men who rowed them across.

"Standby to receive boarding party," Hotrod called. "Secure a line to the five-inch for climbing, Marty."

"Gotcha, Hotrod," Janslotter said and did so. When the raft came alongside, the two men with the boat hooks extended them down to be grabbed and held by the rowers. Jarvis seized the support line and hauled himself up the pressure hull and onto the deck with a hand from the boatswain. Savage came next. Both men looked a bit drawn.

"Welcome aboard *Bull Shark* gents," Turner said with a grin and stuck out his hand to Jarvis. "I take it you've got some news, Pat?"

Jarvis snorted, "To put it lightly, sir. We've had… an interesting few days, haven't we, Chris?"

"That's putting it mildly, as you say, sir," Savage said.

Turner remembered the young man as having an air of arrogant confidence when they'd met in Admiral Lockwood's office in Brisbane. Now, though, it seemed as if something… or someone… had knocked the chip off the man's shoulder. If not entirely, what was there was a sliver of what it had been.

"Well, come on below, gents, and we can get our ducks in a row," Turner said as he headed for the hatch to the forward room. "Ship is yours, Hotrod, mind you don't let her fall overboard."

Jarvis was met with smiles and cheerful greetings when the three officers came below. They had to work their way around the men working below the platform on the two lowest torpedo tubes. Joe Dutch saw the three men come down and clambered up out of the lower section with Sparky in tow.

"Glad to see ya', Pat," Dutch said with a grin. "Who's your pal?"

"My temporary XO, Chris Savage," Pat said. "You guys cleaning house or what, Joe?"

"Had a bad HV surge," Dutch explained. "Went all the way through the boat. We're making sure five and six are functioning properly."

"How's that comin' along?" Turner asked.

"We're gettin' there, sir," Sparky said. "We did find a couple of minor shorts, too."

"Good," Turner said and then smiled at the LPO. "Sparky… I'm sorry I chewed you out earlier. No hard feelings?"

Sparks looked almost dumbfounded at the hand Turner held out. He took it and smiled back, "Aw, hell, sir… no big deal. I shoulda known better."

Jarvis smiled, "Back talkin' again, Sparky?"

"Yeah," Tommy Perkins said in his surfer drawl. "He just don't know when it's time to zip up his tater gobbler."

The men around laughed, and Sparky glared at Perkins, although he couldn't help but smile, "Look who's talkin', *seaman* Perkins."

"You think you fellas can finish this without my eye on you?" Dutch asked the men in the pit, as it were.

"I'll keep 'em in line, sir," Sparky said. "If'n they get a little rambunctious, I'll threaten to set the skipper on 'em."

"Growl," Turner said and led the other officers aft.

The wardroom was packed. With *Bull Shark's* full complement of seven officers plus one, there wasn't room for everyone at the table. Turner and Jarvis elected to stand. Carlson handed out cups of coffee and sandwiches as everyone got settled in.

"Okay, Pat, this is your party, so why don't you fill us in," Turner began the meeting.

Jarvis explained how they'd first sighted the Japanese carrier several days earlier, which he'd already reported ashore. He then described the battle, or lack of one, with the three Japanese destroyers. Savage's face looked drawn and rigid during this. It was clear that he was having a rather difficult time with all that had happened. His loyalties to his captain and his having to face the facts.

Jarvis was open about how he and Waters had clashed and locked horns. Yet he stayed mostly on the topic of the enemy.

"We didn't attack the other day when he was right in our sights, sir," Jarvis said, casting a glance toward Savage. "In my opinion, it was the perfect setup. One strike carrier with one DD escort. Even if a submarine *was* lurking below her keel... I felt that it was worth the shot. The captain, however, didn't. We also disagreed on attacking the three DDs before they found us."

Turner looked at Savage, "What are your thoughts on this, Lieutenant? I know you're one of Waters' staunchest supporters. Do you think he was right not to attack? And do you support Mr. Jarvis now that he's in command?"

Savage shifted in his chair, "Sir... I don't like to second guess my captain. Bernard Waters is one of the most seasoned sub skippers in the fleet. It seems a bit... arrogant... to me to question him...."

"But?" Turner pushed. He could sense that there was more.

Savage drew in a breath and then fumbled in his duty blouse for a pack of Parliaments. He shook one out, slipped it between his pursed lips and struck a match. Once the coffin nail was going, he shook out the match and placed it carefully into the ashtray at the center of the table. The process seemed to give him something upon which to stand.

"I think... well... Mr. Jarvis and I have not always seen eye to eye," Savage began. "But... I think he's right. I think we *should* have gone after that Jap carrier. And the other night... had we attacked first, there might not have been three tin cans on our asses... excuse me, sir."

"Don't worry about it, the swearing lamp is lit," Turner said kindly.

"So yes, sir, until the captain recovers, I'll support Mr. Jarvis," Savage finished.

"Good," Turner stated. "Because I think the two of us need to go out there and hunt that bastard down. The commander of that vessel, or her XO in truth... although who knows now, has made it his mission to destroy *me*. He's gotten it into his head that we're in a personal war. I think that's a dangerous wild card we don't need out here. Things are tough enough without some maniac sneaking around trying to sink us."

"Concur," Jarvis said.

"Problem is, how do we find this crazy Nip?" Post asked. "There's a lot of water out there."

This drew a round of grins, and Jarvis pulled a pencil from his pocket and made several Xs on a chart that Williams had laid out on the table.

"This was our first sighting," Jarvis began, tapping a mark just to the northeast of Guadalcanal's northeastern corner. "He was headed into The Slot from the east."

"Like he was patrolling out in the Pacific… I mean outside the archipelago?" Nichols asked.

"Like last time," Williams opined. "When Pat here gave him a kick up the behind."

"Behind?" Pat needled.

"I'm a good boy, Pat," Williams said sweetly. "Unlike some."

Even Savage smiled at this. He had already noticed the comfortable air aboard this boat. The officers, the men and even the way they interacted. It gave him the impression of a family. A *functional* family.

"Speaking of which," Jarvis said and made a mark on the chart in the far northeastern corner. "Just makes it… this is about where we fought him before, Skipper. And just this morning, we were to the east as well, and it was Chris here who had the deck and who spotted the smoke on the horizon. Right about here… almost due north of us."

"So, he's lurkin' outside the theater," Hazard said thoughtfully. "Maybe sendin' his planes over The Canal and the other islands during the day?"

"It is Tojo time," Turner said. "Frankly, I'm surprised nobody's taken a potshot at us, even though we're forty miles east of Henderson… anyway, I'd guess that he may be doing that, Port."

"Maybe something else, too," Dutch added, tapping the chart. "He's got what, twenty planes? Maybe thirty? A couple of sorties mixing it up with the Marines, and he'd probably lose at least one or two birds each time, right?"

Turner nodded. He thought he saw where Dutch was headed but let the man explain his own thoughts.

"*We* know that Admiral Fletcher's carriers are back out there to our south," Dutch continued. "About a hundred, hundred and fifty miles. The Japs must know that too… but not exactly *where*."

"I see what you're drivin' at, Joe," Pat said. "Maybe *Sakai* is sending out scouts to try and locate our flat tops."

"Then once he does, he'll let Yamamoto know," Savage added.

"And then the Kido Butai, or what's left of it, comes steaming down from Truk in force," Turner added, tapping his chin. "And we get another Midway… hopefully without us being jumped unknowingly this time."

"Problem is that there's a lot of Pacific out there east of the Solomons and south of Truk," Nichols said. "How do we find this guy?"

"We can see by these position indicators that he might be operating within a containment zone," Turner mused. "You fellas found him before in this area… and now there's two of us. We'll need to act in concert."

"Like the Krauts do in the Atlantic," Post said. "Like a wolfpack."

"More or less," Turner said, and then he frowned. "Frank… what do you suppose that thing draws?"

Nichols thought for a moment, "Didn't Mr. Clayton provide us with info on her?"

Turner nodded, "Yeah… but I forget her exact dimensions. She's about five-hundred and fifty feet long and heavier than her original cruiser design."

"Figure at least twenty-two feet," Nichols said. "Maybe a little more."

Jarvis frowned then, and then his face seemed to light up as he caught on to Turner's idea, "Where's the best place to hide from a submarine?"

Turner grinned, "Precisely."

The other men looked confused at first, but Turner was gratified to see that understanding was beginning to dawn on their faces. One by one, each officer sat straighter in his chair, and a slow grin began to spread.

"So, you think he's hanging out in the shallows someplace?" Dutch asked.

"It's a possibility," Turner offered. "Not a surety."

"Like off Cay Sal bank," Nichols muttered, almost to himself.

"Out here in this clear water, even a hundred feet wouldn't hide a boat in the daytime," Jarvis mused. "And that'd be plenty of water for him."

"So, he just floats there in a hundred feet, maybe less," Williams stated. "And uses the long reach of his airwing to scout or attack while remaining safe from torpedo attacks. Not to mention being hard to find on account of the range of his planes."

"It's an option," Turner said. "Remember, he's got something of a ringer on board. Commander Osaka."

"I thought he was on our side," Hazard said.

"He's on *his* side," Turner stated. "There's a distinct difference. Osaka isn't a traitor. He helps us because he wants to spare Japan more grief. But it's for *Japan* that he does what he does… and in order to be able to do it, he must obviously do his duty from time to time."

"In other words," Savage added. "He's probably being asked by this Sato guy to help him."

"Yeah, and he can't refuse without engendering suspicion," Jarvis put in.

"Which means we've got our work cut out for us," Nichols said.

"There's something else, too," Turner said. "The morning fox made mention of another Jap we need to look out for. They call him 'The Sensei.' Apparently, this guy teaches a special destroyer captain's school. Supposed to be the best of the best… and after our experiences with those three DDs the other night… I'm inclined to think that this guy might be out here now. He's reputed to be."

"The only problem I see with this theory," Hazard said, "is that these are all volcanic islands, as are most in the Pacific. That means the depths drop off fast. If you're in a hundred feet of water or less, you're also within a mile or less of shore. Certainly, *Sakai* would be seen by somebody around here, right?"

"Not necessarily…" Savage said slowly after everyone spent a minute or so frowning over Hazard's point. He reached out and tapped the chart in a seemingly empty region north of the Florida Islands. "Although it's not well documented on these charts… I imagine Rand McNally will have their work cut out for them after the war… I've been out here before. There are plenty of small islets and even some sizable islands outside the Solomons boundary. And right about here, if I'm not mistaken, there's a small group of them that might serve."

"Hmmm…" Turner said thoughtfully. "You sure about this, Mr. Savage?"

"Mostly, sir," Savage admitted with a shrug. "It was only once about six months ago… but I'm pretty certain."

"It's a place to start," said Williams and then grinned. "The Savage Islands… apropos, huh?"

"Concur," said Turner.

Jarvis frowned and then reached out and drew a small circle around a point on the chart, "If I may, sir?"

"Go ahead, Pat," Turner urged.

"Suppose that we station S-52 here, about a hundred miles northeast of Tulagi," Jarvis explained. "Then we have *Bull Shark* run a circular patrol starting at Chris' uncharted islands working clockwise out into the Pacific and around to the south. Using us as a pivot. *Bull Shark* is faster, y'see, and she can cover the ground more quickly. Between radar and sonar sweeps, as well as visuals, we should see *something*."

"Even if we cut out the southwestern wedge of that circle, Pat, it's still four hundred miles," Nichols said. "Might take a couple of days."

Jarvis nodded, "Yeah, but at top speed, *Bull Shark* is no more than five hours from S-52 at any given time."

"Hell, we can eliminate the southeastern quadrant, too," Post said. "The Japs won't be out there."

"Probably not," Turner admitted. "So we start at say… three hundred degrees and then work around to a hundred and ten degrees from S-52's center point. Now we're talkin' about two hundred miles or so, and we can do that in a day."

"If *Sakai* is out there, I bet we find her," Jarvis enthused.

"Meanwhile, we leave The Slot undefended," Williams pointed out.

"Perhaps…" Turner said. "But the morning fox also warned of an impending Japanese carrier assault. Lot of activity has been seen around Truk the last couple of days. A lot of message traffic, too… although since the Japs upgraded from JN-25A, Ultra hasn't decoded much. I say let's give it twenty-four hours. If we don't find Sato by then, the two of us come back into the Sealark Channel and station ourselves right in the line of the Tokyo Express. But I think Mr. Savage's suggestion and Mr. Jarvis' plan is a good one. So say we all?"

"So say all of us," the officers, and even Eddie Carlson, almost cheered in response.

25

TRUK HARBOR – TRUK ATOLL
AUGUST 22, 1942 – 1630 LOCAL TIME

At first, no one noticed him enter the CIC. This was hardly surprising, as even though the huge battleship was riding at her anchors in Truk Lagoon, she was still the center of combat operations for most of the Pacific. Men worked at their stations, coordinating radio traffic, analyzing reports, updating plots and most of all, smoking.

The darkened room was filled with a gray fog of burnt tobacco, with enough visible to cast the CIC in a pale bluish-white glow. A scene that would become the quintessential setting for combat, both fact and fiction, for decades to come.

At the center of it all, standing with his hands clasped behind his back, was Admiral Matome Ugaki. He stood over a large plotting table and watched as three junior officers and three enlisted men manipulated their compasses, slide rules and pencils across the vast table in a frantic dance of mathematics and trigonometry.

"I see the hive is busy at work," spoke Yamamoto from behind his chief of staff.

To his credit, or perhaps it was only fatigue that prevented it, Ugaki did not flinch. He simply turned and bowed slightly, "Yes sir."

Yamamoto strode up and stood beside his aid and friend, lighting a cigarette for himself. It was only partly out of the desire to do so. Some of it was simply doing what was expected of him. The act of the great man, casually lighting up as he inspected his men at work.

How odd it could sometimes be, Yamamoto mused to himself. When he was a young man, just getting started in his career, he never could have imagined that one of the most important aspects to an officer's effectiveness was his ability as an *actor*. To portray a role. The role of the competent and steadfast leader. To be what the men expected him to be.

Further fascinating still was how much more of this ability was called upon as Yamamoto had risen through the ranks. The more officers and men that were placed under one, the more one had to hone his skills as a thespian. Now, as the high and mighty living legend that he, laughably to his mind, was to the Navy, Yamamoto's every movement was studied. Every motion, every word… even something so simple as lighting a cigarette held some meaning for those who saw it.

He thought it was preposterous… yet he was wise enough to understand the importance of the thing.

"Have all preparations been made?" Yamamoto asked, knowing the answer already.

"Yes sir," Ugaki said and smiled ever so slightly. He, too, understood the performance. "All three groups report ready to sail. Admiral Nagumo's carrier group is standing by outside the lagoon within short-range radio range."

"Very good," Yamamoto said. "I am most pleased, Matome. With everyone. Please have departure clearance and final instructions relayed through the port director. They will get underway at dusk. Admiral Tanaka may begin now, as his task force is necessarily slowed down by the transports."

"Yes sir," Ugaki said, both admirals pleased to note no less than three adjutants furiously scribbling on notepads in preparation to hurry off to the radio room.

"May I borrow you for a moment, Admiral?" Yamamoto asked.

Ugaki nodded, "Of course, sir."

The two men exited the smokey room and out onto the open deck. Both marveled at the number of ships around them at that moment. Some of them would be departing to accompany Nagumo's Kido Butai, and others were there for a variety of missions and tasks. Yet it was a glorious sight. Dozens of warships and many more supply freighters and transports. It was easy to understand how this out of the way nowhere atoll had become known as the Gibraltar of the Pacific.

In Nagumo's private situation room located one deck down from the bridge and CIC, the two officers stood by the Admiral's plotting table where he'd already arranged his miniature ships. On the table were felt representations of Guadalcanal, Tulagi and the other islands. As before, in such operations as Midway and the Coral Sea, the setup was impressive. Especially impressive when compared to the supposed American forces, which were far less numerous.

"This Guadalcanal campaign is proving to be far more resource-intensive than we originally thought, is it not, sir?" Ugaki commented as he studied the board.

"There is a saying, Matome, that the first casualty of any battle is the plan," Yamamoto mused. "This concept is scalable to any degree, including an entire war. Especially, perhaps, a war fought for control of vital resources. Ironic, is it not? Our home islands, poor by way of certain natural resources, must expend these same resources in greater and greater amounts in order to secure more of them. Food, men and perhaps at the core of it all… petroleum."

"The twentieth century runs on oil," Ugaki agreed.

"Yes… but *think* of it, Matome!" Yamamoto went on, enthusiasm lighting his careworn features. "Men have known of and used hydrocarbons for thousands of years… yet really, not until a cheap and reliable internal combustion engine was developed, did crude oil become the black gold it is today. Just fifty years ago, Rudolph Diesel invented the engine that's now the backbone of civilization. A hundred years ago, this war might have been fought with steam-powered ships… more likely, the majority would still be sailing ships. And even those steamers would have had sails aboard. You can drive a ship with steam, even steam boilers fueled by oil… but you can't launch a heavier than air vehicle with it. You can't run a *submarine* on steam… not for long at any rate. Yet it's gasoline and diesel that powers the

Earth now… and fuels our aggression toward every Pacific nation within our grasp."

"Things change," Ugaki stated simply.

"Don't they indeed…" Yamamoto mused, almost to himself. "Well, my friend… let us not wax philosophical for too long. We're about to engage in a major operation and send thousands of men and hundreds of millions of yen worth of equipment into a conflict over a worthless lump of diseased volcanic rock. How extraordinary… now here is what I would like done. Tanaka will invade Guadalcanal, of course."

"As planned," Ugaki felt compelled to say.

Yamamoto nodded, "I wish Nagumo to detach Ryujo and several escorts to proceed *ahead* of Admiral Tanaka. They will launch a preliminary attack on the island and direct the attention of American forces there."

"A Judas goat," Ugaki said, not without some discomfort. "As with our campaign to take Rabaul in May."

"Yes, Matome," Yamamoto said, a bit glumly. "Let us hope that we don't lose her the way we lost Shoho… but this is a risk we *must* take. Admiral Kondo's force will run interference for Nagumo, and of course… the old man will attempt to locate Fletcher's carriers and do what he *failed* so *miserably* to do in June."

"Let us hope he's more decisive this time," Ugaki agreed.

Yamamoto laughed bitterly, "At this point, Matome, I'd settle for the fool not losing *Shokaku* and *Zuikaku*. Ah, well… please pass this information on. And one more thing, Matome."

"Sir?"

Yamamoto smiled ruefully, yet there was something of a mischievous glint in his dark eyes, "Send a personal message to Nagumo from me. Inform him that I'm counting on him doing his best and that all of Japan's prayers go with him. Tell him that I *know* he won't let them down this time."

Ugaki smiled thinly. The message, on its surface, was encouraging and would sound like a pep talk. However, both men knew, as Nagumo would no doubt know, that it was a veiled warning and perhaps thinly veiled threat as well.

STATION HYPO – PEARL HARBOR, HAWAII

The Dungeon, as the basement room at the naval base was colloquially known, was unlike just about any other military office. Indeed, it was unlike just about any other governmental or civilian office environment, for that matter.

There was something… alive… in the heavy atmosphere of the basement facility. Heavy not simply from the pall of cigarette smoke or from the sounds of human voices, clacking typewriters and the myriad other smells, sights and sounds that made up an open space with a hundred people working in it. No, the dungeon's air was heavy with that special and often unidentifiable electrical charge of emotion. Expectation, frustration, tension, jocularity with an underlying crackle of intense focus.

On this particular day, commander Joe Rochefort found himself in a pernicious snit. Joe was considered by most who didn't know him personally as a bit of a crackpot. A weird guy who worked in bedroom slippers and a smoking jacket or in a bathrobe on those extra-grueling days. His hair was often ratty with tangles, his five o'clock shadow kept round the clock, and a look of deceptive abstraction plastered on his pallid face.

To those who knew Joe Rochefort well, he was an energetic, brilliant, often mercurial and irascible man. To those who knew him especially well, Joe was also nuttier than a pecan log.

On this particular day, which was drawing to a close, he was in rare form. While G.I.s and sailors walked and swam along the beaches of Diamond Head and young surfers paddled their wooden longboards out to catch the last of the evening swells to impress their admiring shore-bound ladies, Joe Rochefort was gulping coffee, muttering to himself and occasionally slamming one random thing against another random thing.

Halfway across the open floor of The Dungeon, Joe Finnegan, Jasper Holmes and Lt. J.G. Joan Turner sat together at a large round table strewn with bits of papers of all shapes, sizes and colors and tried to appear as if they weren't mesmerized by their boss's semi-tantrum. The three of them were frustrated as well, also having gotten nowhere on the new JN-25 code iteration… but they simply couldn't compete with Rochefort's level of perturbation.

"You think he'll blow his stack before the sun goes down or after?" Jasper Holmes asked with a wicked gleam in his eyes.

"I got five bucks says he already flipped his lid, and he's just holdin' it in," Finnegan chuckled.

"Oh, come on, boys," Joan Turner pretended to chastise. "He's frustrated and is a man of deep feelings. He's just scared and lonely and lost… like a little rumple-headed puppy-dog."

The three of them threw their heads back, and peals of laughter rebounded off the walls of the big office. No less than two dozen people joined in, either because they'd overheard or simply needed the release. From across the room, Rochefort swore, kicked his desk, swore again… swore thrice more and then stomped toward the recalcitrant trio.

"You guys are in for it now," said a Marine lieutenant recently assigned to the crypto department. "Old Robe-tilla the Hun is *comin'* for ya'!"

"I assume you magpies are yuckin' it up on account of you've broken JN-25C, right?" Rochefort gloomed.

"I done told 'em they ought not carry on so, Mr. Rochefort sir," said the Marine, a ludicrously over-exaggerated look of innocence plastered across his kisser.

"Shut up, Lester," Rochefort said. "Nobody likes a smart ass."

"Lies will not avail us, Joseph," Holmes said and winked at Joan.

"So what's so funny anyhow?" Rochefort asked, frowning. There was, however, just a glimmer of a smile twitching at the corners of his mouth. "Do you realize that since Midway, we haven't cracked a damned thing worth a fart in a windstorm? At any minute now, Ed Layton or the Old Man himself is gonna bust through those doors and tear us all a new poop shoot."

"Hey, I don't know if you realize this or not, Joe, but this decoding thing is *hard*," Finnegan said with a straight face.

"Yeah, so is maintenance detail in Alaska in January," Rochefort said. "So, if we all don't wanna end up scrapin' frozen turds outta commodes in the Great White North, I suggest we buckle down and come up with some results, for *Christ!*"

"How much coffee have you had today?" Joan asked with real concern.

"Too much, Joanie, like every day," Rochefort said, his pique, as always, effectively damped by Joan.

"Well, it ain't gonna be today, Chief," Holmes said. "Although Joanie here might have come up with another war-winning idea."

"Of course she did," Rochefort said wryly. "What've you got, Joanie?"

"Well..." Joan began modestly, shuffling papers absently on the table. "I know this is gonna sound nutty... but you know that kids game Marco Polo? Where they get in the pool, and one closes their eyes and says 'Marco' and the other kids have to say 'Polo'?"

"Yeah, sort of a hide and seek thing," Holmes said.

"My kids never get tired of it," Finnegan said. "Now that Arty and Dotty are around, it's every freakin' day! Gladys'll probably end up in the booby hatch before October!"

Rochefort said nothing, but his eyes were aglow with dawning realization. He nodded at Joan.

"Well, as you know, the Japanese keep changing their stupid codes on us," Joan said. "Personally, I think it's rather rude myself, but what're ya gonna do."

Laughs from the three men. Around them, other cryptanalysts within earshot were paying much closer attention.

"Anyway, we can't decipher much right now," Joan said. "It's like... we can hear the noise but can't understand the content. But we can *hear* the noise, you, see? We know where the transmissions come from; we know their frequency... I mean the number of times they're sent... we know the address of each radio and the patterns of each transmission."

Finnegan's eyes went wide, "Marco Polo...."

Holmes frowned, and then he seemed to get it as well, "Yeah... yeah! If we can't know *what's in* each message, we can sure as shit take an educated guess. If Truk sends out a long message to some location in the middle of nowhere, and that sends a message back to Truk... we don't know where the messages go, but we can guess based on the response time and possibly pattern… we can RDF the mobile ones and have a rough idea of what they're up to."

"Not bad, Joan!" Finnegan enthused. "Y'know… for a girl."

Joan laughed and stuck her tongue out at him.

Rochefort sparked a pill and crossed his arms over his chest, "So what you're telling me, fellas, is that we got over a hundred people in here, and our only good idea of late has come from our only girl?"

Joan chuckled.

Finnegan shrugged, "What're you tryin' to say, Joe?"

Rochefort shook his head, "Over a hundred dudes… and the girl figures it out."

"Sounds about right," Joan quipped.

"So, based on this brilliant detective method," Rochefort asked when he stopped laughing. "Have you guys got anything?"

Joan looked to Holmes. He cleared his throat and held out a sheet of paper to his boss, "We think Yamamoto is sending a couple of task forces to The Canal. Nagumo and the carriers, two or three, a surface support group and an invasion force. In fact, they're probably underway already."

"Christ…" Rochefort sighed. "Not entirely unexpected, but I'd better go and see the Old Man. Wish we had some confirmation on this."

"We just might soon," Holmes said. "As you know, Joe, Art Turner and *Bull Shark* are operating in The Slot. Tonight's update from them stated that he and S-52 are headed out into the Pacific above the Solomons to try and find some strike carrier group."

"That puts them right in the path of Yamamoto's strike force," Finnegan said, casting a wary glance at Joan.

"An early warning system?" Rochefort asked. "Maybe… but either way, it's time to get the ball rolling. Good work, everybody, especially you, Joan. Why don't you knock off for the night? Go home and see your kids."

Joan nearly protested, yet she stopped herself. Suddenly knowing where Art was and knowing what he was up to was unsettling. She had a nearly overwhelming urge to take her children into her arms and hold them tight.

"He'll be all right, Joan," Finnegan said, taking her hand. "If anybody can get through this craziness, it's Anvil Art."

STRIKE CARRIER *SAKAI* – 100 MILES NORTH OF GUADALCANAL

"A great operation is now underway," Sato said as he, Arawi, Hideki and Osaka sat in what had been captain Igawa's at sea cabin. The evening meal had been cleared, and Sato had condescended to share out some of Igawa's remaining supply of Cubans.

"Let us hope that this time Admiral Nagumo will be successful in locating the American carriers," Arawi said.

"And that the reverse is not true," Hideki added. "That Fletcher's carriers will fail to spot Nagumo's first, as was the case at Midway."

"I believe that the Ame-cohs may have cracked our previous codes," Sato suggested. "There is no proof of this… yet it would certainly explain things. It certainly does not excuse Nagumo's blunders, however. No *code* can prevent *that*, it would seem."

It was unwise to speak so blatantly and disrespectfully about a senior Admiral. However, none of the officers in that room could seriously disagree. Osaka, for his part, shared the view of Yamamoto as regards Nagumo. Nagumo was a timid old man who, in spite of his experience, lacked the grit required to adequately do the job to which he was assigned.

However, castigating a man who was not in their presence would serve no purpose, "We have our own battle to fight, however. I would wager quite a bit that Art Turner and his submarine are coming for us."

"And thanks to your suggestion of using The Sensei, sir," Arawi said with true admiration, "we now know there are *two* submarines out there."

"Perhaps," Sato interjected. "Unless one or both were destroyed."

Hideki exchanged a glance with Osaka and said: "Somehow… I doubt that, sir."

Osaka nodded, "This Art Turner is a wily and resilient fellow. He's coming, I'm sure of it. Did scouts not report sighting possible submarines off Guadalcanal earlier today?"

"Unverified," Sato said and leaned back, puffing languidly. "However… it is likely wise to err on the side of caution. The real question is, what do we do next?"

Both Osaka and Hideki seemed to share the same thought at the same time. They were both put in mind of Kajimora, the former commander of the experimental *Leviathan*. He, too, had been arrogant and enjoyed playing the big man. And he, too, prodded Osaka and Hideki for advice in dealing with Turner.

"We are eager to hear your suggestions, sir," Hideki said, knowing that Osaka was thinking it as well.

"No doubt we will be directed to join the fleet," Sato mused. "We do have this ship and four escorts, which include The Sensei. We also have I-123."

"A great deal of good she did us last time," Arawi mused sourly.

Sato frowned, but then his face became amiable once more, "Indeed, *Yakuin*. Our former captain did not put her to the best use, I'm afraid. Perhaps we can do better this time. What do you gentlemen say?"

"Certainly," Osaka said.

"No doubt," added Hideki.

That appeared to raise Sato's hackles a bit. He was fishing for direct advice and was getting little more than glad-handing. It was beginning to wear on his patience.

"We could simply patrol along the outside of the islands," Arawi suggested. "Sooner or later, if Turner is out there, he will find us and come for us. Between our six ships and our air wing, we should be able to spot him."

A practical, if a bit uninspired, suggestion. Sato frowned at first but then slowly began to nod his head in agreement. Once more, Osaka was gripped with the uncomfortable knowledge that he must act. Must provide a plan that was more likely to succeed while at the same time attempting to give Turner an opportunity as well.

This large fleet action was an opportunity, of that much Osaka was certain. Most things were, in truth. As to what sort of opportunity and how to exploit it, that was another matter.

It was Hideki who provided a different option, "What if, rather than searching blindly, as the American will no doubt be doing… we lay a trap instead."

Arawi cocked an eyebrow, not certain if he should be offended or intrigued by this alternative. Sato frowned over his cigar for a long moment.

"What do you mean, Omata?" Osaka asked, heading off any protests or rudeness from Sato.

"Well…" the CAG began, tapping his ash. "During the last encounter with *Bull Shark*, *Sakai* was stationed not far from here, and the Americans found her."

"No doubt by tracking my seaplane," Sato said. "And in a fog, no less. Damn their radar…."

Osaka thought he saw where this was going, "Yes, they have better radar than we do, that's for certain. Better echolocation as well, I'm afraid."

Sato chuffed derisively, "Are you suggesting we stake our carrier out and *let* Turner find us, Commander?"

Hideki frowned, "Yes… and no. I'm not entirely sure as yet; the idea has only just occurred."

"That didn't work out well last time, Omata," Arawi stated.

"No, but in that instance, *Sakai* didn't know the American was coming," Hideki said. "Knowing that allows us control…."

Osaka thought he saw where this could lead and broke in, "We can choose the time and place. Is that what you're saying, Omata? To set up the board in our favor?"

"Yes, exactly," Hideki said. "We pick the time and place for the meeting and set things up in such a way as to give us the advantage."

Osaka's eyes lit up, "Do we have a chart handy?"

They didn't, but after calling up to the CIC, one was sent to the captain's cabin. It was spread out on the table, and Osaka began to explain the plan that Hideki had inspired.

"As we know," Osaka began, "the standardized charts available today are somewhat lacking as regards the outer boundaries of the

Solomon Islands chain. Specifically on the northern edge. As *we* have been using these waters far more frequently, we've been updating our charts. For example, here, not far from where we are now, there are a series of small islets not noted on the Rand McNally charts. There is one, here, a group of several small islands that may serve our purposes."

"In what way?" Sato asked, leaning forward with real interest.

"Inside these four islands is a sort of bay formed by them," Osaka said. "It would make a passable anchorage in a pinch, as the mean depth is near ten meters. However, around these islands is a sort of failed atoll. A shoal that extends nearly a mile from the shore in all directions and is no more than thirty meters deep."

Hideki thought he saw where his friend was going. By the excited look on Arawi's face, the younger officer appeared to understand as well. It was somewhat gratifying to see that Sato had yet to catch on.

"How does this help us?" Sato asked. "You wish *Sakai* to anchor in this bay? That removes any ASW operation we might engage in."

Osaka shook his head, careful to avoid allowing any contempt to show on his face, "Not the carrier, Captain… but perhaps one or two of our destroyers. No, *Sakai* holds station here… and I-123 can come to rest on the bottom directly beneath her keel, as was the case before. We can position the other destroyers anywhere we like. Perhaps behind the islands or twenty kilometers over the horizon. Once the submarine, or *submarines*, is detected, we spring the trap."

"This seems familiar to me…." Sato mused.

"You've mentioned before that Turner's first patrol was to sink a German Q-ship," Osaka went on. "*They* tried a similar trick to lure Turner into shallow water not far from Florida."

"Which failed," Sato said, his lip curling ever so slightly into a sneer.

"Yes, but they were not prepared well enough," Osaka continued. "And they didn't have the resources we do now. Also, our aim is not to lure Turner into the shallows. He'd be a fool to pass over the fifty-fathom curve in any case. Hell, if anything, we're only presenting a tempting target. What Turner *should* do is to radio our positions in and have the Lunga Point airfield send bombers to attack us. This would, in truth, serve two goals. It would draw air power from the base, which in turn allows our fleet to attack more effectively. It also lets us know that Turner is close. We then have our hidden destroyers race into the combat zone at full speed and close a net around him."

Hideki grinned, "I like it."

Arawi smiled as well, "A very interesting plan, Commander."

"Yes..." Sato said, tapping a long ash into the tray that held one corner of the chart down. "But I'm not certain about I-123. Placing her below our keel does us little good, in truth. I think that rather than having her below us, we place her in deep water further out to sea. She can shadow us, and we will circle the islands or perhaps cruise back and forth in the shallows at four knots. In this way, we will give Turner the *impression* that I-123 is with us."

"And she'll be able to use her sound gear to detect them all the sooner," Arawi added.

Osaka would object that with I-123 closer, sonar-based communication could allow them to exchange information. With the submarine a kilometer or two away, such communication could be overheard. He saw that Hideki was about to make the same objection, but Osaka stopped him with a look and a minute shake of the head.

"It is settled then," Sato said triumphantly. "We will set up a trap and draw our mouse in. No matter what the outcome of Admiral Yamamoto's attack, *we* will successfully rid the empire of an annoying *pest* once and for all!"

Yes, thought Osaka ruefully. *We will...*

26

PACIFIC OCEAN – 100 MILES EAST OF GUADALCANAL

AUGUST 22, 1942 – 2230

Major Al Decker exited the superstructure and moved forward toward the bow of the destroyer *Cavalier*. The night was warm but comfortable and would be, he knew, his last at sea. The small convoy of three destroyers that had left New Caledonia several days before would be entering Sealark Channel and would stand to offshore of Henderson Field before dawn.

It had been an uneventful cruise, with mostly good weather except for a few days ago when the ships had skirted the edge of a nasty tropical storm. It hadn't been too bad, with ten-to-twelve-foot waves and winds of twenty-five knots or so. Now, however, that seemed like a distant memory as Decker looked out over a placid sea on a clear night.

The moon, just a sliver now, had risen and was already a third of the way across the sky, casting her silvery finger upon the light swells and her ethereal glow upon the starboard side of the ship. Ahead of *Cavalier*, Decker could see the destroyer *Blue*, her narrow silhouette visible a mile ahead and her phosphorescent wake reaching back to intermingle with his ship's own bow wave. Behind *Cavalier* was the *Patterson*, an older four-piper that had earned her stripes back in the Great War but was still going strong.

Decker leaned against the bulwark near the anchor gear and bent down below the barrier to light up a Camel. With the ship running at twenty-five knots, the apparent wind was shifted a bit to port and reduced somewhat, although far too blustery to allow a Zippo to keep fire. He snapped his lighter shut and drew deeply on the pill, reveling in the peace of the night.

Over the past few days, the skipper had been kind enough to share radio traffic with Decker. Fleet broadcasts as well as coded reports from The Canal. Decker knew that the Marines on the island were continually harassed by Japanese soldiers, sailors and pilots. He knew that his own men, Oaks, Taggart and Entwater, had fought in an action near the Matanikau and, just two days later, at Alligator Creek. This was probably his and Lider's last night of relative peace.

"Mind if I join you, sir?" Chuck Lider said as his boots thumped along the deck.

Decker turned to the corporal and grinned, "Sure, Chuck. Pull up a plank."

Lider moved to stand beside Decker and lit his own smoke. Like his commanding officer, Lider drew deeply on his cigarette and inhaled deeply of the salt air. He gazed around, and a small smile touched his lips.

"Nice out here, ain't it?" Decker mused.

"Yep," Lider said. "Wonder what tomorrow night will be like."

Decker chuckled, "Not like this, I'm sure. Quite the hullabaloo on the beach as I understand it."

Lider nodded and then appeared to be studying Decker for a moment. Just before the Major could ask why, Lider asked: "How's the wound, Skipper?"

"Not bad," Decker said with just the right amount of bravado. He grinned then. "It doesn't really *hurt* anymore... but I still feel like I've aged thirty years, y'know? Like an old man all of a sudden. My energy just isn't where it should be. I get tired easy; feel like my muscles are getting soft...."

"It'll pass, sir," Lider encouraged. "You been walking the decks every day, which I think is good. It ain't permanent. Might be a few weeks yet before you're ready for the hard action... maybe more... but the fact that you're on your feet and lookin' well only two weeks after takin' a bullet to the lung says a lot."

Decker shrugged, "Says I'm hard-headed anyway."

They fell silent for a time, and then Lider asked: "Sir... what do you think'll happen once we get ashore?"

Decker shrugged, "We'll be digging foxholes to lie in on duty, eatin' canned rations twice a day only... quite a vacation, huh?"

Lider chuckled, "No, I know that... I mean with the team. Think we'll all be together, or will Colonel Edson re-absorb us?"

Decker could only shrug once more, "I can't say, Chuck. It is pretty unusual, an O4 in charge of a fire team with a Sergeant, two corporals and a PFC... I doubt that'll continue. They'll probably put me in charge of a company, and at least for the next few weeks, I'll be a REMF on account of my injury."

REMF stood for rear echelon mother fucker.

"Yeah..." Lider sounded a bit gloomy.

"However," Decker went on, "no matter where they shove *me*, you and the guys are comin' along. Hell, you guys'll all get promotions soon, I bet. But you know how it is, Chuck... we go where the Navy and the Corps needs us."

They fell silent once more. Both men stared forward, contemplating the ghostly form of *Blue* as she cut a furrow through the warm tropical sea. The ship was little more than a sharply angled black blob out ahead. Her starboard side, though, was a ghostly dark gray from reflected moonlight on her hull. So exact were the ships, all arranged in line-ahead, and so perfectly were their speeds, that it was easy to imagine that they were all standing perfectly still. The only sense of movement coming from the long wakes and the gentle corkscrewing motion as *Cavalier's* bow knifed up and through the small swells.

The scene of utter tranquility was suddenly shattered as a brilliant white flash lit up the *Blue,* temporarily silhouetting her tall narrow profile against an impossibly-bright light. An instant later, the gargantuan camera flash was replaced by a dimmer but no less shocking ball of expanding gas, dark red at its outer edge and yellow-white at its center.

As the two men's minds tried to grapple with what they were seeing, a thundering *boom* rolled across the sea, seeming to echo forever. A second or two later, a dragon's breath of super-heated air whooshed across *Cavalier's* decks, so powerful even from a mile distant that it nearly ripped the two men's ball cap covers off their heads.

"Jesus!" Lider finally found his voice. "What the hell—"

His question was cut off by the blaring general quarters alarm. Below the klaxon, men's voices began to shout incoherently. The ship's PA system hissed to life, and some explanation brought the horrific sight into something like focus.

"*General quarters! General quarters! All hands man your battle stations! This is not a drill; repeat, this is not a drill. The ship is now at general quarters!*"

The two Marines stared at one another wide-eyed. Shock and fright registered on both of their faces, now aglow with a hideous crimson light cast by the burning ship ahead of them. They were only guests aboard the destroyer and had no battle station. Yet they were Marines and weren't suited to stand by as simple spectators.

"Come on!" Decker finally said, grabbing Lider's arm. "We'll head aft and see if we can't lend a hand at a gun battery or AA station!"

Decker began to run, although certainly not at top speed. His body, having been violated by a 7.7mm Japanese bullet that had smashed through his shoulder blade, punched its way through his left lung and out his chest, snapping a rib in the process, had robbed Decker of much of his fortitude. It was coming back, as Lider said it would, but he was hardly at one hundred percent.

Seeing this, the corporal slowed his pace to stay beside Decker. No matter what happened next, Lider vowed, he wouldn't leave his skipper's side for anything.

As the men moved toward the superstructure that contained the forward five-inch gun turrets, bridge and gun director, they felt the ship's steam turbines whine and her bow raise as more speed was poured on. In some part of his mind that was so well trained it was no longer a conscious activity, Decker noted that the moon, visible out of the corner of his eye, was sliding aft. The ship was pouring on power and moving to port. He recalled that the explosion he and

Lider had seen appeared to come from the *Blue's* port side, so that made sense.

Not sure why he chose it, nor what he expected to be able to do afterward, Decker began to climb one of the exterior companion ladders to the gun deck. The stairs were steep, but they were, in spite of their name, still stairs and were hardly a hindrance to his progress.

The gun deck was the first deck above the main deck and was where the majority of *Cavalier's* anti-aircraft cannons were to be found as well as the two forward five-inch gun turrets. There was another below, on the main deck and two more aft on this deck, all of which were controlled by the gun director turret mounted above and abaft the bridge.

Decker turned forward and jogged to the twin single-mounted five-inch guns. Each weapon was over fifteen feet in length and was to all outward appearances, just like the thousands of other five-inch, thirty-eight caliber guns mounted on ships across the fleet. There were two seats, one for the trainer and one for the pointer, each controlled by wheels. However, unlike those on *Bull Shark,* for example, these guns were electrically controlled by the gun director crew, although manual control was possible should electrical power be interrupted, of course.

The gun director consisted of a sophisticated set of equipment controlled by half a dozen men. Radar, a stabilizer, optical sights and a fire control computer located, tracked and calculated targets. The director's equipment automatically turned and elevated the guns to ensure a proper aim and that they hit what they were fired at.

Gunnery at sea and in the modern age was a far cry from the glorious age of sail. In those days, cannons were aimed and fired by hand, and more often than not, from less than fifty yards away. Long-range fire of up to a mile and a half was possible, but accuracy was extremely difficult. The problem was that your ship was constantly moving. Pitching, rolling and yawing. If you were firing at another ship, that target was also moving.

In the twentieth century, where speeds of over thirty knots for warships and distances as far as and even *over* the horizon were commonplace, the problem compounded exponentially. The gun director solved this difficulty... not a hundred percent but far better than any human could... by using visual and electronic inputs into an analog computer that would constantly calculate and update the relative positions of your ship and your target. Not unlike the TDC on a submarine, except that the projectiles crossed the intervening space far more quickly. Indeed, the gun director was also used as a torpedo director, aiming the twin torpedo launchers mounted along the *Cavalier's* centerline.

The two five-inch guns were mounted side by side about six feet apart. Between them was an ammunition hatch that led down several decks to one of the ship's magazines. A hoist lifted the fifty-two-pound shells up where they would be retrieved by the ammo handler, passed to the loader who seated them home in the breech and then once the gun was fired, empty shell casings would be passed back down again.

For whatever reason, Decker and Lider were the first to arrive. There was no one manning the guns as of yet.

"Where's the crew?" Lider asked in confusion.

"Alarm just sounded twenty or thirty seconds ago," Decker said, moving to open the ammunition hatch. "Must be on the way. Come on, let's get them ready while we're standing around here with our thumbs parked."

While aboard *Bull Shark*, Decker and his Marines had trained with the crew on the use of their two five-inch guns. They'd practiced pointing, training, loading, firing and maintaining and were fairly proficient at operating the pieces. Each man grabbed a shell and propellant casing from the hoist and moved to one of the guns. A quick inspection, then they began removing canvas covers, pulled the centering pin out, and withdrew the tampion from the muzzle. They then set the direction switches to automatic, allowing the gun director to control the weapons' aiming. After that, they loaded in the first shots and set the ready-fire keys.

By then, a dozen pairs of feet were thumping on the deck as the gun crews arrived. The battery captain, a burly PO1 of about thirty-five, blinked in surprise. He saw two men, one in Marine green drab and one in officer khakis fooling around with his guns. He recognized the marine Major and just managed not to swear a blue streak at the two interlopers.

"Didn't mean to step on your toes," Decker said. "But figured since we had nothing better to do and got here first...."

Curt Palmer, the LPO in charge of this station, grinned crookedly, "Long as you didn't break nothin', sir. Navy tells me these babies are expensive."

Decker chuckled, "Nah... we trained on these aboard a fleet boat just a few weeks back. Got pretty good, too."

"Okay then," Palmer said. "Well, stand by if you like, sir. From what I heard, there's a Jap tin can out there in the dark. Already sent a passel of fish at the poor *Blue*."

Decker scowled, "Yeah, we were on the foredeck when it happened. Why we got here so fast."

Palmer looked to Lider, "I'm short an ammo man. Down with a belly ache. Think you can stand in until I get relief?"

"Sure. First rounds are already loaded, by the way," Lider said. "Corporal Chuck Lider at your service."

Palmer smiled and held out a hand, "Gunner's mate first-class Curt Palmer. Pleased to meetcha. Major... sorry I don't have any job for you, but if you'd like to step back there between the lockers and against the bulkhead and observe...."

Decker grinned, "You mean look all official-like but stay the hell outta your way, Gunner?"

Palmer flashed a set of large white teeth, "As you say, sir... although God forbid, should any of us get hit, I'd be obliged did you step in and take that man's duty."

"You got it, Gunner."

The guns were already in motion. Now that they were readied and set to the control of the gun director, their big electric motors whirred as the weapons, each weighing several tons, were rotated to point off the starboard bow. Men were already at their stations. The pointer and trainer seated, loader, rammer and hot shell retriever standing by. Lider and a short weedy kid stood to either side of the ammo hatch and waited. Beside them, each gun's captain observed his piece and his men while Palmer stood behind the ammo servers and observed everything.

Cavalier was now nearly abeam to *Blue*. Although wounded, the lead destroyer wasn't out of the fight just yet. Decker could see muzzle flashes from her decks as her own five-inch guns roared out, sending their explosive shells over the sea and toward the enemy that had wounded her. In spite of still being capable of fighting, however, *Blue's* way had significantly diminished. *Cavalier* was pulling ahead quickly, making a large swoop out and around her wounded sister to go after the Japanese ship or ships and clear the way for her own torpedoes.

Rolling booms floated to them, lagging behind the flashes of the guns. Then more thunderclaps rumbled, these seemingly from further off. Yet Decker was momentarily confused. Those *must* be the sounds of the Nip's guns going off… but where were the muzzle flashes? All he could see in the direction the five-inch guns were pointing was darkness.

"They came at us from the west, northwest, I'd guess," Palmer was saying. "Put us between them and the moon to light us up… crafty slants… I don't care what nobody says about Jap eyes; them bastards can see like cats at night."

"It's true," Decker said and then realized something. "I was aboard a boat a few weeks ago, and her skipper told me that he ran into some Japs back in May. Said their guns didn't flash like ours… thought that it must be some kind of new flashless powder."

Palmer grunted and nodded his head, "Yeah, that would explain it. Like I said, crafty squints… but they ain't got our radar. We might not see them as yet, but the gun director does; you can count on that, sir."

"Yeah… but then why didn't our radar detect the one that hit the *Blue?*" Lider asked abstractedly as he handed a shell off to the number one gun's loader.

"It ain't our job to have all the answers, Corporal," Palmer said, placing his hands on his hips. "It's our job to serve these beauties and send Tojo a nice big kiss from Uncle Sam!"

"Permission to open fire, Gunner!" one of the phone men stated. "Gun director says fire each to double-check the range."

"Acknowledge that, Lewis," Palmer said. "Okay, boys, you heard what Lieutenant Boyde said. Let 'er rip!"

The starboard gun, gun number one, thundered with a sound like doomsday come at last. All of the men, even the phone talkers, had foam plugs in their ears to prevent deafness. A huge tongue of orange flame spat from the barrel of the seventeen-foot gun, the fire easily as long as the gun itself. Decker felt the deck shiver beneath his feet and again as number two went off.

"Phone talker, inquire as to target distance," Palmer said.

A moment passed, "Eleven-thousand yards, Curt… the L T thinks they're trying to maneuver in closer. Says it's just one DD they believe."

"Twelve and a half seconds of flight time for our shells," Palmer said. "These babies can send off a dozen rounds per minute, and if we're really on our game, even more. Unfortunately, until we got the range and are on target—"

Palmer's lecture was interrupted by the sound of something… no several somethings… tearing through the night and overhead, the wind of their passage ruffling the men's clothing. The sound of a supersonic projectile hurtling past at over twenty-six hundred feet per second was unmistakable.

"Ballsy sons of bitches," Palmer said with an almost eerie calm. "Let's send 'em another, boys."

Once more, Lider and his companion handed off projectiles and propellent cases. Unlike on *Bull Shark's* slightly stubbier five-inch, twenty-five caliber guns, these weapons didn't use an integrated shell and powder casing but kept them separate. This meant that they could swap out different projectiles while still using a universal propellant.

"That was damned close," Decker noted.

"Yeah, and from all I hear, they ain't even got a gun director computer like we got," Palmer cranked. "Just goes to show you what experience does. Gotta remember that your Jap has been at war for a number of years already. We're still new to this game despite having some better gear in places."

"Director reports misses," the phone talker said. "Requests fire again. Jap is maneuvering."

"Guns one and two, salvo fire… *FIRE!*" Palmer roared, sounding excited for the first time.

A whole series of concussions rocked the ship as all five of her five-inch guns, her main battery, sent their vengeful shells off into the night. *Blue* continued to fire as well, and now their third sister was getting into the game. A rolling series of booms sounding to Decker like what a broadside from a frigate during the days of old must've sounded like tore the night open with tongues of flame and thunderclaps.

There was that air-ripping sound again as several shells streaked in. Somehow, without knowing how, Lider realized that they were headed straight for the destroyer. Instinctively, he whirled around and dove, tackling Decker and bringing the two men down on the deck just as the world erupted into a titanic roar of Olympian thunderclaps, volcanic heat and remorseless fury.

The ship was bashed to port, heeling over fifteen degrees as an explosive round detonated just below the level of the deck against the forward bulkhead of the superstructure's first level. A furnace blast whooshed over the gun emplacements, filling the air with shards of torn steel and burning lumps of what had once been the flesh of men.

Decker thought that he might have blacked out for a moment because one instant he was baking in heat and being deafened by a shrieking roar. In the next, the weight of Lider had lifted, and Decker could see again. More than he thought he should, at any rate. There was still a cacophony of noises… although as he sat up and drew in a shaking breath, Al Decker was able to recognize them.

A fire alarm was blaring, there were shouts of urgency and anger… and there were screams. Men screaming in high-pitched womanish wails that few who hadn't seen hard combat could recognize for what they were. The heartbreaking, gut-wrenching cries of a human organism experiencing a level of pain it was not designed to endure.

A hand reached out and hauled Decker to his feet and a sooty, drawn face flickering madly in an infernal vermillion light swam into focus before his eyes, "Sir! You all right?"

"Chuck… what happened… I think so…."

"We took a round just below the rail by the number one," Lider said breathlessly. "The gun bore most of it… but the crew…."

There was fire flickering and lighting the deck. Palmer was still there, directing his men who were wrestling with a fire hose. Other men, men in white navy summer uniforms, were kneeling beside a half dozen men, some of them writhing in agony... the source of the screams... and some blackened husks that were frozen in place.

"Jesus Christ..." Decker said. "Nobody's manning the gun!"

"Can't, too busy fighting the fire," Lider said.

"Fuck that, let's go!" Decker stated, moving toward number two on shaky legs.

He and Lider grabbed a shell and powder case and loaded the now abandoned gun. It was now pointed almost fifty degrees to starboard, and Decker wondered if it was still under control of the Mark 37 Gun Director or not.

Lider flipped up the ramming lever, and the ramming tray slid out. They seated their powder case and shell into the tray, and Lider shoved the handle up, sliding the tray into the breech and causing the breech block to rise into position.

Decker jumped into the trainer's seat and sighted through the optical targeter. He thought he saw a small blob of deeper blackness against the blue-black horizon. Not knowing if the gun was aimed properly or not, he crossed his fingers and depressed the firing pedal.

As he did so, Decker was dimly aware of another scream rising to his right. The sound was cut off by the throaty rumble of the gun, the *chank* of the ramming lever automatically shifted back into the standby position, and the instant whoosh as the gun's compressed air supply blew a slug of air through the breech to clear it of any debris.

Then the scream returned. A high, keening screech that went on and on... God, the man must be in agony...

"Torpedoes!" Lider said, pointing ahead and to the right.

In the dark sea, ten pale fingers of spectral blue were racing away from the ship and toward the horizon. *Cavalier* must have unloaded her entire spread of ten Mark 15s at the Jap.

After ten-seconds and then fifteen, there was no flash of a shell striking. Decker assumed his shot had missed. After several minutes, there was no explosion from torpedoes striking a hull either. All ten fish had gone wide, or the Jap had maneuvered away. Not uncommon, but disappointing.

On the other hand, no more Japanese shells roared through the night to batter the *Cavalier* or her sisters. That in itself was a blessing.

They'd been hit, and several men aboard *Cavalier* had paid with their lives or with severe injuries. *Blue* had fared worse, having a portion of her stern blown off. Yet she was still seaworthy, and with some care and even more luck, she'd make Tulagi a little after dawn.

None of them knew it at that time, least of all Decker and Lider, but the first preliminary shots of the Battle of the Eastern Solomons had been fired.

27
S-52 - 100 MILES NORTHEAST OF TULAGI
AUGUST 23, 1942 – 0810 LOCAL TIME

"All stop, Jack," Pat Jarvis ordered.

"Helm, bridge," Cleghorn spoke into the bridge transmitter. "All stop."

"*Bridge, helm, answering all stop,*" the duty helmsman, Steve Marx, replied. "*Chief Cantone requests putting number one on battery charge for the time being.*"

Jarvis nodded, and Cleghorn relayed the order. The two men lit cigarettes and watched as the way came off the old submarine, and she slowly came to a relative rest, bobbing gently on the low swell. The morning was partly overcast, and from the looks of the cloud formations, Jarvis believed they'd get a line of weather by the afternoon.

"Nice day to scrag some Japs, eh sir?" Cleghorn asked.

"It'll do, Jack," Jarvis mused wryly. "Course, it'd be more dramatic with some lightning and thunder."

"Think we'll have some of that later," Cleghorn said.

Jarvis nodded, "Yup. Looks that way. This is the part I hate though, Jack… this hurry up and wait game. Not my style, y'know?"

Cleghorn grinned broadly, "You came here to smoke cigarettes and kick some jap ass, right sir?"

Jarvis laughed, "Damn straight... and I'm all outta cigarettes!"

"*Bridge, radio... receiving coded message from Big Teeth,*" said the speaker.

Jarvis answered this time, "Radio, bridge... very well. Have Skaggs and Saunders get to work; I'll be down shortly."

"Think we really have a chance of pulling this off, sir?" Cleghorn asked.

Jarvis nodded, "With Anvil Art Turner out there... yeah, I do, Jack. He's one of the rare ones."

Jarvis' head had barely disappeared below the combing of the hatch when Cleghorn smiled wryly, lit another smoke and said quietly to himself, "I don't think he's alone in that, Lieutenant."

In S-52's tiny radio shack, Chief Yeoman Dennis Saunders and Tony Skaggs had completed decoding the message from *Bull Shark*. It was a short message, stating that Turner had arrived at their starting point and was beginning their sweep. He estimated that *Bull Shark* would reach the islands that Savage had indicated before noon.

"And we're off to the races," Jarvis muttered. "Send an acknowledgment and add that we're in position, Yo. I've got to check on the skipper."

Saunders was one of the men aboard who had been somewhat on the fence as regards Waters and Jarvis. Now that the captain had been injured and had been unconscious for the better part of two days, the yeoman seemed to be sliding slowly toward the Waters camp. There was something in his glances or in his tone that made Jarvis think that he, Saunders, blamed Jarvis for the captain's infirmity.

As if by the very act of taking over, which was his duty as executive officer, after all, Jarvis had somehow *caused* the events to unfold. It was nothing the XO could put his finger on, just a sort of back-of-the-mind hunch.

"You think he'll be alright, sir?" Skaggs asked.

Jarvis drew in a breath, "Burke thinks so... but with head cases, it's hard to say. Other than being unconscious, the captain's condition is otherwise good."

"Maybe it's time to get him ashore, sir?" Saunders asked.

Jarvis regarded him silently for a moment. There it was again, just the slightest twinge of... something. Accusation, maybe?

"Burke says that Guadalcanal wouldn't do him any good," Jarvis stated. "At least here, he can rest in a clean environment without the many diseases ashore working on him, too."

"I was thinking more about a naval base, Exec," Saunders said. "Let a real doc take a look at him. Maybe there's something *more* that can be done."

"Which is my intention as soon as possible," Jarvis said. "We'll need to put in in any case, I imagine... but for now, we have a duty to do. Please see to yours, Mr. Saunders, and I'll see to mine."

"Aye-aye, Captain," Saunders replied.

There was a slight emphasis on the word captain. It was subtle, but Jarvis didn't like it. By the flicker of understanding that seemed to cross Skaggs' face, the younger officer had noticed it too. Maybe not for the first time.

Jarvis chose to ignore it, however. It wasn't worth his time to make an issue of a man's internal feelings so long as it didn't interfere with his efficiency. Sticks and stones, after all...

When Jarvis stuck his head through the curtain that served as the door to Waters' stateroom, he found pharmacist's mate Homer Burke leaning over Waters, who was lying flat and still on his bunk. Burke was shining a small penlight into the captain's eyes and listening to his heart with a stethoscope.

"How is he, Doc?" Jarvis asked in a whisper.

Burke was looking at his wristwatch and didn't answer right away. After a few seconds, he pulled the earpieces out and sighed, "Sorry, XO... had to keep count. He's... okay and not, I guess."

"What's that mean?"

Burke sighed, "Christ, sir... physically, he's all right. His head injury was a good one, split the scalp, but I don't think it fractured the skull. There may be a hairline there; I can't tell without X-rays. Yet even if there is, there's not much to be done for him except to let him lie quietly and rest. I don't believe there's any internal swelling, although that would account for his state of unconsciousness."

"Could it be a coma?"

Burke sighed, "Maybe… but it doesn't *seem* right. I mean, it doesn't quite match the usual coma indications I've been studying in my manuals. His respiration and pulse are strong, pupils react to light… temp is good… he's just… well, he's just *asleep,* sir. If I didn't know any better and hadn't treated his noodle bonk, I'd swear he was just tuckered out and having himself a restful cork, as the Brits say."

"I wonder…" Jarvis pondered thoughtfully. "He's been under some strain lately, as you well know… that last mission, this one… is it possible he's just… I dunno… checked out? Like his mind has just thrown up its mental hands and said screw it?"

Burke thrust out his lower lip in contemplation. When he did this, combined with his youth… he was the same thirty as Jarvis himself… the man appeared almost boyish.

Finally, Burke shrugged, "Good an explanation as any, I guess. Though I'm no Sig Freud, of course. Physically speaking, he's okay. If there *is* a fracture or swelling, the swelling should go down on its own. His vitals tell me that much. So, I suppose he'll just wake up when he's good and ready. Until then…"

"Until then, I've got to do his job," Jarvis said wearily. "Thanks, Homer. Best I get back to it then."

"Exec?"

Jarvis paused halfway through the curtain, "Yeah?"

"This boat ain't been the same since that Balikpapan incident," Burke said flatly. "The *skipper* ain't been the same. I hate to say it, specially with him lyin' there like that… but facts are facts. I know that some of the guys aboard, officers and chiefs included, see you as an invader. But… well… they *need* a leader, sir. They're like bratty kids who act out but deep inside, where they probably don't even know it, they need a firm hand to keep them on track. I think you've got that in you, sir."

Jarvis nodded grimly and allowed just a hint of a smile to show, "Thanks, Doc."

USS BULL SHARK – 100 MILES N, NW OF TULAGI

Chris Savage had turned out to be correct. Just before noon, *Bull Shark's* lookouts spotted land on the horizon. A short time later, the ship had come close enough for Turner to confirm what the S-52 officer had told them.

The island was really a collection of four small islands grouped together in a rough diamond pattern. Three of them were little more than mangrove islets, perhaps an acre or two in area. The fourth, the one that made up the roughly western point, was perhaps a half-mile in diameter and featured a low but sharp volcanic peak rising from its jungles. Surrounding these islands were shallows that kept to less than fifty feet until about a quarter-mile offshore and then began to slope gently down to about three hundred where they abruptly began to plunge into deep water no more than a mile from shore.

"Good place for an ambush," Elmer Williams said as, like his captain, he studied the land off their port beam.

"Yeah..." Turner observed absently, examining what he could through his Bausch and Lomb 7x50 binoculars. "No sign of one now, though... Hotrod, let's make a speed run around the perimeter. Just to make sure no Nips are skulking behind that big island over there."

The entire atoll was perhaps four miles across or less, so it didn't take long for the submarine running on the surface to circumnavigate the entire structure. In three-quarters of an hour, they were right back where they'd started.

"All right," Turner said, drumming his fingers on the bridge railing. "Let's proceed on our plotted course. When we get to the other end, we can make a high-speed run back here. I suspect that by tomorrow, or even after dark, this peaceful little out-of-the-way set of islands won't be so deserted."

"If it is now," Williams opined. "Maybe it's me, but... I get the feeling we're being watched."

Turner frowned, "It's not just you, Elmer. The place is giving me the creeps."

"Wouldn't be surprised if Sato put a man ashore on that big island to act as coast watcher," Williams mused.

"Well, we're gonna find out," Turner said. "We'll be back. Okay, Hotrod, let's get on track, and don't spare the whip."

As the fleet submarine's diesels roared up to full power and she headed off toward the east, climbing up to twenty-one knots, a small white shape appeared over the horizon, its aluminum body glinting in the last of the sunlight that wasn't being swallowed by the building storm clouds. The white thing leveled off, skirted the edge of the world and then turned away. It had been visible for no more than five-seconds. Five-seconds in which none of *Bull Shark's* lookouts had noticed. Five-seconds, however, in which the pilot was able to confirm the presence of an American submarine.

AMERICAN CARRIER TASK FORCE – 150 MILES SE OF GUADALCANAL

Commander Harry Felt banked his Dauntless into a wide orbit over the task force as he waited for the rest of his dive bombers and half dozen Avengers to launch and form up with him. It was a beautiful sunny day, and the deep blue ocean was slashed by a twinkling line of golden light that was almost too brilliant to look at directly.

Five thousand feet below him, *Saratoga* and *Enterprise* cruised northeast, with their bows into the trade wind. Surrounding them were the cruisers, destroyers and the battleship *North Carolina* constituting the escorting force. A heartwarming sight, except for one tiny fly in the ointment.

Far off to the south, from his great height, Felt could still make out Task Force 18, consisting of the carrier *Wasp* and her escorting destroyer and light cruiser. Admiral Fletcher had detached them in order that *Wasp* might be allowed to take on fuel oil. As no oilers were available, she'd have to travel nearly a thousand miles to Efate Island before refueling and turning back. A journey of nearly three days.

This left Felt with a vague sense of disquiet. He, like everyone now, believed that the Japanese were coming. Reports had come to the task force to that effect. Nagumo and his carriers, possibly an invasion fleet and more ships were even then steaming toward Guadalcanal. It was why he, Felt, and thirty-five other planes were readying for a scouting and attack run at that very moment.

Yet seeing a third of the carrier force sailing off in the wrong direction didn't sit well with the veteran pilot. Felt hadn't been at Midway, as his carrier had been undergoing repairs at Mare Island at the time. Damage taken not far from these very waters during the Battle of the Coral Sea. Yet Felt knew that the difference between three carriers and two was great. It was true that at Midway, four of Japan's Kido Butai carriers had been sunk… yet he also knew that they had a total of eight and were building more. It was estimated that both *Shokaku* and *Zuikaku*, two large fleet carriers, along with *Ryujo*, a light carrier, were operating in the area. That meant that now, Fletcher's task force was outnumbered. Yes, they did have Henderson Field, which was, in truth, an unsinkable carrier.

Still…

"Looks like the class is all gathered and ready for our field trip, Harry," said Lieutenant Arlo "Trigger" Paxton from the rear seat. "I think we're all ready to take out some flat tops."

Felt twisted in his seat and observed for himself. A nice group of planes. The new Avenger torpedo bomber was a three-seater. A pilot, torpedoman and rear gunner. The Avenger was a considerable improvement over the older Devastators. Faster, tougher and better able to protect itself.

Then there were the thirty other Dauntless SBDs. A good solid plane that could climb higher than anything the Japs could field. However, what the flight lacked, and obviously so, were any Wildcats. They were on their own. Their job to locate and attack any Jap carriers they could.

Felt activated his radio and held up the mic, "Flight leader to all aircraft… climb to angels fifteen and follow my lead. Spread out as discussed at the briefing. Each group keep the next in sight. Fly in line ahead formation. Let's go bag us a hatful of Nips!"

At a little after nine in the morning, a PBY scout had spotted one of the Japanese groups about two hundred miles north of Guadalcanal. The Catalina had ducked low to try and hide over the horizon, but the plane was big and not a fighter, so the jury was out on whether or not the japs had seen her.

What the Catalina had reported were several warships escorting several transports and freighters. *Not* carriers. It was Felt's opinion, and that of both Admiral Fletcher and Captain DeWitt, that this group represented the western point of the Japanese attack force triangle. That they were steaming straight down to put their men and gear ashore on The Canal while Nagumo's forces were further to the east. Not unlike Fletcher's own deployment.

By mid-afternoon, however, it became clear that the Japs had anticipated an aerial attack and had maneuvered their ships away. General Vandegrift sent twenty-one aircraft from Henderson, including a dozen Wildcats, to rendezvous with Felt and assist in the search.

By the time the Marines arrived, however, it became clear that the weather was not going to cooperate. The nearly sixty planes formed up and flew along the edge of a rather nasty squall line for a few minutes before Felt called it.

"I'm afraid the game's gonna be called on account of rain, Major," Felt radioed the Marine flight leader Major Wally Pierce.

"*That's a Rodge, I'm afraid, Commander,*" Pierce replied glumly. "*Lookin' pretty nasty out here and getting' worse by the minute.*"

"*Hey Harry,*" another Navy pilot broke in. "*I think I see something out to the east. I think it might be a submarine on the surface. No wake, though… she's just sittin' out there.*"

"Go and scope it, Burns," Felt ordered. "Swoop in and assess, but do not attack. Let's see if we might not get lucky."

"*That's probably one of ours, Commander,*" Pierce cut in. "*There's two boats out here searching for a carrier group. There's a fourth carrier, called Sakai, I think. Been harassing the islands for a few weeks now. One of those sub commanders came ashore before the invasion, and from what I hear, this Jap carrier has a grudge against him.*"

Felt scoffed, "Really? What kind of crazy shit is that?"

Pierce laughed, "*Ain't no crazier than this war, is it? How you fellas doin' on go-juice?*"

"We're past bingo fuel," Felt said. "Not sure we can get back to the Sara now…."

"*Not to worry, Commander… I know a great hotel not an hour away,*" Pierce said jovially. "*Swimmin' pool's closed, and the tennis courts are bein' repaved, but it's a place to lay your head.*"

"Continental breakfast?" Felt asked wryly.

"*Included, partner.*"

Felt and Trigger laughed, "Roger that, we'll take you up on your kind offer, Major."

"Hell, call me Wally. Just stick to my six, Commander, and I'll give you the guided tour."

Henderson Field was free of rain when the aircraft arrived, but the storm was rapidly approaching. After getting their aircraft squared away, Pierce led Felt to the mess and introduced him to several officers and civilians. Felt and his pilots were shown to what the Marines laughingly called the "guest suites," a set of tents set up behind a wooden Asian-style building known as the Pagoda.

That night, when the rain squalls slackened, the Navy pilots lay on their cots and listened to the sounds of Guadalcanal's nightlife screeching, twittering and cheeping from the nearby jungles. At one point, near midnight, their sleep was interrupted by the repetitious booming of naval guns. A Japanese destroyer was shelling the airfield. It didn't last too long, as the Marines had several shore batteries that could at least fire back and give the Japs pause.

When dawn finally broke, Commander Felt found the Marines already tending to his squadron's planes. They used portable pumps and hand carts to put fuel into the birds and ready them for takeoff. It was a primitive setup, not yet having a fuel truck at hand, but it worked. Luckily there were plenty of men on hand to do the manual labor.

"This ought to get you fellas back to the carriers anyway," Pierce was saying as he and Felt watched the proceedings. "We didn't have much luck yesterday, Harry, but somethin' tells me that today's the day."

"Yeah, I can feel it in my bones, Wally," Felt said and then had an idea. He sipped his coffee… every plane in Felt's group brought a can just in case they had to land at Henderson… and then grinned at his new friend. "Say, Wally… I don't suppose you fellas could make use of a couple of dozen thousand-pound bombs, could ya'?"

Pierce's eyes went wide, "No foolin'? On top of the Joe?"

"No foolin'," Felt said. "Just extra weight for the trip back anyway and considering that Admiral Turner left you boys with your pants down out here… figure it's a fair price for the gas anyway."

"Well, that's mighty white of ya, Harry," Pierce said, shaking the other man's hand. "We'll take 'em, and I'm sure General Vandegrift will be pleased. Hell, maybe we'll get a chance to put 'em to some good use later today."

"I'll drink to that," Felt said, and the two men clinked mugs.

28

S-52 – 100 MILES NORTH OF TULAGI
AUGUST 24, 1942 – 0620 LOCAL TIME

It had been a long day and night. Like his captain, Pat Jarvis was not a man well-suited to idleness. As the pivot in this search for *Sakai*, S-52 had nothing to do but sit still and wait, watch and listen. And for thirteen hours, that's what she'd done.

For thirteen hours, there hadn't been a plane, a ship or much of anything to see. Bad weather came in in the afternoon, and they'd been obliged to steam around in a tight circle so as not to be rocked and rolled at the mercy of the ten-foot whitecaps all evening. Watches had changed; men had eaten and slept as much as they could aboard a ship that moved erratically below their feet.

Finally, at nearly twenty-three hundred hours, the storm had abated, and the sea had begun to calm moderately. They'd also received a radio message from *Bull Shark*. Jarvis had been awakened by the messenger of the watch and had gone to the radio shack in his skivvies.

"This is Little Red, Big Teeth," he said into the handset. "We read, over."

A crackle and then Turner's voice: "*We've reached the end of our tether, Little Red. Been a long day, and we're ready to hit the tiki bar, over.*"

This was prearranged code to be used on an open freq. It meant that Turner was going to head directly for the Savage Islands at top speed. Even so, it would be well after sunrise when they arrived.

"Sounds good to me, Big Teeth," Jarvis replied. "Hey, maybe there'll be a few hula girls, over."

This last was just a bit of prattle that meant nothing. However, on the heels of this short exchange, a coded message from Turner arrived with more detailed instructions.

S-52 was to proceed at top surface speed until false dawn and then submerge and complete the trip to the atoll at test depth. This should get both submarines to the islands at about the same time. At that point, they'd assess and make plans to proceed further. At all costs, S-52 was to remain concealed. Turner wanted the Japs to believe that there was only one submarine hunting them. A set of prearranged signals were passed via the radio transmission that would, if necessary, be broadcast via the sonar when at the islands in order to get S-52 to where Turner wanted her or to engage.

So the boat had run through the night at fourteen knots, burning fuel oil and scanning with her SD radar every ten minutes. They were within fifteen miles of the islands when the air search radar detected something.

"*Bridge, radar... Contact!*" Bobby Gaines, who was pulling double-duty on sound and radar, announced. "*Mr. Savage, we're getting a contact at twenty-thousand yards!*"

"Very well," Savage mused, glancing at Chief Archie Lockner, who was acting quartermaster. "Hmm... sounds like a CAP, doesn't it, Chief?"

"Guess so, sir," Lockner said neutrally. "Hell, I'm just a glorified grease monkey, but it's pretty dark out, don't it seem odd for planes to be up?"

"It's not the flying at night that's really the problem with carriers, I think," Savage said. "It's the *landing* in the dark that's a bitch. Still, it does tell us that *somebody's* out there... better get her buttoned up."

"Good, my engines are grumbling about running wide open so long," Lockner said.

"Clear the bridge!" Savage announced, alerting the lookouts to climb down from the periscope sheers and go below. He depressed the transmitter button. "Control, bridge, prepare to dive the ship."

"*Bridge, control, prepare to dive the ship, aye,*" came Tony Skaggs's voice.

"Oh, and Tony... send the messenger of the watch to alert the XO," Savage said and then drew in a breath.

"Sir?" Lockner asked hesitantly.

"Yeah, Chief?"

"You think the XO... that is...." Lockner tried to find a way to frame his question but was failing. Much to his annoyance.

Lockner was one of the loyal Waters' men, yet since Jarvis had come aboard, he'd tried to keep an open mind. Like every man aboard, he'd heard exactly what had transpired between the skipper and the XO. He knew how Waters had cut Jarvis off at the knees twice and why. Scuttlebutt was already going around the boat about the captain's... issues.

"You're asking *me* if I think he's got what it takes to get us through whatever's coming?" Savage asked bemusedly.

Lockner sighed, "The men are... worried, sir. Lot of the guys who were pissed off about the new XO have now seen the way the skipper's been acting, and... well, they think he's lost his nerve, and that's why he's still out like a light. Now they're having to accept that Mr. Jarvis isn't just the new Exec but the skipper... and knowing his reputation and that of Art Turner...."

"You're aware of my feelings on the matter, right?" Savage asked.

Lockner turned to face him squarely, "Yes sir... at least in the beginning. But rumor has it you might be changing your thinking. Either way... the boys want to know what to expect."

Savage blew out his breath, "I think maybe I was too hard on the man, Chief. Too blindly loyal to Captain Waters that I didn't give him a chance. But I've seen what the man's capable of and I think he's the kind that can lead. I'm not sayin' we're gonna go have beers next time we put in... but I think I'm not as pissed off that *I'm* not the XO instead of him anymore."

Lockner nodded gravely, and then a slow smile spread over his face, "Sir... you *are* the XO right now."

Savage chuffed, "Yeah, be careful what you wish for, eh Chief? Okay, let's get this pig dunked."

CARRIER SAKAI – SAVAGE ISLANDS

"Falcon's flight leader reports no sightings," the radioman in primary flight control reported to Hideki. "But the sun is rising, and their visibility should improve."

"We didn't expect much in any case," Hideki said, turning to Sato and Osaka, who were standing by the situation board.

"No, of course not," Sato said. "However, coded radio traffic from other aircraft from the attack force *did* report sighting a surfaced submarine headed in a southeasterly direction late last evening."

"If that's Turner, he's going the wrong way," Osaka stated.

Sato pondered that for a moment, "Yes... but something tells me he'll be here, Osaka san. Remember, our patrol yesterday morning sighted a submarine leaving the atoll."

Hideki cast a brief glance toward Osaka and then looked to Sato, "You think that was *Bull Shark?*"

"Who else?" Sato asked, waving his Golden Bat in the air for emphasis. "Would an American submarine simply take time to visit an unoccupied and uncharted set of islands? I think not. And had it been one of our submarines... we'd know. No, gentlemen, this Turner was here, and he is coming. I feel it in my bones."

The truth was that Osaka could not disagree. No doubt, Turner had learned of the uncharted islands just outside the official boundary of the Solomon Islands archipelago. He'd deduced that it might be a fine place for *Sakai* to stage an ambush. And after running a circular search pattern and finding nothing, Turner would return to this location under cover of darkness and the sea to double-check himself.

The true irony of the situation was that had Sato and his ego not made such a production of declaring a personal feud with Turner; the American would likely have no idea *Sakai* was now slowly orbiting the four islands. Turner would have had no reason to even *suspect* this. Now, though, he too felt Sato's presence in *his* bones.

Turner knew that the strike carrier was escorted by a destroyer. He would no doubt assume that the three destroyers that had attacked him would be out here as well. He would not know of Captain Yamata, of course. Would not know that "The Sensei" and his *Viper's Fang* was also now engaged in hunting him.

Yet Turner, now alerted, would be on his guard. He'd not only be *expecting* Sato to pull something… Turner himself would be searching for a way to turn the tables on his self-proclaimed nemesis. To Osaka, the entire business was foolish, yet perhaps there was a way to make things come out right.

Sato was arrogant and supremely confident. To some degree, this was understandable. After all, he had an ASW-capable strike carrier at his command. A ship that was both fast and maneuverable. A ship that could also field fighters and dive bombers. As if this weren't enough, Sato had at his fingertips four destroyers, and on one of which was Japan's greatest anti-submarine warfare expert.

What did Turner have? A submarine that could travel below the surface to great depths. A heavy armament of guns for a submarine along with six forward and four stern torpedo tubes. He *may* also have another submarine working in concert, but there was no proof of that.

Long odds for the American, to be sure.

Longer still in that there were three fleets of Japanese warships bearing down on the Eastern Solomons at that very moment. Three aircraft carriers, a powerful surface battle force and an invasion group. All of that and *Sakai* against a lone wolf.

"Are you with us, Commander?" Sato suddenly asked, breaking into Osaka's thoughts.

For a brief moment, Osaka experienced a genuine flush of true rage aimed at the man. He'd never liked Sato, and his opinion of him hadn't improved any, despite the captain protem's seeming respect for Osaka's experience.

Yet, at that moment, Sato was suddenly the embodiment of the sickness that had infected his people. This manic belief in their divine right. This total conviction that they could do whatever they wished simply because they *could* and because whatever they wanted was theirs by *right*. In Osaka's view, such madness could only lead the nation down a single, dark path. A path that ended in a bottomless pit from which no rescue was possible.

"I was thinking that perhaps I should make a detailed report to Admiral Yamamoto," Osaka said. "He should be aware of every piece of information we have in order that he might best execute—"

"I'm sorry, Commander... but no radio transmissions can be permitted at this time," Sato said in a reasonable tone, yet his eyes flickered with something unpleasant. "The danger of radio direction finding, you know. As well as intercepted transmissions. I'm afraid this is too important an operation to jeopardize."

Hideki's belly tightened ever so slightly. While Sato's words *sounded* reasonable enough, the premise was flawed. All of them knew it, and Hideki began to wonder if this might not be the beginning of a rift between Osaka and the new captain.

Ever since Osaka had confided in him about his doings and his feelings on the war, Hideki had been extra vigilant. He knew that there was no love lost between Osaka and Sato. He believed, and rightly so, that sooner or later a difference of opinion would pit the men against one another, and a fissure would open that could swallow them all.

"Low risk under the circumstances, Captain," Osaka said neutrally, hoping that the title would appeal to the man's vanity enough for him to relent. "And besides... we *want* Turner to find us. That is, if I don't mistake, the *purpose* of laying a trap, is it not?"

"I want him to find us on *my* terms, Commander," Sato said, his voice suddenly less amiable. "Not to lead him here by the nose. Permission denied. I'm sorry, but any attempt to send any outgoing radio transmission must be viewed as a mutinous act."

Hideki flinched and opened his mouth to protest, but Osaka beat him to it. In a flat and emotionless tone, he said: "Of course, Captain. I wouldn't think of such a thing."

Sato smiled thinly. A smile that did not reach his eyes, which were still two cold black chips of flint, "Of course not, Commander. Perhaps you will lend your expertise to the next phase of our problem."

Osaka nodded slowly, "Indeed. I shall ponder it."

He turned on his heel and strode out of the compartment. Hideki watched as a flash of satisfaction lighted upon Sato's face and then was smoothed over again.

"Commander, I would like you to launch the entire Zero wing," Sato said. "Have them fly out to approximately one-hundred and fifty kilometers to the... east, southeast... and then head back for *Sakai* twenty meters off the deck at as low a speed as possible."

"Sir?" Hideki asked, containing his own emotions.

Sato puffed and smiled, "If the American submarine is out there, she may be running at periscope depth. Further, if reports are true and she has two types of radar, one for air and one for the surface, the aircraft will be too low for the air radar, and Turner will no doubt be sweeping *forward* with the other to locate us."

"I see..." Hideki said. "I shall have the planes armed with depth charges then, shall I?"

"Exactly," said Sato. "If Turner is coming, which I believe he will be... it will be his *last* mistake."

USS BULL SHARK – 15 MILES FROM THE SAVAGE ISLANDS

"Contact!" Chet Rivers said in quiet excitement from his sonar station, where he and Joe Dutch were both monitoring. "Light slow screws, sir... bearing zero-one-zero... range five thousand yards."

"Think that's our Pat, fellas?" Turner asked.

"Probably," Dutch added. "The machinery signature sounds familiar... although it *could* be a Jap sub as well, Art."

"She's headed three-two-zero," Rivers put in.

Turner nodded, "Yup, that's Little Red all right. What's her speed?"

"Reading... five knots, sir," Rivers replied.

"I don't suppose you can tell me her depth?" Turner inquired.

Dutch himself smiled grimly, "Not without being over top of her, certainly not from this far away. She is on batteries only, though, so she's submerged."

"I figured that," Turner said. "Phone talker, alert maneuvering to standby to answer bells on the growlers. Frank, radar depth. And get the snorkel open. Might as well use the damned thing for once...

y'know, since the spies went and ripped off the Norwegians and since we're the only boat on Earth to have one… probably."

"Kinda funny, isn't it, Art?" Elmer William's head asked from the open hatch to the control room. "Web Clayton once told me that he thought the Norwegians wouldn't even have one on an operational boat for another year and a half yet."

"I guess that's the intelligence game for you, Elmer," Turner said, reaching a Lucky Strike out of the pack on the chart table. "There's the *official* set of books… and there's the super-secret winky-wink *real* set, I guess. You tell somebody eighty years from now that old *Sharky* here had her a snorkel, and they'll probably say you're full of bologna."

"I believe we're simply special," Hotrod Hernandez opined from his position at the chart desk and DRT.

"*You're* special, that's for sure," Mug Vigliano tossed over his shoulder.

"It is infinitely gratifying to this humble and sexy peasant that a goomba such as yourself would see that, *amigo*," Hotrod quipped.

"I really can't understand how we've survived all this time," Williams mused before he dropped out of sight, leaving chuckles behind him.

"Radar depth," Nichols announced. "Diesels standing by, Art."

This last was almost unnecessary. The entire boat vibrated with the rumble of her four big diesel engines starting up. Turner ordered the search scope raised and Vigliano to head for the other submarine at all ahead full.

"Anything up there, Ted?" Turner asked as he pressed his face to the rubberized eyepiece and began a full rotation sweep.

"Negative on the sugar dog, sir," Balkley reported. "Switching to the sugar jig now…."

The sun was still low on the horizon, but it was up there. Turner could see a moderately disturbed sea, its surface still heaving somewhat from the previous day's storm. Over the four-to-six-foot swells, he saw nothing. At forty-five feet, the periscope's head was twenty-three feet above the surface, giving Turner a horizon of about five miles.

"Sir…" Balkley began, sounding uncertain. "I think… I think I just got something on the SJ… faint, but a definite contact."

"Lay it on me, Ted," Turner ordered.

"A contact… maybe more than one, low on the horizon bearing zero-four-zero," Balkley said. It's faint, and I'd estimate a range of about twenty-four thousand yards. Moving fast, though… near two-hundred knots, sir."

"Which means," Turner said thoughtfully. "A plane, or a flight of planes. Probably forty miles away at cruising altitude… headed where, Ted?"

"About due east, sir," Balkley said. "I'm losin' 'em, though…."

Turner nodded, "Dipping below the hill. Hmm… if I'm right, and I always am—"

Dutch, Hotrod, Rivers, Vigliano and even Balkley coughed significantly and hid their smiles. Turner grinned broadly, grateful for the high spirits. He couldn't help but feel that the men would need all they could get before this day was through.

"As I was *saying*," Turner pretended to grump, "in my most humble but indisputably accurate opinion… they came from the atoll ahead. My guess is either *Sakai* sent them out to join the big fracas today, or Sato is trying to pull a fast one on us. Have a squadron of Zekes do an end-around, come up on our sixes and drop a few care packages on us."

"That's some fine thinkin', Captain," Williams said from below.

"Why they pay me the big bucks, Elmer," Turner said, hitching up his shorts importantly and drawing another round of laughs. "Okay… please mark those aircraft on the plot, Elmer. Let me know when we're over S-52 as well. We're gonna need to have a few words."

It was just under fifteen minutes later when Williams reported that they should be above the other contact. Hotrod held up a maneuvering board and nodded.

"Kill the rock crushers, Frank," Turner ordered. "Once we're on batteries again, Mug, give me an all ahead two-thirds bell. Five knots."

The ship went quiet again, and Mug turned his engine enunciators. A pair of jangling bells came immediately in response, "Maneuverin' ansiz' two-thirds and five knots, sir."

"Okay, Chet, you're on," Turner said. "First, give me their depth, if you please."

"Two-hundred feet, sir," Rivers reported immediately.

"Very well," Turner replied. "Frank, take us down to one-hundred feet. Let 'er rip, Chet."

By using short, low-powered bursts from the JK sound heads slung below the keel, those with the active pinging capability, *Bull Shark* could send coded messages through the water to the other submarine. S-52 could then reply in kind. By lowering the power nearly to zero, the sound waves would be so weak that they'd disperse quickly. The conversation should be undetectable by any passive listening gear more than a mile away.

"They acknowledge and welcome us to the show, sir," Rivers said. "Standing by for orders."

Turner thought for a long moment and moved over to study the chart. Hotrod had a penciled point and half-circle where their course would intercept with the fifty-fathom curve of the atoll. It was dead-ahead. As he studied the chart and the hand-drawn islands on it, a plan began to form in the captain's mind.

He had no idea where Sato was. No idea how many escorts he had. In order to accurately fight this fight, Turner needed some data. He needed to know if the bastard was planning a nasty surprise for him, too. No doubt he was, as this man's obsession seemed extreme even from the first moment that Turner had spoken to him on Guadalcanal.

Sato wanted to win this contest... no, he *needed* to win it. So, it would be no stretch of the imagination to assume that he'd set up the board to his best advantage. He had an aircraft carrier with ASW capability, probably several destroyer escorts and possibly a submarine, too. He certainly had aircraft and would use them.

What did Turner have?

Two submarines, one of which was old and couldn't dive half as deep as his own. He had stealth... but that only went so far and worked against him as well.

To Turner's mind, there was only one thing to do. Although he couldn't control the location or the game... he *did* have control over when it got started. That'd have to be enough. He'd use a simple strategy that had worked for him before.

"Inform Pat that we're gonna use him as a hat," Turner said to

Rivers finally. "We'll duck under him and proceed at four-hundred feet until the bottom starts to rise. We'll then come abeam. Inform S-52 that at that time, once we near the fifty-fathom curve, to prepare for a full-power active ping from us. Then I want them to shut down and become a hole in the water. That clear?"

Rivers nodded gravely as he made notes on a scratch pad, "Yes sir… sending now."

The sonarman went to work with his gear. After a moment, he turned back to Turner with a smile playing at his lips, "S-52 acknowledges, sir. They also sent back an inquiry."

Turner grinned, imagining Pat Jarvis' face when he heard the message read to him, "Go ahead, Chet."

Rivers cleared his throat, "Mr. Jarvis asks what happens *after* they shit their pants, sir."

29
THE SAVAGE ISLANDS
AUGUST 24, 1942 – 0930 LOCAL TIME

Sakai had just completed her third orbit of the odd little four-island atoll. She steamed in a slow circle, moving at no more than four knots and making a single loop every ninety minutes or so.

The shallow bottom was no more than forty meters below her keel. There was nothing between it and the bottom, of course, but that's not what Sato hoped his enemies would believe. The I-123, which had escorted them, was sitting on the bottom at the fifty-fathom curve. Her job was simply to wait and listen and to report anything she heard if possible. Should the situation present itself, I-123 would attack any other submarine that crossed the curve.

In the CIC, the ship's radio gear was tuned into the fleetwide frequency. To the east was Admiral Nobotake Kondo's surface attack fleet, consisting of six heavy cruisers, the seaplane tender Chitose as well as six screening destroyers. This force was meant to charge the American carriers after dark once they'd been found.

North of these, Admiral Nagumo was headed south with the remainder of the Kido Butai with his two heavy carriers, two battleships as well as screening cruisers and destroyers. Even then, the light carrier Ryujo was passing to the north of *Sakai*. She and her escorts were to join Admiral Tanaka's invasion force. The idea was, and Sato found this particularly amusing, that Ryujo was to stake herself out as a tempting target for the aircraft of Henderson Field and Fletcher's carriers to focus on. Sato thought this was foolish, as Ryujo was only slightly larger than *Sakai* herself and didn't have nearly as large an airwing as would be required to defend herself.

These matters were, to Sato, rather unimportant and somewhat disconnected. For although they would be happening all around him, they did not directly affect him. Not unless he was ordered to send his own airwing to attack the Americans or to defend Tanaka. He sincerely hoped that would not be the case. His twenty planes, only half of which were fighters, would be needed to defend his carrier or even attack Turner if the opportunity arose. The moment that *Ryujo* launched her airwing and sent them away, she was a dead duck if found by the Americans.

On the plotting table before him, several men worked to keep track of Sato's own force. Captain Yamata had agreed to position his three destroyers to the northwest, fifteen kilometers away from the largest of the four islands. Just out of sight over the horizon from the shallows. Should Turner be detected, Yamata's force could come steaming into the fray in less than twenty minutes and catch the arrogant American in a pincer.

The remaining destroyer, the one that had been with *Sakai* for several weeks now, also made a circuit of the islands but in the opposite direction from the carrier. This ship moved at a much greater speed, closing a circle every thirty minutes. Sato was certain that nothing could get near his ship, let alone past her, without meeting with immediate destruction.

"Where are our fighters, Commander?" Sato asked Hideki as he entered the CIC.

"They've completed a large circuit and are headed back to us," Hideki reported, casting a furtive glance at Osaka. His friend stood by stoically, sipping from a cup of tea. "As requested, they are twenty meters off the deck and flying just above stall speed. Even so, they should appear on radar before ten a.m."

"Excellent," Sato said. "With the sun higher in the sky, they should be able to sight anything submerged at less than sixty meters. What do you say, Commander Osaka?"

"Concur," Osaka said and sipped.

"Nothing to add?" Sato asked a bit peevishly.

"You seem to have things in hand, Captain," Osaka said neutrally. "Nothing occurs at this time. Perhaps when and if our quarry appears, I might have a suggestion… if you're interested."

"As you say, Osaka san," Sato said almost in a sneer. "We will see."

Omata Hideki knew Osaka well enough to know that the man was fuming. Yet Osaka had an admirable ability to contain his emotions. The way that Sato seemed to sneer and make use of the familiar respectful "san" was beginning to irritate Hideki just to observe it. He could only imagine how his friend felt.

The Combat Intelligence Center was an interesting compartment. Both noise and quiet somehow existing simultaneously. There was the low murmur of voices as men compared data, made reports and talked to one another. There was the occasional crackle of a radio transmission or sonar feed on a loudspeaker. There were the mechanical sounds of equipment and the low rumble of the ship herself, all combining into a melodious burble that soon became part of the background. When something changed, however, it was noticed by all.

The sonar technicians, two of them, had the passive listening gear outputting to the loudspeaker. When the low whine began and then began to grow in volume, it drew everything and everyone to silent attention. The ghostly wail rapidly grew into an enormous echoing screech and then a resounding gong as the high-powered sonic wave impacted with the ship's steel hull below the waterline.

"Localize!" Sato all but shrieked excitedly.

"I'd say our opponent has entered the field of play," Osaka said casually to Hideki and smiled ever so slightly.

Sato laughed cruelly, "And gave away his position and his presence. Completely obliterating what small advantage he had! Perhaps I overestimated this Turner."

Osaka almost laughed but managed to keep his voice neutral, "I would not underestimate him, Captain. He may have exposed himself temporarily... but he's also gotten a good picture of our forces as well. Turner is no coward and no fool. He would rather face you on equal footing. He is, in essence, slapping you with his glove and inviting you to face him in a duel."

Sato laughed, "Then he's truly a fool. His bold move will not show *Viper's Fang* and her sisters... it will only deliver him to hell all the faster."

"I have the probable origin point of the active ping, sir," one of the sonarmen said eagerly, handing a slip of paper to Sato. "Approximately four thousand meters to the southwest."

"Exactly where I *thought* he'd be," Sato said with a chuckle. "Radio, inform *Lanotei* to vector directly to that location and begin an active search and destroy."

"Sir!" the radio technician replied. "Incoming message from *Ryujo*, sir. They are reporting to Admiral Nagumo that an American flying boat has located them and the invasion force and is shadowing. Admiral Tanaka reports that he is reversing course."

"And so it begins...." Osaka muttered.

"Commander Hideki," Sato barked. "Have our dive bombers launch and vector them to *Ryujo's* position to act as temporary support. When we've recovered our Zeroes and refueled them, we can offer further assistance. They're doing no good sitting on the flight deck."

"*Hai*," Hideki said and turned to go.

"Should we not attack Henderson?" Osaka asked. "Rather than sending dive bombers to act as fighters to defend *Ryujo?* If... no, *when* the Americans come for her, they'll need fighter support, not clumsy dive bombers."

Sato considered him with narrowed eyes for a long moment, "Thank you, Commander. I am in no need of your suggestions at this time."

Osaka bowed slightly at the shoulders, "Very well, then I shall make myself useful elsewhere."

As he and Hideki left, Osaka began to ponder the situation. Turner's bold move could be effective, except for the fact that he didn't know just how large a force his opponent had at his command. He didn't and couldn't know of Captain Yamata's destroyer squadron. In spite of gaining an accurate picture of the situation as he knew it, Turner was still walking into a trap.

This weighed heavily on Osaka's mind. On the one hand, he should be glad that his enemies were walking into certain defeat. Yet he also knew that part of his duty was to accelerate Japan's eventual surrender, and a man like Arthur Turner was quite useful toward that cause. Osaka respected and liked him and didn't *want* to see him and his crew die.

There was more, however. Perhaps at that moment, Osaka most of all loathed the idea that Turner's death would come at the hands of Takashi Sato. A man whose arrogance and self-importance fell far short of his actual ability. A man not *worthy* of an adversary such as Turner. A man who could only win this contest by *cheating*.

No… no, that wouldn't do. If Sato was to win, then it would have to be on fair terms. That was, perhaps in the final reckoning, justice. Let Sato and Turner face one another in a fair game. Then, at least, the best man would have a chance to win the day.

S-52 – 3 MILES AWAY

"Holy cow, sir!" Bobby Gaines exclaimed. "*Bull Shark* just lit up the whole area!"

Jarvis chuckled, "That's Anvil Art for you."

"With all due respect… is he nuts?" Savage asked from the hatchway.

"Nope," Jarvis said, lighting a Camel. "He's shrewd. He knows that sooner or later, our enemies will discover us. Art is just getting things started on his terms. *Forcing* the Japs to make a move. It's worked before. What've you got from that ping, Bobby?"

Gaines listened, "Got a set of three fast heavy screws, XO… had them before, though, a set of twin fast lights further off and… something… a stationary return almost on our nose. *Bull Shark*, of course, and she's beginning to move off to the north."

"Crawford, make our depth three-hundred feet," Jarvis said. "Helm, all ahead one-third, make turns for two knots. Rig ship for silent running. Bobby, give Mr. Savage what you've got on those contacts. And I want to know more on the stationary one, too."

"The big one, that must be the carrier, is continuing a course around the atoll, sir," Gaines reported. "The other is a tin can, about nine-thousand yards off, headed in the opposite direction. The stationary one... the return sounded *metallic*... but that's all I got. A bit muddled, too. Like something metal with a heavy blanket thrown over it, if that makes any sense."

"Do you have the position?" Savage asked.

Gaines gave it to him. The temporary XO met the temporary Captain's eyes.

"That's weird...." Jarvis said. "Plot that, will ya, Chris... I have a hunch."

Savage disappeared and returned with a slip of paper. At the same time, Jak Cleghorn plotted everything on the chart desk as well.

"That carrier has been running at slow speed for a while now," Jarvis said. "As he's done in the past. Making like there's a Jap submarine under his keel."

"According to our chart," Savage said. "Which, I admit, could be wrong... it's only based on my memory... he's in a hundred, hundred and fifty feet of water on that course."

"Yeah..." Jarvis said. "Yeah... he *wants* us to think he's got a sub under his ass... but I don't think so. I'll bet you any money that Bobby's muddy return is a Jap sub sitting on the bottom nice and quiet like. Just waitin' for a chance to pounce. What's the depth where she is?"

Savage frowned, "Maybe three hundred feet... again, I'm guessing at these depths, XO."

Jarvis frowned and came to a decision, "Chris, turn the plot over to Jack. You come up here and work the TDC. I think we're gonna send that Jap a few care packages."

"A blind shot at depth?" Savage asked incredulously. "We don't really even know—"

"The faint heart never won the fair maiden, Chris," Jarvis said. "And I want to take away any advantage this Sato character has. What's the range, bobby?"

"Three thousand yards, sir."

"Start me a solution, Jack," Jarvis said as Savage reluctantly slid into the chair at the TDC. "You too, Chris. Alert the torpedo room to open their outer doors and set depth on all weapons to three hundred feet. Speed high. It's a shot in the dark… but my gut says it's the right one."

BULL SHARK – OPENING FROM S-52

Chet Rivers made essentially the same report. As soon as the active ping went out, Turner ordered Vigliano to come to a three-four-five and make turns for three knots. The captain was exercising a bit of land warfare combat doctrine that he'd learned from his recent stint with the Marine Raiders.

You never fired from the same place twice.

Originally, Turner had ordered Jarvis to remain stationary and quiet. Lying in wait for whatever might be alerted by the ping. However, when that odd stationary return had come in, and Jarvis had elected to continue on course, Turner approved.

It was difficult, in truth, to pinpoint the origin of an active sonar ping. If the receiving vessel was close, it became easier. Within a thousand yards or so, the sonar operator could be certain to within a hundred yards or so. However, the further away the originating ship was, the greater the cone of probability. *Sakai* was about three miles off, and she would be able to guess to within a thousand yards or so where the pulse had come from. Perhaps less if her sonar techs were really on the ball.

However, the stationary object, which was definitely metal, was half that distance. This object, if Turner was right, was a Japanese submarine lurking on the bottom and waiting for a hapless Yank to cross over him. At that distance, the Jap could guess the origin point of the sonar pulse to within one or two hundred yards easily. More than enough to home in on the other boat's machinery noises.

Now the two American submarines were moving apart at a combined rate of about four knots. Even should *Sakai*, the closest ship, go to full speed and head directly for their position, it would be at least fifteen minutes for her to accelerate and close the distance. By then, S-52 would be at least one-thousand yards away.

And would the Japs attack?

The thought bloomed in Turner's mind white-hot and sent a shiver of excitement up his spine. The Japs *knew* where their boat was, right? So, would they race in to that position and start depth charging the area and risk hitting her?

Of course not!

Which meant that, unless the Japanese submarine moved, there was probably a thousand-yard circle of safety around her. That meant that even if the Japs echolocated a submarine within that circle of safety, they *couldn't* attack! Further, should the enemy submarine begin to move, then the American subs would have a better sound profile to home in on. They could hound her or... or even fire on her!

Turner wished he could somehow send a telepathic message through the intervening water to his torpedo officer. To somehow communicate his thoughts to Pat. Yet he couldn't, and using sonar communications would only give things away at this point. He had to hope that Pat was having the same thoughts as himself and would come to the same conclusions.

For the moment, Turner had other fish to fry.

"Joe, call down to Sparky and Murph," Turner said. "Have them open the outer doors on all tubes. Have them do it manually, though. Nice and slow and nice and quiet like."

Dutch, who, as acting torpedo officer, had a sound-powered telephone around his neck, made the calls. He received acknowledgments and reported this to Turner.

"Very well. Bet the phone talkers in the torpedo rooms didn't report *everything* their LPOs said," Turner mused. "Okay... we're gonna let Pat worry about that submarine. Chet, what about our other targets?"

"Sounds like the carrier is maintaining her course," Rivers said. "No change in screw noise or anything... but the DD is powering up. Range nine-five-zero-zero yards... screw noise increasing... turn rate... thirty knots, I think. CBDR, Skipper. She's headed right for us, or almost. Course is... one-nine-zero."

"Right for her submerged comrade, in other words," Turner said. "Just our luck, we happened to come up on the bastard almost dead on. Sato guessed that's where we'd come in from… crafty prick. Well, he's comin' alone, so he's asking for it. Keep the plot going on him, and keep your ears on *Sakai* Chet. Let's hope that this is Sato's first mistake. Sending a lone tin can after two angry boats. What's his bearing, Chet?"

"Zero-one-five relative… triple zero true," Rivers reported. "Having some trouble tracking S-52, sir… she's running slow and quiet."

"Very well," Turner said. "Mug, right standard rudder. Increase speed to all ahead two-thirds, steady up on course three-five-five. Plot, double-check me on that and give me an intercept course, please."

Orders were acknowledged, and the boat began to turn toward her enemy. The two natural adversaries, the destroyer and the submarine were now rushing at one another at a combined speed of thirty-five knots.

Even at that speed, it would take the two vessels about ten minutes to close with one another. In that time, *Bull Shark* would be about a mile north of the theoretical Japanese submarine. He crossed his fingers and hoped that in that time, S-52 would get clear of what might be a very uncomfortable bit of ocean.

"Target is the DD," Turner said to Dutch. "Order of tubes is seven, eight, nine and ten. Give me a three-degree spread, Joe."

"What's your desired firing range?" Dutch asked and then squinted at Turner. "Stern tubes? What…?"

"We're gonna go right under his belly and send our fish straight up his skirt," Turner said, that old predatory gleam in his eyes. "If I'm right, she'll power down right about the time we get close so she can get a good return from her echolocation. We're gonna zip under her and fire at point-blank range. We need five hundred yards of torpedo run, Joe. We'll figure it out when we get close. It'll depend on speeds."

Everyone in the conning tower and down in the control room crossed their fingers and, to a man, smiled in anticipation. They were going to get a little payback for their last pasting, and when Anvil Art Turner's blood was up, it seemed as if the very air in the boat was

395

charged with electricity. Their *Bull Shark* had a taste for blood and was about to launch an attack on her favorite prey… Japanese shipping.

S-52

"If that sub is sitting on the bottom, Chris," Jarvis was pondering. "Then we'd have to figure the Japs know where she is, right?"

Savage was looking mildly unhappy and pale sitting at his torpedo data computer, "Yeah, you'd think so…."

"So, the Japs probably won't send depth charges down near her, right?" Jarvis went on, absently snapping his fingers as he thought.

"I wouldn't think so… I mean that'd be…" suddenly, the thought hit Savage, and his eyes widened.

"Exactly," Jarvis said, rubbing his palms together briskly. "What's a safe radius from depth charges, do you think?"

"Probably a half-mile or so," Savage said. "Like what we use when doing an indoctrination depth charging. Plus, the boat is on the bottom, so that could make it worse, maybe."

"Okay, so let's assume a thousand-yard radius," Jarvis said. "A safe zone where the Japs *won't* drop charges on their friends… I hope."

"Sir! *Bull Shark* is increasing speed and altering her heading," Gaines reported. "So is that further contact. I think… the further contact is headed this way, and *Bull Shark* is headed for her! Holy cow… is Captain Turner *charging* them?"

Jarvis laughed, "Wouldn't be a bit surprised… how long to intercept?"

Gaines worked the math in his head, "About… ten minutes, sir…."

"Range to the Jap submarine?" Jarvis asked.

"Uhm…" Gaines didn't quite know, as there was no sound return now.

"Twenty-eight hundred yards, bearing approximately three-four-five, Skipper," Cleghorn reported.

It was odd being called that. To Jarvis' mind, he was still the XO, filling in for the indisposed captain. And even at that, he was only the XO for this patrol.

Yet he thought of the talk he and Elmer Williams had had not long before. How Jarvis had explained that, like it or not, Elmer *was* the skipper because Art Turner wasn't aboard. Jarvis supposed that was true for him, too. So long as Waters was down for the count, Pat Jarvis was the captain for better or worse.

The skipper then smiled wolfishly, "Helm, left rudder. Steer two-niner zero."

The balls were in motion now. The great tumblers of fate had been set loose to click into whatever place they desired. There was no turning back and no takebacks.

The battle of wits, brains and brawn between Art Turner and his two submarines and Takashi Sato and his six ships and twenty airplanes was now irrevocably and inevitably set in motion, and no force on Earth could stop it.

This was fitting, as less than a hundred miles away, a lone PBY was circling over a group of warships, transports and an aircraft carrier, sending reports back to her home base and any other Allies who would listen.

The World War… the *second* world war… raged across the Pacific, in the Atlantic and on and above Europe and Africa. In the Eastern Solomons, men fought against other men for possession of small bits of mostly worthless land. Great fleets and their weapons of destruction drew ever closer in a mighty conflict.

And at a small uncharted atoll just outside the boundaries of the Solomon Islands, two men moved their pieces onto a chessboard and opened a game that could have but one outcome.

Death.

Death for one… death for some… or death for all.

No matter the outcome, one thing was certain. Death would have its due and would most certainly not go away from this day unslaked.

30

The *Asashio*-class destroyer *Inatei* raced through the sea, parting the bright turquoise waters with her knife-like cutwater and throwing up a prodigious bow wave that creamed halfway down her light gray flanks. On her upper decks, men manned the 127mm deck guns, although there was little chance of them being used. Aft, sailors readied one-hundred-and-fifty-kilogram depth charges on their racks and in the throwers that sent them out thirty meters to either beam.

On her bridge stood her skipper, a youngish man of thirty who had recently graduated from The Sensei's destroyer command school. Although he was glad for the training and very pleased by his instructor's approval of his performance… he was grateful not to be attached to Captain Yamata's squadron all the same.

It wasn't that he begrudged the man anything. On the contrary, Yamata's tough but fair education had no doubt vastly improved the skipper's own skillset. However, he wanted an opportunity to prove himself. To pit his hard-won knowledge against a real foe. To do so *without* his former teacher looking over his shoulder.

"Helm, reduce speed to one-third on both engines," the skipper commanded. "Sonarman, begin active echolocation. Search frequency."

The destroyer's way came down quickly, dropping from thirty knots to a comparatively sedate ten. While still faster than any submerged submarine, this low speed would allow her two sonar operators, one on the active gear and one on the passive, to better hear their undersea enemy without the roar of the ship's own engines fouling the sound profile.

A submarine was out here; of that, there was no doubt. The Amecoh fools had been arrogant enough to send out a powerful active sonar pulse. This most certainly gave their position away and removed any advantage in stealth they might have enjoyed. A stupid and, to the skipper's mind, an almost childish blunder. Suddenly, however, in his mind, he could hear Yamata's firm but calm voice speaking to him, as if the man were truly hanging over his shoulder instead of twenty kilometers away.

"Never underestimate your adversary, Goto," the teacher reminded. "Always assume that a submarine commander is *not* a fool. They don't give fools such commands, after all. No... assume he's crafty. Craftier than you, in fact. You are fighting yourself as much as him. Combatting your own assumptions and pre-conceptions."

The sonar ping *had* come from the general vicinity of I-123; it was true. And it was also true that until the submarine moved, there was a charted area where depth charges could not be dropped.

"Contact!" the sonarman said from the passive gear. "Submerged contact bearing zero-zero-zero... range one-thousand meters... speed five knots... no, increasing now... six... seven...."

"Combat frequency!" Goto exclaimed. "Lock in on him! What's his heading? Yakuin, alert depth charge crews to launch on your command... when I give the word."

"The submarine is headed right for us, sir!" cried the active sonarman. "Speed now nine knots! Depth one hundred meters."

"Yakuin, have them set their depth triggers to one-hundred meters!" Goto said and resisted the urge to smile triumphantly. He must remember his dignity, after all. "Helm, increase speed to two-thirds all!"

Even should the American fire his forward torpedoes just then, the two ships would close the gap before they could arm themselves. Still, should evasive maneuvers be necessary, a higher speed would aid them.

"Depth change on target!" the sonarman reported. "Coming up... ninety meters... eighty... sixty!"

Goto suddenly realized his mistake. The American was counting on his active pings finding him. It would then give the destroyer hunting him data to use in setting their depth charges. Now, though, with the two ships nearly meeting, it was nearly too late to alter them.

Nearly... but not quite.

Goto gritted his teeth, "Range to target?"

"Two hundred meters and closing rapidly," the sonarman reported. "Depth now thirty meters... holding at thirty meters."

Goto swore he could almost see the submarine's dark shape down in the depths ahead of his ship. This was impossible, of course, not with the sun off the starboard bow and still only a few hours above the horizon.

"Yakuin, belay my last to the depth charge crews, order them to set depth on all weapons to forty meters," Goto said. "We have them now!"

"One hundred meters!" the sonarman nearly shouted. "Fifty... they will pass beneath our keel shortly, sir...."

Goto smiled triumphantly, "In twenty seconds, order depth charges to be launched."

The destroyer's sound beams echoing off the American submarine's hull and bouncing back seemed to fill the ship with their rapid, high-pitched pinging. The rush of water, sonar pings and churning propellors made any reliable data impossible to gather now, but it didn't matter.

"Depth charges away!" the first officer reported.

Goto ran out onto the port bridge wing to observe. As he watched, canisters rolled off the racks on the ship's squat fantail while others were flung out to port and starboard. These hurtled through the air, tumbling end over end before splashing into the sea and plunging downward toward their foe.

Thunderous booms rocked the destroyer as first two, then four and then eight depth charges went off, their concussive waves blasting upward and erupting from the sea in massive geysers of foam fifty feet high.

It was then that Goto had a flash of insight. This flash caused him to make another decision. A decision that would be his final error.

What if the submarine had dived deep again?

"Helm!" he roared back into the navigation bridge. "Hard right rudder! *Quickly!*"

The true pity of it, at least from the *Inatei's* perspective, was that Goto had guessed correctly. *Bull Shark* had angled down at a thirty-degree bubble just before crossing beneath the destroyer's bows. By the time the depth charges went off, the boat was at two hundred feet. The charges still rocked and rolled her, smashing light bulbs, loosening cork insulation, as well as men from what they'd felt were secure positions. Bruises and cuts were earned, one or two minor leaks broke out from over-stressed feed line fittings, but it was nothing as compared to what they delivered in return.

Tubes seven through ten were fired in quick succession. The four torpedoes streaked for the stern of the DD at forty-six knots, slowly spreading out from one another in an ever-widening fan. By the time their wakes could be seen on the surface, somewhat obscured by the disturbances from the charges, the four Mark 14 fish had spread out to cover a fifty-yard swath of ocean.

Had the destroyer not turned, at least one of the two inner fish would have struck her. Yet her rapid and wide turn exposed her starboard side to the two right-hand torpedoes, and the screaming steam engines propelled the two weapons into the steel side of their prey like hungry adders striking a rabbit.

The explosions came six seconds apart. The first blew off thirty feet of the destroyer's stern and ignited the depth charges resting there. A massive fireball rolled into the sky, hurling steel fragments, burning debris and unidentifiable lumps of what until a few seconds before had been men.

The final torpedoe's torpex warhead blasted open the ship's side, allowing tons of seawater to smash into her starboard boiler room, igniting the boilers and setting off a cataclysmic explosion that literally ripped what was left of the ship in two, tossing over one hundred feet of bow into the air to tumble three times before settling into the roiling, frothing sea.

What was left of her burned even as she sank, the twisted, blackened hull bearing no resemblance to the sleek war machine she'd been.

"Periscope depth!" Turner called even as the last of the stern torpedoes was blasted out of the tubes. "Phone talker, alert after room to close outer doors and begin reloading. Mug, back us down to two-thirds!"

It had been a rocky ride. Turner's ploy to rise toward the destroyer in hopes that they'd reset their depth charges to a shallower trigger had worked. However, *Bull Shark* could only plane up and down so quickly. When the charges set to a hundred feet had gone off, the boat had only been at two-hundred and descending.

However, it was always better to have tooth shakers explode *above* a submarine rather than below, as the majority of the energy of the blast was forced upward by physics. The charges had rattled the boat severely but had also actually pushed her downward and away.

"Periscope depth!" Nichols called up.

"Up attack scope," Turner ordered, and the slim periscope rose. He bent down to the deck, snapped the handles down and rode her up. "Okay... got her... Christ... that's a kill for sure. Mug, right standard rudder. Let's circle back to where S-52 should be."

"Skipper..." Chet Rivers was pressing his hands to his headphones and frowning. "I'm getting... something...."

"Can you be more vague, Chet?" Turner joked.

Rivers continued to frown, "Sorry, sir. It's... well... I'm not sure... oh, damn! It sounds like propellors, sir! Aircraft incoming... can't quite tell from where, though."

Turner spun the scope and stopped when he was facing a bit forward of the starboard beam. "Oh, shit... Zekes! Coming in low on the deck! Down scope! Frank, hard dive! Hard dive!"

Below at the diving station, Frank Nichols exchanged a worried glance with Chief Buck Rogers before ordering, "Full down on all planes! COB, flood negative and bow buoyancy."

"You think they saw our scope, Art?" Dutch asked.

"If not the whole boat in these gin-clear waters, Joe," Turner said unhappily. "Elmer, take a fathometer reading. Get us close to the bottom."

A low-volume ping and Turner heard Williams tell Nichols that it was five-hundred and sixty-five feet deep.

"How far away were those planes, sir?" Hotrod asked.

Turner pursed his lips in thought, "They were pretty low, no more than a hundred feet, I'd guess. Four miles, maybe five… two or three minutes away. Probably armed with depth charges. I counted ten planes, probably from *Sakai*. Even if they guess right, it's only ten ashcans. We'll stay rigged for depth charge for now."

"Now passing one-five-zero feet," Nichols intoned.

"Splashes!" Rivers announced. "Two… four… six… ten, sir! Spread out, though. Not a good pattern… but a few are close."

The sea roared as first one, then another and then another depth charge exploded. None were very close, and each one had been set to a different depth. The object was clear. The aircraft had laid down their entire load of ten charges in a random pattern and at random depths in hopes of hitting something. Reasonable enough, but mostly a waste.

Except that it happened to work, at least partly.

The eighth charge to be dropped had been set to a depth of two-hundred and twenty feet. In an unfortunate twist of fate, the pilot had misread his depth selector. He'd *meant* to set the charge to three-hundred feet, but in his haste, he only glanced at the selector and hit the release button, overly excited by the rest of his squadron's actions and eager to score a hit for himself.

His erroneously set depth charge exploded no more than ten feet ahead of *Bull Shark's* bullnose just as the boat was nosing through two-two-zero feet. The explosion smashed the tip of the wooden deck, sending debris rattling and clunking along the boat's hull as she drove through it. One of these bits of debris, a six-foot-long steel support stringer, jammed into the vents of the bow buoyancy ballast tank and tore two of the vent covers off. As the tank was already flooded, this had no immediate effect. However, it did render it impossible to blow the seawater out. The concussion wave also sent enough energy down into the tank and its associated air supply valves to rupture one.

"Flooding in forward torpedo!" fireman Wilbur Dockerty exclaimed.

He was acting phone talker stationed in the after battery compartment. His job was to collate damage reports from other compartments and relate them to the damage control officer and then return any orders. Dockerty was relatively new to the boat, having transferred aboard at Brisbane. This was his first taste of real combat, and by the pale look on his nineteen-year-old face, it wasn't as much fun as he'd thought it would be.

"How bad?" Porter Hazard, acting DCO, asked. He cast a quick glance at Henry Hoffman and the ship's cooks, who doubled as his attendants.

"Uhm…" Dockerty waited, his face glistening with flop sweat. "Pretty bad. An air line burst that feeds the bow buoyancy tank, and water is coming in fast!"

"Understood," Hazard said calmly. "Take a deep breath, Wilbur. You ain't up there, son. Tell them to compensate with salvage air and get a patch on. Ask if Sparky needs any assistance."

Dockerty took several long deep breaths and then spoke into his sound-powered telephone set. A few seconds went by, and then he said: "Forward room reports they're on it and think they can get it under control, sir."

Hazard nodded, "Very well. Make a report to the XO, Wilbur."

Bull Shark continued to dive, now moving faster due to the extra water weight forward. Frank Nichols eased up on the bow planes and blew the negative tank to the mark. He had the men at the air manifolds put extra air into the forward trim tank and auxiliaries. The dive continued but at a more sedate pace.

. . .

Less than two miles away, the S-52 hung motionless at three hundred feet, the muddy bottom less than fifty feet from her keel. According to both Cleghorn and Lockner's calculations, they were no more than five hundred yards away from the stationary Japanese submarine.

However, without some kind of reading or sound to triangulate on, it would be impossible to aim their weapons at the enemy boat... if she was even truly there.

"What about an active ping?" Savage suggested, lounging at the TDC and smoking a Chesterfield.

Jarvis frowned, "We can't pull that trick too many times, Chris. The problem with an active pulse, as you know, is that it's global. It goes out in all directions. We might ping the Jap, but we'd ping *Bull Shark,* too. The Nips already know we're out here; I don't want to give them any more advantages. Speaking of our friends, Bobby, what've you got on *Bull Shark?*"

"I think they got the DD, sir," Gaines said. "But I'm picking up depth charges... ten, I think."

That tightened Jarvis' gut for a moment. However, if there was more bad news to report, Gaines would've done so. He would've done so without being asked.

Instead, the young man frowned at his gear and then turned back to Jarvis, "Still picking up faint, light screw noises, sir. Bearing zero-nine-five. Range... three-eight-zero-zero yards."

Jarvis nodded with relief. He hadn't expected the worst, but it was still hard for him, knowing that his boat... his *true* home... was out there somewhere without him aboard. He wondered if this was how Turner had felt when he was ashore on Guadalcanal.

"I want that Jap boat," Jarvis said suddenly after a moment of silence.

"Well, without active sonar or them making any noise," Savage offered, "not sure what we can do about it, sir."

Jarvis drummed his fingers on the periscope barrel next to him, "No... unless they're stupid enough to alert us to their exact position, or we're stupid enough to ping them... *hearing* is out for now. They're close, though... I can feel it in my balls... so if we can't hear 'em, what does that leave?"

"We can send Tony out with a mask to look around for them," Savage joked.

"Hey!" Skaggs called up from the control room. Evidently, he'd come forward from the after battery compartment where he was stationed as DCO.

A round of barely audible chuckles from below and the conning tower. Jarvis had to smile. That was the first laughter he'd heard aboard that wasn't secretive or at someone's expense. Just good-natured joshing.

"Unfortunately, of the five senses, hearing is the only one a submarine's got," Cleghorn offered solemnly. "Can't smell, touch or taste the enemy, now, can we?"

"Sautéed Jap?" Steve Marx said from the helm and laughed.

"You're forgetting one," Jarvis said, snapping his fingers. "Sight."

"Not submerged," Savage added. "We're limited to sound only."

"Why?" Jarvis asked, rapping his knuckles on the periscope barrel. "We got eyes. A pair of them, in fact. Nothin' sayin' we can't raise the scope underwater, now is there? In this clear tropical sea, visibility is a couple of hundred feet. Probably not as much on the bottom... but still... the clarity of the water helps. Down this far, the light level is probably thirty percent of surface strength... but that should be enough to spot something."

"Yeah, if we're within maybe fifty yards," Savage argued. "A pretty wide margin for error, isn't it?"

"We know the approximate location of that sub," Jarvis pontificated. "I think we could creep up on him and get within fifty yards or so. All we need is a glimpse. A confirmation of where he *really* is, and then we back off and send him a little torpex smooch."

"One problem, sir," Cleghorn said reluctantly. He hated to rain on the parade, but it must be said. "Our scopes leak. It's bad enough at periscope depth. Lowered as they are, it's fine... but you raise them at this depth and with the pressure being five times what it is at periscope depth...."

"It'll be a salty monsoon in here... and we could permanently rupture a seal...." Jarvis muttered. "Sweet baby Jesus in a jumper... Well, we only need a quick look when we think we're close. It's an option. Marx, ring me up an all ahead one-third bell. Make turns for one knot. Bobby, keep your ears peeled. We're gonna tip-toe along here and find that God damned Jap, even if we have to stick a white cane out the friggin' window."

31
KIDO BUTAI – 250 MILES NE OF GUADALCANAL
AUGUST 24, 1942 – 1220 SHIP'S TIME

Admiral Chuichi Nagumo once more found himself on the observation deck of an aircraft carrier on the verge of battle. He was, somewhat to his astonishment, still in command of Japan's mighty Kido Butai, the combined fleet. Although in truth, the term was going out of use and the less romantic label First Fleet was being applied.

Perhaps, in some way, this was a rebuke by Admiral Yamamoto. Kido Butai had something of a ring to it. It sounded majestic, grandiose… powerful. Of course, the once-mighty carrier fleet of eight aircraft carriers had been brutally sliced down the center, with one side still operational and the other now resting at the bottom of the Pacific Ocean some three hundred kilometers northwest of Midway Atoll.

A rebuke indeed. Under his, Nagumo's, command, four mighty carriers, *Kaga*, *Akagi*, *Hiryu* and her sister, *Soryu*, had been destroyed by American aircraft within a span of hours on June 4. It was little consolation that *Shokaku*, his current flagship, was once again at sea after having been damaged at the battle of the Coral Sea in May. Yes, there were new carriers being constructed… yes, the Americans had lost *Yorktown* at Midway… yet the latest intelligence reports showed that, in spite of what the IJN had believed, that was the only carrier lost at Midway.

The Americans still had *Enterprise*, *Hornet*, *Saratoga* and *Wasp*. What the Japanese Navy did *not* know was where these carriers were. Certainly, at least two or three of them would be somewhere south of Guadalcanal. That much had been hinted at by scouting missions and intelligence reports. It only stood to reason. Yet Nagumo did not *know*, and this bothered him more than he could express.

Carrier battles were of a different variety altogether. There were no lines of battle or firing of shells from just over the horizon or racing through the sea and sending torpedoes back and forth in some mad, twisted ping-pong match.

No… carriers fought each other from hundreds of kilometers away. They didn't fight with guns or torpedoes… not directly at least… but with aircraft. It had been shown now in several major engagements that the side who spotted the other first was likely to be the victor. So, in order to win carrier battles, a commander must be decisive and cunning.

Was he cunning? Perhaps. The powers that be wouldn't have left him in the position of such an important command unless *they* thought so. His chief of staff and aid, Admiral Kusaka, would have said that Nagumo was crafty… yet what would Isoroku Yamamoto have said?

Nagumo actually found himself chuckling sardonically. Yamamoto had said little, and yet, he'd spoken far more in his silences and in the words he *did not* say, than in his direct speech. Nagumo knew that his superior had been livid after the Midway debacle. Yes, any battle could be won or lost, and luck most certainly played a part. However, Nagumo had hesitated, dithered and changed his mind *twice* on that fateful morning of June 4, and it had cost him four carriers and a failed invasion. Nagumo had achieved nothing positive. They'd lost four invaluable and irreplaceable ships, dozens of their best pilots and had not even seized hold of that worthless sand speck into the bargain.

Nagumo had no doubt that if he didn't have the personal backing of Tojo and Hirohito himself that Yamamoto would have ordered Nagumo to come aboard the *Yamato*. He would then have strangled Nagumo with his bare, rage-fueled hands.

So now here he was, forced into almost the exact same position.

His carriers were to shield another invasion force. They were to locate and destroy Frank Jack Fletcher's task force and see that the Americans lost their toehold in the Solomons. He must act and act decisively.

And he must pray.

"Sir," Kusaka's voice said quietly from behind Nagumo. The man didn't want to disturb his superior when he was so obviously in deep contemplation.

"Yes, Kusaka," Nagumo said finally, turning to face the slightly younger man and smiling. "You have something for me?"

"Admiral Hara reports that he and *Ryujo* are within safe striking distance of Guadalcanal," Kusaka reported. "He also reports that the flight of dive bombers from *Sakai* are reporting low fuel and that they must depart. Admiral Hara also says that the enemy flying boat is still popping up over the horizon."

Nagumo nodded, "We must thank *Sakai* for their support. Would that they could join *Ryujo* in this action. Even their limited airwing would be useful… but they have other fish to fry at the moment. As for the American plane… well, we must assume that they are aware of *Ryujo's* position by now. What are your thoughts, my friend?"

"We could order Hara to alter course," Kusaka suggested. "To get out of the area to avoid a counter-attack."

"No… we can't do that," Nagumo said reluctantly after several moments of pondering. "It's not just a matter of *Ryujo* attacking the airfield, Kusaka… they are meant to draw an attack. To divert carrier and ground aircraft away from us while we hunt down Fletcher. When his planes come for *Ryujo,* we'll then have a better idea of the location of the American carriers."

Kusaka's belly tightened. They'd discussed this already, of course, and both men knew what Nagumo's proclamation meant. They were sacrificing the light carrier to the cause. There was no question of that. Even with cruiser and destroyer escorts, the light carrier's limited supply of Zeroes wouldn't be able to stop fifty or sixty American planes. As they'd all seen at Midway, it took but two or three hits from the large bombs the Americans carried to doom even a huge carrier like *Kaga. Ryujo* wouldn't survive.

Yet if Nagumo could trade her for *Enterprise* or *Hornet,* two of the carriers that had been at Midway, it would be considered a victory indeed.

"Yes sir... but I do not like it."

Nagumo nodded gravely, "Nor I, Kusaka... nor I."

The chief of staff waited once more. He could see the misery of the decision playing on Nagumo's face. Unfortunately, no matter how much advice Kusaka gave, it was still up to the Old Man to give the final word.

"Tell Admiral Hara to launch his attack," Nagumo stated. "This should dovetail nicely with Rabaul's attack force. They should rendezvous over Lunga Point by early afternoon."

"And the larger carrier force?" Kusaka asked.

"We must wait, my friend... we must wait," Nagumo said. "But this time, at least, our aircraft and those on *Zuikaku* will be used *only* against Fletcher. The sun will not set this day before we have wreaked a terrible vengeance on him."

USS *SARATOGA* – TASK FORCE 61 – 150 MILES SE OF GUADALCANAL

"Updated report from the Catalina, Admiral," Captain DeWitt Ramsey said, stepping up to Fletcher, who was enjoying a cigarette on *Saratoga's* observation deck.

Frank Jack Fletcher had been pacing since before sunrise. Sometimes on the navigation bridge, sometimes in the CIC and sometimes out on the deck. He'd stare out over the sea as if his eyes, and his eyes alone, could see beyond the horizon and locate Nagumo's carriers.

"Nothing from our scouts?" Fletcher asked in mild irritation. "For Christ's sake, DeWitt, we've got half a dozen scouts out from us and *Enterprise,* and not one of them has seen anything?"

"Not as yet, sir," Ramsey stated. "It's a big ocean, and Nagumo could be anywhere within a thirty or forty-thousand square mile area. We'll find him, though, of that, I'm sure."

"As he's sure he'll find *us,*" Fletcher replied gloomily. He sighed and offered Ramsey a faint smile. The man had something to say, and he deserved to be heard. "What's the word from that Catalina?"

"They say that *Ryujo* has been spotting birds on deck since noon," Ramsey stated. "They're launching Vals, Bettys and Zekes. By the looks of it, they're launching everything they've got. The Catalina had to duck over the horizon and leave the area lest one of those Zeroes comes after her."

"They're lucky that hasn't already happened... do they have a probable course?" Fletcher asked, although there was only one possibility. The IJN light carrier was northwest of Guadalcanal.

"They believe southeast," Ramsey said. "Which could mean Henderson Field or... or us."

Fletcher snorted, "I doubt they're headed for us. That'd be just plain idiotic. Nagumo may be many things, but stupid isn't one of them. Certainly, his boss isn't... no, those birds are meant for the Marines, certain sure."

"Shall we launch an offensive against *Ryujo* now, sir?" Ramsey asked hopefully. "Commander Felt and his guys are ready to go, as you can see."

Fletcher moved to the port side of the observation deck and looked down on the flight deck. Felt's entire dive bomber squadron had returned from Guadalcanal after daybreak and had been refueled and re-armed. They sat on the flight deck and were all ready to fly. Once they took off, a squadron of half a dozen Wildcats and as many Avengers would quickly be sent up from the hangar and sent with Felt.

"Not yet," Fletcher said thoughtfully. "Let's give it a little time. I'd prefer to send Harry after the big boys rather than waste his talents on *Ryujo*. It doesn't take a brain surgeon to know that the Japs are staking her out specifically to draw our attention *away* from Nagumo."

An hour later, however, Fletcher couldn't hold back any longer. By then, the IJN light carrier's planes would be most of the way to Guadalcanal. This was confirmed by the radar techs who reported aircraft at long range, about a hundred and eighty miles off. Upon hearing this, Fletcher ordered Felt's flight to be sent up with orders to proceed to *Ryujo's* position and destroy her.

At the same time, unseen and unheard, a lone Aichi floatplane droned southward, her pilot and observer scanning the horizon ahead for any sign of ships. It would be over an hour yet, but somehow, the aircraft would go unnoticed until it was nearly on top of Task Force 61.

COMMANDER HAROLD D. FELT – *SARATOGA* STRIKE FORCE - 1423

Harry Felt flexed his fingers as he peered through his windscreen at the partial cloud cover below him. His thirty-eight planes, consisting of Dauntlesses, one of which he flew, the new Avenger torpedo planes, and their Wildcat escorts had climbed to angels twelve upon leaving the task force. They'd stay below the required oxygen ceiling for most of the flight to conserve their O2 supply. After about forty minutes, he'd ordered everyone to climb to thirty-six thousand feet for their final approach.

From his experience and from other reports, the vaunted Japanese Zeroes did have a drawback when it came to their operational ceiling. At angels thirty-six, the American aircraft would be several thousand feet above the Zeroes' operational ceiling. It was one trick the Wildcat pilots used, especially at Henderson. They'd climb up high and then dive down on top of the Zekes.

Another advantage of coming down from this great height would be that the sun, now only a little past its summer zenith, would be behind the aircraft. This trick had proven most effective in the past, especially at Midway. Even roaring out of the sky at full throttle and nearly straight down, the Dauntless would still take nearly two minutes to reach bomb release altitude. If the Zeroes were down close to the deck, as they'd been when Wade McCluskie had dived on *Kaga* just a few months ago, they'd be all but useless. Should the Zekes be up high, why then the Wildcats could tangle with them while Felt and his SBDs dove and the Avengers went low to launch their pickles.

"Got 'em, skipper!" Trigger shouted excitedly. "Think that little toy boat way down there is the Nip flattop!"

"Okay, Trig, keep your skivvies on," Felt replied with overly exaggerated aplomb. His heart set to hammering in his chest. "No need to get riled up. Just a war is all… All right, put me on the horn."

The bombardier also acted as radioman and opened the general channel to the rest of the flight, "Stepping up to the mic… the silky sounds of Smokey Felt and his orchestra…."

Laughter over the channel and Felt had to suppress a grin, "Looks like we found Tojo, boys. We're goin' in three waves. Avengers, you circle down and get to the deck. Wildcats, follow us in and watch for Zekes. Your priority is the Avengers. Dive one, then Dive two, and then I'll take the final plunge. You fellas ready?"

"*Ready!?*" came the incredulous response from Lieutenant Eddie Baker, dive one's flight leader. "*I've had a five-foot hard-on for the past fifteen minutes!*"

"*Guy's always gettin' his centimeters and feet scrambled!*" guffawed Lieutenant Mike Waggoner, leading Dive two. "*Now get your stubby ass down to the deck and make way so that I can show you clowns how a* real man *sinks him a carrier!*"

Laughs and cheers and catcalls filtered over the channel from the pilots and their crews. Felt's face was nearly split in two by his grin. His men needed this kind of apparently careless bravado. They were about to dive down into a fleet of ten ships with their ack-ack going like mad. They'd all heard or had seen pilots smashed into the sea or burn in midair during an attack. They needed the spirits.

"Okay, you turkeys," Felt said. "You can yuck it up later when we update the greenie board. For now, let's go to work. Dive one, you're away!"

Felt throttled back to let Baker get ahead. After a moment, the eight planes of Dive one threw up a wing, rolled over and nosed down into an eighty-degree full-power dive. Even as Felt led his planes into a slow orbit, he could swear that the winding up roar of the diving planes' engines reached him.

The radio squawked and crackled, and voices began to flood over the channel. Felt could hear Baker's bombardier calling out the altitude by the two-thousands. Finally, after an eternity, Baker screamed the release order and Felt banked his bird so that he and Trigger could peer down through six miles of sky at the sea below. There were a few wisps of clouds, but the tableau below was in no way obscured. The carrier, made tiny by perspective, was suddenly surrounded by pinpricks of white foam. Felt counted eight microscopic splashes and cursed under his breath.

"Your turn at the plate, Mike… let's see whatcha got!" Felt ordered and watched as the nine planes of Waggoner's group accelerated into their dive.

Once again, to the consternation of Felt and the men of the second dive attack, every bomb splashed harmlessly into the sea. One or two exploded, sending up huge plumes of water tantalizingly close to *Ryujo,* but none came close enough even to cause minor damage.

It was strange, Felt thought as he maneuvered to lead his own planes down to the deck. No one had reported a single Zeke. The ships below were sending up streamers of bright tracer rounds, their elongated fingers tearing through the sky in intermingling cones of death. In spite of the Japanese gunner's zeal, however, not a single Dauntless had been hit as yet.

But where was *Ryujo's* cap? Where were the Zeroes or even bombers to defend her?

"You're not getting off this time, bitch," Felt muttered to the defiant carrier below, steaming at over thirty knots and weaving to avoid destruction. "Not from this guy you ain't… Dive three! On my six! And look sharp, boys! These goddamned half-ton eggs we're carrying ain't cheap, huh? Don't waste 'em!"

"Tallyho!" Trigger whooped as Felt threw his ship over and shoved the throttle to the stop.

Now there was no doubt that he could hear it. His Pratt and Whitney radial engine revved up from a modest throaty hum to a roaring, almost shrieking scream. Wind howled around the canopy, buffeting the plane and making the men's teeth chatter as the Dauntless powered down at more than two and a half times terminal velocity. The air rapidly thickened around them, and the sounds of the engines, the howl of the wind and the continuous shuddering of the airplane grew in intensity.

This was what it was all about. This was why Felt had joined up. These eighty seconds of sheer, thrilling terror in which a man lived on the true razor's edge of life was nearly impossible to describe to anyone who hadn't lived it themselves. He'd once *tried* to explain it to a buddy who had never flown, let alone in combat or dived on an enemy.

"It's sort of like that first drop on a big roller coaster, y'know? Except... an order of magnitude more frightening and exhilarating," Felt had declaimed. "No... it's like this, Stew... imagine you're having the best sex of your life, and you're about to hit the finish line... and then you blow your stack, but instead of that usual three seconds, it just keeps going on and on and *on!* And the whole time, you're also afraid that at any second your heart will explode... and you have to try and think through this, to remember to watch your altimeter and your oil pressure and fuel and all the other minutiae that a nice head-busting orgasm would make it tough to do. Then at the last second, you gotta throw on the brakes and pull out... no pun intended... or you die! It's just... well, it's just nutty is all."

"Twelve thousand!" Trigger was screaming.

Christ, had he dropped twenty-four thousand feet without even realizing it?

"Ten... eight... *six!*" Trigger was almost hysterical. "Good line up, Harry! Keep her steady now! Four... two... eighteen hundred... sixteen... hit the brakes! Bomb's away!"

Felt applied his air brakes a second before Trigger's finger squeezed the release mechanism. The Dauntless seemed to jerk upward as if on a rubber band, causing the restraint to dig into the men's shoulders, chest and waist painfully. Felt gritted his teeth through the two Gs of acceleration, threw the stick over, and felt his vision grey out slightly as the G forces increased and suddenly went to port.

"A hit!" Trigger whooped. "A hit, skipper! We got that slant-eyed son of a bitch!"

Felt glanced to the side and saw a pillar of oily smoke rising from the center of the light carrier's flight deck. The pillar was joined by a massive tongue of flame that reached toward the sky, tossing out bits of something into the air and sea.

"Woo-hoo!" Felt exalted as he banked his aircraft and began his evasive climb to get away from the anti-aircraft fire. As he cleared the immediate danger, Felt saw three more hits erupt on the carrier's deck and swore that a pillar of fiery water shot into the air near the vessel's port bow.

"*YEAH!* We got 'em, fellas!" Felt whooped in delight. "Damned fine work! Now, unless you all got dates I don't know about, what say we make for Henderson and run down that Jap's planes, huh? Give the Marines a hand. We got plenty of ammo in the cannons!"

Felt's victorious squadron flew toward the southwest. No one razzed any of the men who'd missed. That was part of the game and why dive-bomb attacks made use of so many planes. On the surface of it, hitting a five-, six-, seven- or eight-hundred-foot ship would seem easy. Yet from fifteen or twenty thousand feet and more, those thousands of square feet of deck looked like a postage stamp. It was remarkably difficult to do. Yet when it happened, every plane in the attack shared in the glory. They were a team and were as one. One single, dedicated machine bent on victory.

At the same moment that *Ryujo* received her mortal blows, the lone floatplane sent out hours before by the cruiser *Chikuma* also sighted the battleship gray coloring of warships below them. The plane emerged from a raft of puffy clouds, and the two pilots were momentarily stunned and shocked to see multiple ships only a few miles ahead of them. Two of the ships were very clearly big American carriers.

Both men were so surprised that their reaction time was slowed. The pilot recovered first, punching his observer lightly in the arm and ordering him to get on the radio and report the position. Yet even as he did so, angry lances of crimson streaked up toward them from the screening battleship, cruisers and destroyers. The co-pilot had hardly finished his report, struggling to maintain control over his voice as his partner threw the aircraft over into a wild hairpin turn in an attempt to escape the fate that raced toward them.

It would prove useless. The sturdy Aichi floatplane was struck by a hammer blow, then another and then by many blows. The big shells ripped the plane apart, igniting fuel, and turning what was left of the men and the machine into a rapidly expanding ball of fire and death.

Yet it hadn't come soon enough to prevent the radio report that made it back to *Shokaku*. A radio report that set multiple waves of Japanese aircraft into the air with murderous intent.

32
KIDO BUTAI - 150 MILES N, NE OF GUADALCANAL
AUGUST 24, 1942 – 1525 SHIP'S TIME

All was quiet.

He lay on his bed, although there was something odd about that. For one thing, bright sunlight was streaming in through large bay windows. That in itself was odd, yet he couldn't understand why. The bed was far larger than it should have been. In some vague part of his mind, he felt that there should only be enough room for him to lay on, not spread out in great comfort.

And there was no sound… all was silent, and the familiar low vibration that he knew should even then be gently caressing his bones was gone. The bright and even cheerful room didn't just feel wrong; it suddenly filled him with an inexplicable dread. A dread that was even then closing its cold hand of fear around his heart.

Then, suddenly, the light was gone. No… not gone… diminished nearly to night. That's when the sound came, and his fear expanded into a paralyzing terror.

There were screams from somewhere, and then the entire ceiling of the room and most of the walls were rent, torn violently away to expose a vista of ocean that stretched off into eternity. Save for one huge dark shape that blotted out the sun.

Something so monstrous that his mind couldn't begin to catalog it looked down on him from high above with huge, cold reptilian eyes. The flesh of the thing... no, not flesh... it was scaly and as dark green as seaweed... and it was slick with damp. The thing's hideous mouth yawned open, and a roar that seemed to echo through time and space nearly deafened him. A huge, clawed hand seized him, lifted him high into the air, his silent screams unable to find voice.

He was now face to face with the monster, far up in the air. Its massive eyes studied him and the mouth, wide enough to swallow a boxcar, began to move in a grotesque approximation of speech.

"You are needed in Command, Admiral!" the monster's screeching, roaring voice said deferentially.

Nagumo shot bolt upright on his bunk, sweat beading on his forehead and beneath his shirt. The knocking from his door brought him back to reality, and he drew in a steadying breath.

"Yes?" he asked far more calmly than he felt.

"Admiral, we have word of *Ryujo*," a muffled voice said. "Admiral Kusaka wishes your presence on the navigation bridge."

Nagumo got to his feet and began to put on his white summer uniform jacket. Even as he followed the messenger down the corridor and up one level to the bridge deck, he pondered the dream. What might it mean? He'd always put great stock in interpreting his dreams... and that one was certainly ominous and did not instill confidence.

"Ah, Admiral san," Kusaka said gravely. "I thought you should be told... *Ryujo* has been attacked and evacuated. Admiral Hara has escaped and transferred his flag to *Jinsu*. There is no hope for the carrier... as we feared."

"No, my friend, no... we knew this going in," Nagumo said. "But now we must make certain that they did not lose their ship and that those who did not live didn't die in vain. Launch the attack group now. Have *Zuikaku* launch theirs fifteen minutes later. What is the status of our air cover?"

"Twenty Zeroes orbiting," Kusaka said. "Ten at one thousand meters and ten at five thousand meters."

"Good," Nagumo said. "Once the attack flight has launched, ready the relief fighters. Same orders for *Zuikaku*. We will not be caught unawares this time, Kusaka... not *this time*."

On the flight deck of the big carrier, three dozen airplanes lined up and were catapulted toward history. First, the torpedo bombers, then the dive bombers, and finally, the escorting fighters winged into the mostly clear sky. It was a glorious sight to behold, made even more so when the *Shokaku's* sister carrier sent the same number of planes into the sky. Thanks to the ill-fated scout, Nagumo now knew exactly where to find Fletcher's task force, and there *would be* retribution on that day. It would be Fletcher whose heart would break as he watched his precious carriers slip below the waves...

"Sir! Sir!" a lookout from outside all but shrieked. "Dive bombers incoming!"

Nagumo's belly performed a neat and nauseating barrel-roll. His exaltation of a moment before now had the taste of bitter ashes. Had that been what the dream was trying to tell him? That his arrogance was about to get them all destroyed?

The fleet's anti-aircraft guns began to chatter and thump in response. The Admiral couldn't help but be taken back to early June when he stood on the observation deck of *Akagi* and watched in fascinated horror as tiny black dots fell from the sky and delivered fiery death to his mighty fleet.

"It's only a small squadron!" Kusaka shouted almost into Nagumo's ear as the two men raced outside to see for themselves. "Look! The Zeroes are on them!"

It was true. The ten high-orbiting fighters pounced on the slower Dauntlesses. Immediately, two of them exploded into black-orange fireballs. Another two were picked off even as they dove toward *Zuikaku*. Two of them, however, made it through, and they grew from tiny black dots into the deadly shape of bombers with remarkable swiftness. From their bellies, two black shapes separated and plunged down... down...

The ship was jolted, rocked first to port and then to starboard. Kusaka and Nagumo reached out to clutch one another's arm to steady themselves, but the disturbance was short-lived.

"No damage!" someone shouted. "Near misses only!"

Kusaka's eyes gleamed with triumph, "The Americans have had their go, sir! And now our seventy-two aircraft will have *theirs!*"

Nagumo, despite everything, found himself smiling, "And let us pray that they do, Kusaka san."

USS *ENTERPRISE* – 135 MILES SE OF GUADALCANAL

"Message from Saratoga, Captain," the messenger of the watch said as he stepped up to the situation board. "They've detected three dozen aircraft on radar, headed this way. Bearing roughly zero-two-zero true."

Captain Arthur Davis ashed his Marlboro into a tray resting on the lip of the table. It was damned near overflowing with dead butts and ash. He stared at the pile of burnt cigarettes for a long moment, feeling as though he should find some deep significance in them. Sort of the way Julius Caesar would take the auspices before a battle.

There were no entrails to read here, though. No patterns in the smoke. For all that hokum, Davis had always believed that Caesar did it to appease his men. He'd been successful because he knew where to position his troops and how to manage them. Now Davis and *Enterprise,* along with Ramsey and *Saratoga,* had to put their men in the right place and at the right time.

"Anything else, petty officer?" Davis asked in that stoic, confident captain's tone that they all so expected to hear.

"Yes sir," the younger man said with evident eagerness. "We're clear to launch our attack birds and get our Defenders up."

"Acknowledge that," Davis said. He stepped over to where Rear Admiral Thomas Kincaid stood with the ship's CAG, Lieutenant Commander Max Lesley, conferring softly. The two men, one in his early thirties and the other close to fifty-five, looked at the ship's captain expectantly.

"We're a go," Davis said. "Max, get your attack birds aloft and then spot the Wildcats. We got thirty-six japs inbound, and I'll bet dollars to donuts that's only half of them."

"Aye-aye, Skipper," Lesley said and moved to the nearest telephone set.

"How you feelin', Art?" Kincade asked as he lit his pipe.

Davis flashed him a grin, "Better with that bowl going, sir. The boys kinda think your pipe is their good luck charm… and I'm one of them."

Kincade smiled thinly, "Glad to hear it. Wife is constantly on me to give the thing up… but… well, now I've got a good excuse, don't I?"

Davis grinned, "Yes sir… excuse me a moment… helmsmen, right standard rudder. Come to course one-two-zero. All ahead full. Standby to receive course correction from flight director."

The huge ship's four propellers began to churn the sea into froth as she turned and accelerated into the steady fifteen knot southeasterly trades. Far out on the horizon, Davis could see the distinct profile of *Saratoga* doing the same. The two ships were a dozen miles apart, but from the lofty height of the navigation bridge, Davis could easily see the other big carrier's hull.

Douglas SBD Dauntless dive bombers and Grumman Avengers soared into the blue sky. The two carriers sent as many planes up as had their Japanese counterparts. It now remained for each attack wing to seek its targets and do its best… or worst. Before the sun set on this day, everyone knew, the balance of naval power in the Pacific could change once again.

Next came the F4F wildcats. Twenty-four from each carrier. A smaller number of aircraft than the seventy-two now incoming, yet these Wildcats had but one job: to attack the Kates and Vals and keep their weapons away from the carriers. They'd have to tangle with the Zekes, too, but the Wildcats at least had the advantage over the bombers.

"Let's go down to PriFly," Davis suggested to Kincade once the ship was on course and the Wildcats had lifted off.

The two men went down one level and found Lesley working with the flight coordinator and the row of radio techs. The room was not unlike the CIC or navigation center of the ship, with a situation board and men working plots at its center. However, there were also officers and assistants posted to coordinate with gun crews along with several individual radio sets for the radiomen to communicate with the aircraft flight leaders and coordinate the action.

Almost immediately upon entering, however, both Davis and Kincade could see that chaos was brewing. Nearly twenty men were chattering, exchanging reports and shouting over one another. Radar techs were updating their supervisors, who were updating the plotting party, and Lesley and the flight coordinator. Other men were relaying radio reports from planes and to the planes from Lesley. It was barely controlled chaos, and both senior officers stayed out of the way but watched everything with close attention.

"Cats one through six, engage!" Lesley ordered, and the radio tech went to work. He cast a glance over to the captain and admiral. "We've met the Japs sir. Wildcats are engaging."

In the sky, thousands of feet above the sea, nearly a hundred planes merged into a great buzzing, cloud-like, gargantuan hornet's nest. Red and green tracers flashed across the sky, radial engines roared, and metal birds winged and soared and looped around one another. Sometimes in pairs, sometimes in threes and sometimes in half a dozen or more. Each jockeying for position and advantage.

Over the radio and in the flight control centers of both carriers and the radio shacks of all the escorting warships, dozens of garbled messages flew through the ether. Pilots shouted reports, requests and warnings at their ships and at one another. So much so that it became impossible to make any single conversation out.

"...*on my six... break, break, break!*"

"*Badman four... Badman four, you got a pair of Zekes....*"

"*For Christ's sake, Tucker... watch your ass, he's—*"

"*I'm hit! I'm hit! Parrot six... going....*"

"*...splash one Val! Take that you fuckin'—*"

"*Mayday! Mayday!*"

"*Watch it, three!* Enterprise! Enterprise! *Evasive! You've got incoming....*"

That last message was chillingly clear. Davis sprang forward, taking hold of a phone talker by his sleeve and opened his mouth to shout something, but his words were drowned out by a tremendous thundering boom that shook the entire ship like a paint mixer. Several alarms began to blare at once. Collision alarms screeched, fire alarms blared, and dozens of voices began to shout in fear, anger and confusion.

Davis ran to an inboard viewport where admiral Kincade was pointing down to the flight deck and shouting something incoherent. Davis nearly slammed the man into the viewport as he slid to a stop to peer out and see what the admiral was so excited about.

Enterprise's captain swore his heart skipped a beat when his eyes beheld the sight two decks below and astern. A furious orange-white pillar of fire rose like some insane blow torch near the after elevator. The tongue of flame shot fifty feet into the air, belching greasy black smoke and bits of debris that flew up and twisted like a fourth of July fireworks fountain.

"My God..." Kincade said. "How far down did that one get...?"

Seconds later, a second Val made it through the screen of Wildcats and curtain of flak from the carrier and her escorts. This one's bomb landed only a few dozen feet from the first, punching down through the flight deck and exploding in a flight magazine, igniting ordnance and sending another dragon's breath of flame roaring into the sky. With it came bits of steel and hunks of burning wooden flight deck. Around the fires, men raced, first toward them and then away. Others were thrown across the deck like rag dolls. Some living and some flaring like human torches.

"God help us...." Davis muttered in awed horror.

The final strike, coming shortly after, hit the flight deck near the number two elevator. Once more, the great ship bucked and heaved, and debris went soaring... but the damage, at least seen from flight control, seemed light.

Davis and Kincade met one another's eyes. It was bad, but somehow both men knew that their mighty carrier was still in the fight. How they knew this couldn't be explained, but both fervently believed she'd survive the day.

Several decks down from the flight deck, below the waterline, things didn't seem so optimistic. The first five-hundred-pound bomb had plunged through the flight deck, hanger deck and several more, its mass and kinetic energy smashing through level after level after level until it could penetrate no further.

427

The bomb, dented and warped by impacts and heat, stopped its plunge in the center of the firemen and boiler maker's mess. The resulting explosion was mostly contained by the compartment, the majority of its fiery destruction following the holes it had punched and rising to lick at the sky.

Unfortunately, there were thirty-five men who had been released from battle stations to head to the mess and grab a quick cup of coffee and a sandwich. Their deaths, which were horrific, were at least mercifully instantaneous. The compartment was filled with fire and pressure, and anything that wasn't solid steel was blasted into bits and nearly vaporized. Great gouts of white-hot fire and debris coughed out into the passageways, adding four more lives to the thirty-one who'd died while grabbing a quick snack. Several other men were wounded as they rushed into the scorching heat with whatever came to hand in order to fight the blaze that was consuming the mess and threatening to flow through the rest of the deck like a volcanic eruption.

On the hangar deck, about midway along, aviation machinist's mate Bernard Peterson suddenly found himself flat on his back and didn't know how he'd gotten there. The last thing he remembered, he was racing across the deck toward an emergency equipment station to try and activate one of the fire suppression hoses. A bomb had struck aft… then another and a huge wave of flame…

Peterson struggled to sit up, becoming aware that half his body seemed coated in hot coals. He looked down at himself and saw that his flight crew coverall was half blackened, and on the blackened side, standing out starkly against the flaking carbonized fabric were several patches of bright red. Blood… his blood. he absently took hold of a jagged bit of metal with his sunburned, or so it appeared, fingers and pulled it from the flesh of his right thigh, releasing a fresh warm gush of deep red.

The world around him had gone mad. Men ran back and forth; some lay on the deck and didn't move… just laid there like lumps… couldn't they hear the alarms? Couldn't they see the fires?

Peterson tried to stand, and a wave of nausea nearly dropped him to the deck again. Blindly, he reached out and flailed, his left hand finding something solid to steady himself. The petty officer clung to this whatever it was while the nausea crested and broke on the shores of his guts in a foaming explosion that sent what remained of his lunch hurtling out and onto the deck in a chunky pinkish gout of vomit.

"Oh... Christ..." Peterson groaned, squeezing his eyes shut and praying to God for the dizziness to end.

It passed, or at least the wave retreated to something manageable. Peterson began to lurch across the deck once more, forgetting about the fire hose that had only been a few feet behind him and instead being drawn by the sounds of weapons fire and screams from the flight deck twenty feet over his head. He made it to the nearest companionway and stumbled up the steps like a drunk, clutching the handrails and using his other hand to push off the risers lest he fell face-first on their checkered metal surfaces.

Finally, he seemed to burst out into bright sunlight all at once and was immediately overwhelmed by the chaos that reigned. Fires blazed from the craters in the thick wooden decking that made up the flight deck. Avgas and oil spills snaked across the huge surface, some burning like rivers of fire. Around and between the destruction lay men. Some were unconscious, some burned and some with missing limbs. Fifty feet away, Peterson spotted a man dragging himself toward the rim of the deck, one of his legs was gone, and a gory crimson snail trail led thirty feet away to where a blackened and bloody something hideous lay abandoned against the brightly painted deck. Peterson began to move then, understanding for what the man intended blooming as white-hot in his mind as the fires that had singed him. He tried to cry out, tried to find a way to dissuade the man, who he now realized was screaming in an odd, almost dazed way. Like his mouth was on autopilot, and he was only screaming because he thought he was supposed to rather than from any stimulus of pain.

Yet Peterson, his own body burnt and peppered by shrapnel and his head foggy from a concussion, was too late. The legless man reached the edge of the deck and pushed himself off with one final mighty heave of his good leg and his one good arm... oh Jesus... and vanished from sight.

Not far from where the wounded man had committed suicide, Peterson saw a 20mm Oerlikon crew tending to one of their men, who lay on the deck and moaned pitifully and kept yelling that he couldn't see, couldn't see!

He lurched over to the three men, "Who's the gunner here!"

"Kendrick!" one of the sailors said, pointing at the wounded man. "His eyes… I think he mighta took some flak!"

Peterson bent down, nearly vomiting again, and inspected Kendrick. He had to forcibly pull the man's hands from his face. The face was singed, and there was a dark oily substance covering most of it, but no damage to the eyes.

"He's got oil in his eyes!" Peterson said. "One of you get him below and find a corpsman. You there, help me with the gun. You're my new loader! Come on, dammit! The fuckin' Japs are comin' in for another run!"

Peterson shoved the man toward the hardened ammo locker while he himself slid the butt strap over his backside and took hold of the weapons' handles. He could see that two belts still fed into the twin mount and swung the gun around, pointed it skyward toward a flight of three tiny white Zekes and squeezed the triggers.

Davis had left flight control after the third bomb had detonated. By the time he reached the bridge, his executive officer had managed to calm everyone down and gotten them focused.

"Neil, what's the sitch up here?" Davis asked as he barged in and nearly went ass over tea kettle when his foot slid on a loose sheet of paper on deck.

"We've lost some engine power," the Exec said. "And we're getting no response from the rudder. She's over to right standard from our last maneuver and won't answer the helm!"

"We've got fire in a dozen compartments on three decks, sir," the damage control officer broke in. "Firefighters are putting out bedding… oil fires… the works."

"How about the flight deck?" Davis asked.

"Getting those blazes under control," the DCO replied, his gaunt features having gone ashy even under the sheen of sweat there. "We'll have steel plates rigged. I've got Chief Bill Smith on the horn for you, sir."

Davis took the offered phone and noticed Kincade rushing onto the bridge and moving toward him, "Chief, this is the captain, go ahead!"

"*Sir, I'm outside the steering compartment,*" the forty-three-year-old chief machinist's mate reported and coughed. "*I can see a blaze in there, and I think it's knocked out the primary rudder control motor. I've got a fire suit and an O2 tank, and I'm gonna go in and try to switch over to number two manually.*"

Kincade was close enough now to hear the conversation over the phone clearly, "Christ on a soda cracker...."

Davis met his eyes and nodded grimly, "Chief... you think you can get to it without getting cooked?"

A long pause, "*Hell, sir... it's gotta be tried, don't it? If not me who.*"

"If not now when," Davis replied. That had been a running joke between himself and the chief, a man with whom he'd served for several years. He drew in a breath, knowing that his next words might send a good man to his death... to join the nearly one-hundred others that had been reported. "Chief... Bill... go ahead and give it a go... but if you think it's too risky...."

"*I'll get her goin' again, Skipper... you got my word on that.*"

Smith had been as good as his word. In just five minutes, he'd not only fought his way past the flames and activated the auxiliary rudder motor, but he'd also organized a firefighting party and had doused the blaze in the steering compartment. Within an hour, the Japanese aircraft having long departed, *Enterprise* was under control and making twenty-four knots. Damage repair crews had contained the fires and had plated the flight deck. The huge ship was now beginning to recover her aircraft, at least the Wildcats.

After landing his Wildcat, which had no less than sixteen holes of both 20mm and 7.62mm delivered by two Zeroes, Lieutenant Fred Mears made his way wearily to the starboard quarter companion. The stairs led down into the hangar deck near one of the ship's after five-inch and anti-aircraft weapons galleries. The stench of burnt things...

things that shouldn't be burning caught the pilot's attention, and he turned from continuing to the pilot's locker room to check it out. He had to admit that his curiosity was getting the better of him. He'd seen his beloved Big-E take those three punches and some part of him simply had to know how bad it was.

In the next moment, as he passed through the open blast door, the horror he experienced entirely wiped away any curiosity he'd been nursing. The scene before him was like something out of Dante's worst nightmare.

There were nearly twenty men still in the gallery... or what had once been twenty men. Every single sailor there had been roasted to a blackened husk. Their bodies had burnt so hotly and so fast that most of them hadn't even had time to realize they were dying. Their clothing and hair were gone, but the coal-black shells of men still held their shapes like wrought-iron statues. Some men lay on deck in grotesque positions, as one would expect. Yet the true horror came when Mears saw that there were men still seated at their guns. One man still had his charcoal hand on the elevation wheel of his weapon. Another had been caught in the act of opening a breech, his body frozen like black ice when the indescribable heat must have washed through the place like a tidal wave.

Mears stood there agape for a long, long time. He couldn't speak, couldn't move... at one point, he thought he might have raised a hand to cover his mouth, but he wouldn't remember that part later.

Yet what he would remember... what would haunt his dreams for the rest of his life, were those charred things that had once been living, breathing American sailors. The nightmares wouldn't last too long, as sadly Lieutenant Mears, who served bravely on that day and at Midway before, would die in a tragic airplane crash while leaving San Diego in June of 1943. He would be returning to duty after a much-deserved shore leave.

In something of an ironic twist, neither *Enterprise's* nor *Saratoga's* attack groups found Nagumo's carriers. By the time the sun was nearly kissing the western horizon, the Kido Butai had turned north, thinking that they'd sunk an American carrier and damaged another, and Fletcher had ordered the entirety of Task Force 61 to head south for much-needed fuel.

Two hundred miles north, the last group of *Enterprise's* attack group, flight three hundred, was beginning to run low on fuel. Lieutenant Turner Caldwell, who was in charge of the group, consulted with his second in command on the subject.

"What do you think, Harry... think we can find Big-E before it's pitch out there?" Caldwell asked.

There was a pause over the radio circuit before Harold Beule replied, *"Dunno, Skipper... I kinda doubt it, and Thumbs concurs. We got what, thirty, forty minutes of good light left? Even if we push it to the firewall, our girl is at least an hour away."*

Caldwell sighed, "Yeah... but Henderson is half that. Guess we're gonna go visit the Marines and check out their new digs."

Beule laughed, *"Been there once already... didn't land, it was still in jap hands that day... but was happy to drop a nice easter egg on the slants then."*

"Well, I guess that makes you our tour guide, Harry," Caldwell said, making up his mind. "Take point and lead us to Jarhead city."

The planes banked lazily and put the setting sun a bit to starboard of their noses. They flew for Guadalcanal, never realizing that the Japanese surface fleet and the carriers they proceeded were no more than ten minutes over the horizon.

33
THE SAVAGE ISLANDS
AUGUST 24, 1942 – 1920 LOCAL TIME

After seeing *Inatei* explode and break into multiple pieces, it became clear to all that Turner had arrived. It also became clear that he'd scored the first point in the contest. It was at this point that Sato began to worry.

It wasn't so much that he was afraid that the loss of one escort would doom him. It was more that he had expected to win so easily and now must face the fact that Turner wasn't going to allow that to happen.

He considered several options. First, he thought of calling for Captain Yamata's three-ship squadron to join the fray and hunt down the submarine. It was one thing for Turner to aggressively attack a single destroyer. This was more of a fair match. It would be another entirely for him to try and sink three of them... especially with Japan's most celebrated anti-submarine warfare officer in command.

Yet there was another factor to take into account, although Sato had no proof of it. There was a strong probability that Turner was not alone - that there was another submarine with him now. I-123 could easily confirm this, yet she had been ordered to remain still and silent for the time being. Two submarines against three destroyers could be a different matter altogether. Without knowing their location, the two boats could strike simultaneously and even the odds.

Then there was *Sakai* to consider. She had recently recovered her combat air patrol of ten Zeroes. Her Aichi D3 dive bombers were en route and would need to trap within the next hour or so. This put the ship in some danger, as so much attention must be paid to recovering the aircraft. She would be vulnerable.

So, Sato had ordered the strike carrier to proceed into the center of the semi-lagoon formed by the four islands. Lieutenant Arawi had objected, saying that the passages were narrow and that the mean depth of the lagoon was only about a dozen meters.

"Excellent," Sato had objected. "We only draw eight. As for the passages, we will proceed carefully, Yakuin. Once inside the lagoon, we will be able to recover our planes and launch again without needing to worry that half a dozen torpedoes will suddenly appear during the process."

Arawi looked pained, but he recognized when a command had been given and when he was expected to obey, "*Hai*. Shall I order a change of armaments, sir?"

Sato had turned to Hideki and Osaka, who'd come back to the CIC after a time. He cast a questioning glance at Hideki.

"I suppose that all aircraft should be loaded with depth charges," Hideki had stated. "The dive bombers can hold two each. This gives us a mobile attack force of thirty charges should we need them."

"Concur," Sato said. "Order the flight and hangar decks to do as the CAG suggests. And what of you, Commander? Have you any thoughts on how we might find or draw Turner out into the open? He has scored a kill and may now be hungry for more."

Osaka did indeed have an idea. An idea that might, in fact, level the playing field. It was risky and would require him to take a definite step that, if discovered, would be difficult if not impossible to explain. First, though, he had a question.

"What of The Sensei?" Osaka asked. "Should he not be called in from his standby position to go on active search and destroy?"

Sato snapped a lighter in front of a Golden Bat and made a show of deep consideration, "Not just yet, commander. If Turner and possibly his ally see those three ships and possibly identify them as the same ships that harassed him several days previous... he may elect to disengage altogether. Aside from my personal desire to sink the man, there is another consideration. By keeping two American submarines occupied, we are preventing them from hunting down our fleets. Just as *Ryujo* is acting as a decoy for the American airplanes, we must keep hold of our tiger's tail. Is it not so?"

Osaka nodded, "Indeed, Captain. Most wise. Then I suggest this: we send instructions for I-123 to go on an active search scan. In all likelihood, Turner knows she's out there, even if he can't prove it."

"Will this not expose I-123 to danger?" Arawi asked.

"Not very much," Osaka said. "A submarine is only vulnerable to a torpedo attack on the surface. Use her as you did the last time you faced Turner. Simply as an underwater beacon that occasionally broadcasts an active ping. It'll drive Turner mad and give us a clear picture of where he is, at least on the southeastern side of the atoll... or wherever I-123 moves."

"Will this not identify our position, Commander?" Sato asked with an arched eyebrow.

"We have a direct line of sight out to the I-123 from here," Osaka said. "On low power, our message will not travel outward very far. Even should the Americans hear it, it will be in code in any case. Also, what of it? It isn't as if Turner will come charging in here on the surface during daylight hours."

Sato had chuckled and nodded, "Very well. Compose your message and give it to sonar."

Osaka's message was simple, and he encoded it and wrote it on a sheet of paper for the active sonar technician to send. As he stood behind the two men, one manning the active sound system and the other the passive, he showed no outward sign of nervousness. Yet what he was doing was risky.

It was one thing to sneak communiques to Webster Clayton by overseas phone or telegraph. He had a series of contacts who could physically carry information to other contacts who could then send it. He had even sent a direct radio transmission once or twice to a ham radio operator under Clayton's employ. Yet what he was doing now was so bold as to almost seem arrogant. To send a coded message to Japan's enemies right under the nose of a ship's captain.

"Sir..." the sonar technician frowned. "I think... that is... I think I'm not getting any response from the active echolocator."

"You *think*, sailor?" Osaka feigned annoyance. This was entirely expected, and he knew that the man's gear was indeed not transmitting, and he knew why. "What of you, son? Are you detecting our broadcast?"

This last was asked of the other tech, the one on the passive listening set. The young man frowned, adjusted his equipment and shook his head.

"Nothing, sir."

"Dammit!" Osaka snapped, loud enough to draw the attention of the captain.

Sato and Hideki moved across the CIC to the sonar alcove. The captain inquired: "What is it?"

"There seems to be a short in the echolocation system," Osaka said. "We're not pinging."

"Then I suppose this plan of action is out," said Sato.

"Not necessarily, Captain," Osaka said. "Let us have the repair crews trace the circuit and locate the malfunction. It's probably a simple matter of a frayed wire or bad resistor someplace. I am well-versed in sonar equipment. I'll go down to the auxiliary sonar station and transmit under local control. Should we not locate the damage shortly, I can even remain there and supervise our sonar techs from that location so as not to lose any ASW capability."

"Very good," Sato said. He considered Osaka for what seemed a very long moment. "Please proceed, Commander... and thank you."

"*Hai*," Osaka said and bowed at the shoulder.

BULL SHARK – SOUTHEASTERN EDGE OF SAVAGE ISLANDS

It had been over three hours since the sinking of the Jap tin can. Since then, the boat had gone quiet and still. Turner had ordered the submarine secured from silent running and from depth charge but had passed the word for the men to go about their business as quietly as possible. This wasn't hard, as the tension of battle still hung in the air like a soupy fog.

Turner had won the first round of this boxing match, but it was far from over. Even if *Sakai* were now alone, she still had twenty airplanes at her disposal as well as her own ASW capabilities. And these included several dozen depth charges.

Not long after the destroyer, or what was left of her, had settled to the bottom, however, *Sakai* had done something strange. Chet Rivers said that she was moving toward the atoll and that her machinery signature was becoming garbled and muddy. After a time, it was apparently swallowed up entirely. Or the ship had killed her engines, which was unlikely. It had been Elmer Williams who suggested that the carrier might have gone inside the lagoon formed by the large island and the three smaller islets.

"Then we've got him trapped," Turner said with a wolfish smile. "We can take a peek with the scopes and maybe even send a few pickles in there."

"Maybe…" Williams had explained as he and Art stood at the master gyro table in the control room. "According to Chris' information, though, the passages into the lagoon are a bit twisted. Depth is good, obviously, but it might not be possible to send a fish straight in."

Turner had sighed then, "Of course not. God forbid we should catch a break. Either way, though, we've got him bottled up. We can report this position, and somebody can send a squadron of dive bombers after him. Only problem with that is that if the carrier has planes up, they'll spot us when we come up to radio depth."

"Not to mention they could use RDF to locate us," Andy Post said as he entered the control room with a clipboard in hand. "Then vector in bombers of their own to spank our bottoms."

"Worst case scenario," Turner said with a slight smile. "Is we wait until dark. Once the sun goes down, the carrier loses the advantage of her airwing. Then we and S-52 can creep inside that lagoon in the dark and give them a surprise. Our two five-inch guns and S-52's four-inch plus torpedoes... old Sato is gonna wish his father never met his mother, by God!"

So, they had waited as the hours ticked slowly past. Turner took that time to tour the boat, speaking to the men and getting a visual and local update from each compartment. Any minor damage from the previous depth charging had been cleaned up. Inspections were performed on vital electrical and plumbing systems.

The pasting they'd taken several days before from the squadron of destroyers had left the boat with quite a few casualties. That damage had been repaired, but much of it was patchwork or jury-rigged. Turner was having every item gone over twice and reinforced if necessary.

He was now in the forward room, conversing with Sparky and his gang. There had been some flooding here when the bow buoyancy tank had been damaged. The flooding had been contained, and the water pumped out, but the tank itself had not been able to be blown dry.

"My guess is we got damage up on the bow," Sparky said, pointing directly overhead. "That charge probably blew off a chunk of our nose, and some debris jammed a vent or broke one off."

"Like that time in June," Tommy Perkins added.

"What happened?" Hazard, who was the watch engineer while Nichols got some rack time, asked.

Turner grimaced and shook his head, "We tangled with a Jap light cruiser and this monstrosity of a submarine about seven hundred miles from Midway a day or two before the big dust-up. Took some ashcan damage. Got some debris caught in the vents of MBT number six-A. Had to unjam it and weld the vent shut."

Hazard shook his head, "Anybody ever tell you fellas this submarine binness was dangerous?"

Perry Wilkes lit a smoke and chuckled, "Yeah... but the stories sure do get the broads goin', sir."

Sparky chuffed, "It *might* get the broads goin'... if'n we ever got some shore leave, sir."

Turner laughed, "Yeah, ain't it the truth... how about our pickle cannons, Sparky?"

Sparks sighed, "Number five and six are on the fritz, sir. They's got electrical shorts, blown impulse valves and the outer doors are jammed part-way open. Can't close 'em with electrical, and we tried with the Y-wrenches, and they only went about three-quarters of the way."

Turner sighed, "Great… well, that still leaves us with eight tubes in all. What about the torpedoes in those tubes?"

"Ain't none in there now, skipper," Sparky said. "We unloaded to do the electrical inspection, as you ordered before… but without having them fully functional, we didn't reload."

"Well, that's something anyway," Turner said. "Gives us use of all of our remaining fish at least."

"This lady could really use some time in a drydock, sir," Tommy Perkins put in.

Turner sighed, "Yeah, we've been beatin' her up pretty hard the last few months and a couple of days in port isn't gonna cut it. I'll see that we get our two weeks in Pearl after this or know the reason why. Okay, fellas, good work."

The 1MC circuit hissed open, and Andy Post's voice echoed through the ship, *"Captain Turner, please report to the radio shack. Incoming message."*

"What in the hell?" Hazard asked. "We're three hundred feet down."

Turner shrugged, "Sonar, I'd guess. Let's go see."

The two officers moved aft and were intercepted by Eddie Carlson with a couple of mugs of coffee.

"God bless you, Eddie," Turner said.

Hazard grinned, "I don't suppose you'd consider marryin' me, would ya', Eddie?"

Carlson scoffed, "No way, sir! My mama told me to hold out for a doctor or a nice, dreamy ship's captain at least."

Carlson and Hazard laughed aloud, and Turner shook his head, "Jesus Christ… we better surface soon and refresh the air down here. Buncha goddamned whack-jobs."

Turner was somewhat confused by the fact that he'd been asked to the radio room and not the conning tower and the sonar station. However, when he saw that Post was standing with Chet Rivers inside the tiny compartment and scanning the codebook, he figured he knew the answer.

"Sir... we've picked up a sonar message," Post said. "Well... Chet here picked it up... it's repeating, and part of it is in Jap code... don't think we're gonna crack it, but at first, I wasn't sure, so we ran it through our decoding procedures."

"Understood," Turner said, impatient to get to the point but not wanting to push.

"Well sir," Rivers said, "the first part is in code, as Mr. Post says... but the second half of the message is in plain Morse. English words and letters, too."

"You fellas gonna let us in on the secret or not?" Hazard asked with just a hint of pique in his tone.

Post smiled sheepishly, "Sorry sir... it's just... odd. Here's what we've got. As I say, the messages repeated three times, and it's the same each time."

Turner accepted the bit of notepaper and examined the message, "Let's see... I 1-2-3... SS... 3 DD with ASW expert NW 15km... hmm... if I read that right, then we've got a Jap submarine out here called the I-123. We knew that, mostly. Then I think there are three destroyers to the northwest of the atoll about nine miles offshore with an anti-submarine warfare expert with them. Well, I'll be damned...."

"Who sent this?" Hazard asked.

Turner frowned, "Well... if I had to guess, I'd have to say Shadow. Commander Osaka. He was taken back to *Sakai* as far as I know... maybe he's still there."

"Or it's a trap, sir," Post opined.

Turner shook his head, "I don't think so, Andy. My gut says no. After all, this doesn't direct us to do anything, just gives us a picture of what we're facing... evens the odds, you might say. Buck!"

Rogers stepped away from the chart table and moved to the crowded open door to the radio shack, "Sir?"

Turner showed him the note, "I think we're getting a helping hand. Plot me a course around the atoll. I want to stay right at the fifty-fathom curve, or close to it, and end up one-hundred and sixty degrees from where we are now, on the northwestern side."

The COB examined the paper, and his brows rose, "You think this is Shadow, sir?"

Turner nodded. Rogers had actually met Osaka when he'd gone aboard the doomed *Leviathan* back in June, "I do, Buck. Either way, it's something to investigate."

"I wish we knew what this gobble-dee-gook was before the Morse," Rogers muttered. "Must mean—"

From outside the ship, a low whine began to grow rapidly louder. It quickly rose in pitch and volume until it thumped against *Bull Shark's* steel flanks.

Turner grinned at the COB, "Well, Buck, I think you just found out what the code said."

S-52 – TWO NAUTICAL MILES FROM *BULL SHARK*

Jarvis tapped the piece of notepaper thoughtfully, "Plain Morse code… and in English, too…."

"Think it's legitimate?" Chris Savage asked from beside him at the gyrocompass table.

"I think maybe yes," Jarvis said. "There's a Japanese officer by the name of Osaka who's been helping us out. Sending intelligence to an OSS man we know by the name of Clayton. Anyway, I think he's aboard the *Sakai* and might be telling the skipper what's out there waiting for us. Makes sense, too."

"Or it could be the Japs tryin' to lead us into a trap," Savage opined.

Jarvis sighed, "Maybe… but it does make sense. And since the carrier seems to have vanished, maybe inside the islands… it's something to sink our teeth into."

Before Savage could respond, a high-pitched ping resonated through the sea and gonged off S-52's hull. It was a powerful blast and couldn't have come from far away.

Not long after Jarvis had ordered S-52 to creep closer to the suspected location of the Japanese submarine, he'd ordered them to come to a stop. The truth was that without looking through the scope, which he was advised might be a bad idea, on account of the pressure

443

and that once the seals blew, it might be impossible to stop the leak, he could either run past the Jap or plow right into him.

Now, though, an active sonar ping had just been sent out from very close aboard. Jarvis was halfway up the ladder before the echo of the sonic impact had faded away.

"Bobby?" he asked as his head cleared the hatch combing.

Gaines knew what he wanted to know, "Bearing three-four-zero, sir... range five-hundred yards. I've got another contact bearing one-zero-five at three-eight-zero-zero. Probably *Bull Shark*."

"Then we got the bastard!" Jarvis said. "Chris, get up here!"

Savage was actually hot on Jarvis' heels and practically bowled him over as he bounded up the hatch and moved to slide into the TDC seat, "Workin' on it!"

"Christ, he knows we're here now," Jarvis said. "Damn, five bills... glad we stopped. Chris, I want all four tubes. Set depth on one and two to two-hundred and ninety feet. Three and four to two-eighty. Two degree spread."

"Sir! Mechanical transient!" Gaines half exclaimed, and half gulped. "Assess electric motors engaging and... and torpedo doors opening."

"Ballsy slope," Jarvis muttered. "He's gonna try for us. Come on, Chris!"

"I'm workin' on it," Savage said tersely.

Jarvis had the absurd shot that if this were a movie, it would be now that the score would soar and drums would beat. A rapid, tense staccato roll as Tyrone Power or Glen Ford worked his gear...

"Forget the solution, Jarvis said. "Set gyro for number one to three-four-five, number two is three-four-zero. Same for three and four! Come on, come on!"

"Ready!" Savage called out excitedly.

"Fire one!" Jarvis ordered and counted down the six longest seconds of his life. "Fire two... fire three... fire four! Close outer doors. Helm, all back two-thirds, left standard rudder! Diving officer, ten degree up bubble!"

"Fish running hot, straight and normal!" Gaines enthused.

It was literally a shot in the dark. They had a good chance of hitting, as the Japanese sub was likely bottomed at three-hundred feet. However, Jarvis knew several things that made him uncomfortable.

First, his torpedoes were not modified. There was a better than average chance the magnetic exploders wouldn't function. Second, whether they did or not, the Mark 14 tended to run ten to fifteen feet below the set depth. That was a large margin for error when trying to hit the hull of a submarine that was no more than sixteen feet tall, not counting the deck or conning tower. His four fish might slam into the bottom short or sail harmlessly over the I-123's decks.

The likelihood of a counterattack was low, of course. The Japanese had the same problem, at least as far as determining the precise depths of another submarine. That's why Jarvis had ordered S-52 to begin moving. By the time the Japs got a fish underway, the American submarine would simply no longer be where she had been. Hopefully, the Japanese boat would take longer to get underway. At least for the thirty-seconds the torpedoes needed to travel the short distance between the two submarines and arm themselves.

"More mechanical transients," Gaines said. "I think *Bull Shark* is getting underway, too, sir."

"Time?" Jarvis asked even though he was counting down in his own head.

"Ten-seconds," Savage replied tensely, his fingers crossing of their own volition.

"Put sonar output on the squawk, Bobby," Jarvis ordered.

A switch was hit, and the scream of steam-powered torpedo engines filled the conning tower. Everyone counted down the seconds for the first torpedo. There was what sounded like a prolonged thump.

"Miss on number one," Gaines said glumly. "She plowed into the bottom."

Six-seconds passed, and then what sounded like a gonging. The second torpedo had found the mark but had failed to explode. Jarvis let fly a string of foul oaths.

"Maybe it'll do some damage," Cleghorn said with a shrug. "Forty-six knot missile striking a ballast tank could do somethin' maybe...."

"Torpedo three... six, seven, eight... ran through the target bearing, sir," Gaines said flatly.

Jarvis sighed, "Damn these torpedoes! What the hell does BeauOrd expect us to—"

Thwack—BOOOOOOM!

The unique sound of a torpex explosion rolled through the boat with such volume that it hurt the men's ears. Almost immediately, the shockwave of the initial explosion struck the boat, buffeting her and forcing her bow down by nearly thirty degrees. Fortunately, the reverse movement and the up-angle on the planes kept her from striking the seabed.

After a long moment, the shock of what happened wore off, and Cleghorn was the first to recover himself.

"You got him, sir!" the quartermaster howled exuberantly. "Nailed that slant-eyed son of a bitch!"

The conning tower and control room erupted into cheers and exclamations of joy and pride that flowed outward and through the entire ship like a wave of its own. Every man aboard couldn't help but smile and beat his chest, figuratively or literally. For the first time since the patrol began, S-52 had made a kill. A damned unlikely one, at that.

Jarvis let the ruckus go on for a few seconds and then held up his hands, "All right, you monkies! As you were, for Christ's sake. Let's have a little dignity on deck. We still got a job to do. We're not out of the woods yet."

The men got themselves in hand and refocused on their tasks. Yet now, whether they be hard-liner Waters supporters, indifferent to who was at the con, or in Jarvis' corner… they were all filled with a sense of pride and purpose they hadn't felt in weeks. Without realizing it or without any conscious thought from anyone, the entire crew had suddenly solidified into a unified working unit. All for one and one for all.

All that is, except perhaps for one of them. For in his stateroom, Lieutenant Commander Bernard Waters' eyes suddenly popped open. He was more than a little bewildered, somewhat disoriented and filled with resolve to find out what the hell was going on aboard his ship.

34

Pat Jarvis pressed his face to the eyepiece of the search scope, being certain that the brim of the rain hat was redirecting the seawater away from his face. The sun had set, although there was still plenty of light for the time being. That wouldn't last long, however, as in the tropics, night and day changed hands faster than jujus in a jazz club.

After hitting the I-123, Jarvis had decided that it might be possible to do something more. Although they probably couldn't get a torpedo inside the lagoon without going in themselves... not a comforting prospect... there was another way to reach the fortified *Sakai*.

"It looks clear," Jarvis said, rotating through a complete circle. "No aircraft visible... and there's the bastard! I've got the carrier, Chris, just forward of the starboard beam. Not even totally hull up from this level... hmmm... I think I see some birds coming in, too. Range is maybe three miles. Stand by to surface the ship. Sound battle stations gun action."

Chris Savage gawked at him, "Sir! We're gonna go topside and lob shells at them?"

"Unless you want to take her into the lagoon and send a few pickles their way," Jarvis suggested. "I'm okay with that, but it seems a bit risky."

"Oh, sweet Jesus...." Savage said. "They've got AA emplacements and five-inch guns, too, you know."

Jarvis nodded, "I do know that. But they're more or less *trapped* in there, XO. We can maneuver. Even a few good shots might make all the difference. It *might* even force them to come out and play."

"What about those three tin cans your Jap buddy warned us about?" Savage pressed.

Jarvis looked at him sternly, "Mr. Savage, in case you haven't been following the papers or tuning into Tokyo Rose lately, we're at war with these people. War is risky. It's dangerous. It's a ball-breaker. We don't win it by playing it safe. Might as well go home then. We do the unexpected. We act with bold decisiveness. *That's* how you win a war against an enemy that's driven by almost spiritual dedication. Hell, it's what your *captain* did not long ago, isn't it? Go topside and slug it out with a Jap destroyer?"

Savage flushed slightly, "Yeah, and look what happened! We lost eleven good men, including our XO."

"Tough titties," Jarvis snapped, true anger now evident in his voice. "I'm sorry for that, Chris, I really am. It's a tragedy when young men, when good men, die, even in a war. It sucks that your first officer was killed. It's a shame that the psychological effects of that battle have stolen captain Waters' fire, or so it seems. It's understandable. But let me tell you something. Just because your decisions cause the death of some of your men doesn't make them *wrong!* Captain Waters was *right* to surface and attack that DD. Losing men is the price we must sometimes pay for victory. I know that's a shitty deal, but it's the way war is. Now I'm tired of explaining myself. I'm tired of coddling you men through your hurt feelings. This is a fuckin' *war*, we're in the middle of a fuckin' *battle,* and I *will not* hear any more arguments! Either you follow my orders or relieve yourself."

Savage's shame was bright on his face now, "Hey, I was just doing my job as XO! Offering—"

"Bullshit!" Jarvis snapped. "You're scared, Chris. You're scared of no longer being hidden and facing your enemy head-on. And you know what? That's okay. It's *normal,* for Christ's sake. Everybody else is scared, too, including me. But we've got to fight through that fear. Use it to keep our senses sharp, but we *cannot* let it dictate our actions. Do you understand?"

Savage opened his mouth and closed it again. He drew in a breath and nodded, "Aye-aye, sir."

Jarvis reached out and squeezed his shoulder, "Good man. I know you got what it takes, Chris. I know you all do. This is the goddamned S-52, for Christ's sake! The boat that went toe to toe with a *Fubuki* and cleaned her clock! Now let's bag us a Jap strike carrier, huh?"

Everyone cheered, even Savage, who couldn't help but smile. As the cheers died down, a single pair of hands clapped slowly. Everyone turned to see Captain Bernard Waters halfway up the hatch from the control room, a white bandage wrapped around his head.

Jarvis waited, wondering what would happen next. Now that Waters was on his feet, the entire situation might dramatically alter.

"Stirring words, Exec," Waters said, his voice neutral. "You really believe in what you said?"

"Yes sir, I do," Jarvis stated without hesitation.

Water's brown eyes met his temporary first officer's blue ones and held them for a long, long moment. Jarvis thought he saw something in them, something that might be a plea and maybe even hope.

"I guess guys like you and Anvil Art Turner are what our country needs," Waters said. "Men that can push through it. Take a punch and keep on coming. Guys that don't crack under pressure."

"Any man can stumble, sir," Jarvis said, trying with his words to tap into that special something that all ship's captains have inside them.

"Sometimes you don't regain your footing, Pat," Waters said softly, regretfully.

"And sometimes you *do*," Jarvis replied firmly.

Waters sighed, "Exec, continue with your attack."

Jarvis stepped back from the scope and pulled off the sou'wester, "No sir. The deck is yours, sir. Forward room is reloading, gun crew has been called. We're rigging for surface and can run on one engine for a recharge. This is your boat, Captain. This attack should be yours to run."

For another pregnant moment, Waters hesitated. He closed his eyes, drew in a deep breath, and clenched his jaw, "Very well, Exec. Please take command of the gun party. Mr. Savage, you stay where you are. We might need to fire a few fish before this is over."

S-52 surfaced, started her diesels and lookouts were posted. The crew for the four-inch deck gun was posted, and the men stationed to act as a munitions train were ready.

As Jarvis was about to go up the ladder to the bridge, Waters stopped him with a hand on the shoulder. The older man leaned in close and whispered so that only Jarvis could hear.

"You sure about this?"

"Yes sir," Jarvis said without a moment's thought.

Waters smiled ever so slightly, "Thank you, Pat."

"So, Commander Osaka," the unpleasantly smug voice of Takashi Sato spoke from the corridor outside the sonar control room. "Yamamoto's pet sending secret messages to the Americans. How wonderfully droll... what would the great Yamamoto say... what *will* he say, when he learns that his favorite protégé is a *traitor*."

It had been some time since Osaka sent his piggybacked Morse code message via the active sonar array. He'd stayed down in the bowels of the ship and monitored the passive sound heads. When he detected the active ping from I-123, he knew that the signals he was sending had at least reached them. Then, moments later, a thunderous underwater concussion rolled through the shallows and into *Sakai's* electronic ears. Osaka knew the sound all too well. A torpedo had struck and exploded. Based on the odd sound of the impact, he'd determined that it had been an American torpedo.

I-123 had been destroyed. Perhaps Turner or his companion had been nearby and had capitalized on the active ping to home in on the submarine. Osaka's heart went out to them. He had no wish to see any of his countrymen killed... yet he supposed that it couldn't be helped. Still, the feelings of guilt and shame were there, threatening to boil to the surface and, he was certain, eventually would, whether he liked it or not.

Now, here stood Sato, his burly shape filling the hatchway. On his face, the captain wore a wicked smile, and in his hand, he held a Nambu semi-automatic pistol.

"A traitor, Sato?" Osaka shot back. "I think not."

"Really?" Sato seemed to be enjoying this immensely. "You sent information to the Americans about our forces, Osaka. Did you not realize that we could monitor your activity? Did you *really* think that the repair crews would fail to find the cable that you deliberately cut?"

"All I have done, Sato, is give you what you claim you want," Osaka said coolly. "I've taken away your advantage… your cheat. I've given Turner enough information to know what he's up against. Now you must face him on an even playing field. Night is falling, and now you will have to use the cunning which you believe you possess. Or were you hoping to use lies and treachery yourself? As you did when you murdered Captain Igawa?"

Sato laughed cruelly, arrogantly, "Pure speculation, Ryu. Captain Igawa was wracked by guilt, you see. He took the only honorable way out for him."

Osaka laughed then. He couldn't help it, "You fool, Sato! Do you think a seasoned and decorated ship's captain like Igawa would kill himself over his ship taking minor damage? Perhaps a coward like you would do so, but *not* him. Oh, and it's not pure speculation. You see, I've had some time to do a little investigating of my own. During the course of that investigation, I have uncovered evidence that it was *you* who perpetrated Igawa's suicide."

Sato's smugness flickered for just a moment before he asked, "Evidence? Nonsense! You are lying, Osaka."

"No, *Captain*, I am not," Osaka said, getting to his feet and facing the other man. The two meters between them crackling with tension. "You see… Captain Igawa's personal typewriter was damaged. It so happens that several letter strikers had broken off. He put in a request that his yeoman replace it. Further, this same yeoman, who also served as your clerk, reported that your own machine was beginning to show signs of wear. Specifically, the letters T and the E were beginning to come out slightly crooked. Had been for nearly a week. And do you know what he said when I showed him the captain's supposed suicide note? He said that he thought that was strange because all the Ts and Es were crooked… just like every one of *your* typed messages. What do you say to *that, Commander?*"

Sato's face blanched and then began to redden as his self-satisfied expression morphed into one of dark rage, "I say that you should have left well enough alone, Osaka. I say that you leave me no choice but to kill you now. How fortunate for me. I had sufficient reason to do so because of your treachery, but now, I can kill the only man who knows the truth about that fool Igawa. You were foolish to reveal what you know… but it is of no matter. It only gives me an even better reason to execute you now, and, in my report, I'll expose *your* treason. An elegant solution, and I have you to thank for it."

"He's not the only one that knows, you idiotic pig," came another voice from out in the corridor.

Sato sidestepped and glanced through the open hatch to see Omata Hideki standing behind him, holding a Nambu of his own. Hideki did not wear a smile, only a grim expression of disgust.

The tense silence was broken when the ship received a mule kick that knocked all three men off their feet. The impact was accompanied by a thunderclap and the screaming of tortured steel as a four-inch explosive round smashed into the carrier's port bow just above the waterline. Although two decks above the sonar room, it was nearly directly overhead, and the rumble was so loud it temporarily drowned out the alarms.

Osaka scrambled to his knees just as Sato did the same. In his fall, the captain had lost his gun, which now lay on the deck almost equidistant between the two men. Sato's eyes met Osaka's, and then both men lunged.

Osaka wasn't trying for the pistol, however. He knew there was no need, as any second Hideki would recover himself. Instead, the pilot and submariner doubled up his fists and slammed them into Sato's solar plexus, deflecting the man's try for his gun. Sato threw out an arm wildly, connecting with the side of Osaka's head and setting off bright fireworks behind his eyes.

Again, the ship was rocked by the impact of a shell, this time further aft and further up, possibly on the flight deck. The two combatants took no notice, however. The men fell to rolling on the deck, punching and grabbing for one another's throats. At one point, both men got their hands on the other's throats and began to squeeze, each man's airway closing while he closed the other's.

"I always knew… you were a traitor…." Sato rasped.

"And… I always knew… you were a fool!" Osaka croaked back.

More rumbles and booms now. *Sakai's* own gun crews were firing back at whoever had taken to attacking them. Hideki wished he could go on deck and find out what was happening. The thought of being fired upon while stationary inside a small lagoon with nowhere to maneuver was uncomfortable in the extreme. He also knew that this contest before him must end, for the ship's sake, if for no other reason.

Ryu Osaka was a fit man, lean and strong. Yet Sato outweighed him by at least ten kilograms. In a contest of brute strength, it was probable that Osaka would lose. All that was required was for him to begin to pass out, and Sato would have him. It couldn't be allowed. Whatever the consequences, Omata Hideki couldn't let his friend die. Not for his own sake, let alone the fate of Japan.

Hideki swallowed hard, stepped forward and placed the barrel of his gun against Sato's head. Without a single word, he pulled the trigger and Takashi Sato's plans, schemes and ambitions splattered across the sonar console in a fountain of chunky bloody brain matter.

Osaka got to his feet and looked down on the dead captain in shock. Not for the fact that he was dead, but for what would happen next. He stared at Hideki for a long moment.

"It was necessary," Hideki stated, slipping the gun into his jacket pocket.

"Yes," Osaka said sadly. He removed a grenade from his own pocket. "As this is. Come, we must get to the bridge. I doubt we can save the ship, but we must see to the crew."

Hideki's eyes bulged at the sight of the explosive. He backed out into the corridor and watched as Osaka pulled the pin and then tossed the grenade beneath the sonar console along with the pin. He then slammed the hatch shut and propelled Hideki toward the watertight hatch just a few meters away. Behind them, a muffled roar shook the deck plates beneath their feet.

Osaka followed Hideki through the hatch and then sealed it, "We'll report flooding in this compartment. Come, we must get to the flight deck. Are there any aircraft ready to fly?"

Hideki blinked in surprise, "I don't know... standard procedure is to begin refueling immediately, at least for the zeroes intended for tomorrow's CAP. But Ryu... it's one thing to fly at night and another to *recover* planes...."

Osaka sighed, "I'm not worried about recovering them, my friend. I'm concerned about getting as many men as possible off this ship should it come to that. Come, we have much to do."

Captain Hitake Yamata was a patient man, but even his deep wellspring was not bottomless. As the sun disappeared below the horizon, it dragged with it any remaining vestiges of the captain's willingness to stand by and wait for instructions. The Americans were out there. They'd already proven *that* when the bright explosion from nearly twenty kilometers to the southeast had rolled into the afternoon sky.

Yet Sato had requested that *Viper's Fang* and her two escorts remain over the horizon and hidden. Why? Was it because Sato was cunning, or was it that he wanted to hog the glory for himself?

For Yamata's part, he cared nothing for glory. He had glory and accolades enough for any man. He was out here in the field to do his duty. To hunt down and destroy the American submarines that were preying on Japan's merchant fleet. On his nation's invaluable life's blood.

As the hours crept past and sonar watch after sonar watch was changed, Yamata's legendary patience continued to fray. Now, with the light fading and the advantage to the submarine growing, he decided it was time to act. He had no fear of what Sato might say. After all, Yamata was a full captain and his superior officer.

"Daki," he said to his Yakuin, the *Viper's Fang's* official captain. "Order *Viper One* to proceed in a counterclockwise course around the atoll. Inform them to maintain their highest sonar speed. Should they detect anything, they are *not* to attack but to track the enemy submarine. Then put us on a clockwise course around the atoll, first get us to the fifty-fathom curve. No more than ten knots, Daki. Active search on echolocation the entire time. We have predators to snare."

"*Hai*," Daki said. "Do you think we can find them, sir?"

Yamata smiled thinly, "If they're out there, Daki, then we'll find them… or they'll find us. Either way, the time for waiting has ended."

With twilight coming on, Art Turner had ordered his submarine to radar depth. He extended the snorkel and activated two of his diesels to charge the batteries. He left the other two inactive. He wasn't intending to speed up. In fact, his sedate two knots would minimize the feather line of the big snorkel on the surface. Even at night, this could be seen by a sharp lookout as the foamy phosphorescence left a glowing line like some great ghostly chalk mark upon the dark water.

Once the I-123 had pinged, Turner had ordered *Bull Shark* on a circular counter-clockwise course around the atoll just outside the fifty-fathom curve. At two knots, it would take most of the rest of the day to come around to the northwestern side where, if Osaka's message was right, a trio of destroyers sat quietly six miles out to sea, just over the visible horizon.

At forty-five feet, the SD and SJ radar heads were only a few feet above the water. That meant that the surface-search SJ only had a horizon of about two miles. A destroyer's masts were about sixty feet high, so the absolute furthest the submerged boat could expect to detect them was ten miles, and even that was not a sure thing. However, the periscope's eye was twenty feet higher, and with a clear night, the human eye might pick up the dull reflection of a grey hull before the electronic eye might.

To that end, Elmer Williams was now taking his turn and dancing with the one-eyed lady. Ted Balkley was carefully focused on both of his radar panels, and Chet Rivers was all but lost in the world of sounds below the ocean's surface.

"Contact!" Williams, Balkley and Rivers said so nearly perfectly in unison that Turner almost laughed out loud.

"I've got something," Williams went first. "I think a couple of masts, bearing zero-three-zero."

"Confirmed, sir," Balkley said. "Faint contacts, three of them, same bearing, range fifteen-thousand yards."

Turner looked to Rivers with a raised eyebrow. If he'd picked up the destroyers on passive sonar, that meant that they weren't just sitting idle out there. The young sonarman nodded, as if he'd read Turner's thoughts.

"Light, fast screw noises, sir… one seems to be faster than the others… two at a slower speed," Rivers reported. "Can't tell their turn rates yet; it sounds like they're starting up from an all stop."

"So, the game's afoot, eh?" Turner asked no one. "Mug, all stop. Frank, stand by to kill the rock crushers. Not just yet, though. Pump as much juice into the batteries as you can."

Bull Shark's creeping speed quickly fell off to nothing. The submarine, most of which was beneath the surface, rocked gently in the light swell, her periscope and radar masts peeking above the darkening waters. Everyone on board waited. No one spoke, as if by doing so, their low voices would somehow cross the eight miles of water and alert the Japanese to their presence.

Turner couldn't blame them. That cryptic ASW expert tag certainly gave him pause. If this was the same trio of DDs he'd faced days earlier, then he knew that their commander was shrewd indeed.

After several minutes, Rivers pulled back his earphone cups, "One DD is making fifteen knots, sir. The other two are making ten and headed almost straight for us… and they're pinging on search frequency. I can barely hear it over the screw noise, but it's out there."

"Where's the third guy headed?" Turner asked.

"Taking a one-six-zero," Balkley said. "Moving away from the other two."

"Spreading out," Williams opined. "Splitting up to encircle the atoll and look for us… and S-52."

"Whoa, sir!" Rivers suddenly jumped, cupping his headphones

again. "I just heard... something... sounded like an explosion from the southeast. Can't be sure; it's awfully muddy...."

Williams twirled around, spinning the periscope to look back toward the islands. There was a gap between the big one and a smaller islet to the north. He thought he saw something in there, probably the *Sakai*. After a moment or two, he yelped in surprise.

"Gunfire!" he said. "I saw a flash and then an explosion... can't tell if it's the carrier firing or...."

Turner chuckled softly, "Or if Pat's lobbing shells at them. Christ... well, not much we can do. We've got our own fish to fry. Secure diesels. Mug, all ahead one-third. Secure radar masts. Down scope. Frank, take us down to one-hundred feet. Sound battle stations torpedo. Joe, alert both rooms to open outer doors on all tubes... well, except for five and six of course... have them set depth on all weapons to six feet and speed high."

"We're gonna try for those tin cans, Art?" Williams asked, knowing the answer, of course.

Turner grinned, "*You're* gonna try for them, Elmer. I'll con her; you handle the attack. We gotta get out of their sonar sphere, though. Helm, right standard rudder."

"Maneuverin' answerin' all-ahead one-third," Mug replied. "Sir, my helm is right standid'."

"Standid'," Dutch mused after relaying his orders through his sound-powered telephone.

Turner moved over to the chart desk and joined Hotrod Hernandez there. Both men shared the maneuvering board and made notes based on Porter Hazard's information. Hazard was leading the plotting party below.

"What do you think their effective sphere is, Chet?" Turner asked.

"At ten knots, if they're making full sweeps, which I'm sure they are... I'd say no more than two-thousand yards, sir," Rivers stated confidently.

"You hear that, Port?" Turner called out. "I want a course that just skims that circle."

"Aye-aye, sir," Hazard said. A moment went by. "I suggest three-two-five."

"You heard the man, Mug," Turner said. "Keep us at three knots. Joe, here's what I want to do… when those three ships are about two-thousand yards off the port bow, I'm gonna rise to periscope depth, and Elmer is gonna make an observation with the attack scope. We're gonna fire all four forward tubes with a negative gyro. Lead them well ahead of the DDs course. Then we'll swing to starboard, and I want the after four tubes fired but with a slight positive gyro and a five-degree spread. You with me?"

Dutch frowned, "You're gonna try and get them to dodge to port when they see the first four and then hit them with the after four?"

"Exactly," Turner said. "I'd love it if the first four hit something, but I think it'll be Murph's pickles that really do the job, if at all. Two-thousand yards is a long shot with tin cans. But I'm hoping that their jig to port will cut that down enough that they run smack into our next volley. If nothing else, it keeps these two guys from going after Pat. They'll be *real* interested in us."

"Terrific…" Turner heard Buck Rogers say with a sardonic laugh from the control room.

"One-zero-zero feet," Nichols called up.

"Frank, when we shoot our after fish, I want an immediate hard dive," Turner said. "Take a fathometer reading as soon as the after fish fire and get us down as deep as you can. You call the speed settings."

"Aye-aye, sir," Nichols said and then: "Bow buoyancy is still flooded, keep in mind. Buck and I are having a devil of a time holding depth as it is."

"I haven't forgotten, Frank," Turner said. "I'm counting on that helping us out… and relying on you two boys to keep her in hand."

The seconds ticked by with agonizing slowness. On his and Hotrod's maneuvering board, Turner ticked off the distances in five-hundred-yard increments. Below at the master gyro table, Hazard, Chief Weiss and Fred Swooping Hawk did the same on a larger scale. So far, according to Rivers, the Japs weren't zigging. No need; they were hunting and not *trying* to avoid a submarine.

"Mark!" Hazard called up from below even as Hotrod opened his mouth to do the same.

"Periscope depth, Frank," Turner ordered. "Elmer, you got six-seconds."

"Plenty of time," Williams breezed with more bravado than he felt. He crouched on the deck, almost bent over and kissing it. "I'll ride her up, Ted. Stay with me!"

"I'm on it, sir!" Balkley, who was now the periscope assistant, replied, holding up the control remote.

"Seven-five feet…" Nichols called out. "Seven-zero feet…"

"Up scope!" Williams snapped.

The attack scope began to rise, and the XO flipped the handles down and let them pull him to his feet. As he rose, he turned the scope to the approximate location of the approaching Japanese. "Stop! Okay… final bearing… mark!"

"Three-two-zero!" Balkley said excitedly.

Williams twisted the range finder knob and lined up the stadimeter. "Range… mark!"

"One-nine-five-zero!" Balkley called.

"Angle on the bow is three-two-zero port! Down scope!" Williams ordered with far less cool than he'd have liked.

"Now, Frank!" Turner ordered. "Joe?"

"Shoot!" Dutch said.

"Weapons free, Joe, let 'er rip!" Williams exclaimed.

"Mug, full right rudder!" Turner snapped out.

"Give me six knots, Captain!" Frank called out.

Mug was already setting the enunciators.

"Can you use the current info for your aft tubes, Joe?" Turner asked between shots.

"Yes sir!" Dutch said excitedly as he pushed the plunger down for number four. "All forward fish away… give me a mark when we're ready."

He played the TDC knobs, adjusting settings for the four after tubes even as the submarine turned away from her quarry. In his mind's eye, Turner saw the destroyers moving across the face of the sea and his submarine slowly turning away. When he thought it was right, he glanced quickly at the gyrocompass repeater above Mug's wheel and turned to Dutch.

"Shoot!" he ordered.

As before, four jolts shivered through the submarine and into the feet and legs of the men on her decks. Below, Nichols and Rogers worked together to adjust trim tanks and planes in order to keep the boat from hobby-horsing with the sudden loss of six tons of weight from astern.

"Now, Frank! Full down bubble! How deep?" turner asked.

"At least a thousand feet of water now," Nichols called.

"Let's hope we find a thermal," Turner muttered. "Or this crazy-ass gambit actually tags one of those suckers…."

"Torpedoes in the water!" a lookout on *Viper's Fang* screamed into the night.

Yamata ran from the navigation bridge and out onto the port wing, "Where away!?"

"Port bow, incoming at an angle, sir!" the young man said from his perch above the bridge.

Yamata looked out onto the dark sea. Sure enough, four fingers of bubbling eldritch light were extending toward them. No, not *exactly* toward them. The torpedoes were aiming for where the two destroyers *would* be nearly two minutes into the future.

Very clever, Yamata thought. The commander of the submarine was no fool. He knew that with such a distance and firing upon such maneuverable ships, he'd have to lead his shots like an anti-aircraft gunner trying for a distant bomber.

Yamata spun back to the archway, "Helm! All ahead flank! Left full rudder!"

The mighty *Fubuki*-class destroyer's steam turbines whined as they ramped up to full power. Her stern was pushed down, and her knife-like bow rose as the ship surged forward and began to turn to port, out of the path of the incoming torpedoes.

Without looking, he knew that *Viper Two* would match her leader's move. It would come a few seconds behind, naturally, but that skipper was a sharp-eyed bird, Yamata knew.

As his ship circled to her left and out of danger, a disturbing thought crossed The Sensei's mind.

Why only four?

If it were the *Bull Shark,* then they had six forward torpedo tubes. Sending all six out in one spread would greatly increase their odds of hitting something...

He turned aft and saw that his sister ship had made her turn and was now nearly in *Viper's Fang's* wake. Yamata looked off the starboard bow, watching as the four torpedoes raced past, their bubble trails clearly visible even in the dark and the scream of their steam-driven motors already beginning to diminish.

That's when the idea popped into his mind, and the smile that fought so hard to spread across his lips turned into a jaw-dropping realization. Fear seized his heart, and a cold trickle of sweat broke out along his spine.

"Helm! Reverse your turn!" Yamata shouted, unable to move. "Quickly!"

He was nearly tumbled off his feet as the ship suddenly began to turn to starboard, the centrifugal force instantly changing from a pull to the right to a pull to the left.

As Yamata watched, wide-eyed with shock and grudging admiration, four more ghostly streaks reached out for him. There were several horrifying seconds when the outcome was in doubt, but the captain saw that the turn had come in time. *Viper's Fang* would clear the torpedoes, if only by a few mere meters.

The four torpedoes streaked by, whining in their furious hunger for Japanese steel. Yamata shook his fist at them and laughed out loud.

"A good try, my American foe! But not quite—"

His boasting was interrupted by two simultaneous events. A mental explosion of understanding that preceded the torpex explosion by only a fraction of a second. Yamata had time to turn and see *Viper Two's* bow blossom into a flowering rose of destruction. Flames, smoke and burning bodies soared into the night sky as fifty feet of the destroyer's bow disintegrated. The ship instantly began drowning in hundreds of tons of Pacific Ocean. The stern rose as the bow greedily gulped in seawater.

Then another torpedo struck, blasting away much of the fantail and turning the upper decks into a holocaust. For a long moment, The Sensei could only stare, dumbfounded, as the mighty destroyer was broken and burnt even as she plunged into the dark depths.

Once more, this Turner fellow had scored a devastating point in this fight to the death. Now, Yamata and his *Viper's Fang* were alone with a ferocious enemy lurking somewhere beneath their feet.

35

"They're startin' to home in on us, sir!" mess attendant first-class Apolinario Avellino shouted back to Jarvis from his position as rammer on the four-inch deck gun.

"Yeah, I can see that, Double-A!" Jarvis replied, his binoculars glued to his face. "But you guys are locked in. That last one hit the flight deck; give me two up and five right!"

Two bright flashes from *Sakai* nearly blinded S-52's XO as two of her five-inch guns bellowed out in reply to the upstart pest that had dared to fire on her. The air was ripped apart as two shells arced in and dropped into the sea to the submarine's portside. Only about a hundred feet to port.

"Ready!" the gun captain called.

"Fire!" Jarvis ordered.

The four-inch gun, smaller and shorter than *Bull Shark's* two five-inch twenty-fives, was still a considerable weapon. It thundered and sent its forty-pound explosive round soaring into the night. With the strike carrier little more than a mile away, only half visible behind the mangrove islet between her and S-52, there wasn't even time to call "shot out" before the projectile found its mark.

On the tower of the carrier, a small orange-white fireball bloomed into life. It wasn't quite at the level of the bridge but impressively close.

"We're gonna have to get outta here, Exec!" Captain Waters said from behind Jarvis on the bridge. "They've almost got us bore-sighted. One good hit and we're toast!"

"It's your show, Skipper!" Jarvis said.

There was a pause and the submarine's two diesels revved up to full power. Waters leaned forward, "I've ordered an all back full bell. We'll stay in line so you can at least keep the azimuth!"

More booms and more Japanese shells fell. This time, one to either side of the boat. Although now that she was beginning to move backward ever faster, they were a few yards short. Still, it wouldn't be but one or two more before the party would end rather abruptly.

"Hell, we're gonna go for broke, fellas!" Jarvis said. "I think I know where those guns are mounted… nice of these nips to use flashing powder… okay, give me same elevation, but ten left."

"This is it, Pat!" Waters said. "We gotta get outta here and down cellar before their friends round the corner."

"Aye-aye, sir!" Jarvis moved forward and looked over the trainer's shoulder at his sights. He thought they might be lined up right, but it was a shot in the dark… literally.

"Okay, Branson… give it to 'em!" Jarvis called out and stepped back.

Branson depressed the firing pedal, and the stainless-steel gun boomed one last time. A tongue of crimson fire leapt from the barrel as if in defiance of their enemies.

"Secure the gun!" Jarvis shouted. "Secure ammo hatch! All hands below!"

A tremendous rolling thunderclap and the executive officer looked up to see a rolling cloud of fire expanding along the carrier's bow just below the lip of her flight deck. By some miracle, his shot had landed inside the port gun gallery and turned it into a firestorm of death and destruction.

"Nice shootin', Tex!" Waters whooped in *his* Texan drawl. "Now, let's get this lady wet!"

The last of the men clambered up to the bridge and down. Jarvis was the last, and Waters held out a hand to be shaken. The two men clasped hands and grinned at one another like wide-eyed kids.

"Sir! Sir!" a voice called up through the hatch. It was Bobby Gaines, and he was so excited he hadn't even bothered with the communications system. "Picking up something on radar, sir! Faint and distant... but range is eight thousand yards and closing."

With only an SD set, the sonar operator doubled as radarman most of the time on the S-boat. Both officers did a full scan of the horizon. If the SD set was picking up something on the surface, then it wouldn't be far, as the range suggested. The gear was designed to look into the sky and didn't usually catch surface objects too far away.

"There!" Jarvis shouted, pointing off the port side, a bit aft of the centerline. "I think that's a tin can, sir!"

Waters met Jarvis' eye, "Well, then let's go find out, Exec!"

They dropped down the hatch, and Jarvis secured it. Waters grinned at his first officer.

"Think you can take her down ass-first, hotshot?"

Jarvis chuckled, "Pfft! In my sleep, Skipper."

The maneuver wasn't entirely uncommon, but it could be tricky. With the submarine running at twelve knots in reverse, it would take time to slow her down and then move forward again until enough speed was gained to allow her to smoothly dive and break the surface suction. This might take several minutes, and if the Japanese ship had spotted them and had gone to flank, she could close the distance by over a mile in that time.

"Rig ship for dive!" Jarvis said over the 1MC. "All stop! Close main induction! Rig out bow planes... okay, helm, give me all back full-on batteries... Crawford?"

A pause, "Green board, sir!"

"Open all MBT vents," Jarvis ordered. "Get me a fathometer reading, too. Flood safety and negative tanks. Stern planes on rise, bow on dive... Trim me down by the stern but watch the bubble, diving officer. Nothing past ten degrees."

"Depth reads one-two-five feet, XO," Tony Skaggs called up from the control room.

Jarvis frowned, "Christ, we gotta get out to sea."

The boat tilted down, and air roared as it was blown out of the flooding ballast tanks by inrushing seawater. Inside the pressure hull, the safety and negative tanks filled as well, making the ship negatively buoyant.

"She's buckin' a bit!" Marx said from the wheel.

"Hang on, Steve, we're almost there," Waters said calmly.

"Forty-five feet, conning!" Lutz called out.

"Close main vents," Jarvis said. "Ease up on the stern planes. All stop, helm. Left full rudder."

S-52 eased her angle slightly and began to turn, her stern moving to the right. As the way came off and her nose came around toward open sea, Waters ordered an all-ahead one-third bell and a depth of one-hundred feet.

"What've you got, Bobby?" the captain asked, smiling at Jarvis. "Nicely done. I still think you're a pain in the ass, though."

Jarvis shrugged and lit a Camel, "So does my mom."

"I think they might've spotted us, sir," Gaines reported. "Turn rate indicates twenty-five knots. Bearing zero-nine-zero relative. Range now five-thousand yards."

"She's got a bee in her bonnet," Waters said. "Is she alone, sonar?"

"Appears so, sir...." Gaines said, twiddling his knobs.

"We got two choices, men," Waters stated, glancing around the conning tower. "We can evade or fight. I think I know what our crazy Exec wants to do. How about the rest of you? Chris?"

Savage sat at his TDC and smiled thinly, "With all due respect, sir, I say we bag the son of a bitch."

"Let's get 'em, sir!" Skaggs called up from below.

"That goes double for me, Skipper," Lutz added.

"Okay then," Salty Waters stated, drawing a breath. "Mr. Jarvis, please take over the plotting party. We're gonna paint this Jap's flag on our conning tower in the morning."

A cheer went up from every man in earshot.

"Now passing three-zero-zero feet," Nichols reported.

"Frank, increase your bubble to twenty degrees," Turner ordered.

"Mug, back her down to all ahead-one-third. Make turns for four knots. Then put your rudder hard left."

Enunciators chimed, reports were acknowledged, and the boat tipped forward another ten degrees. Above them and astern, the dreadful spectral whine of a search sonar beam pursued them. Behind this sound, distant but steadily increasing, was the relentless churning of steel blades through the sea.

Ooooo-eeeee... ooooo-eeeee...

The sonic beam reached out and down, reaching, grasping... hungry for contact. It began to swing from astern slowly forward along the port beam as *Bull Shark* turned west.

"Joe, how long on the reloads?" Turner asked.

Joe spoke quietly into the sound-powered phone. With the ship now rigged for silent running, the noisy job of reloading torpedo tubes would necessarily have to be slowed down to minimize... there was no way to eliminate... the metallic clunks and clangs and rattles of the evolution.

"Maybe a half-hour if they're gonna keep it quiet," Dutch reported finally.

Turner drummed his fingers on the periscope barrel and pondered. He smoked an entire Lucky Strike before he spoke again, "We got one of them... but something tells me that we didn't get lucky and get this ASW ringer the Japs have. I've got a feeling this guy isn't gonna be easy to shake. Let's hope we find a layer soon."

"Four hundred feet," Nichols said. "No layer yet, Skipper."

Turner frowned. He could take his boat deeper, had before... yet this patrol had seen a good deal of pounding. *Bull Shark* had her weak spots now, and that was a concern. Fresh out of a drydock, Turner would do almost anything with his boat, confident in her ability to take it.

After this past week, however...

"Dutch, tell the rooms to hustle," Turner decided. "To hell with it. It's one tin can against us. Their ten torpedoes against our ten... er... *eight*. Our two five-inch guns, Pom-pom and Oerlikon, against their deck armament. Their high profile against our low. If worse comes to worst, we'll duke it out toe to toe."

There were a number of groans and then irreverent chuckles. Turner had gained a reputation for such ballsy maneuvers. It was both a source of pride for the men of *Bull Shark* as well as a true asshole tightener.

Of course, until the torpedo rooms completed reloading their tubes, the ship wasn't able to avail herself of all the options Turner listed. There was another consideration, too. No matter what happened, *Sakai* must *not* be allowed to escape.

Earlier, when the boat was running at radar depth, Turner had sent an encoded report with coordinates to Pearl. He requested that as soon as possible, a carrier strike or even a B-17 strike be sent to the Savage Islands to deal with the flattop. Yet that wouldn't happen until daybreak. Until then, the carrier could decide at any time to get underway. If so, and if Turner and S-52 didn't stop her, Sato would slip away to fight another day.

"Attack freq!" Rivers declared. "Turn rate decreasing to twelve knots, sir."

"Four-five-zero," Nichols called. "Skipper, our phone talker is reporting we've got leaks in the forward room and motor room."

Turner sighed. He thought so. With the bow buoyancy tank open to the sea and pressure damage from that aerial ashcan, some things had been rattled loose. There was also a patch on a feed line in the electric motor compartment that had been patched twice now.

"How bad, Frank?" Turner asked, fumbling another cigarette between his lips as he did so.

"Moderate," Nichols called up. "They're compensating with salvage air."

Ping... ping... ping...

Chu, chu, chu, chu...

"Continue your turn, Mug," Turner said. "Where is he, Chet?"

"Bearing two-zero-zero, range two-thousand yards and closing fast, sir," Rivers reported.

Then something odd happened. The destroyer's sonar beams found their target, gonging off *Bull Shark's* steel hull as if someone were outside with a hammer banging away. Immediately, the surface ship altered course and drove right toward the slower submarine.

Rivers reported that the tin can was reducing speed, and when they were right on top of *Bull Shark*, the sound of their active echolocation changed. It reduced power dramatically and began to ping off the boat in what at first was an erratic pattern.

"What the hell…?" Williams muttered as he stuck his head up through the hatch.

"Put it on the loudspeaker, Chet," Rivers said.

The odd long and then short and then long pings went on for several seconds. It was Hotrod who first understood. His brown eyes went wide.

"*Madre cabron!*" he exclaimed. "It's Morse code, sir!"

Turner grinned, "I'll be damned… it *is!* Let's see…."

"Message is beginning again, sir," Rivers said.

"*Bull Shark… Bull Shark…* well-played… must withdraw… look forward to another game… know that I could've had you… Yamanna?" Turner didn't quite catch the sign-off.

"Yamata," Hotrod corrected.

"That's one for the books," Williams said.

Even as he spoke, the sound beam vanished, and the destroyer five-hundred feet overhead began to accelerate. Their screws powered up and moved off, slowly diminishing with speed and distance.

"Think it's a trick, Art?" Williams asked.

Turner shook his head in bewilderment, "I don't know, Elmer… he *is* leaving the engagement rather hastily… maybe called away by his fleet? I dunno… but I'm not going to sit down here and second guess it. Elmer, give me a direct course to the closest atoll channel into the lagoon. Diving officer… periscope depth."

"Here he comes, sir," Gaines reported. "Making turns for ten knots, range one-thousand yards, and he's on attack frequency!"

That was obvious to everyone aboard S-52. The lone destroyer must have seen them firing and was now running down the slowly diving and escaping submarine. What was also obvious was that, unlike *Bull Shark*, S-52 didn't have nearly the depth capability.

Current naval intelligence reports stated that the Japanese depth charge didn't operate below four hundred feet. S-52's test depth was only two hundred. And while the boat had gone down to four hundred in the past, even a little deeper, it was still well within the range of Jap ashcans. And should the intelligence reports prove false… which the men of *Bull Shark* could attest to… then there was no ducking below the max depth to escape. Their only salvation would be to find a halocline above four hundred feet, and there was certainly no guarantee of that.

"I've got an idea," Waters suddenly said, glancing over at Jarvis, who was halfway through the conning tower hatch.

There were groans from the men in the tower and from below, but on Jarvis' face, a slow grin began to spread. That made the other men groan even louder.

"What would Anvil Art do in this situation, Exec?"

Jarvis chuckled, "Surface and hit them with deck guns, range alongside and board her in the smoke. Bring back a prize."

Waters laughed, "Yeah, I'll bet. Well, what he would do, I'm sure, is be aggressive. Keep us at three-hundred feet, Mr. Lutz. When that bastard above drops his first load of tooth shakers, I want you to blow every tank we got and give me a thirty-degree up bubble. Steve, I'm gonna order a full-speed bell, so be ready."

Now the men were cursing under their breath. Jarvis met the captain's eyes and nodded in understanding.

"You're gonna shoot to the surface or to periscope depth and send him every tube we got," Jarvis half-asked and half-stated.

"Exactly," Waters said and turned to Savage at the TDC. "Christopher, I'm gonna shotgun the forward tubes. Zero gyro but with a ten-degree spread. Probably not gonna have much range to work with, so be sharp."

"Aye-aye, sir," Savage said. "What settings?"

"Fast and depth twelve feet… no, scratch that. Make it four feet," Waters said. "Go ahead and alert maneuvering to set their single fish that way, too."

The active pings grew louder, as did the destroyer's screw noise. The twin propellers churned overhead, resounding through the ship like doomsday. The active sonar was now ping-ponging as the surface ship crossed over their heads.

"Splashes!" Gaines said a few seconds later. "Eight, sir!"

They might have just enough time. A destroyer had to move away from the location of her depth charges because if she was too close, the force of the explosions pillaring up through the sea could damage her. So, the ship had to be moving quickly enough that by the time the charges went off, she was clear.

With the target swimming at three hundred feet, it would take the tooth shakers thirty-seconds to descend to that depth and explode. At ten knots, the tin can would move away at five yards per second. That gave at least a hundred- and fifty-yard separation. Then the ship must turn around and come back, although generally this wasn't done right away, and the turn itself would put more distance between the destroyer and the submarine.

In this case, S-52 was headed almost directly southwest and the Japanese ship southeast. Waters did the calculations in his head and knew it wouldn't be enough distance for his torpedoes to arm.

"Belay my last for the time being," he ordered. "Steve, hard right rudder. Come to three-one-five. Once you do, ring me up an all-back full bell, you hear?"

"Yes sir…" Marx said, not understanding but complying.

Everyone went silent as they waited. Waited for the tell-tale clicks that were the depth charges' hydrostatic pistols initiating the explosives.

It came then, a series of gargantuan hammer blows that rocked the ship from side to side and set her to bucking like an obdurate bronco. The pops of bulbs exploding and sending tiny shards of glass flying, steel hull plates and frames screeching in agony, and loose objects banging around accompanied the tremendous *wha-boom* of each depth charge.

"Where is she!?" Waters shouted after the last charge went off.

Gaines' face was coated in a fine sheen of sweat as he settled his headphones back over his ears, "Uhm… moving directly off the bow, sir!"

"Okay, dive, let her rip!" Waters said. "Marx, all back emergency!

We dove arsy-versy, and now we're gonna *surface* arsey-versey! Get ready, Chris!"

Another roar surrounded the men as high-pressure air was blown into the ballast tanks, pushing hundreds of tons of seawater out and making the ship considerably more buoyant. The bow tilted forward, and everyone's gut lurched as S-52 felt as if she were being yanked upward by cables.

"Two-five-zero!" Lutz called out; his famous cool gone now. "One-eight-zero… one-five-zero… Christ, we're headed up fast!"

"Jap is still headed off," Gaines said. "Range now four-hundred yards… I think he's making his turn, sir!"

"One hundred feet!" Lutz called out. "Seventy… fifty… thirty… hold on!"

Impelled by eight knots of stern way and a large positive buoyancy, S-52 broke the surface of the sea stern; first, her ass end coming so high out of the water her two bronze propellers spun madly in the open air for several seconds, their RPMs momentarily ramping up far above the usual rate. With no water resistance to stop them, they hummed and bit at empty air before the stern crashed down again, sending up massive sheets of spray out to port and starboard for several hundred feet.

"Jesus Christ!" Marx gulped, fighting his wheel even with the help of hydraulic power.

"Up search scope!" Waters called. He peered through, "There he is! Almost made his turn… he might even see us… yup, here he comes! Steve, left standard rudder. I'm gonna aim with the ship."

"Turn rate increasing on target!" Gaines shouted.

"Yeah, he's gonna try and run us down," Jarvis said. "His last mistake."

"Damn skippy," Waters said. "Okay… meet her, Steve! Chris?"

"Set!"

"Fire one!" Waters ordered and counted down from six. "Fire two… fire three… fire four! Helm, hard left rudder, all ahead flank!"

S-52's stern began to turn even more sharply to port. Even with the engines now moving ahead, they couldn't kill the stern way so quickly. Not before the nose of the boat was facing more than ninety degrees away from the Jap. Then her props bit, and her backward momentum slowed, stopped and then began to move forward again.

"Fish running hot straight and normal!" Gaines reported.

It was a huge gamble. If the torpedoes missed, S-52 would be at the mercy of the destroyer. Even should they find their mark, they were not modified, and there was a better than average chance the torpedoes would simply fail to explode.

But S-52 and her captain's luck was with them on that night. The very first torpedo went home, slamming into the bow of the destroyer and blasting it open like a can of sardines. In one of those improbable circumstances that would likely never happen twice, the second fish drove itself into the gaping maw where the DDs cut water had been and exploded against an inner bulkhead, sending a huge fireball plowing through the ship's vitals and blasting out the stern in a death-dealing dragon's fart.

"Got 'em!" Waters whooped.

Cheers rose through the ship. Men laughed, cheered and pounded each other on the back. Pat Jarvis stepped up to the captain and extended a hand.

"Give you joy of your kill, Skipper," Jarvis said and met the older man's eyes. "And for getting some payback."

Waters felt his throat tighten as he seized his Exec's hand. He swallowed hard and grinned, "Thank you, Mr. Jarvis… thank you."

What happened next was somewhat anti-climactic.

Bull Shark surfaced, and her SJ radar confirmed that a surface contact was exiting the area at thirty knots. The ship was already several miles to the east by the time Turner stepped up onto his bridge for a much-needed breath of fresh air.

The passage between the large island to the west and the small mangrove islet to the north was substantial, and even in the light of the sliver of moon and the stars, Turner and the lookouts could easily make out the bulk of *Sakai* in the center of the lagoon. The strike carrier's stern was almost directly facing them. It was too dark to try and navigate inside the passage. There was just no way to know where the channel might be or what its shape might be. Let alone if there was even sufficient depth.

However, Turner had Hotrod bring the ship to a stop a little more than two miles from the carrier. It almost seemed a letdown, this easy target now sitting idle and unable to evade what was coming.

"I hate to blast them like this," Turner said to Elmer Williams, who stood behind him and Hotrod.

"No choice, skipper," Williams said. "They started it."

"I know," Turner sighed. "It just seems… unsporting. Nothing for it, though."

"We have a saying in the village where I was born," Hotrod stated in his exaggerated Mexican farmer voice.

"Oh, here we go…" Williams muttered and grinned.

"A man who would sneak onto another man's property and steal his chickens should not be surprised when *that* man comes for his pecker," Hotrod said somberly.

Turner threw back his head and roared with laughter. Williams shook his head and managed to recover first.

"Lotta chicken farms in Long Beach, are there, Ralph?" Elmer inquired.

Hotrod and Turner looked at one another and then back at Williams. In perfect unison they said: "*Si*."

"*Bridge, conning,*" Joe Dutch said over the speaker. "*We're set. Fire anytime.*"

Turner's humor dampened immediately, "Very well… fire one, Joe."

The boat juddered as the twenty-foot-long weapon rocketed from her bow. The three men watched in maudlin fascination as the bubbling finger of doom stretched out ahead and toward the carrier. Turner wondered what was going on over there. Did they know *Bull Shark* was out there? Did they see the wake? Were they trying to rig machine guns to shoot the torpedo?

Whatever it was they did or did not do, it had no effect. There was a tremendous flash, a rising pillar of fire and water from the stern, and several visible hunks of burning somethings spiraled into the night sky.

Almost in afterthought, the echoing *whump* of the impact reached the submarine accompanied by a caldron's breath of air.

"Now they're trapped," Turner gravely declared. "Our work is done."

A silence fell. It was a victory but somehow not particularly sweet. In a way, it seemed more like an execution.

"*Bridge, radio… I'm getting a call from the Japanese ship, sir… and Captain Waters,*" Arnie Brasher called up, sounding bemused.

The three men on the bridge met one another's eyes before Turner replied, "Patch them in, radio."

"*Bull Shark, this is S-52. How do you fair?*"

Turner smiled thinly, yet wondering what was happening over there now that the captain was calling and not Jarvis, "We're in one piece, Captain. How about you fellas?"

"*We just bagged us a Jap tin can, and we're otherwise nominal.*"

"Excellent, Captain Waters. I believe we also have the skipper of *Sakai* on with us."

"*Not exactly, Captain Turner. This is Commander Ryu Osaka speaking.*"

Somehow Turner wasn't surprised, "I see… and Commander Sato?"

A pause, "*He was killed by a shell earlier this evening. I have assumed temporary command of what's left of Sakai. I regret to inform you, Captain, that I'm not authorized to surrender.*"

"*Then we'll blast you and your crew into shark meat!*" this was Waters.

Turner thought for a long moment. No doubt there was a more complicated explanation for Osaka's taking command. He'd love to hear the story, but of course, he couldn't ask without blowing Osaka's cover.

Then there was the question of the carrier. Even if the Japanese surrendered, the two submarines were in no position to take so many prisoners. Further, the Japanese fleet was out there somewhere. They could be called in, or that other destroyer could come back. Like it or not, Turner felt there was only one recourse.

475

He cleared his throat, "We couldn't accept your surrender in any case, Commander. We haven't the facilities."

A short laugh from Osaka, "*For what it's worth, your torpedo has ruptured the hull astern. The running gear is smashed, and we're taking on water. Sakai will be on the bottom in a matter of hours… although several decks will still be exposed.*"

Trapped in other words, Turner thought. "Commander… in the spirit of all wrecked seafarers throughout time, I feel it my duty to warn you that by daybreak, your ship will no doubt come under aerial attack. I suggest you get your men off and to the island for retrieval. I must report your disposition, of course. I suppose that either your countrymen or our navy will show up first. I can't say which."

A short laugh from Osaka, "*A sporting chance, eh? Well, it's appreciated, Captain Turner. My men and I will take it.*"

"You're just gonna leave them, Turner?" Waters broke in indignantly.

Turner shrugged, a useless gesture over a radio link, "What do you suggest, Captain? We can't take on a thousand prisoners. Or would you have us continue to fire on them and shell them while they're helpless?"

Another pregnant pause, and finally, Waters said: "*Understood. I concur.*"

Turner didn't say that whether Waters concurred or not, Turner's decision would stand. Instead, he said, "I wish you good luck, Commander Osaka."

"*And I you, captain.*"

"Well gents," Turner said, inhaling deeply of the tropical night air. "I don't know about you, but I think we've earned a trip back to Pearl. We'll stop off at Guadalcanal first and then come hell or high water, our girl is headed for a comfy birth at the submarine base, and our boys are headed for two weeks at the Royal."

"Sounds good to me, sir," Hotrod said with a toothy grin.

Williams smiled, "I bet Joanie will be pleased."

"You know what, Elmer?" Turner asked, smiling at the thought. "I bet she might. I'm awfully charming."

EPILOGUE

"Permission to receive the gangways, sir?" Chief of the Boat Paul "Buck" Rogers asked the bridge.

"Permission granted, Chief," Ensign Andy Post, who was officer of the deck, replied, beaming.

He'd conned *Bull Shark* into Pearl Harbor and toward the submarine base, past the 10-10 dock and smoothly into her berth. It was his first time, and Turner had insisted that he add this skill to his set.

Mooring lines were secure, and the two metal brows were snaked out from the pier and settled onto *Bull Shark's* decks near the fore and aft end of the conning tower. All the officers and men who could be spared from actually operating the boat were on deck in their best khakis and dungarees. At the foot of the entry brow, two well-known figures with admiral's stripes stood by patiently waiting.

Turner and Williams went down to stand by Paul Rogers as Admiral Chester W. Nimitz and Admiral Robert English stood just at the edge of the platform. They both turned and saluted the colors, and then Nimitz spoke for both of them.

"Permission to come aboard, Captain?"

"You're more than welcome, sirs," Turner said with a smile and held out a hand. "It's a real pleasure to see you both again. On behalf of the men of *Bull Shark*, you honor us with your visit today."

Nimitz smiled, "Poppycock. It's a privilege for us, believe me, Art."

"That goes double," Bob English said, shaking the offered hands. "Yet another patrol as successful and crazy as anything else we've come to expect from Anvil Art and his merry men!"

Nimitz chuckled, "There's so much work to be done, gentlemen. And you and others are showing us how it needs to be laid out. For that, I, and the American people, thank you."

"It's an honor, sir," Turner replied.

"Now, for the good news," English said. "You and your boys are finally gonna get your two weeks, Art. You've sure as hell earned it after the last few months. And don't worry about your girl, here. We'll get her fixed up as good as new. Better. Uniform of the day is summer whites and shined shoes, XO. The busses will be here by fourteen hundred to take your men over to the Royal. I'd like to offer that you take your time with your materiel condition reports… but I'll bet they were ready yesterday."

Williams smiled a bit shyly, "Yes sir."

"Excuse me a moment, gents, I'd like to have a word with old Buck Rogers," Nimitz said, walking away a few paces to speak to the COB.

English's good humor dampened somewhat, "He's damned proud of you fellas… but he's a bit troubled by what happened aboard S-52. Captain Waters radioed in his after-action report, of course… but we've taken notice that several updates came from *your* torpedo officer, Art. Charlie Lockwood and I both are somewhat disturbed by what happened between those two."

Art felt a twinge in his belly, "Sir… from all I know and have heard, Mr. Jarvis simply did his duty."

English raised a hand, "It's not that we're saying he did anything wrong, Art. No general court or anything like that… but until I speak in person to him and Salty Waters… well, there are just some uncomfortable questions that will occupy us shore jockeys for a while. S-52 is due in next week. We'll see then. And I think that having you sit in on the meeting might not be a bad idea. However, that's then, and this is now. I happen to know that a certain very pretty WAVE is anxious to speak with you, Captain. I'm certain that if I don't let you cross the brow within the next sixty-seconds, she's gonna have my ass for a Sunday roast!"

Turner looked back to the dock and there indeed was Joanie in her Navy uniform. She looked pretty and radiant, and his heart felt like it was about to leap from his chest. Standing beside her with big smiles on their faces were his two children.

'Uhm... excuse me, sir... Elmer..." Turner managed to say without his voice cracking.

He rushed across the brow and into the waiting arms and squeals of his family. Arty Jr. chattered and hugged him fiercely, Dotty squeezed and kissed him and started to cry... and Joan, her eyes brimming with tears, regarded him with an evident hunger.

"Hey sailor," she said, her voice quavering, "you come into this port often?"

"Not often enough, baby," Art said, his own vision blurring as he took her in his arms. "God, you're a sight for sore eyes."

They held each other hard, clinging desperately as if terrified to let the other go. The kids started to giggle and scuff their toes on the concrete, but their parents seemed to pay them no mind.

"Was it bad?" Joan asked quietly into her husband's ear.

"Bad? No... just straining," Turner said. "It's always a roller coaster ride. I'm a bit worried about Pat, but otherwise, we're in good shape. Probably get another damned medal."

Joan chuckled, "They're a dime a dozen for old Anvil Art, I hear... but I've got something to reward you with, and it can't be pinned to a blouse."

Turner's heart began to thump, and there was a definite tightening in his uniform trousers.

A WEEK LATER...

The tension in Admiral English's office was heavy when Art Turner arrived. Bernard Waters, Pat Jarvis and Chris Savage were already there. Sitting behind his desk was Bob English, his uniform crisp and tie straight. As if it was vital to maintain a sense of formality in this small gathering. That was not encouraging.

"Thank you for coming, Captain," English said, waving Turner into an empty seat beside Jarvis. "Sorry to break you away from your family like this."

"Of course, sir," Turner said.

"All right then…." English shuffled a small stack of papers on his desk. Probably updates from both S-52 and *Bull Shark*. He settled a pair of gold-rimmed readers on his nose and frowned. "We have ourselves a bit of a… snafu here, gentlemen. I wouldn't call this a mutiny, not by any stretch. Yet having the executive officer take command of a submarine after being relieved by the captain… and gents, I know that nobody is pointing any fingers in their reports, but I've been in this game a long time. I'm damned good at reading between the lines. And what I'm reading is troubling, to say the least. Captain Waters, your unit cohesiveness fractured, and you and your XO were at each other's throats during a combat patrol. For Christ's sake… during potential *combat!* This is no good, gents. And you're prevaricating and buck-passing in these reports ain't gonna fly, dammit. I want to know the truth, and I want to know it now. Not to yank anyone's short and curlies, but to make sure we can *prevent* this sort of garbage in the future."

The three S-52 officers fidgeted uncomfortably in their seats. For his part, Turner remained still and quiet. He knew very little of the details himself.

"With all due respect, sir…." Waters began, casting a quick glance at the others. "I take full responsibility for any breakdown in the chain of command and in-unit cohesion. It's my job as captain to maintain that… and I dropped the ball. Mr. Jarvis only tried to do his duty. If anything, he did his best to encourage me to do mine."

"I concur, sir," Savage added. "The fact is that after that last patrol where we lost so many men and our old XO… we sort of closed up, if you see what I mean. Mr. Jarvis comes in to take the XO slot… comes from a decorated boat with a celebrated skipper… you know, sir…."

"And some of you acted like spoiled brats and were jealous,"

English said, although without much rancor. "And you, Mr. Savage, were pissed off because you didn't get to be the exec."

"Yes sir," Savage said, shame-faced. "We gave Mr. Jarvis a pretty hard time... but he came through when it really counted, sir. He's definitely XO material... hell, Skipper material, to be honest."

"I agree," Turner said but no more.

"Another thing," Waters said, drawing a breath. "Some of the men, including Pat here, thought that I'd lost my nerve after facing that tin can off Balikpapan. And... they were right. I should have excused myself on those grounds before taking the boat out again. I should've been man enough to face my demons and not try to hide them at the cost of my ship and men. With respect, sir... and I know I *personally* owe you for my command... I think that it's well past time I stepped down."

English looked uncomfortable at this, yet he didn't protest. Turner still held his tongue, not entirely disagreeing with Waters. The man had tried to pretend he wasn't shaken up from that incident. He'd shied from battle and been reckless during a storm. And he tried to make Jarvis the scapegoat for his deficiencies, on top of it all.

English frowned and met Jarvis' eyes, "Do you concur, Lieutenant?"

"No sir, I do not," Jarvis said matter of factly, surprising everyone. He drew in a deep breath. "Anybody can stumble, sir. I'm sure I could've done a better job working with the captain. Perhaps I failed and let my pride get in my way, too. I could've handled things better, I'm sure. But in the end, sir... the boat, the men *and* the captain rose to the challenge when it came. To let go of a man with Captain Waters' experience would be a shame and a loss to the fleet. In my humble opinion, sir."

Savage looked at Jarvis in surprise and grinned. Waters only looked stunned. He blinked rapidly and cleared his throat but had no words.

"Well, Barnie," English stated, "I can't think of a better endorsement than that. The fleet needs you, and in the fleet you shall stay. S-52 has taken a pounding, but I think a month or two at Mare Island should set her to rights. That old boat still has some fight in her. That leads me to my next points of business. First, I think that Mr.

Savage here can take the time to leave his boat and head to New London for PXO school. He should return ready to take the position, Barnie, if you agree."

Waters nodded and smiled, "I think that's a grand idea, sir."

"As for you, *Pat*," English said sternly. "Your comportment during this last patrol is hardly what I'd call fitting for a Lieutenant in the United States Navy."

Jarvis flushed, stiffened and hung his head slightly, "Yes sir."

"However," English glowered, and then his face broke into a shit-eating grin. "It is the kind of nutty foolishness we've come to expect from Lieutenant *commanders* like Anvil Art here. Congratulations, Lieutenant commander Jarvis!"

Turner laughed, and Jarvis's eyes went wide, "I… uhm… thank you, sir…."

"You've earned it, son," English said. "And you and Chris here can share a flight back to Connecticut. You're headed to PCO school. Not sure when we'll have a command for you, but a few months ashore and then a PCO tour and 1943 just might be your year. What do you say to that, Art?"

"Well, sir, I hate to lose my best torpedo officer," Turner said. "But far be it from me to hold back one of my officers… no matter how much his selfish pursuit of his career might leave all of his friends in dire straits. It's fine, though… we'll *manage* somehow."

"I hate you, Art," Jarvis said and laughed.

"Better get packed, Commander," English said. "I'm sending S-52 out as soon as she's got fuel and grub. By the way, a friend of yours is in Connecticut right now, Art. Mush Morton is getting ready for his prospective commanding officer school. He and Pat here will be classmates. I'm hoping to put him aboard *Wahoo* when he gets his certificate. She's got a good XO now. Smart, young guy by the name of O'Kane. Anyway, with Morton and O'Kane and Turner and now Jarvis out there, the Japs oughta be surrendering by New Year's!"

Hands were shaken, and pats whomped on backs. English shooed them all out. Turner offered to take them all out for drinks at the officer's club. Waters said he'd be happy but would like a word with Jarvis in private first.

"I want to thank you for what you said, Pat," Waters said when they were alone.

"I meant it, sir," Jarvis said.

Waters smirked, "Hell, we're both O4 now... anyway, I appreciate it. Not sure if I agree, but it was kind all the same."

Jarvis met his gaze, "I believe what I said, Barnie. Yeah, maybe that mission shook you up, but I think you found your way back. A hotrod gets a flat, you change the tire. You don't junk the whole car. A man stumbles, he steadies up and keeps powering through it. You've still got a lot to offer, and the nation needs that right now."

Waters nodded, "Maybe... but what the nation needs most, and I'm glad to see it's getting it, is men like you and Art Turner and Mush Morton. Aggressive young men who know how to push the envelope."

Jarvis clapped him on the shoulder and grinned, "And we learned everything we know from guys like you, sir... well, almost. C'mon, the skipper's buying, and I'm not one to turn down free hooch!"

Waters chuckled, "Now you're starting to think like a skipper."

A WORD FROM THE AUTHOR

Ahh… alas… here we are, slipping safely into port after another exciting adventure! Isn't it a bummer when good things come to an end? I know it personally tightens my jaws when I get down to the stub of a fine cigar.

Fortunately, however, for those of us who enjoy good stories, there are lots more out there to tide you over until the *Bull Shark* heaves into view once more. Obviously, there are my books, which I'll list for you below. However, I'm pleased to announce something that you might like to take advantage of.

I've recently been added to Tropical Authors, a small catalog of authors who write water-related action, adventure, crime and thrillers. Anything on, near or below the water. Check it out:

www.tropicalauthors.com

Also, if you enjoyed this book, please give her a glowing review on Amazon and/or Audible. If you didn't like it… then don't trouble yourself, hahaha.

A WORD FROM THE AUTHOR

Additionally, if you have not yet done so, I strongly encourage you to visit my website and join my free email list. I generally send out updates, deals and other goodies once per month or so. No spam, no constant stream of sales requests… just a private club of the most intelligent and beautiful readers on Earth!

www.scottwcook.com

You can also follow me on Facebook at:

www.facebook.com/swcwriter

I sincerely appreciate you reading this book and all the others, and fear not, I am diligently tapping away at the lappy even as we speak!

Scott W. Cook
Amateur historian, scribbler and handsome crackpot

Printed in Great Britain
by Amazon